The Candidate's Daughter

Catherine Lea

Published by Brakelight Press

ISBN: 978-0-473-26175-7

The Candidate's Daughter is a work of fiction.

Names, characters, businesses, places, events and incidents are either the products of the author's imagination or used in a fictitious manner. Any resemblance to actual persons, living or dead, or actual events is purely coincidental.

Cover Design, Deanna Dionne at CustomIndieCovers.com
Formatting, Polgarus Studio
Editing, Sara J. Henry
Author Blog: http://cathylea.wordpress.com/

DEDICATION

For my Girl. What will I do without you?

CHAPTER ONE
DAY ONE—2:24 PM—KELSEY

Six years old. Even from here the kid looked small for her age.

Kelsey lowered the binoculars and squinted off down the street.

"Is that her?" Lionel asked and reached back. Kelsey handed him the binoculars while Matt shifted forward in his seat and rested both arms across the steering wheel, his attention on the child.

"That's her," he said.

They'd been sitting in this junker Camry for half an hour now, freezing their asses off while they waited for school to finish and the last remaining students to leave. November in Cleveland and no functioning heater, the car was an ice-box. The instant Kelsey saw the kid, it was like someone had flicked on a switch. Now all she could feel was heat flashing down her back and sweat prickling under the wig. She adjusted her jacket and loosened her collar, watching the woman and the child exit the Special Children's Center and make their way to the street.

"Ready?" Lionel said.

Matt checked the street front and back. "Not yet. Wait for it ..."

Kelsey lifted the binoculars again, leaning forward so she could get a clear view of the kid. Holly McClaine's mousey brown hair was cut into a bob and secured back from her face with a headband; she wore a windbreaker two sizes too big over a checked pinafore dress, fawn-colored tights and plain brown shoes. Her left hand was on the strap of her Dora the Explorer backpack, her right one in the grip of a woman Kelsey recognized as her teacher, Audrey Patterson. While Holly stared straight ahead, a worried frown creased the teacher's brow. She pulled the child's hood up, then turned and shrugged her shoulders against the icy wind, searching the street for a car that was never going to come.

Matt checked his watch. "Okay," he said. "Now! Go, go, go."

Kelsey opened the left rear door, got out and headed down the street, drawing the collar of her jacket up over the dagger tattoo on her neck. "Hi," she called, flipping back a strand of her long brown hair and smiling as she crossed and trotted towards the teacher and the kid.

Audrey Patterson gave her the brief smile, but otherwise ignored her and continued scanning the street, until Kelsey paused next to Holly, dropped to one knee, and said, "Hey, Holly, I'm taking you home, baby."

The teacher swung on her, automatically gripping the child's shoulders and pulling her in, saying, "Excuse me?"

Kelsey straightened, offered her hand. "Oh, I'm sorry. I'm Amy, Lizzie's sister. You must be Audrey. Lizzie told me all about you. Says you're a terrific teacher."

Audrey's frown softened but the skepticism remained. She took the proffered hand. "Nice to meet you," she said, although the snap visual she gave Kelsey's jeans, Metallica tee-shirt and fringed suede jacket told her something entirely different.

"Oh, yeah, I didn't have time to change. Airports, huh?" Their eyes met, locked. Right there Kelsey saw the distrust and her heart did a flip.

Audrey flashed another zero-degree smile. "Thank you for coming, but Holly's car will be right along." Then she turned her attention back to the empty street.

Kelsey followed the teacher's gaze. "Oh, so Lizzie didn't call?"

"Elizabeth? No. Was she supposed to?"

Kelsey gave her a lopsided grin. "Jeez, I swear she'll forget her damn head one of these days. She's been so busy with all that campaign sh ... stuff with Richard and all, and yeah ..." She shrugged.

Another tight smile. "So I believe. And I think he'll be a great state senator."

"Yeah well, he'll have to get voted in first. Way he's going, that'll never happen. Anyhow, everything back home's gone all to hell. That's why I'm here." She smiled down at the kid. "Oh yeah, and Sienna. Y'know, like the nanny? Lizzie told me she's gone to her mother's. Yeah, so anyway, she told me to pick Holly up—Lizzie, that is, y'know."

Holly looked up at Kelsey, open-mouthed and without a hint of expression. Her puffy eyes were red-rimmed and lightly crusted with the yellow flakes of pinkeye. They were set in a round, flat face that bore the trademark scar of a cleft lip running from just under her nose to her upper lip like a jagged crack. Below that, her round pink tongue peeked from her open mouth. Apart from the scar, she looked like any other Down syndrome kid Kelsey had ever seen.

"I'm sorry but that's out of the question," Audrey told Kelsey, like she was speaking to an idiot. "School policy dictates that we secure confirmation from the parents before we release any child into the custody of anyone other than his or her authorized guardians."

Kelsey stuck her hands on her hips and shifted her weight. "Oh, right." It pissed her off when teachers and rich assholes talked down to her like this. "Well, I guess Lizzie should have told me that before I drove all the way across town," she said, a little more sharply than she'd meant to.

Audrey stepped back and pulled Holly in a little closer. "I'm sorry, what did you say your name was?"

"Amy. Amy Pace. I just flew in yesterday from Idaho. Shit of a place," she added and grinned. When nothing came back she directed a smile down at Holly, and said, "Well, I guess there's nothing I can do but go home and wait."

Audrey said nothing, just stared at her, both hands still firmly on the child.

"So, I guess I'll have to see you back at your mom's, huh?" she told Holly.

Audrey's flinty glare never faltered, so Kelsey tipped her head, said, "Fine," in a *have it your way* tone, then turned and started walking away.

This was the part where Audrey Patterson was supposed to call her back. According to Matt, she'd be relieved the sister had come to take the kid home so she could run along to the phony meeting he'd set up for her. That wasn't happening. Kelsey crossed the street, shaking her head and wondering yet again why she'd let Matt and Lionel talk her into this dumbass plan. When she glanced back, Audrey was watching her, only now she had her cell phone to her ear and was talking on it.

"*Shit.*" Now Kelsey didn't know what to do. Matt and Lionel would be watching her from the car and going nuts. She spun on her heel, and crossed the street again, trotting back towards Audrey Patterson and Holly.

"Y'know, if you phone the house," she called as she approached again, "Sienna could tell you who I am. I mean, if that's what you need. That's all you have to do." She shrugged; cool, casual.

Then remembered she'd just told her the nanny wasn't there.

When the teacher turned back to her this time, the tilt of her head, the sharp, knowing little smile all told Kelsey one thing—Audrey Patterson knew something was going on, but she was the one in control here. "That won't be necessary," Audrey said as her eyes went straight to the uncovered tattoo. "I'm sure Holly's car will be right along." Then she angled the child around and began shuffling her back up the path toward the school.

Kelsey turned, gave the street another once-over, wondering what the hell to do next. By the time she came to a decision, a couple of cars had gone by and Audrey Patterson had steered Holly halfway back to the front door. Once they got inside it would be too late. So, she went after them.

Audrey had just got to the door when Kelsey threw her arm across, barring their way. "Give her to me," she said quietly. "I'll take her now."

"Excuse me—" Audrey began, and tried to push Kelsey aside. Without even thinking, Kelsey gave her a shove that sent the teacher reeling backwards and crashing into a trash can beside the door. For the briefest moment, Kelsey hesitated and thought, *What the hell am I doing?* Her first instinct was to stop and check that she was okay. Instead, she grabbed Holly by the hand, scooped her up like a sack of potatoes, and ran for the car. The backpack fell to the ground with a clatter of pens but Kelsey didn't look back. All she could hear was Audrey Patterson screaming for her to stop.

Kelsey leaped out into the road with the kid in her arms, but a car appeared from nowhere with a screech of brakes and a blast of its horn. She twirled away, looked right and left, then ran for the car. She ripped open the door and tossed the kid in as Matt started it up, yelling, "Get in!" Kelsey jumped in after Holly but just as she reached to close the door, a hand grabbed her arm, and there was Audrey Patterson, teeth bared, eyes wide, clinging on like her life depended on it. Kelsey jerked away, trying to break Audrey's grip while Lionel leaned over and swatted her. Matt hit the gas, grinding through the gears, swearing and yelling, but Audrey Patterson held on even tighter.

Kelsey tried prying the woman's hand off, but she had a fist like a bear trap and her fingers wouldn't budge. "Slow the fuck down," Kelsey yelled to Matt, but he wasn't listening.

Audrey stumbled, almost fell, and Matt screamed, "Shut the fuckin' door," and swung the car left then right.

Still Audrey Patterson hung on. But now they were dragging her along, her feet pedaling against the speeding blacktop, trying to keep up.

At the corner Matt spun the wheel so hard Kelsey almost went out the door and Holly wound up in her lap. When Audrey Patterson finally lost her grip, Kelsey reached out, grabbed the swinging door and slammed it. Matt hit the gas again, but almost at once they heard a bumping on the side of the car.

Matt yelled, "Open the door!" His eyes were riveted to the side mirror. "She's caught in the fuckin' door. Open the door."

Kelsey threw open the door, then immediately slammed it again. She turned just in time to see Audrey Patterson tumbling over and over on the blacktop as they sped away.

"Mitha Pannathon," said Holly. She looked like she'd taken the whole experience like a routine trip to the mall.

Kelsey's heart was pounding, her hands shaking. She ripped off the wig and raked her nails through her short-cropped blond curls. "Huh? Oh, Mrs. Patterson, yeah, sure." Through the rear window she could see Audrey Patterson lying in a heap on the roadway while people rushed toward her. "Yeah, she's fine," she told Holly. "She's waving goodbye."

"Holy shit," said Lionel. "Holy fuckin' shit."

Matt's eyes were switching from the road to the rearview mirror. "Everybody just stay calm. Just stay …"

Behind them the wail of a siren split the air.

"Oh Jesus! Hang on tight," said Matt. He swung hard right at the next street, then took a left, smashing the stick-shift through the gears. "This piece of shit …"

Kelsey leaned forward, gripping the front seats. "Go down the Theatre route. Two blocks in there's a shortcut to the parking building."

"I know, I know," said Matt. He twisted the wheel and the tires screeched as they flew around the next corner then spun into the next. The left wheels mounted the curb and they flew down between stopped cars and terrified pedestrians, but the cop did the same. People jumped out of the way and shouted abuse after them. Kelsey grabbed the armrest with one hand and Holly with the other. When she looked down, the kid smiled up at her.

Suddenly Matt swerved and they all rode air as the car flew over the first incline and crashed down on the underground ramp. Tires squealed as they twisted and turned deeper and deeper into the parking garage. The cop drove straight past but in a matter of seconds he backed up and Kelsey knew he'd soon be behind them again.

But now there were two sirens.

They hit the fourth level down just as a car pulled out and cut the cop off. On the fifth level Matt slammed on the brakes and twisted the wheel, skidding sideways to pull into a slot. Kelsey grabbed Holly, hugging her close as they all leaped out. Matt fumbled in his pocket for a key, unlocked a blue Ford SUV and they jumped in. Matt fired up the engine while Lionel twisted in his seat, searching for the cop. Kelsey buckled Holly up and turned her attention to the rear window.

"All clear," said Lionel, so Matt slammed the truck into reverse, swung it around and threw it into first. They shot forward to the end of the row, and stopped. Then, calmly, quietly, he drove out of the building while three cop cars went screaming past. "Everybody okay?"

"I think I'm gonna throw up," said Kelsey.

CHAPTER TWO
DAY ONE: 3:09 PM

The SUV turned into the driveway and the instant it came to a halt, three doors flew open. Kelsey waited for Holly to scoot across the seat towards her, and lifted her out while Matt waited with the blanket. He tossed it over the child in Kelsey's arms, and guided them to the house. Lionel opened the front door, checking the street for prying eyes, and slipped in behind them, shutting the door and locking it.

"Wah-hoo!" Lionel yelled. "Blue skies, crystal clear waters, here we come." He and Matt bumped fists while Kelsey pulled the blanket off Holly and brushed her hair back from her face.

"You okay?" Kelsey asked her.

"Holy shit," said Lionel, staring down at the girl for the first time. "Holy shit, you see this?" he asked Matt and pointed. "She looks like a gopher."

"Shut up, Lionel," Kelsey said, wheeling Holly around and steering her toward the stairs.

Behind them he was laughing and saying, "Oh man, she's like one of those Goofy Gophers from the cartoon show—we got us a Goofy

Gopher," he said, and laughed so hard he doubled over with his hands on his knees.

Even from the bedroom upstairs, Kelsey could hear Lionel braying like the jackass he was.

"Naff," said Holly. "Naff an' naff."

Kelsey opened the Walmart shopping bag and searched through the children's clothes they'd bought the day before. They all looked too big. "Huh?"

"Nine-a naff."

"*Nine-a naff*? Oh! Oh yeah, Lionel's laughing. Whole street can hear Lionel laugh. He's an idiot. Here, try this on." She took out a crumpled tracksuit and shook it out.

"No naff a' me," Holly said, shaking a little finger. The words came out so fiercely, they made Kelsey look up.

"Hey, nobody's laughing at you. Ignore Lionel. He's an asshole."

"Ah-ho."

Kelsey gave her a half grin. "Okay, so maybe not that word. Maybe we'll stick with 'jackass.'"

"Nack-an."

"Yeah, a nack-an. And we'll keep that between you and me. Here, take your dress off. We don't want your expensive clothes getting all mussed up, do we?" She slipped the dress up over the child's head and checked the label. "Target. Oh, wow. So, no expense spared, huh? Oh," she said and stopped short when she saw the wet patch on the child's leggings. "I see you had a little accident, too, huh? Take off your undershirt and panties and I'll get 'em changed." She peeled Holly's soiled clothing off, noting the yellow coloration of faded bruising across her buttocks. "What happened there? Huh? Did you fall down?"

Holly looked up at her and said nothing, the emptiness of her stare so deep it almost echoed. But out of nowhere, a smile bloomed across her face. She bunched her little fists to her mouth and folded over laughing. To Kelsey the transformation was so stark, so sudden, it was like looking at a different child.

"Fah down. Oopny oop. Ah fah down," Holly said, and giggled all the harder.

"Oopty, oop's right." A smile caught the corners of Kelsey's mouth. And when the kid doubled over helpless with laughter, Kelsey found herself chuckling along with her. She was still smiling and stepping the child into a pair of clean panties when the door opened and Lionel leaned in. His eyes went straight to Holly. "So, what's happening?"

Conscious of his gaze, Kelsey angled herself between Holly and Lionel and pulled the panties up. "What do you want?" she said as she reached for the track pants.

He leaned on the door frame, grinning. "Well, look at you. Little mama, huh?" he said, angling his head to look around her. "Little mama and the Goofy Gopher."

Kelsey pulled Holly in close. "Get out, Lionel." Still shielding Holly from his gaze, she pulled the sweater over the child's head and tugged it into place.

"You got a new mama there, huh, Goof?" He folded his arms and leaned a shoulder into the door frame. "Hey, Goofy, are you deaf or somethin'?"

Kelsey felt an instant flash of irritation. "Don't call her that. And she isn't deaf."

Lionel's grin solidified and his expression switched to something more calculating. "Aw, shit, she don't know what I'm sayin'. Do ya, Goof?"

Kelsey tucked in the child's undershirt and adjusted the sweater. Then, she shuffled Holly in behind her and turned to face him. "Was there something you wanted?"

Lionel said nothing. Just looked from Holly to Kelsey.

"Then get out."

He gave her a wink, shut the door as he left.

Kelsey clamped her mouth shut, holding back the torrent of words she would have let go if there wasn't a child present. She pulled back the comforter on the bed and waited for Holly to climb in. Now, staring down at the kid who looked back up at her with her pink eyes and open-mouthed wonder, she couldn't help but smile. "You snuggle down there, missy. Try to get some sleep. It's nap time."

Holly wiggled into the bed but just as Kelsey tucked the comforter around her, a little hand popped out, snatching at the air. "Ninny, Ninny," she pleaded.

"Ninny? What's a ninny?"

"Ninny Nion," Holly said and snatched at the air again. "Wah Ninny Nion."

"You want your nanny? You mean Sienna ...?" But before Kelsey could finish, Holly's eyes widened and she let out a howl that made Kelsey jump. "Hey, hey," she said, but Holly sucked in another breath and howled even louder. Her arms flayed and feet kicked, and all Kelsey could do was grab her wrists and pin her down. "Hey, whoa there. Sienna's not here. You hear me? She's not here. She's all gone."

Holly fell silent. She sucked in one long hiccupping breath and drew the back of her sleeve across her eyes. "Nenna ah gong?" she asked. "No Nenna?"

"Nope, no Sienna. She's way gone. And she ain't comin' back."

Holly reached out again. "Wah Ninny Nion."

"Oh, I got it. You mean *Lilly Lion.*" When Holly's eyes lit up and she snapped her hand again, Kelsey said, "Okay, so Lilly must be your favorite toy, right?" She touched her finger to the end of Holly's nose. "Well, I'm sorry, but I don't have your Lilly Lion. Listen, though, I'll make you a deal—"

But before she could finish, the door behind her opened and Matt leaned in. "What the hell's goin' on? Why's she yelling like that?"

Kelsey tucked the comforter up around the child, then turned. "Nothing. Everything's fine."

Matt regarded them both, and dropped his shoulders. Twenty-four years old, Matt was as good-looking as the day Kelsey met him—maybe better. Thick brown hair, strong white teeth, great body. He was the one who had planned all this. Right down to the last detail. He had covered bases no one else even thought of. Like mailing the ransom note out the day before so it got there at the perfect time. Kelsey would never have thought of that. She would have just called on the phone like you see in the movies. Matt told her the cops could track you down if you called on the phone. But how many people passed through a different part of town one day and were gone the next? So if you posted a letter from any particular part of town, how would the cops ever trace it? The rest was in the timing. That's what he'd said.

Even now she still didn't understand why they couldn't just call on the phone. But there you had it. Matt was the smart one. Kelsey's old man always said she was dumb as a sack of hammers. But she had enough clues to know smart when she saw it. And Matt's ingenuity, his cleverness, his ability to make something out of any situation; those were the things she loved most about him. Though lately, he had so much on his mind he hardly seemed like the same guy.

He raked his fingers through his hair and said, "I'm going to get something to eat. You want something?"

"I'll go," she said.

"We'll both go."

"No," she replied so sharply that he shot her a look. "I'm not leaving her with Lionel."

"I don't know why you don't like him."

"It's not that," she lied. "It's just … what if he gets strung out? He can't look after her if he's out of it. Anyway, she needs some shit for her eyes. They're all red and itchy. They're driving her nuts."

Matt spread his hands and let his gaze circle the room in exaggerated wonderment. "So, why's that our problem? Why do we have to get it? Why can't her rich parents shell out their money for it? It's not like they can't afford it."

"Well, maybe they would. Only they're not exactly here."

He considered it. "Okay. You go. Don't talk to anyone, keep your head down and stay low. Don't go blowing this. We've come way too far to screw it up now."

"Just keep an eye on her."

Kelsey followed him to the door and looked back. Holly lay tucked under the covers, grinding her little fists into her eyes. "Just keep checking on her. Make sure she's okay," she said and pulled the door closed.

Downstairs Matt dug in his pocket and came up with ten dollars. "Quit worrying, will you? We'll take good care of her."

Matt was Kelsey's world. She never trusted anyone like she trusted him. She'd trust him with her life. She wouldn't trust Lionel to butter her toast. If she'd had the choice, she'd have taken Holly with her. That option wasn't on the table. So she'd have to move fast.

CHAPTER THREE
DAY ONE: 3:51 PM—ELIZABETH

Elizabeth McClaine sat on her wide, black sofa in the living room of her luxury lakeside home in the better part of Bay Village, nibbling her thumbnail. She was still reeling from the news the man sitting across from her had just delivered, and wondering why her husband was taking so long to get there.

She had just checked her watch for the umpteenth time, when she heard the front door close. She immediately got to her feet.

"Elizabeth, where are you?" Richard called out.

Once upon a time, everyone called her husband Mac. It didn't matter who they were—architects, company board members, laborers slogging for minimum wage for his construction conglomerate; they all called him Mac. The minute he'd declared his run for the U.S. Senate, he'd become Richard. Alice, his steel-belted campaign manager, had decreed it. No one argued. They wouldn't dare.

"I'm in here," Elizabeth called out, and pressed her white fingers to her lips, frown lines highlighting the worry in her eyes.

As soon as he entered the room, he crossed straight to her, placing a protective hand on her shoulder. "I got your message. What's happened?" At forty-nine, Richard was the picture-perfect politician—handsome features, perfectly styled hair, a smattering of gray at the temples. His gaze flicked first to the martini glass on the coffee table, then to the man who had risen from the seat opposite his wife.

Their visitor was probably between fifty and sixty but looked older. He wore a woolen coat a year past its best, and one size too big. The two deep creases down his face and bluish pouches under his eyes gave him the look of a chronic insomniac. "Mister McClaine," he said, with a nod.

"It's Holly. She's been kidnapped," Elizabeth told her husband in a strained voice. "This is Detective Delaney," she added, gesturing toward the man. "Holly's gone, Richard. Someone's taken her."

Richard flashed his election-drive smile and extended his hand, then checked himself and frowned. "Kidnapped?" His attention swung from Elizabeth back to the detective again. "What do you mean kidnapped?"

Delaney reached into his pocket and produced a square of standard white paper in a sealed plastic bag. He handed it to Richard.

"It's a ransom note," Elizabeth said. She folded her arms across her chest, watching him smooth out the plastic bag so he could read the note.

His eyes zipped back and forth across the scrawled words within. When he got to the dollar value, he sucked in a breath like he'd been hit in the gut. "Jesus," he said.

"They want ten million dollars for Holly's return," Elizabeth said.

"Ten mill ... Jesus Christ." Richard clapped his hand over his mouth and turned to scan the room while the information sank in. Then he turned and waved the plastic bag in Delaney's direction.

"This is unbelievable. What…?" he began, and swallowed hard. "What happens now?"

"I was just telling your wife that a full investigation is underway, Mr. McClaine. We're doing everything we can."

"When did this happen?" asked Richard. "Are you sure it's Holly they've taken?"

The detective dredged a notebook from his jacket pocket and flipped through the pages. "At approximately two-thirty this afternoon, a witness saw a young woman running from the scene with a child. We've accounted for everyone else in the class and your wife has identified a child's backpack that was dropped at the scene. It was your daughter's."

Richard turned to her. "And you're sure it's hers?"

"Yes, of course I'm sure," she said, a little more sharply than she'd intended. She slipped a glance at the detective and modified her tone. "It's her Dora the Explorer backpack. And Holly's the only child in the class the police haven't located. My God, Richard, her teacher was run down in the street. They took Holly and dragged Mrs. Patterson along the roadway and now she's in the hospital. What kind of person would do something like this?"

"Is Audrey going to be all right?"

"I'm afraid there's been no word on her condition," Delaney replied. "Mrs. Patterson was unconscious when she arrived at the hospital. I haven't heard anything further."

Elizabeth clasped her hands to her mouth, whispering, "Dear God, this can't be happening."

Richard read through the note again, frowning and shaking his head. He looked dazed, as if he could barely take the words in. "So, where are the police, the FBI? Who's investigating this?"

Delaney's chin lifted an inch. "Right now our department is handling the case, Mr. McClaine. Reinforcements are being pulled in out of the field as we speak."

"Yes, of course."

Delaney consulted his notebook again, and took out a pen. "What can you tell me about your nanny, Miss Sienna Alvarez?"

Elizabeth frowned. "Sienna? Why?"

"Have you spoken with her today?"

Elizabeth exchanged a look with her husband. Then he said, "No. Should we have?"

"We haven't heard anything from her," Elizabeth added. "I've been trying to contact her. I have no idea where she is."

"Do you think she had something to do with this?" Richard asked, tilting his head to see what Delaney had noted down. "Did you try calling her on her phone?" he asked his wife.

"Well, of course I did," she replied. Again, she shot a glance at the detective, and softened her voice. "Her phone was turned off."

Delaney nodded. "Can you think of anyone who may have a grudge against you, made any threats, perhaps?"

"No one," said Elizabeth.

"Have you seen anyone acting suspicious? Unusual cars driving by the house, that kind of thing? Perhaps anyone who might have taken an unusual interest in your daughter …?" Delaney asked.

Elizabeth shook her head and looked to her husband, but he'd hardly noticed anything beyond his campaign these days. "Not that I've noticed."

Delaney nodded, made a note.

"They said not to talk to anyone," Elizabeth told the detective. "That's what it says in the note—that if we go to the police, they'll harm her. What happens if they find out you've been here?"

Delaney tucked the notebook into the breast pocket of his jacket. "I have officers following up the school incident and questioning witnesses. There's no way the police couldn't be involved. But rest assured, any information you've given me stays with me." He regarded each of them. "Don't worry. We're already working on a number of positive leads. But remember, if you think of anything that might help us—no matter how insignificant it seems, I need to know immediately. If you can't get hold of me, leave a message." He took a stack of cards from his pocket and handed one to Richard, one to Elizabeth.

She glanced down at the card without reading it. "We will. Thank you."

"I'll need a recent photograph of your daughter, Mrs. McClaine," Delaney said, giving the room a quick scan. "And a description of what she was wearing this morning."

Elizabeth followed his gaze across the sideboards and dressers where no family portraits or mementos were apparent. "Upstairs," she said. "I'll go and find one."

"I'll ah … I'll come and help," said Richard.

*****

Emptiness echoed off the walls in Holly's room and the air seemed somehow colder in here. Elizabeth hugged herself, feeling as though the dead of winter had suddenly descended on her.

Richard peeped out into the hallway and quickly closed the door. "Why now? Five days to the election. Five goddamned days," he groaned as he stalked across to the window.

"I can't believe this is happening," Elizabeth said. She let her gaze trace the room where toys and clothes were positioned like props on a movie set. It was as if the past six years had been erased; as if she'd awoken from some ghastly nightmare, only find herself plunged into something worse.

Richard had one hand cradling his forehead, the other on his hip. "I cannot believe they sent one policeman—*one,* for chrissakes. I'm running for the United States Senate. Where's the FBI? Have they even been informed? I wouldn't be surprised if this detective shut them out—trying to keep the case in-house. His *solve-rate*—that's what this is about."

Elizabeth wasn't listening. "Who would do this? Someone must have been watching her—stalking her. And now she's out there, all alone. She could be anywhere by now. She could be out of the country. How are we ever going to find her?"

Richard's eyes narrowed on a point just beyond the glass. "It'll be somebody who knows us—they've probably been watching our movements, waiting for their chance. And now they expect us to hand them ten million dollars to get our own child back." For some moments, he said nothing, just stared out with his nostrils flared. He checked his watch. "I've got a press conference in half an hour." He dredged out his Blackberry and checked the screen. "I'll have to cancel that. *And* the rally in Columbus tomorrow. Jesus, I'll have to reschedule my whole week. I don't even know where to start," he said, and shut it down again.

Elizabeth was opening drawers, aimlessly searching them, then pushing them back in. She was trying to remember the last time she had even seen her daughter, much less spoken to her. "I don't like that detective. I feel like he's accusing us of something—of being bad parents; of not caring about her." She shoved one drawer back in with a bang and pulled out another. "What were we supposed to do?

Keep her with us every minute of the day? That's ridiculous. And would she want that? I doubt it."

"I'd like to know what happened to Holly's car," Richard said. "We pay that driver to take her to school every day and pick her up. Have the police even spoken to him? He'd be the first one I'd be talking to."

Finding no photographs in the dresser, Elizabeth crossed to the highboy and pulled out the top drawer. At the very back, she found a school photograph. It showed Holly's round, flat face smiling into the camera with her pink puffy eyes and scarred upper lip. She stared down at it for some seconds while an avalanche of emotions crashed down on her. That old familiar pain—already she could feel it leaching back. She had borne it for three long years until she had finally wrenched herself free of it. At a distance she was safe. She could shut off her emotions. Such a respite may have been tenuous, but it let her breathe. Now that respite was gone and reality had come gushing back to fill the void. She drew in a deep breath and stiffened. "Here, I found this. It's her school photograph."

Richard stepped across to look over her shoulder at it. "Don't we have a better one?"

"If we do, I don't know where." She crossed to the closet and parted the dresses and sweaters hanging inside. She had no idea what was in the closet let alone what wasn't. She took down a dress, checked the label. Then a second, and a third. "What? I don't understand. These are all Target brands. I give Sienna two thousand dollars a month to buy clothes for Holly. What's she doing with the money?"

Richard was standing in the center of the room, looking around as though he'd just woken to find himself somewhere he didn't recognize. Then the words hit him. "What? Two thousand dollars?

Don't we pay her enough? Maybe it's time we got rid of her. She skulks around here watching every move we make. She never smiles; never speaks. I don't even know why we employed her."

Elizabeth shoved the dresses back into the closet. "Don't be ridiculous. We need her. And besides, it doesn't matter whether you like her or not, Holly adores her."

"You want to keep someone working for us—in our home—when she's stealing from us?"

Elizabeth crossed to the dresser and pulled open another drawer, realized she'd already searched it and pushed it back in. "Now you're being over-dramatic. She's not stealing from us. I'll talk to her about it when she gets here. There'll be some simple explanation."

"*If* she ever gets here ..." Richard said, and let the implication hang between them.

"What do you mean, *if* she gets here?"

"Well, think about it—Holly's suddenly kidnapped, Sienna disappears ..." He spread his hands as if to say, "Need I say more?"

"Sienna would never do that. She loves Holly. Anyway, she doesn't have a tattoo."

"It's exactly what the police will be thinking. Tattoo or no tattoo, she'll be top of their suspect list."

She was about to object when Delaney's voice echoed up from the bottom of the stairs. "Mr. McClaine, is everything all right up there?"

Richard crossed quickly to the door, opened it, and leaned out. "Yes, fine. We'll be right down." He closed the door again. "Dear God, I don't believe this."

Elizabeth pulled out more drawers, hunted through them, and pushed them back in again. Finally, she cast a helpless look across the room and shook her head. "Well, I have no idea what she was wearing when she left this morning. Why don't we just give the kidnappers whatever they want so we can get her back? At least then we can get on with our lives again."

Richard ignored her. His gaze was fixed toward the window, staring vacantly into space. "That's out of the question," he said absently.

"Out of the question? What do you mean, out of the question? The note said if we pay the ransom, we'll get Holly back." When he still said nothing, she took a step closer. "Are you listening?"

"Pay it? Did you see what they're demanding, Elizabeth? We're not talking nickels and dimes here. They want *ten million dollars.*" His eyes narrowed at the thought. "Wait till I get my hands on these bastards. Who do they think they are?"

"What does it matter how much it is? When the police catch them, we'll get the money back, won't we?"

He snorted. "I doubt that. The money will be wired from one offshore bank account to the next. That's how these people work. We'd never see it again."

"Does that matter? We'd have Holly back." Elizabeth looked down to find she was holding one of Holly's sweaters. She folded it, feeling the softness, the warmth, while the image of that tiny baby scorched into her mind—the memory of holding her in her arms, of gazing down, searching for her beautiful angel—the child she had prayed for; the child she had lived for, would have died for. But in her place was something damaged, something dreadful. All her maternal instincts told her to hold on to her, to love her, protect her; but something deep down inside was already urging her to run.

She pushed the memory away along with the sweater. "She's our daughter, Richard," she said. "We have to do something. She's out there all alone. She needs us."

"Well, we can't just hand these people ten million dollars." He glanced back to find her staring at him. "It's not that simple. We don't …" he began, then looked away.

"What? We don't what?"

"We don't have the money," he said quickly, and turned with his back to her.

Elizabeth blinked at him. "Don't be absurd, of course we have the money. We have plenty of money."

"*Had* plenty of money, Elizabeth. Past tense." He went to the window and stared out across the pool and the surrounding gardens, avoiding her.

Elizabeth frowned, as if he'd told a joke she didn't understand. "What are you talking about?" When he said nothing, she stepped towards him. "Richard?"

"I'm saying," he said, turning on her like it was her fault, "that we don't have ten million dollars. We don't have one million dollars. If they were asking for a thousand, we probably couldn't pay it."

"You're telling me we don't have a thousand dollars in the bank?"

He turned back to the window. When he spoke again, his voice was almost a whisper. "I thought I could turn the situation around. It just kept getting worse." He pressed his fingers to his face and heaved out a breath through them.

"So, how much money *do* we have?"

"Jesus, Elizabeth, how many times? We have *no* money. It's gone. We've been living in the red for the past two months. And even if we had the money …" He sucked in a deep breath, straightened and rolled his head to ease the tension in his neck. "We'll talk about this later. Let's give the photograph to this detective and get him out of the house."

Elizabeth felt as if something cold and dark had wrapped itself around her, squeezing every atom of breath from her. If the depression she'd suffered over the past six years had been bad, this was becoming ten times worse. "What about the stocks? What about the company accounts, the offshore bank—?"

"Shhh, keep your voice down," he hissed. "What have I just been telling you? They're gone. Between the campaign and Ray Townsend with every state official in his back pocket … look, let's get downstairs before this detective—"

"But surely—"

"Listen to me. Do you know where I was when I got your message? I was out at the East Flight construction site over in Painesville telling two hundred and fifty employees—people who believed in me—that as of today, they're out of work. Right now, two hundred and fifty men are on their way home to tell their families they could be on the street by this time next week."

"Then we'll get loans …"

"Elizabeth, you're not listening. We've been hemorrhaging cash for the past twelve months. All our accounts are in the red, our line of credit is stretched to the limit and our assets are gone. This election was going to drag us back from the brink; stimulate the economy, stimulate industry. Now this happens."

Elizabeth lowered herself onto the bed, fighting to absorb it all. "The house," she said in a moment of clarity. "We could take out a mortgage on the house. That would at least give us …" She saw the look on his face and stopped mid-sentence. "What?"

He folded his arms, dropped his chin to his chest, and quietly said, "The house is already mortgaged to the hilt."

She got to her feet, eyes wide. "You took a mortgage on our house without telling me?"

He said nothing. His expression said it all.

"Then we have to find her," she said, pointing off toward the windows. "We have to get out there and—"

"And what?" he interrupted. "Go door-knocking, asking people if they've seen our child? Every man, woman and child in this state knows us—knows exactly who we are. How far do you think we'd get before we were swamped with reporters and tabloid newspapers? And then what would happen? The kidnappers would kill her. You want that?"

His words hit her like a physical blow. She could barely think straight. In a matter of hours, her whole world had changed in ways she could barely comprehend. This morning she had a child, a home, a life of normality—if not one of happiness. Now, a thunderous wave had crashed through their lives, picking up everything she'd known and loved, carrying them away while the heavens rained twelve kinds of hell down on them. "But we have to do something. We can't just leave the police to find her while we carry on like nothing's happened."

At the sound of footsteps on the stairs, Richard crossed to the door, opened it and called out, "We've found a photograph, Detective. We're coming now."

There was a pause, then Delaney said, "If you would, Mr. McClaine. We need to move quickly on this."

"We'll be right along." Richard closed the door again.

"So, what are we going to do?" Elizabeth whispered. "If we have no money to pay the ransom, how are we going to get her back?"

"This is what the police are for. They'll find her," he said.

"What about your father?"

"No," he snapped, and looked to the door again. "That's out of the question. My father stays out of it. I don't want him or my mother involved. Not yet. I'll think of something," he added, although he didn't sound convincing.

Downstairs, Delaney stood at the picture window with his phone to his ear, looking out over the garden. He ended the call and turned to them as they entered. "I'll need the name of the driver that picks Holly up from her school."

"Of course," Richard said. He got out his own phone, found the number and waited while Delaney noted it down.

Elizabeth passed the photograph across. "We found this. I'm afraid I have no idea what she was wearing. Sienna takes care of dressing her," she added, with a stinging glance at her husband.

Delaney took a pair of eyeglasses from the breast pocket of his jacket. He slipped them on at an awkward angle and gazed down at the child who stared back up at him from the photograph. A sad smile deepened the creases on his face. "She's a very pretty little girl."

Elizabeth stiffened and folded her arms defensively to her chest. "Yes. Yes, she is. She's very special," she said in a chilly tone. She knew exactly what was coming next.

The detective tucked the photograph into his right-hand breast pocket and took off the eyeglasses, folding them carefully, and slipping them carefully back into his jacket pocket. "And her ...?" he said, touching his finger to his upper lip.

"Oh. The scar," Elizabeth said, hugging herself a little tighter while a wave of anger flashed through her. *Here we go*, she thought.

From the day Holly was born, Elizabeth had endured the morbid curiosity of spiteful people who were supposed to be her friends; perfect women with their perfect children and their perfect lives, all peering into the crib and saying, *Oh, isn't she beautiful*, when it was plain as day she was not. "She was born with a cleft palate and lip,"

Elizabeth explained flatly. "The lip was operated on, but she had a reaction to the anesthetic and the palate is still—"

"—we couldn't put her through another operation … until she was stronger," Richard chimed in. He placed an arm around his wife's shoulders. "The first one was traumatic enough. We nearly lost her."

"Yes. She's very frail," Elizabeth said, bending her head to touch her middle finger to her forehead. When she lifted her head again, her words sounded strained. "And she doesn't communicate well. She talks in … mumbles. Whoever has her won't have the first clue of what she's saying. Oh, Richard, where is she?" she said, bunching her fist to her mouth as he pulled her in close.

Delaney drove his hands into his pockets and dropped his gaze briefly to the floor. "I need to get back. I'll be in touch as soon as we have some information. And listen," he said in a tone that made both of them look up. "Stay near the phone. These people haven't given you a time or place for delivery of the money. But they will. When they do, I'll have a tap on the line and someone with you day and night. In the meantime don't talk to anyone, don't leave the house." They both nodded. "I'll have an officer here as soon as one's available. Trust me, we're going to get these people," he said.

And just like that, he left. For some moments Elizabeth stood watching after him. Somewhere out there was her child. In some dark, despicable corner of the world, someone had her hidden away. Richard was right—they had no other choice but to leave it to the police.

And pray they'd find her alive.

CHAPTER FOUR
DAY ONE: 5:22 PM—KELSEY

Kelsey checked the map again. She'd turned the GPS off in case Matt could somehow retrieve the route she'd traveled from the memory and find out where she'd been. That's the kind of stuff he could do. That's how smart he was. She wasn't smart. All she could be was careful. She turned the SUV into Remington Drive and cruised into Belle Vue, slowing for a hundred yards or so, before stopping two doors down from the house at 243.

The place was huge. It sat like a castle in the middle of vast, manicured gardens full of roses and ivy and perfect hedges. Kelsey had never seen gardens like that outside of a public park. Then again, Kelsey didn't come to this part of town too often.

A woman ran right by the car. Designer sweat pants, designer running shoes, Gucci sunglasses; she loped along with her hair flying behind her like she'd just jumped out of a shampoo commercial. Kelsey watched her jog to the end of the street and disappear around the corner. People could run in this kind of neighborhood. You didn't see people run in Kelsey's neighborhood unless they had forty cops right behind them.

She turned her attention back to the house.

On the driveway just inside the gate sat a sleek black Mercedes convertible with the top down. Kelsey knew cars. She'd spent time boosting a number of them for a chop shop. This was a Mercedes Benz SL550 Roadster—a 32-valve V-8 engine that churned out close to 400-horsepower without breaking a sweat. Stylish, sexy, the thing drove like a bullet and handled like drugs on wheels. She stole one once. She knew how to get into it, how to drive it, how to take it apart. And she was fast. Her fingers were nimble and strong. She could strip a machine like this down to its barest components almost as fast as Matt could.

But that's where Matt came into his own. He had the brains. In two seconds flat he could calculate the value of those components down to the last dime, without even using a calculator. Or at least he could until early last year. That's when the chop shop got busted and it all went to hell.

But you didn't chop a car like this. Kelsey's boss, Jesse Milano, would have had customers lined up around the block and back for the complete unit. One thing Jesse knew was how to make money. Which was just as well because it took plenty of cash and a high-priced lawyer to keep him from doing a significant stretch inside. These days his workshop was strictly legit. Or so he said.

But the car wasn't the reason Kelsey was sitting outside 243 Belle Vue Drive on this chilly evening. The house it was sitting in front of was.

She ducked her head, scanning the front of the house, the upstairs windows, along the roofline, down the side; searching for any convenient point of entry, any weakness. She couldn't see one. The alarm would be set, and with the owners out, the place would be shut up like a vault. That didn't mean she couldn't get in. But she needed the cover of night.

Kelsey hit the ignition, drove to the end of the street, then headed to more familiar territory and the drugstore on the corner of Chester and East 55th. She pulled into the lot, checking the immediate vicinity for cops before getting out.

After locking the car, she walked quickly to the door of the drugstore and stepped inside. Three women were standing in line at the counter in back of the store. Two of them glanced across at Kelsey as she approached. That's when she remembered the wig. She'd been wearing it because it hid the dagger tattoo that ran down the side of her neck. She should have been wearing it now. Without thinking, she put her hand to her neck and hesitated.

"Yes, can I help you?" the pharmacist called from behind the counter. He was looking straight at her. All three customers also turned to look her over.

"Yeah, ah," she said, twiddling with a strand of hair just behind her left ear, shielding the tattoo as she moved forward. She felt conspicuous, like everyone knew who she was and what she'd done. She gestured towards the far end of the counter. Probably assuming she had a delicate matter to consult him on, the pharmacist followed her.

"I need something for eyes," Kelsey told him in a whisper.

"Oh, right," said the pharmacist, as if he'd guessed what the secrecy was all about. "Eye drops will take away the redness by constricting the blood vessels, so you don't want to use them for—"

"No, no. I need something for Pinkeye. Like, for all the yellow shit … I mean, y'know, the itchy, flaky stuff." When he narrowed his eyes, and leaned in to search hers, she added, "Oh, no, it's not for me. It's for my little girl."

"Ah, I see," said the pharmacist. "Well that's a whole different matter. Have you taken her to a doctor? Because if it's bad enough, she'll need a prescription. You let these things get out of control, it could jeopardize her sight."

"Well, no. She just got it," she said. "And you know—doctors, huh? You gotta rob a bank to see one. Plus I don't have insurance."

"Well, the best over-the-counter option I can suggest is Patanol. How old is your daughter?"

"Ah, ten," she replied. Then silently cursed herself when she realized she would have been twelve when she'd had her.

"Well, without seeing her …" he said, then looked up when the doorbell dinged. "Be right with you, Al," he called genially to the person who'd just entered.

Kelsey glanced back over her shoulder. The person walking right up behind her was a cop. Her heart thudded so hard against her ribs, she was sure he could hear it.

The pharmacist had moved in behind the counter where he reached up and plucked a tiny bottle off the shelf. "I'd say you should start her off on the point-one solution. Use it twice a day until it's cleared up. But if it gets worse, take her to the doctor." He rang it up, and said, "That's thirty-three, seventy-six."

"What? Oh, jeez," said Kelsey. She didn't know if she had that much. All she had was the money Matt had given her for the food, plus a couple of quarters of her own. She hurriedly counted it out but it came up eight dollars short. She was scrambling for more change in the bottom of her pockets, aware that the cop had moved across to stand right next to her. She could feel his eyes on her. Despite the chill in the air, beads of sweat flashed onto her forehead. She turned her back to the cop while she dug deeper into her pockets. "Hold on, I got some change here …"

"How's it going, Al?" the pharmacist asked the cop.

"Busy. We just pulled in a suspect for that robbery over on East 65th. Guy had just got out last week from his last robbery. You'd think they'd learn," he said and chuckled.

Kelsey was about to tell the pharmacist she'd come back so she could get out of there, when she heard him saying, "What's this I hear about a hit-and?run outside a school for special-needs kids. They said the teacher got knocked down."

"News travels fast," the cop said, tipping his head.

"In here it does. One of our customers has a child at the same school. She said the police were over there interviewing people."

"It's a bad situation. Teacher's in the hospital. She's lucky to be alive."

The pharmacist clicked his tongue. "At least they got a witness. Apparently, it was a girl with a wig on and some kind of tattoo on her neck."

Kelsey's hand went straight to the tattoo, fidgeting with the hair behind her ear as she tried to casually turn away from him.

"A teacher for special-needs kids, if you please," the pharmacist added bitterly, and shook his head. "A woman like that doesn't deserve to get run down in the street like a dog."

The cop shifted his weight and nodded in agreement. "Don't worry, we'll get her. We already got some solid leads."

"Well, I hope they string her up," the pharmacist said. "The things people do these days. Do you want to take that?" he asked Kelsey.

"Uh, no I don't have enough money," she replied. By now she had her back to them, still pretending to search her pockets with one hand, then both hands. "I got some more in the car. I'll be right back." She reached back, put the bottle on the counter, and walked straight to the door.

"Hey, just a minute," called the pharmacist.

Kelsey froze.

All she could hear was the blood pounding in her ears. Slowly, she turned around. Both the pharmacist and the cop were staring at her, along with both assistants behind the counter and all three customers.

"Make sure your daughter gets plenty of vitamins. Fruits and vegetables are best," said the pharmacist.

Kelsey nodded stiffly. "Sure. Thanks."

"You got time for a coffee?" the pharmacist was asking the cop as Kelsey shut the door behind her.

Outside, she took a few deep, steadying breaths, then went straight to the car. The instant she pulled the door closed, she turned the ignition and hit the gas. Dusk had already drawn an icy blanket over the city. She checked her watch: 7:28.

She had to get back to the house. And she had to do it fast.

CHAPTER FIVE
DAY ONE: 7:28 PM—ELIZABETH

The second Delaney was out the door, Richard went to the bar and poured himself a drink. Just as he tossed the first shot back, his phone rang. He pulled it out of his pocket, glanced at the screen, and answered it. "Blake, what's happening?"

Blake Ressnick, Richard's press secretary. He used tactics Elizabeth considered dirty, and he thought everyone admired him for it. His frequent quips were blatantly sexist, bigoted and homophobic, and he once suggested that Richard would have fared better had he been single.

Elizabeth had told Richard she didn't like Blake. Richard told her it didn't matter what she liked and didn't like. Blake had made impressive gains in Richard's ratings. Even Elizabeth had to admit that. She just wished someone else was leading the charge.

Still on the phone, Richard nodded a couple of times and said, "Yes, yes, put her on." He gave Elizabeth a look, then turned his back to her again. "Alice, hello. Yes, listen I'm… yes, yes, I know but I'm not going to make the press conference. Jesus, you don't have to tell me, but there's no … No, I'm not at liberty to discuss it right now."

After a few more nods and murmurs, he turned a pained look on Elizabeth, and said, "Well … we got a note in the mail. It's Holly. She's been kidnapped."

Elizabeth's jaw dropped and she turned to face the windows. Alice Cressley. Of course he'd tell Alice Cressley. She was Richard's campaign manager and the only person Elizabeth despised more than Blake. She ran his campaign like a political boot camp and kept all Richard's dirty little secrets tucked away, thinking Elizabeth was too stupid to know. Sharp eyed, sharp tongued, she fired out orders like throwing knives and ate grown men alive. At sixty-five she had the personality of a machete and the features to match. There wasn't one pleasant attribute Elizabeth could assign the woman.

She picked up her glass and drained the remnants of her drink while she waited for Richard to finish the call. He hung up just as she was putting the glass down again.

"That was Alice," he said. "She's on her way over."

"Why tell her? Detective Delaney just told us not to speak to anyone."

"Are you kidding? Alice is my campaign manager. I had to tell her."

"Why? Why did you *have* to tell her?"

"Without her and Blake, how far do you think I'd have got? There's no way I can keep this from her."

An icy silence fell between them. Then Elizabeth said, "So, what's she going to do?"

"Fix it. That's what she does."

"How is she going to fix it, Richard? We have no money, no idea where our child is, and an election in five days. What the hell can Alice Cressley do to fix this?"

"Whatever she has to," said Richard, pouring himself a second shot. "That's what I pay her for."

*****

Elizabeth had been debating whether or not to get herself another drink when the doorbell chimed. Richard turned from where he stood over by the window while she went for the front door.

As soon as she opened it, Alice Cressley stepped inside and pushed straight past her, tossing a dismissive "Mrs. McClaine," at her by way of greeting while she went in search of Richard.

In contrast to Elizabeth's loose gray trousers and shell pink blouse, Alice wore a deep turquoise pant-suit fitting so tightly around her bird-like frame that it was a wonder she could breathe. A dark green-stoned brooch nestled at the throat of her cream silk blouse, her auburn-colored hair was swept up in two severe drapes that sat on either side of her face like folded wings.

"Mrs. Cressley," Elizabeth muttered as Alice crossed the foyer and headed on into the house, saying,

"Where's Richard? This is terrible, terrible news."

"He's in the living room," Elizabeth called. "Don't mind me," she added in a flat tone, and closed the door. "Just go on through."

As if on cue, Richard appeared at the living room door. "I'm in here, Alice. Come on in," he said, gesturing her through.

"What's happened? Fill me in," Elizabeth heard her saying. "What did the police say?"

Elizabeth followed her into the living room where Alice had already peeled off her jacket, flung it across a chair and sat down. "How about some coffee?" she said to Elizabeth, and snapped her fingers. "I'm running on empty here. I've been up to my ass in opinion polls since five this morning. We're doing okay," she told Richard. "But what's this about your daughter? What are the police doing?"

Not in the house two seconds and already she was handing out orders. Elizabeth tightened her lips and went to the kitchen. She took three cups from the cabinet, then paused. What the hell was she doing? This was her daughter they were talking about here. This wasn't a referendum on healthcare initiatives. It wasn't a debate on immigration policy. Her daughter had been kidnapped. She had been taken from her school in a violent act that had left her teacher in the hospital. Elizabeth had every right to hear what this woman planned to do about it.

She left the coffeepot sitting on the counter and went straight back into the living room to sit at the far end of the sofa. "Coffee won't be long," she lied.

"So, this is how I see it," Alice began, sitting forward like she was about to regale them with the highlights of a movie she'd seen. "All the way over here, I was thinking, 'How do we run the election *and* get your daughter back home?' There's no easy fix. You have to understand that if we continue on with the election—even if Holly is found—"

"Alive," Elizabeth interrupted. "Dear God, they have to find her alive," she added, and pressed her hand to her mouth.

"Of course they will," Alice said. "But even so, continuing on with the campaign will make you come across as uncaring. That's an image we cannot afford."

Richard rested his elbows on his knees and drew both hands down his face. "So what do you have in mind?"

Elizabeth sat rigid with her breath held.

Alice waited a beat, letting the suspense build. "I say we go public."

"We can't do that," Elizabeth said.

Richard sat back, deflated. "She's right. It's out of the question."

"Now, wait. Before you go making any rash decisions, listen to me," Alice said. "What I've got in mind will bring your daughter home, and win the election. If we do this right, we achieve all of our objectives."

"Go on," said Richard.

"The police told us not to talk to anybody. They also told us to stay home—near the phone," Elizabeth said.

Alice turned on her. "And why do you think that is, Mrs. McClaine? I'll tell you why. First, they want you out of the way; and second, the media will hang them out to dry if they fail. Believe me, it's their own asses they're protecting here, not your daughter's."

"This is the police," Elizabeth insisted. "We can't just ignore them."

Alice dropped her head. "I understand your feelings, Mrs. McClaine, but tell me, why do you need to stay home? You can take your phone with you. They'll have a tap on the line. It's not like your phone is fixed. You can divert all your calls to your cell phone. There is nothing to stop you leaving this house."

"Okay, but," said Elizabeth, floundering at the obvious truth, "maybe they think we could drop the call at the critical moment or—"

"*You have an unlisted number*," Alice said slowly. "How are they going to call if you have an unlisted number? They're not. That's why they sent you a note."

"She's right," Richard said. "Where would they get our number?"

This was typical. Elizabeth knew this woman would turn him around. This election had sucked up every moment of his time for as long as she could remember. Nothing existed beyond it. It was a wonder Richard even recognized her these days.

"What about the officer Detective Delaney is sending over?" Elizabeth asked. "Shouldn't we at least wait for him?"

"Officer? What officer?" Alice said. "The police should have had somebody here already. How long are you supposed to wait? Hmm? Listen to me," she said before they could answer. "Law enforcement budgets in this state have been cut to the bone under this administration. Police in this city are stretched to breaking point. You'll be lucky to get someone here before the middle of next week. Tell me this, Mrs. McClaine, are you willing to place your daughter's life in the hands of a police department that takes two weeks to attend to a street shooting? Because I sure as hell wouldn't."

Alice was referring to a recent front-page story in which two men had been shot dead in a rival gang incident. All witnesses had suddenly gone mute, and two weeks after the event—big surprise, still no arrests. The story was an attempt to highlight the effects of recent budget cuts in law enforcement across the state. Instead it had left the police department looking incompetent.

"I'm sorry if it sounds harsh, but these are the facts," Alice told Richard. "The police don't have the time or the resources to deal with even the everyday crime in this city. If you wait for them, they'll throw you up in front of a camera and get you to squeeze out some tears hoping the person who took your daughter will have a heart. Well, I'm telling you right now, they don't have a heart. If they had a heart your daughter would be here at home with you." Alice sat even further forward, determined. "Richard, think about it—I'm offering you a solid, workable strategy. We go public; take it to the people. We have a window here. As soon as this policeman arrives, that window closes. Forever."

Richard chewed his lip while he considered it. "So, let's hear what you've got."

Alice leaned forward, a determined glint in her eye. "Okay, so here's the plan going forward. We hit it hard, and we bat for the bleachers. I can get back-to-back media coverage; we'll have the story across every network channel, on every TV, in every home. We get your name, your face up there: 'Richard J. McClaine,'" she said, framing her hands as though it was already in neon. "It'll be in full public view, so every man, woman and child in this city can see your grief, feel your pain. They will know what it's like to lose a child. They will see you reaching out—"

"When the police told us not to speak to anyone, I'm assuming that included the press," Elizabeth said sharply, and wondered why she was even bothering. "They said—"

"Elizabeth!" Alice cut in. "With all due respect, you're not seeing the big picture. How could we possibly keep this quiet? How long do you think it'll take before the media notice one of the leading candidates in a race for the *United States Senate* just vanished off the radar? Hmm? With only five days before the election? My God, it's a wonder they're not jumping all over it now. But listen," she said, addressing her comments only to Richard now. "I can leak it. I have a contact with every newspaper in the state and an ear in Townsend's camp. First, we put the story out in the papers, then we drop the word on Townsend that your daughter's been abducted. You know what he's going to think? I'll tell you what he'll think—he'll think you're out of the race. He'll think this election is a done deal. This is a simple strategy. It buys us time, it buys us media exposure, it buys us an advantage. Because when we strike, Townsend won't know what hit him."

She sat even further forward, eyes narrowed, determined. In a low, confident voice, she said, "One word, and I can have an entire PR machine ready to roll within minutes. I say we get this out there, right here, right now, overnight. We catch the early edition of every paper in the state, and right off, we're ahead of the game. Every man, every woman, every *child* will wake up tomorrow morning thinking they slept in a time capsule. The news will be everywhere—on the TV, the radio, in the office canteen. They won't be able to move without hearing your name."

"So, how is this going to help Holly? How does this bring our daughter home?" Elizabeth asked, wondering why she was wasting her breath.

Alice broke the connection with Richard and took an infuriated breath. "It'll help her because Mr. and Mrs. White-bread America will know exactly what your daughter looks like. It'll help because if anyone tries to move her, someone will see her, and that someone will call it in through our hotline. This will work, Richard. But I need your okay on it."

Elizabeth got to her feet. "And what if the kidnappers panic and kill her? Did you think of that? What if, while you're so desperate to keep your campaign on the rails, these people murder our daughter?"

"Mrs. McClaine—Elizabeth, please. Come, sit down," Alice said and patted the seat next to her. "I understand your concerns. But trust me," she said, in a calm, consoling voice. She reached to take Elizabeth's hand but Elizabeth pulled hers away. She'd seen Alice perform this switch so many times she'd lost count. She didn't know which she trusted less—the Alice who held nothing but contempt for her, or the Alice who pretended to care. "What this is about, Elizabeth," Alice said in a voice thick with exaggerated passion, "it's about control. Who has it; who doesn't. I'm warning you, don't wait for the police. Remember little Christobel Hopkiss? That child was taken two days before her fifth birthday. Six days later, they found her body. Who do you think was running that investigation?"

Elizabeth sank back to her seat and felt her breath go.

"Delaney," Richard supplied quietly.

"Exactly," Alice said. "That man only has one strategy for a case like this. He plays everything so close to his chest, even the parents don't know what's happening. Let me ask you something—how many people in this state knew who little Christobel Hopkiss was before she was found strangled? Did you? Because I didn't. Trust me, in a case like this, everything depends on circumstances you have no control over. At least this way, we have control at our end. If you ask me, I'd say we have a much better chance of getting your daughter back if you have the whole country behind you."

"And I wouldn't have to abandon the campaign," Richard said. "A lot of people out there are depending on me."

"*Exactly*, Richard. Everybody comes out a winner. We get control, we handle it. That's what this is all about."

Richard hesitated, thumb and forefinger to his mouth. He let the moment stretch, then he said, "Okay. Let's do it."

Elizabeth wasn't so sure. She was about to make another objection when the sound of a key in the front door drew their attention.

Elizabeth jumped up. "It's Sienna. Oh, thank God," she said, and made for the foyer, then stopped in her tracks. Not only did she have to tell Sienna that Holly had been kidnapped, she'd eventually have to fire her, regardless of what happened. A shot of acid flushed her stomach and she felt ill.

Sienna stepped into the room wearing a loose-fitting sweater, jeans, and a blue anorak that hid any hint of the slim figure beneath. Her dark brown hair was pulled back from her face in an untidy bunch, while her clear skin and large brown eyes gave her the appearance of a girl younger than her nineteen years. She gasped in surprise and clutched the front of her sweater, while her startled gaze crossed each in the room, finally settling on Elizabeth.

"I'm sorry. I leave my coat here," she explained and gestured to the foyer. "I get it, then I go."

Elizabeth crossed to her. "No, wait. Where have you been? Why weren't you here for Holly today?"

The girl blinked at them as if she hadn't understood. "I got a call," she said, the lilt of her Spanish lending her words a poetic cadence. "Someone call me on my phone. He tell me my mother have an accident. I try to call you, but you don't answer, so I leave a note on the kitchen counter. Then I go straight away. Why? What's happen?"

"Oh my God," Elizabeth said. "Is your mother all right?"

"She is fine. She wasn't in no accident," Sienna said. "Somebody is playing a joke. I drive right across to my mother's—tree hours," she said, shaking three fingers at them. "When I get there, no mama. I get in the car, I go to all the hospitals; I call her doctor. I'm thinking, 'Oh my God, my mother is dead.' I turn around to come back, and Mama walk in the door. I say, 'You okay, Mama?' She say, 'I'm fine.' She say she been to the beauty parlor. So, I get in the car and drive all the way back again. Why? What's going on?"

"Well, at least we know why you didn't call when Holly didn't come home," Richard said.

Sienna moved into the room. "Holly? Why? What's happen?"

Elizabeth placed a comforting hand on the girl's shoulder. "Come with me," she said. "I need to speak with you. Through here," she said and motioned to the door. When she glanced back for confirmation, Richard gave her a curt nod, so she followed the girl to the kitchen and closed the door.

Sienna went straight to the counter, took a small square of paper from the surface and handed it over. "See? Here is the note I leave. I try to call. But there's no answer," she said again.

Elizabeth took the note, focusing her attention on it without reading the words. After a moment, she folded it, running her thumbnail firmly down the crease. "Holly's been kidnapped."

Sienna gasped. "Kidnap? But why? When?"

"This afternoon. They're demanding money for her return. That's probably who called you. They wanted you out of the way so they could … take her." She cleared her throat and continued. "Anyway, I know this has come as a shock to you, but …"

"But who would take her?" Sienna asked, as if the notion of someone kidnapping the child was completely out of all reason. "Why would anybody even do that?"

"We don't know. The police are investigating. The thing is, Sienna, I know how much you love Holly and how much you love working here …"

Sienna's expression shifted, as if she could see what was coming. "Yes. So …?"

Elizabeth drew a faltering breath. "That's the thing, you see. Without Holly here … well, you may as well go home. I'm sorry, but with all the—"

"You are *firing* me?" Sienna's eyes widened and she stepped back.

"No, of course not. But …" Elizabeth massaged her forehead with her fingers. She was wishing she'd let Richard deal with this. He was the communicator. He was the one people listened to. He was also the one who wanted to get rid of the nanny. "Look, I don't know what's going to happen and I'd rather not discuss this now. When Holly comes home, then we'll talk about the terms of your employment—"

"What do you mean 'term of my employment?' I don't understand. I done nothing wrong. I was at my mother's. You go ask ..."

"Sienna, I'm not arguing about this—"

"So what about me? I got rent to pay. I got to make repayments on my car."

Elizabeth's mouth dropped open. "Holly has been *kidnapped.* Have you even been listening to what I'm saying?"

The girl lowered her eyes. "Yes, Mrs. McClaine. I'm sorry."

For the longest time, she said nothing. Just stood with her head bowed.

Elizabeth raised her hands briefly and dropped them. "I'll make sure you get your money, but I don't know what else I can tell you. This is all so ..." She drew in a breath, huffed it out. "I'm sorry. Go home. There's nothing you can do here."

The silence stretched. Elizabeth reached out to the girl, meaning to break the tension with a few consoling words. But when the nanny's eyes lifted, instead of that sweet, smiling girl who had gushed over Holly at their first meeting, Elizabeth found herself staring into the cold and bitter glare of someone she hardly even recognized.

Sienna quickly turned away. She snatched up her purse, hugging it close to her chest. "I have to go."

"No, wait." Elizabeth crossed the kitchen to cut her off. She grabbed her by the arm and jerked her around. "Where were you today? Where did you go?"

"I already tell you. I'm at my mother's. Go ask her, if you don't believe me. I done nothing wrong."

Sienna went to pull her arm away but Elizabeth tightened her grip. "Why didn't you call me? You were supposed to be looking after Holly. That's what I pay you for, dammit."

"I try to call you. I already tell you all this."

"So, what? You just drive off? Not knowing if she'd get home?"

"This is not my job. This is the driver's job. Now leave me alone." She jerked her arm free, shouldered the door open and stalked out, leaving Elizabeth wilting at the shoulders, and wondering if she could have handled that any worse.

Furious with herself and sickened by the exchange, she snatched up the note and cast it angrily into the trash, then turned for the living room. But out of nowhere, a single sob welled up and burst from her lips before she could stop it. She clapped her hand to her mouth. "No," she whispered to herself. "No, no, no. Not now." She blinked hard at the ceiling, patted the tears from her eyes, and pulled herself back together again.

By the time she reentered the living room, Elizabeth was the epitome of politician's dutiful wife again—calm, collected, in full control. Richard and Alice, on the other hand, were both on their feet, gaping open-mouthed at the door Sienna had just stormed through, slamming it as she went.

Richard immediately turned on her. "You fired her?"

"Of course not. Why would I fire Sienna? I was trying to explain the situation to her."

"Well you didn't do a very good job," Alice said. "The girl thinks you just fired her. At this rate, we'll have an employment dispute and the entire Hispanic community hammering down the door. Jesus Christ, this is all we need."

"How could you let her go like that?" Richard said, gesturing after the girl. "Why didn't you discuss this with me first?"

"Me? You're the one that wanted to get rid of her ..."

Alice raised a calming hand. "Forget it, Richard. "I'll pay her out. It's not an issue. Seriously, Mrs. McClaine, we've got enough problems here. I'm beginning to wonder whose side you're on."

Elizabeth felt her cheeks flash hot. "I'm on my daughter's side. Whose side do you think I'm on?"

"Well, right now you're not doing her any favors. The press gets one whiff of this fiasco, the only media we'll be featuring in is the tabloids."

"What the hell do we do now?" Richard muttered, and massaged his jaw.

"I told you, I'll handle it," Alice said. "Now, go change your clothes. I've got a press conference set up for nine-thirty. I want you in smart casual—nothing expensive, leave out the Armani. In fact, go one better. Go drab. You're stressed; you're pressured. Drab under these circumstances is understandable. Elizabeth," she said, giving her a brief appraisal. "You'll be fine as you are."

Elizabeth said nothing. She didn't much care what the woman thought.

"Come on, people," Alice shouted, clapping her hands as Richard flew up the stairs. "I want harassed, I want home-style, I want 'I just got home and ripped my tie off and I haven't had time to eat.'"

Elizabeth pursed her lips and crossed to the liquor cabinet.

Alice watched her. "With all due respect, Mrs. McClaine, drinking right now would be a very bad idea."

"I think I'm a little tired of your ideas, Mrs. Cressley," Elizabeth said and reached for a glass.

In an instant, Alice crossed to her, stepping in so close, they were almost nose to nose. "You listen to me, and you listen good," she said in a low voice. "I'm sixty-five years old; your husband's candidacy is on the line here. I've been in this business many, many years, and to date, he's my best shot at the White House. If you think I'm going to let a drunken housewife stand in my way, try me."

The two women stood silent, locked in a battle of wills for ten solid seconds. Then Richard appeared at the top of the stairs. "Let's go," he said. "I'll take my car."

Alice broke away and snatched up her bag. "You're not taking that car, Richard. You take that car, people see ostentation. People see money they don't have. We're working against a Democrat incumbent in tough times here. People think you're waving your money in their face, they'll tell you to go to hell. We're taking my car."

"How do I look?" he asked, straightening the collar of his pale pink shirt and rolling up the sleeves.

"Good, I like the color choice," Alice said. "Now go get in the car before this policeman gets here and the whole plan is shot to hell."

They locked the house and went straight to Alice's car. Richard got into the passenger's seat, leaving Elizabeth in the back like an unwanted accessory.

"Okay, here's how we play it," Alice said. She started the engine, wrenched the shift-stick into gear, and reversed into the street. "I didn't have time to get a speech drawn up, so, you're flying solo. But here are the rules ..." She glanced across to find Richard consulting his Blackberry again. "Are you listening to me?"

"Yes, yes, I'm listening," he said, and put the device in his pocket.

Alice slammed the car into drive and stamped her foot on the gas, her eyes swiveling from the road to the rearview mirror. "You do not talk money. You do not talk politics. You make one remark about politics, this crowd will take you to the pit. And believe me when I say I'll be the first with my foot in your back. You hear me?"

Richard had one hand on the dash, the other gripping the seat. "I do," he said.

"You start off by placing your arm around Elizabeth's shoulders. You have to give the impression of a solid unit here. Then you open by addressing your absence in the closing stages of a hard-fought political campaign."

"So, I mention the campaign at this point?" he asked.

"No. I am not saying that," she said. As they approached a red light, Alice stamped her foot so hard on the brake, all three in the car bent forward like reeds in a hurricane. "Just listen to what I'm telling you."

Richard nodded.

"You go on to say that your six-year-old daughter didn't return home from school, and that you've subsequently discovered that someone has taken her. Pause for effect, let it sink in. Then you say, 'We don't know who is responsible.'"

Richard nodded, hanging on her every word.

When the light turned green, Alice pressed her foot to the gas and they sped away again. "While you're speaking, imagine there's an audience in front of you. Chances are there'll be no more than six people present—doesn't matter."

"Are you going to bother mentioning the girl had a tattoo and a wig?" Elizabeth asked. "Or isn't that part of the show?"

Alice shot her a look in the rearview mirror. "Do you want to panic these people? Do you want them to kill her?"

"Of course not," said Elizabeth.

"We're not dealing with political terrorists here," she said. "We're not dealing with any kind of strategic genius. These people are stupid. Anyone who sends a note the police can take fingerprints off is a moron. Anyone who does that and doesn't include details for the money drop is stupid beyond belief. Now, they have to send another note. My guess is they'll have the money transferred from one bank account to the next. But the minute they give the police that first account number, it'll be traced, so they'll send another note giving you a two-minute window to deposit the funds, then they'll transfer it."

"That's if we manage to raise the money in time," Elizabeth said, aiming the remark at her husband. Her tone had acquired an edge. She was sick of sitting in the back of Alice's car. She was sick of the sound of Alice's voice. All she wanted was to get away from this dreadful woman and get a drink.

"If these people have any brains at all," Alice said, "the money will go to a location where the United States government can't retrieve it." She pulled the car to an abrupt halt in front of her office block, wrenched on the parking brake, and yanked the keys from the ignition. "So, then you go on to say how you just got home and found the note. Make it their fault. Make them realize *they* messed up. Finally, you look straight down the barrel of the camera and you ask the kidnappers for one more day. Wait here, while I get my other briefcase."

"You think they'll buy it?" Richard asked. "The extra day?"

Alice turned in her seat. "Listen to me. The kidnappers are expecting the money at noon tomorrow. Once they've heard your speech—and believe me, they will be listening—they will know they can't have the money when they wanted it because they screwed up. But you must ask for that extra day. I can't do this without it. We need the momentum; we need the exposure. I want the American public to see a man who'll go to the ends of the earth for his daughter. I want them to see a man who will move heaven and earth to get his child back. Then you thank everybody, the end."

"What do I say?" Elizabeth asked her.

"You don't say a word. Let Richard do the talking. That's what he's good at." Alice got out of the car and went straight to her building, leaving Richard and Elizabeth sitting in the car in an icy silence for almost three minutes.

When Alice returned, she got into the car, twisted the key in the ignition, and picked up from where she'd left off. "So, immediately after the speech, Richard and I will head on downtown. I took out a lease on some space there. It's not much, but it'll be campaign headquarters for the next few days. Elizabeth, you can go home straight after. And don't drink anything. I need you alert. If anything happens, they'll want to interview both parents."

Elizabeth snorted. "What, are you afraid they'll find my daughter and I'll be too drunk to speak coherently?"

Alice pulled the seat belt down and snapped it into place. "Those are your words, Mrs. McClaine, not mine."

"Your opinion of me must be so low, Mrs. Cressley. Are you sure you can trust me to be on my own?"

Alice met her gaze in the mirror again and held it. "If you want the truth, no, I don't trust you. And it's nothing to do with opinion. It's past experience. Unfortunately, I need you to be at home when the next letter arrives."

Elizabeth said nothing. She didn't have to. As they pulled back out into the traffic, she folded her arms across her chest and turned her attention to the passing landscape.

The instant they hit the freeway, Alice checked her watch. "It's now eight-thirty-five. It'll take us approximately twenty-two minutes to get there from here." She turned briefly to check the traffic behind them, then hit the gas. "Hold on to your hats, kids. We're in for a bumpy ride."

CHAPTER SIX
DAY ONE: 8:35 PM—KELSEY

By the time Kelsey pulled the SUV back into the safe-house driveway, the sun was down, the temperature had dropped into the thirties, and the streetlights were on. She collected the three bags of McDonald's, checked the package in her pocket, and went inside.

As she closed the door, Lionel and Matt turned from where they were sitting in front of the TV, and Matt got to his feet. "Where'd you go? Canada?"

Kelsey gave him one of the bags, another to Lionel, who snatched it out of her hand and tossed it on the coffee table. "I went by the drugstore to get some shit for her eyes. Then I got stuck in traffic."

"Next time, call," Matt said, as he opened his bag and drew out the Big Mac. He peered into the bag then frowned up at her. "Is this it? Is this all you got?"

"I didn't have enough money. I had to get some for Holly."

"Don't know why we have to feed her," said Lionel. He was sitting back gripping the arms of the chair like it was about to throw him out. Kelsey watched him for a second. She could see the telltale signs: the irritability, the tight angry features, the greasy sweat. Hands trembling, knee bouncing; he was strung out. Lionel spent the better part of his life either strung out or getting clean. He was mean when he was sober, unpredictable when he was high. Strung out, he was ten times worse. Even now his pupils were so dilated they looked like black holes in his face.

"What?" he said, knee still jiggling, shoulders twitching.

She shook her head, said nothing.

"So how much was this eye stuff you got for her?" Matt was asking her.

She tossed the car keys down on the coffee table. "I didn't get it. It was thirty-three bucks."

Matt's mouth dropped open. "Holy shit, we're in the wrong game. We should be robbing drugstores at those prices." And he chomped into his burger.

"I'll take Holly's up to her," Kelsey told them.

"And tell her to shut up," Lionel told her without taking his eyes off the TV. "She's been blubbering up there since you left. Fuckin' neighbors'll hear. Next thing, we'll have ten thousand cops banging on the door." Irritated, he sat forward and cupped his hands over his nose and mouth, and squeezed his eyes shut like he was fighting for some kind of control.

Kelsey turned the unspoken question on Matt, who glanced across at his brother. "He's fine. Just go," he said, and stuffed the last of his burger into his mouth.

Upstairs Kelsey opened the door and peered in. She could hear Holly sobbing beneath the folds in the covers.

"Hey, hey, what's up?" She closed the door and went across to her. When she sat down on the edge of the bed and leaned across, the little lump under the comforter fell silent. "I got something for you. Do you wanna see what it is?"

The covers parted and Holly's face appeared, eyes red and swollen from crying, a trail of mucus streaming from her nose.

"Oh man, look at you. C'mere." Kelsey took a tissue from her pocket and wiped it across the child's nose. "Don't go making a big noise. You'll just piss 'em off downstairs. Here," she whispered. "Look what I got." She reached into her jacket pocket and drew out a misshapen cardboard package that was dripping red juice. "It's strawberries. They're a teensy bit squashed. But they'll still taste good." She opened the top and passed one to Holly who was now sitting up and peering into the pack.

"Nawmerry?"

"Yeah, strawberries. I didn't get the stuff for your eyes, but the pharmacist said you gotta eat fruit. You need the vitamins. My mom used to get me strawberries when I was little." She picked one out and gave it the child. "Hey, hey," she said when Holly pushed the whole berry into her mouth and crushed it. "You're not supposed to eat the green part. You throw that out." But Holly had plucked another from the box and stuffed that one into her mouth along with a third and a fourth. "Or not. Long as it's not poison. I guess if it was poison, it'd say on the pack." She turned the packaging, searching over the print. "Nope, no warnings or nothin'. I guess you're in the clear."

A red trail of drool snaked down Holly's chin. She dashed her sleeve across it and selected another strawberry, holding it up for Kelsey.

"Nah. You eat 'em." Her eyes fell to the child's arm. Red welts had risen on the skin where she had been scratching. "Shit, now we got fleas. Terrific. There's hardly enough room for us in the bed without extras. They'll be in this shitty cover." She got up, drew the comforter off and shook it hard twice, then replaced it on the bed, tucking it in around the child.

Kelsey smoothed the comforter and sat down again. "I bet you don't get fleas where you come from," she said as Holly crammed strawberries into her mouth, barely chewing before taking another. "Good, huh?" She wiped the trail of juice from the corner of the child's mouth once more and smiled down at her.

Holly paused, mid-chew. "Wah Ninny."

"I told you, I don't have your Lilly Lion. I'm sorry." She watched her for a while. "I guess you'll be home with your mom and dad soon anyway. You'll have your Lilly Lion and you can eat strawberries every day if you want."

"Snoomin."

"Huh?"

"Snoo-min," Holly said again.

"Stupid? Who says you're stupid? You're not stupid."

Holly wiped her mouth on the back of her hand. "Nanny."

"Your nanny? Sienna? She says you're stupid? Well, ignore her. She's a bitch."

Holly's face crumpled and she let out a wail.

Kelsey grabbed her. "Hey, shut up, shut up. What did I just tell you? You'll piss 'em off. Then they'll be up here. We don't want that, do we? No. So, just keep quiet, okay?"

The child clapped both hands to her mouth and sat back, staring wide-eyed at the door.

"And if Lionel said you're stupid, ignore him, too. I told you, he's an asshole—I mean a jackass, right?"

Holly shook her head. "Nanny."

"Oh, your daddy? Your dad said you're stupid? Well, he's a jackass, too. Let me tell you, there's a bunch of 'em out there. My dad took out the top prize for bein' a … jackass. But that's how I got my name. Money—Kelsey Money."

"Nangsie Mommy," Holly said.

"Huh?"

"Nangsie Mommy," she repeated and pointed to Kelsey.

"Oh, that's right, Kelsey Money. That's a laugh. Never had any money, probably never will. And you know what? He wasn't even my real dad. My name was Kelsey Terrasone. My mom married Vic Money and he adopted me. She always said she married into money. Which was a fu …" She stopped short of using the word, surprising herself, and smiled at her own reaction.

"Well anyway, that was a hilarious joke because none of us had any money. Ever. Vic Money was about as much use as diet crack. He did one good thing, though. He taught me to fight. See this?" She sat up, pulled up her sleeve, and flexed her right arm until the bicep bulged. "Look at that. Tough, huh? I still work out, too." She rolled the sleeve down. "I'm fit and I'm good. I can go toe-to-toe with guys way bigger than me and still put 'em on their ass. I won a medal once." She smiled, shook her head. "Only one I can't beat is Matt. He's real good. Trick is, you gotta keep your guard up. Jab and move, jab and move." She held up her fists—like Sugar Ray, ducking this way and that. She dropped her hands, massaged her fingers across the knuckles. "Anyone can move, but if you drop your guard, you're sunk. I used to spar with Vic."

Kelsey's smile faded. Her voice dropped as the memory pulled her back there. "He used my mom as a punching bag. I came home one day, he's beating on her. I jumped in, punched him right in the kisser. Beautiful right jab," she said, rounding her fist and demonstrating the stroke. "Broke his nose, knocked him clean on his ass. Fifteen, I was. Just fifteen years old," she whispered. "That was hilarious. You should have seen the look on his face."

She could almost see it playing out right in front of her. Vic Money had gotten straight back up and punched her full in the face. She'd woken up an hour later to find Vic gone and her mother dead on the kitchen floor.

"Stupid bitch," she muttered, and blinked to clear her eyes. "She should'a left like I told her." For a while, Kelsey was silent, lost in thought. When she turned back, Holly was sitting wide-eyed, mouth open, strawberry stains across her face. "Listen to me, will you—blabbering on and on. You should'a told me to shut up." She smiled and touched the kid on the nose. "Anyway, doesn't matter now. I got Matt. He takes care of us. He's smart. He always knows exactly what to do." She swung her legs around and up onto the bed, leaning back next to Holly, and pulling her in close. Holly snuggled into her side. "I'm gonna talk to him tomorrow. Find out when you can go home to your mom."

Just as they were settling down, there was a shout from downstairs, Matt calling her name.

"Shit. What now? Wait here," she said. "I'll be right back."

Downstairs, Matt was pacing the room while Lionel lounged back, eyes fixed on the TV.

"What's going on?" she asked.

Matt stopped and dropped into a chair. "We had a visitor," he said, like it was her fault.

"A visitor? Who?"

Lionel turned his head to her, a stupid grin on his face. "Stick Clemmons," he said.

Kelsey stuck her hands in her pockets, said nothing. Stick was Lionel's drug runner. *Typical*, she thought.

"Home delivery," Lionel added with a grin. "How's that for service."

Matt leaned forward, palms pressed to his eyes. "So, how many fuckin' people know we're here now? Huh?"

"Just Stick," said Lionel, broadening the grin. He looked like a different person when he was high—mellow, calm, agreeable. When he was like this, you could almost trust him. Almost. He frowned briefly, held up a finger. "Oh. And Wayne. Just Stick and Wayne. That's all."

"Jesus Christ," Matt said, and rocked his head back. "You told Wayne Clemmons? You might as well have told the whole fuckin' world."

"Calm down, I didn't tell the whole world. Just Stick and Wayne, that's all. How else am I supposed to get well? Huh?"

Kelsey kept her mouth shut. She wanted to see how this panned out. From long experience, she knew Matt never stayed mad at Lionel for more than three minutes or so. She couldn't understand it. No matter what the guy did, how bad he screwed up, Matt always forgave him.

Right now Matt was leaning on his knees, massaging his temples in frustration. "You should have waited, that's all I'm saying."

"For what? I gotta get fixed, don't I? What?" he said when he saw Matt's expression. "Okay, so you want me rolling around on the floor in agony, do you? You want me pukin' my guts up all over the place?"

"No."

"You want me completely useless? Because, you know I can't do a fuckin' thing when I'm like that, right?"

"I know."

"And that's what would happen."

Matt's shoulders slumped. "I know, I know."

"You have no fucking clue what it's like being dope-sick," Lionel went on. "I wouldn't wish that on my worst enemy."

"Look, it's okay, man. I just don't want anyone knowing where we are, is all. It's just … it's okay."

And there it was, right there: the big turnaround. Kelsey hated Lionel, hated his big mouth and his lousy attitude. But most of all, she hated the hold he had over Matt.

They fell into an uneasy silence, Matt and Lionel watching TV, Kelsey pretending she wasn't there. Matt turned to Kelsey, as if he'd just noticed her. "So what were you doing upstairs? You're with that kid more than you're with us."

"No, I'm not." She slid into an adjacent chair, one foot propped on the coffee table, the other tucked up with her arm resting on her knee. "You want me to keep her quiet, don't you? Her eyes are sore and there's like, a million fleas in the bed. How'd you get this place, anyway? It's a shit-heap."

"Doesn't matter how I got it. It's only one night, so quit bitchin'."

Lionel cut the tension with a yelp. He was laughing and pointing to the TV where an old rerun of *Gilligan's Island* was playing. "Oh man, I love this show," he squealed like a kid. "Goddamn, this shit makes me laugh. Look at it, look at it."

Matt grinned along with him. "We used to watch this when we were kids."

Here we go, thought Kelsey. *Another "when we were kids" episode.* She slid a little further down in the seat and waited for it.

Lionel spread his hands. "You hear that? Now that is funny. You gotta admit, this guy is hilarious."

"Remember that time you ran away?" Matt said. "Now *that* was hilarious. Eight years old, you were gone two days. The old lady didn't even notice." And he laughed.

Lionel said nothing, just grinned at some point in front of him and shook his head.

"And remember that time ..." Matt said, and pointed at him.

Any minute, thought Kelsey. *Lorraine Purcell, any minute now.*

"... when you were playing high school football—quarterback, no less." Matt raised both hands, as if to quiet a nonexistent crowd. "Man, you should'a seen this guy, Kelse. Top of his class and Mr. Popularity all in one. One of the teachers asked him once, she goes, 'So, Mr. Subritzski, what are you planning to be when you leave school,'" Matt said, mimicking a woman's high-pitched voice with a snooty accent. "And this guy turns around, looks her straight in the eye and he says, 'God.' Just like that, 'God,' he tells her." And he burst out laughing again.

Lionel grinned even wider. "Yeah, I remember that. Oh, and there was the time with those two girls, huh? Remember them?"

"Oh, yeah. Man, that was funny. They came running right over to you, right in the middle of quarter-finals. It's like, a minute to go and both of them run up to you, pull up their tops and show you their titties—"

"—and then they ran off." Lionel scratched at his face. "Those were good days, brother, good days."

Wait for it, Kelsey thought. *Any minute.*

Matt pointed to Lionel. "This guy," he told Kelsey, like she hadn't heard it a million times before, "he was a legend. Give him a football, and he was like, 'Dust, assholes.'"

Lionel said nothing, just sat there, wallowing in the reverie.

Kelsey forced a smile. Okay, so maybe she was wrong. Maybe Lorraine Purcell would get a rest this time.

"And that time," said Matt, "when there was you and me—"

Nope, thought Kelsey.

"And Lorraine Purcell—"

Here we go, she thought.

"Upstairs in the bedroom. And I'm bangin' her, but she's like, 'I want more, I want more ...'"

"Oh, man," said Lionel, tipping his head back, "that woman could not get enough."

Kelsey kept her eyes on the TV.

"And so I'm done, right? And she's still yelling, 'Gimme more, gimme more,' so you jump in and the next thing—"

"The door opens," Lionel chimed in, "and there's her old man standin' there."

Kelsey had heard this stupid story so many times she could just about mouth it along with them.

Lionel shook his head, laughing now. "And he says, 'What's my daughter doing here?' and you say—"

"And I say, 'same as you're doin' to my old lady downstairs,'" Matt added, slapping his knee and doubling over with laughter again.

Kelsey didn't know why they had to keep bringing up the same goddamn stupid story. It wasn't even funny. She scratched at the corner of her eye as though she had something in it. Matt's laughter finally tailed off into a grin. When he turned to Kelsey, the grin evaporated. "What's wrong with you now?"

"Nothin'," she said with a shrug. "Nothin's wrong."

Matt leaned back. "I dunno, every time we start having fun, you get all shitty."

"I'm not shitty," she lied.

"You look it."

She did a slow head-shake, bottom lip jutting. "I'm not."

Lionel slipped one of Matt's cigarettes from the pack. "Women," he mumbled.

Sometimes Kelsey would study Lionel from across the room. She could not reconcile this dreg of humanity with the brilliant hero Matt talked so much about. She figured it must have been the drugs that had turned him into a complete waste of space.

After almost a minute's silence, Kelsey swiveled around in her chair, knee up. "Listen," she said, trying to sound casual, "we need to talk."

Matt pulled a cigarette from the pack on the table, stuck it in his mouth and lit it. "What about?"

"Well, when do we get the money?"

"Tomorrow. I told you." He tipped his head back and blew a plume of smoke in the air.

"Yeah, but what time? And who's taking Holly home?"

"Why?"

"I'm just thinking—it's probably best if I do it."

"Why?" Matt said again.

"Yeah, why?" said Lionel.

Matt had been her life. She could trust him to the ends of the earth. Lionel was a different story altogether. He was ten people in one skin and you never knew who was up front. "Because when I was in the drugstore today, a cop came in."

He had grabbed the lighter off the table and started flicking it, over and over. "Oh, yeah, that's a real good reason," he told Matt.

Matt took another pull on his cigarette. "So … ?"

Kelsey shifted in her seat. "So, him and the pharmacist were talking about the kidnapping, saying how they know that some lady did it. They were saying she had like, a wig and a tattoo and stuff."

"Is that right?" said Matt.

"Who told them that?" asked Lionel, still flicking the lighter.

"He was saying there was a witness," Kelsey told them.

"A witness?" said Matt.

Lionel stopped flicking. "I didn't see nobody."

"Apparently some lady saw me. But I'm the only one they know about. So, they think there's only one kidnapper."

An unspoken message ran between Matt and Lionel. Then Matt said, "But they don't think anyone else is involved, right? Like, they didn't see me and Li in the car?"

"No, of course not," said Kelsey. "So, I'm thinking that if they don't know about you and Lionel, then I should be the one to take her back. Y'know, in case shit goes down."

Lionel went back to flicking the lighter again. "If … we take her back."

"What do you mean *if* we take her back?" said Kelsey. "That was the plan, Matt. That's what you said." She got to her feet and took a step back.

"Sit down and shut up," Matt said. "Everything's under control."

"The plan is," Lionel said, like he was explaining it to a two-year-old, "if her old man doesn't pay up, I pop her—boom! Pwah." He made a gun of his fist then splayed it like an explosion bursting in slow motion from the side of his head. "Then it's the big cement swim." And he grinned and held his nose like he was descending into deep water.

"Now, hold on a minute …" Kelsey said.

"Will you both just shut up?" Matt said. "We stick to the plan. They pay, the kid goes home." He let it hang, and Lionel shrugged.

Now Kelsey was starting to realize just how little she knew about the plan. Well, that *was* Matt's department, wasn't it? She couldn't have planned something like this. She wouldn't know where to begin. But now there were questions. Like …

"So, how do we get the money?" she asked. "Like, it can't be cash. I mean, that's a lot of cash."

Lionel huffed. "What's your problem? You think he's stupid all of a sudden?"

"It isn't that," she said.

Matt was making out like he wasn't listening, but now they were both staring expectantly at him. He did a double-take and groaned. "Okay, okay. Listen up and shut up, because I'm not explaining it twice." He waited it a beat, then said, "The money gets transferred into a bank account, right? The reason we're doing this in two stages is that if we give them the account number, the cops will be on that account in like, two seconds and then they'll suck the money back out before it's even settled."

Kelsey nodded. That made sense.

"And then …" Matt paused to stub out his cigarette. "It gets transferred into an off-shore account." Then he settled back again, eyes on the TV.

This time both Kelsey and Lionel sat up.

"Off-shore?" Lionel asked. "You mean like, another country off-shore?"

Matt drew an exasperated breath, clapped both hands to his face and growled in frustration. "No. Out in the fuckin' lake off-shore," he said, gesturing vaguely off towards the door. "Off-shore to Kelly's Island off-shore. Three fuckin' feet off-shore," he said and shook his head. When he saw the confusion on Lionel's face, he reined in his anger and said, "Yes, of course another country."

"You didn't say nothin' about any other country," said Lionel.

"Well, that's how this kind of shit goes. I'm the one planning it all, remember?"

"Yeah, you're the one planning it," Lionel said, "but where's the money going after that?"

Matt bit his lip, hesitating. "Okay, so … I was going to open an account in Mexico, right?" Kelsey and Lionel said nothing, just blinked at him. "But then Raul down at Stacy's Gym told me that the U.S. government can get illegal American money out of the banks down there."

Kelsey and Lionel shared a look that suggested they both had the same question. "So where's it going now?" she asked.

Matt stalled a few seconds. Then he licked his lips, and said, "Well, I got …" They waited. "Somalia," he said at last and snatched up the cigarette pack.

"What?" Kelsey and Lionel both said at once.

"Somalia?" said Lionel. "They're goddamn pirates over there—like, for real pirates. Those assholes will steal anything that ain't nailed down."

"Listen. I'm not stupid. I asked Delmar about it. He's a Somalian. He's got family back there. They're the ones that set up the account."

"You told Delmar about the plan?" said Lionel.

"Yeah, that's right," Matt told him. "I told him everything. I told him where we got the kid, how we got her. I even showed him my dick. What do you think I am? A half-wit? You wanna do this; you wanna do all the planning, be my guest. You tell me where else you put ten million dollars of ransom money. America's got agreements with every other fucking country in the world so if money from any kind of illegal shit goes there, the American government can just go in and suck it straight back out." He dipped his head and raked a hand through his hair. "Satisfied?"

"So, if it's in Somalia," Kelsey asked gently, trying to avoid getting him even more steamed up than he already was, "how do we get it out?"

Matt clenched his teeth so hard she could see the muscle at the side of his jaw working. "The money," he said with forced patience, "is in Somalia for, like, *one minute.* Then it gets transferred back to a second account I got set up. Okay?"

A slimy grin creased back one side of Lionel's mouth. "Now that's smart. That is very smart."

"So, anybody got any other questions?" Matt asked in a tone that suggested he wasn't going to listen anyway. Neither of them did. "If we stick to the plan, we can't go wrong."

"Sure, okay," said Kelsey. "But once her old man pays, she goes back, right?"

"Is that part of the plan?" he asked her.

"It was."

"Then it still is. Eight o'clock tomorrow morning, we head out to the next safe-house. From there we go to the last point and we dump her there."

Lionel waggled his eyebrows at her and made a gun of his fist again. "Pop, pop."

"Why can't we just take her home?" Kelsey asked. "I could do it."

Matt tipped his head back, eyes up to the grimy ceiling again. "For chrissakes ..." he started, but Lionel interrupted him, yelling,

"Shut up. Look." He was pointing to the TV. A banner across the top of the screen read: "Breaking news: U.S. Senate Candidate Richard McClaine's Daughter Kidnapped."

"Turn it up," said Matt.

CHAPTER SEVEN
DAY ONE: 9.30 PM—ELIZABETH

The space Alice had rented was on the second floor of an office block down by the theater district. The large central room was lit by a panel of overhead lights that lent everyone below a greenish hue, and a temporary lectern had been erected on a small podium at the front like a school classroom.

Contrary to Alice's words, there were more than six people present. The place was packed wall-to-wall with reporters holding up iPhones and microphones, while photographers snapped shots of anything that moved, and cameramen and their assistants ran cables left and right. At Alice's right side stood Blake Ressnick, stroking his chin and looking pensive. They looked like two warlords overseeing operations. All around them the scene was abuzz with reporters jockeying for position while camera lights flashed and doors opened and shut as more and more people pressed into a room growing stuffier by the minute. Directors crouched in front of the lectern, checking camera angles and sound equipment and lighting, yelling orders to cable runners, demanding they bring this here and that there so they'd get the best shot and the clearest sound. Alice's P.R.

machine was like some kind of juggernaut that had rolled straight into action and it looked ready to crush anything in its path.

Elizabeth stood steely-faced behind a large pair of sunglasses. She was poised at Richard's right-hand side with his arm clamped around her, his fingers pressed into the flesh of her right arm. She wanted to remove them, just lift them a little for her own comfort. She did not dare move. She couldn't help wondering how much of this was campaign momentum and how much was due to the "leaked" news of their daughter's abduction. Nothing seemed real.

As she waited for the countdown to nine thirty to tick away, she glanced across at Alice, who gestured for her to remove the sunglasses. Reluctantly, she reached up, drew them off her face, folded them and clutched them in her right hand. She knew she looked dreadful. Her shoulder-length blond waves were tousled and lank and she hadn't reapplied her lipstick—Alice had instructed her not to. Now she felt naked and vulnerable. Every magazine would have these photographs for all eternity to roll out whenever they might want to chop her down. She turned to ask Richard to release his grip on her arm when she heard someone call:

"... three, two, one, and rolling ..."

Richard lifted his head, pulled her in close and let his gaze range out across the room as Alice had instructed. "Thank you all for being here at such short notice. Some of you ... many of you, will be wondering why, in the closing stages of a hard-fought campaign for the United States Senate—a campaign that ..." Across the room, Alice drew a furtive line across her throat. He cleared his throat, dropped his eyes momentarily. "My wife and I came home this afternoon to discover our daughter missing." He let the moment stretch, then said, "After a considerable search, to no avail, we received news of an incident outside her school ..." Alice spread her hands, questioning. "… and upon …" He let his face crumple a moment, sucked in a breath, and continued, "… upon discovering a letter not one hour ago, it appears our little girl has been abducted."

A shower of lights and cameras blazed for a full twelve seconds. Elizabeth blinked against them, biting her lower lip. She raised her eyes to the paneled lights above. The heat from them was almost unbearable. She couldn't let anyone see how small she felt. The press would have a field day.

"And for those …" Richard continued as the drone from their audience died down. She felt his grip release. "For those of you who don't know, our daughter has Down syndrome." There was a moment's hesitation as the words caught in his throat. His grip on her arm tightened, fingers pressing hard into Elizabeth's arm again, this time biting to the bone. Elizabeth looked up at him. This wasn't staged, this was genuine. For a fleeting moment Elizabeth recognized something in her husband she hadn't seen in a long time. She turned toward him, placing a comforting hand on his chest. But just as suddenly, it was gone. His fingers relaxed and the politician was back.

Richard lifted his head, standing tall, confident. "Whoever you are who took our child, we will do anything you ask—*anything*. We will meet your demands. All we want is our little girl back home with us. Please," he said, and looked straight down the barrel of the camera in front of him, "please, don't hurt her. She cannot speak. She cannot communicate. She has a scar on her face from surgery to her mouth and she cannot form words." He paused, searching for words. When he spoke again, his voice was soft, quavering. "She is only six years old. She is innocent. Please, don't hurt her. We want her back. But we need more time. We've had only one hour …" He looked out across the faces, all turned to him. "… but in order to meet your demands, we first need to know that she is safe. And we need one more day."

"Mr. McClaine, I have a question," shouted a female reporter from the front row. Elizabeth recognized the face, but couldn't recall the name. The articles she wrote made it clear she was biased toward Ray Townsend, one of the country's most influential senators, and the incumbent Richard was running against. Every microphone in the room swung to her. "Does this mean you are no longer challenging for a seat in the U.S. Senate?"

"Mrs. Frazer, with all due respect, this isn't the time for electioneering. My daughter is all that matters right now. I'm sure that you, and any American parent, will appreciate that."

Elizabeth saw Alice's eyebrows rise in approval of the comment.

"Have the police been informed?" It was a guy from somewhere in the middle of the pack. "And if so, what has their reaction been?"

"When are the police issuing a statement?" someone else asked.

Richard raised both hands, patting the air, calling for quiet. "The police have been in contact with us. They have advised us to do exactly as instructed, but we have to wait for another communication. As for a statement," he said, and raised his hands. "I don't know when the police will be issuing one, but I'm sure you'll be notified."

"Mr. McClaine." It came from a woman sitting on a chair in the front with her pen aloft like she was working the floor at the stock exchange. She wore a tight red skirt, black blouse under a matching red jacket that was buttoned beneath an ample bosom, red high-heel pumps; feet crossed to one side at the ankle. Her short dark hair was pulled back from her face; notebook on her lap. A sudden hush descended on the room as everyone held their breath.

"Yes," said Richard coolly, nodding in her direction. "Miss du Plessis."

The woman cocked her head. "Does your daughter have a name, by any chance?"

Elizabeth saw Alice's head drop into her right hand. When she raised it again, she looked ill.

"Oh, uh … of course," Richard stammered. For a moment he was lost for words.

Elizabeth leaned to the microphone. "It's Holly," she said. In that split second, the image of that tiny baby lying in her arms flared in her memory—the tiny perfect hands, the tufts of honey-blond hair, that dreadful hole in her face where her little lip was split …

Elizabeth blinked the image away. Not now. Not in front of all these cameras, in front of all these people.

The room remained still. A sea of faces turned on her, all waiting. "It's Holly," she said in whispered voice that sliced through the air via the speaker system, freezing the room and everyone in it. "My daughter's name is Holly."

"Please," Richard said, pulling his wife in with one arm and holding out his hand out to fend off further questions. "Please," he said again against the buzz of chatter flooding back into the room once more, "this is very difficult for both of us."

A voice from the back called, "How much are they demanding?"

"Do the police have any leads on who took your daughter?" someone else yelled. And the room erupted into a million questions.

"Thank you, thank you, everybody," called Alice. She had cut her way through the crowd and was stepping up to the lectern. "I'm sorry; we're going to have to end it here. Mr. and Mrs. McClaine have been through a terrible ordeal in the past few hours and they need to gather themselves. They will be available later, but as you can appreciate they're in for a very long night and they need to rest. If you have any further questions, I'm sure they'll be answered in due course. A call center has been set up and the numbers to call with information are ..." She turned to Blake who raised a finger, signaling the affirmative. "Yes, according to my colleague, the numbers are currently trailing across your screen. If you have any information, please, please call. All information will be treated as confidential. For those wishing to donate, you may do so on the call center number. Thank you all."

As the din of voices rose once more, she turned and grabbed Richard by the elbow, steering him down off the podium and gesturing towards a corner. "Over here."

They squeezed between reporters and cameramen and stepped over cables, nodding and smiling at journalists and film crews doing last wraps and packing away sound equipment as they made their way to the corner.

"What did you think?" Richard asked Alice. "Did I come across okay?"

Alice maneuvered him around and gave him a long-suffering look. "Fine, very good. But we have company."

Elizabeth turned to meet the stony glare of Detective Delaney, who was making his way around the edge of the crowd, moving towards them with his hands in his pockets, and a uniformed officer in tow.

"Jesus," Richard muttered.

Delaney strode across and stopped in front of them, regarding each in turn. "Good evening," he said. "Mrs. Cressley."

"Detective," she said.

He turned his attention to Richard and Elizabeth. "Did I, or did I not tell you two to stay at home and to speak with no one?"

Over his shoulder, Elizabeth spotted Blake shouldering his way towards them.

"What's going on?" he asked as soon as he got there.

Alice gestured at Delaney with a flick of her hand. "The police have finally made an appearance."

Blake turned to him. "Can't this wait, Detective? Senator Shepherd has an urgent meeting with Richard. We're on a schedule here."

"No, it can't wait," Delaney told him. "This is a police inquiry, if you don't mind. And Mr. and Mrs. McClaine should be at home as previously instructed."

Blake seemed to consider his position. "I'll ask Senator Shepherd if he can wait," he told Richard.

Richard nodded, and as soon as Blake had left them, Alice turned on Delaney. "Listen to me. You left these people with no police presence or support. What were they supposed to do? Wait until their daughter turned up dead?"

"Thank you, Mrs. Cressley. I'll be speaking with you next."

"Excuse me, Detective," she said. "But this is nothing you wouldn't have done. The difference is, we did it, and we did it two hours sooner than you would have."

Delaney narrowed a glare on her. "May I have a word with you in private, Mrs. Cressley?" And he motioned to a clearing a few feet away. "Would you excuse us?" he said to Elizabeth and Richard.

Alice hesitated and gave Richard a look of forced tolerance. "Do I have a choice?" she asked Delaney.

"No, Mrs. Cressley, right now you do not," he replied, and ushered her a few feet away. The second officer stepped across with them and stood to one side, scanning the room with his hands clasped behind his back.

A few moments later, Blake reappeared, sidling up next to Richard. "The senator will call you later," he said.

Richard nodded again, and they stood in silence, watching Delaney and Alice. Delaney's expression remained impassive as he spoke but Alice was obviously rattled. She gestured this way and that as she put her side forward, huffing out a breath every now and then, and spreading her hands in consternation.

"I wouldn't worry," Blake told Richard. If anyone can put him straight, Alice can. I'll start wrapping things up here, shall I?"

Richard slipped back his sleeve and checked his watch. "Let's give it another half hour."

"What do you think they're saying?" Elizabeth asked her husband.

"I have no idea. Whatever it is, she doesn't look happy."

"She never looks happy."

"Dear God, don't let them arrest her," Richard said.

"Yes," Elizabeth said without emotion, "wouldn't that be terrible." She let her gaze slip across to the rest of the rapidly emptying room. Off to one side, she could see the woman in the red skirt and jacket, Miss du Plessis. She turned just as Elizabeth spotted her. For a moment, their eyes locked, then Elizabeth quickly looked away.

"I need to make some calls," Blake told Richard. "If anything happens, call me. Mrs. McClaine," he added by way of a farewell. And he cut his way into the crowd and vanished.

Alice and Delaney broke from their discussion to join Elizabeth and Richard again.

"Thank you for your patience," Delaney said to no one in particular. "Now let's get a few guidelines set in place—"

"Are you arresting her?" Elizabeth interrupted.

"Why, Mrs. McClaine? Would you like me to arrest her?"

Elizabeth wanted to say, *"Yes. Take her away. She's a menace and a bully."* Instead she met Alice's icy blue eyes and simply shook her head.

"This is how it goes from here on in," Delaney told them. "You are welcome to have Mrs. Cressley continue with your campaign or any other damned thing you want, I don't care. Fact is I'm willing to let you run another television slot later this evening to follow up from this one—as long," he said pointedly, "as it's in conjunction with our own press release. But anything and everything you do must be carried out with the express approval of my office, or not at all. Do you hear me?"

"But what about—?" Richard began, but Alice jumped in, saying:

"—just yes, Richard. That's my advice."

"Then, that's fine," he said.

"Mrs. McClaine?" Delaney asked.

"Yes, yes, that's fine," Elizabeth muttered. Behind him, she could see the du Plessis woman had approached and was now hovering on the sidelines, waiting to speak to them. So this was how it would be. Everybody would want a piece of them. Not that that was any different from any other day, but now everybody would be scrutinizing her, questioning her, reminding her of her failures as a mother. The very thought of it sent a shot of irritation through her. If only she could get a drink. One vodka martini would do. Maybe two; three, if she wanted—the hell with Alice Cressley.

Delaney turned, saw the woman. "Yes, Miss du Plessis. Is there something I can do for you?"

"I wanted to speak to Mrs. McClaine for a moment, if I may."

"After I'm done, you certainly may."

She regarded each of them. "Then I'll wait." And she turned on her heel and retreated.

When the woman had achieved a suitable distance, Delaney turned back to them. "So this is what we have to date: We have four sets of prints from the letter and the envelope. One is yours, Mrs.

McClaine. We have no others on file. I suspect they'll be from the postal workers who delivered the letter."

"So, what are you saying? That they used gloves?" asked Richard.

"That's my guess," Delaney replied. "Everybody watches *CSI*, everybody knows the procedure. But it's not all bad news. We have a positive ID of the woman. Our witness picked her out of our records—which was fortunate because she's not the only female on our books with a tattoo down the side of her neck."

"Your records?" said Elizabeth. "You mean she's been in trouble before?"

"She's known to us," he said. But there was more, Elizabeth could see it. Perhaps sensing her question forming, he added, "She was once arrested in connection with the murder of her mother."

"Oh, my God," said Elizabeth. "She killed her own mother?" Now, she really did want that drink. All she could think of was going home and pouring herself a couple of stiff vodka martinis and washing all of this away.

"I don't believe she's working alone," said Delaney. "I believe she has at least one accomplice who drove the car. That could be her long-time boyfriend, Matthew Subritzski. It seems most obvious, but of course we have no evidence to support that. Right now, I need one or both of you to stay at home in case they call, or a second letter arrives. I'll take you there myself, if you like."

"That's out of the question. I have to stay here," said Richard. "Well, with so much going on ..." He gestured to what was now a rapidly depleting crowd.

"I'll go," said Elizabeth. In fact, she couldn't wait to get out of there. She'd go home and close the door on the world.

"Fine. Officer Wallace is on his way over here. He called on your home earlier today but of course, you weren't there," Delaney said.

"As soon as he gets here we'll get going. Officer Kennedy here will be stationed with you, Mr. McClaine." Behind him, the young policeman stepped forward and nodded.

"I hope you've got the house under constant surveillance," said Alice. "That's the first thing I would have done."

"We have an unmarked car doing regular checks at five-minute intervals, Mrs. Cressley. I do know my job," he told her. "If we have an obvious presence at the house, they may not send the next letter. No letter, you don't get your extra day."

"I hope they're looking after her," Elizabeth said in a small voice. Despite the fact that she couldn't remember the last time she'd seen her daughter, she'd never felt so far from her.

CHAPTER EIGHT
DAY ONE: 9:56 PM—KELSEY

"The hell do they mean, another day?" Matt asked again. It was the third time he had said it, and neither Kelsey nor Lionel were coming back with answers. "What the hell is wrong with these people?" he demanded, spreading his hands in disbelief at the TV anchor who now babbled on in muted silence.

Every now and then, pictures taken from various angles of the street outside the school flashed up across the screen, alternating with the school photograph of Holly. "And how come they only just found out? The goddamned letter was delivered in the three o'clock mail. Three o'clock, for chrissakes! What is it now? Almost ten. What the hell were they doing all this time?" he asked Kelsey and Lionel.

"They're too stinkin' rich to open their own mail," mumbled Lionel, switching from screen to screen on his iPod, searching for something to listen to. He was already coming down from his all-too-brief high. Frustrated, he tossed the iPod down on the coffee table, snatched up Matt's cigarettes, extracted one from the pack and lit it. "I say we tell 'em to go fuck 'emselves. They give us the money, or we pop her. Plain and simple," he said as wisps of smoke snaked from his nose and mouth.

"But what if they can't get the money right away?" Kelsey asked. "What if they don't have the cash sitting in the bank and they have to sell some stocks or shares or whatever? What time does the stock market close?"

He glanced at his watch and the corners of his mouth drew down. "I dunno, hours ago, I guess."

She shifted in her seat. "Okay, so we told them twelve noon. Another day'll make it twelve noon on Saturday. Ten million's gotta be tougher to find than the hundred grand we were going to ask for. And what difference does it make?"

Matt pressed his fingers to his eyes. "For chrissakes. What do you mean, 'what difference does it make'? We're sitting here like a bunch of morons waiting to get sprung, is what difference it makes. Every minute we've got that kid and no money, they're getting closer," he said, pointing off to somewhere out front. "That's the difference."

"But, we're gonna take her home after, aren't we?" she asked.

Matt's entire body tensed up. "Will you shut up about taking her home? You don't shut up about it, I'll go up there and fuckin' kill her myself."

She fell silent. When he was like this it didn't pay to aggravate him. Problem was he'd been like this a lot more since he lost his job on the construction site six weeks ago. But he was smart, he'd come up with something. And he wouldn't do anything stupid. She knew that much. Matt picked up his phone, checked the screen, put it down again. Kelsey wondered if he was expecting a call. It wasn't a good time to ask.

"Okay," he said at last, and sat down again. "This is how it goes down from here …" He paused, turning his head towards the window where a background din outside had been slowly rising. Jaws clenched in irritation, he got to his feet, went to the window and parted the dirty curtains.

Out front, cars had been driving up and down the street, sound systems booming and sending vibrations through the house at regular intervals. Up until now they had ignored it—well, this kind of neighborhood, what did they expect? And whereas before, the loud rhythmic thumping of rap music came and went with the cars, now it droned on in one long, low-level series of vibrations that punched through the walls and the floor and rattled the windows. "What the hell's going on out there?" Matt angled his head against the glass, looking up and down the street before narrowing the source of the racket down to the house opposite.

Kelsey moved in next to him, also peering out at the house. Lights were on and music poured out of the open windows as though it had mass and energy and a life of its own. Beefed-up guys in gang colors, and girls in tight jeans, puff jackets with fur-lined hoods, and high leather boots were sitting out on the porch, or milling around with bottles and cigarettes in their hands, yahooing and laughing as they wandered in and out of the house. Cars lined either side of the street and every now and then, a shriek of laughter rang out above the music.

"A party. Shit," said Kelsey. "They better not wake Holly up."

Matt growled in irritation, and was about to say something when his phone rang. He snatched it up off the coffee table, checked the screen and answered it with, "About fuckin' time." He listened, grunted a couple of times, then said, "*I* changed the amount. You got a problem with that?" Whoever he was talking to said something, to which he replied, "Yeah, whatever." Then he hung up. "We'll give them until three," he told them as he tossed the phone back down.

"Who was that?" Kelsey asked. It got her a filthy look but no reply.

Lionel was slouched back in his chair, blowing smoke rings, watching them wobble and dissolve in the air. "Don't know why we're givin' them an extra three hours. We should just get our money and get the hell outta here."

"I think we should give them the day," said Kelsey. "Maybe they need it, y'know. And it's only like, one more day."

Matt turned on her. "What'd I just tell you? That's another day we have to stay low, another day the cops have to find us." He began stalking back and forth, shaking his head and darting aggravated looks at the window where car headlights intermittently swept the room as more and more people arrived.

Then, the music got louder.

"Jesus Christ," Matt groaned. "How are we supposed to stay here, keeping low and staying out of sight when we got half of Cleveland just across the street?"

"Y'know, I heard of kidnappers that kept people for days, sometimes weeks," Kelsey told him in a conversational tone, trying to sound reasonable. "I mean, there's no hurry. I can look after her. I can make sure she stays out of sight."

"In Somalia they keep 'em for goddamn years," Lionel muttered and blew another smoke ring. "End of the day, they always come back dead." He turned a grin on her.

"Will you quit bitching about Somalia?" Matt said. "I told you the money's ..." He stopped, scrubbed at his face, seemed to gather himself. "We'll get the money, okay? We'll get it."

"They're gonna want to know she's alive," Lionel muttered casually.

"Will you shut up and let me think?" Matt sat down and buried his head in his hands. "Okay, this is the deal. We give 'em the day. But that's it. Saturday noon, we're gone. Gimme a sheet of paper."

"But then we'll take her home, right?" said Kelsey.

Matt just gave her a look.

Lionel leaned forward, slid a sheet of paper from the ream they had bought two days prior, and held it out. Matt pulled a pair of white cotton gloves from his pants pocket, slipped them on, and snatched another sheet from it. "No prints, see? That's why I'm the one in charge here," he said, showing the both of them the new sheet of paper. He perched on the edge of the sofa, took out a pen and wrote several lines.

"So, how do we prove she's alive?" Kelsey asked. The last thing she wanted to do was annoy Matt any further. Annoy him more than this, you were likely to wind up with a smack in the mouth for your troubles. But some questions had to be asked.

He gave it a moment's thought. "We'll send a photograph." He took his phone from his pocket and placed it on the table.

"How are they going to see it?" Lionel asked. The whole situation seemed to be amusing him. "Are you gonna email it to them?" he said and chuckled. "How about we stick it on Facebook," he added and laughed.

Matt froze for a full four seconds, his flinty gaze directed at a point a few feet in front of him, his breath rasping. "No," he said with forced calm. "I'll give them my phone and the memory card. And I'll also give them my name, my address and my date of birth. How's that?" he said through clenched teeth. "We'll take a photo of her with today's paper, then we'll print it out. Anybody else got any smartass comments?"

"So how do we print it out?" asked Kelsey.

"Everyone thinks I'm a fuckin' idiot. Nobody thinks I can think for myself," he said and threw the pen across the room where it hit the wall and broke. He folded the sheet of paper roughly, stuffed it into an envelope. "Whichever of us delivers the note can go by Walgreens and print out a copy of the photo in one of the kiosks there. Then they'll stick it in this here envelope and go deliver it. Got that? Everybody happy?"

Kelsey nodded. "Yeah, sure. That's a good idea."

"I know it's a good idea," he told her. "That's why I thought of it."

"Only we don't have today's paper," Lionel added. He was now lounging back in his chair with his feet crossed on the coffee table, watching the TV and taking a last drag on his cigarette.

Matt said nothing, just glared at him. Then he said, "I know … wait here." He went to the front door, leaving the door open for the music and laughter to flood in from outside while he disappeared. A few seconds later he came back in with a handful of junk from the mailbox. He kicked the door shut and flitted through the circulars and foldouts, tossing the discarded papers on the floor, until he came to a yellow sheet of paper advertising specials for a local computer store. "We'll use this. It's a one-day sale and it just came today. It says 'tomorrow's specials' with tomorrow's date, so it had to be delivered today."

"I'll go," said Kelsey. "I'll deliver the letter."

The two brothers hesitated.

"It makes sense. I'm the only one they've seen. If I get caught …"

"Yeah," said Lionel. He scratched at a scab that was developing on his cheek. "She's right. She should go."

Matt gave it some air. "Yeah, that makes sense. You take it, but make it fast. Her folks are still downtown so now's your best chance.

You go to Walgreens, drop the letter, then get straight back here, y'hear? Drive to the speed limit, take the backstreets, and don't go stopping along the way," he told her. "And be careful. They'll have the street staked out. Pick your timing. Don't fuck it up."

"I know, I know. I'll be quick as I can. We better get a good photo. Just let me check on her first."

*****

Upstairs the bed was empty. Kelsey's heart almost stopped until she saw Holly over at the window, peering down at the commotion across the street.

"Hey, get away from there." She scooped the child up in her arms and carried her back to the bed. "Those are mean sons of … people down there. You don't wanna let them see you up here. You hear me?"

"Wah Ninny."

Kelsey sighed. "I already told you, I don't have it, so shut up about it." Holly's brow furrowed. Her chin crumpled and the corners of her little mouth turned down. "Oh hey, I'm sorry." She tucked the child into the bed and sat down on the edge, leaning over her with a hand each side. "You gotta stay with us one more day, okay? Matt's gonna come up soon and we'll take a photo of you so your mom won't miss you too much. And the time'll go like that," she said, snapping her fingers. "I promise, in no time at all you'll be back with your family."

Holly's eyebrows rose in the middle, forming an inverted V, and her mouth puckered. "Ninny," she whimpered.

"I just *said* …" Kelsey stopped herself. Something was irritating her—something she couldn't put her finger on. It was as if some small piece of her world had shifted—a change so small that every time she tried to nail down exactly what it was, it slithered away out of reach and disappeared. "I don't have your lion. But I'll get it, okay? I'll get your Lilly Lion. I'm going back to your house to get the stuff for your eyes anyway. You're gonna be with us an extra day, so you're gonna need it. So, I'll get your damned lion while I'm there."

Holly's face lit up. "Ninny?" She giggled, wriggling in the bed and kicking her feet.

Despite her irritation, Kelsey smiled. "Yes, Lilly. Doesn't take much to make you happy, does it? But, don't tell Matt. He'll go ape-shit." She leaned close down over the child, and whispered, "It'll be our little secret, right?"

Holly peered up with her red, swollen eyes and her damaged lip, and grinned. "Nuvs Ninny Nion," she said, drawing both her little fists across her chest. Then she ran her hand back over her hair in one deliberate movement.

"Oh, believe me, I know you love Lilly Lion. Hey, and you can do that signing language. Wow. And that means love." Kelsey held her fists crossed at her chest. "You know somethin'? That means you know a whole other language." She smiled down at this strangely beautiful child. "And you taught me something. That makes you real smart—smarter than me, because I only know one language."

Holly frowned. "No." She clamped her little fists across her chest again. "Nangsie Mommy mart. Nuvs Nangsie Mommy." *Kelsey Money smart. Loves Kelsey Money.*

Kelsey leaned low again, took the child's face in her hands and looked hard into those crusted eyes for the longest moment. "Don't talk shit," she said and sat up. "Now listen up. I gotta go now because if I don't, we'll miss the opportunity. Then we'll be sitting up shit street and no one will be going anywhere."

"Agh, agh," Holly cried out, her hand snapping for Kelsey.

"No, I can't. Soon as we got this photograph, I gotta go. But Matt's here. He'll look after you." But even as her words hit the air, something deep down in the very pit of her gut shifted once more—that small, insignificant niggle. Like a tiny pebble tumbling down the rock face of an enormous precipice with a barely audible *click, click, click* as it bounced off the hard, cold surface, plummeting into the depths below. Kelsey could not identify the source of the movement; she didn't know what had dislodged it. But there it was—creating ripples in her world and making its presence felt.

"Listen to me," she told Holly. "I'm gonna take you home to your mom. Not right now, though. I can't. But when the time comes, I will. I promise."

"Snay wah Nangsie Mommy," she said, using her sign language as she fought to mold the words with her scarred lips and her thick tongue. "Snay wah yoo." *Stay with you.*

"No. No you can't stay with Kelsey Money. I got nowhere to keep you, no home or nothin'. You got a beautiful home with all your toys and stuff. I gotta take you home. On Saturday, okay? But you gotta listen to me. Are you listening?" The child blinked up at her. "If Lionel comes up here, if he comes anywhere near you, you holler. Just open up and yell. Matt will come. He'll help you. You hear? But, I'm warning you, he'll be pissed as hell. He'll yell and make a performance out of it like you don't know what. But don't worry. He won't hurt you." There was that distant *click, click, click,* once more. "And I'll be back before you can even count."

CHAPTER NINE
DAY ONE: 10:07 PM—ELIZABETH

Elizabeth had her purse clutched to her chest as she headed towards the door of the makeshift control/campaign room that was now Richard's campaign central. All she wanted was to get home, kick off her shoes, and get away from all these prying eyes. Perhaps once she was alone, she could figure out how the hell she was going to get her child home. Because from what she'd already seen, she needed more than one incompetent policeman and Alice Cressley's PR circus to find her.

Just as she reached for the door, however, the unmistakable sound of Alice Cressley's voice cut across the din, calling her name. Elizabeth froze, debating the wisdom of just walking out and not looking back. She decided against it and slowly turned.

"Did you hear me?" Alice said, as she approached.

"I did. I was wondering if I should simply ignore you."

"Then you made an excellent choice." Without waiting for a response, she stepped aside, indicating to the woman who was standing behind her. "I'd like you to meet Diana du Plessis. You may remember she was sitting in the front row during Richard's speech."

Terrific, she thought. "Yes, I was just …"

"We meet at last, Mrs. McClaine." Diana du Plessis smiled and extended her hand.

Alice cut in, saying, "Miss du Plessis will be accompanying you to the hospital to visit the teacher tomorrow. At ten o'clock, she'll join you to attend an open day at the school."

"Is that so," Elizabeth said. "And since when did you start organizing my calendar, Mrs. Cressley?"

"Since your daughter got kidnapped, Mrs. McClaine. Would you excuse us a moment?" Alice took Elizabeth by the arm, angling her around, and guided her off to the side.

"Of course," Diana du Plessis replied, as though she hadn't noticed.

As soon as they were out of earshot, Alice dropped her voice. "Now listen here. I am tired, and when I'm tired, I become even more cantankerous than I normally am. I've gone to great pains to organize an exclusive with this woman—and before you go butting in—" she added as Elizabeth tried to protest, "—this could be the difference between getting your daughter back and getting her killed. Diana du Plessis may be a bleeding heart liberal I would not cross the street to spit upon, much less read the trash she writes, but she has clout. She writes *human interest* stories, which means we can pick up an entirely different demographic. This is a very large, well-informed vote we may otherwise have never had access to. Richard and I have already given her exclusive rights to the story, which will run in four of the biggest newspapers in the state first thing in the morning. All you need to do is stay sober and nod. Do you think you can do that?"

"Is there nothing you won't do for a vote?" Elizabeth asked her.

Alice moved an inch closer. "You want the truth? If hiring Tarzan to lope from tree to tree with his balls swinging around his ankles meant I could secure one more vote, I'd be stringing vines instead of wasting my time talking to you."

Elizabeth stiffened. "Do you always have to be so crass, Mrs. Cressley?"

"Yes, Mrs. McClaine, I do. That way people listen to me."

"Please excuse me." Diana had stepped a little closer, fingering her watch to indicate time was against her. "I really must go. I'll call by your house at eight o'clock in the morning, if that's not too early," she said to Elizabeth.

"Of course." Elizabeth forced a smile. "I'll look forward to it."

Already she could see how this was going to pan out. Yet again, she would be thrust into the midst of those holier-than-thou teachers at the Special Children's Center for the Disabled, made to feel inadequate as they went about their daily routines, proving to her once again that even without the bonds of familial attachment, they had something she so patently lacked—the ability to accept and love her own child, a child she couldn't even—

Elizabeth felt her entire body spasm. She swallowed hard and she placed a finger to her lips, checking furtively around to see if anyone might have noticed. If she didn't remain vigilant against these emotions, it was only one small step to the edge. She could not fall down that hole again. Not after everything she'd done to prevent it. She lifted her head high, smiled at the few remaining malingerers, and went in search of Detective Delaney and Officer Wallace.

She had to get home. She needed that drink. And to decide what she'd do next.

CHAPTER TEN
DAY ONE: 10:15 PM—KELSEY

Kelsey drove through Cleveland's old Brooklyn neighborhood, and after finding the Walgreens closed, she took a detour and headed to a late-night photo shop she knew along Biddulph Avenue.

It was just as she made the first turn that she noticed the headlights behind her. She drove slowly, watching in the rearview mirror. When she stopped at the lights, she could see the outline of a guy in the car behind her, talking on a cell phone. In the occasional sweep of passing headlights, she could just make out a thin face and long strands of thin hair hanging to his shoulders. She watched him for a while, and when the light turned green, she pulled away and turned left.

The car behind followed and her heart picked up a beat. At the next intersection, she took a right and he followed. Sweat broke across her forehead. She'd been driving for several minutes, wondering what to do, when she hit the brakes and pulled over and the car went straight past. She tracked the car to the end of the street, where it turned and disappeared out of sight.

Kelsey blew out a breath. Tension had tightened the muscles across the back of her neck and shoulders. She rolled her head, hearing the click in her vertebrae. After a minute or so, she pulled out and hit the road again.

When she reached the photo store, she parked in an inconspicuous slot away from the streetlights. The air was still, the streets quiet. A few cars passed, but no cops. She pulled the key from the ignition, got out, and walked quickly inside.

The photo kiosks were situated at the back of the store. Kelsey walked past the first kiosk where a couple were sitting, laughing at the images flashing up on the touchscreen in front of them. She found a seat as far from the couple as she could, pulled the memory card from her pocket, and slid it into the slot.

A grid of images jumped up to fill the screen. Matt had taken six photographs in all, each showing Holly holding the yellow advertising foldout in front of her like a mug shot card. Kelsey checked around again, then clicked on the last photograph taken. It opened to show Holly staring wide-eyed into the camera without expression. Exhaustion had caused her tiny frame to droop and the foldout had slipped into a position that rendered the text unreadable. The one before it was better, although this one showed her looking up with her mouth open, asking Kelsey for Lilly Lion once more. Kelsey had feigned incomprehension. And when Holly's little chin had crumpled at her reaction, Kelsey had wanted to reach out to her and tell her that of course she was listening, that of course she understood, and that she'd get her damned Lilly Lion if she'd just be still.

The photograph immediately before this showed everything they needed. The little face stared into the lens as instructed, eyes showing pink, tongue peeking between her parted lips. Kelsey hit the print button and closed down the shot.

Just as she went to close down the album and extract the memory card, a splash of blue in one of the photographs caught her eye. It was among a series of shots she didn't recognize. She clicked on the first. It showed Matt and Lionel laughing and pretending to fight each other. Wasn't that just like them? A couple of idiots when they got on the juice together. In the next one Matt was obviously holding the camera because they were both crushed together, grinning and pulling faces when the button had clicked. The next showed them dancing among a bunch of people with the splash of a blue dress just behind them. It looked to Kelsey as though they were at a party. She checked for the date, wondering when they were taken—the 23rd. That was last Saturday. Matt had told her he was going bowling that night. Not that it made any difference, but she found herself wondering why he would lie about such a thing. He went to parties without her. It had never mattered before.

The next photograph back showed a slim black man she recognized as Delmar, the Somali refugee who was arranging the bank account for Matt. She still couldn't believe the money would go there. She was convinced it would never come back. The next showed Delmar in conversation with Lionel. The subject must have been serious. Neither of them was smiling. Kelsey flicked back a couple more, wondering where the party was and why they wouldn't have asked her along, when an image of Matt and a girl stopped her short. She tapped the thumbnail on the screen and the image leapt up to fill the space in front of her.

"Maria fucking Puentez." She glared at the screen. Maria had long flowing hair with a splash of bleached blond in the front, brilliantly white teeth, eyes painted up and blazing like the Fourth of July. In this shot, she was wearing a low-cut azure blue dress, her plump round breasts straining against the satin fabric, nipples puckered beneath. Matt had always called her a whore. He said she probably carried diseases medical science didn't even know about. But in this picture, she was clinging to Matt like a star-struck lover, and he didn't look like he was objecting. The next shot showed Lionel pointing towards whoever was holding the camera and laughing in the foreground, but behind him the image showed Matt and Maria locked in a passionate embrace and kissing. The next had Maria, Matt and Lionel all toasting, the next ... well, it didn't matter. Kelsey couldn't look at any more. She felt as though Maria Puentez had leaned out of that screen and scratched her heart out.

Had she missed the signs? Was there something she had or hadn't done? Kelsey was no genius—even she was the first to admit that, but Matt had only ever referred to Maria as an empty space on legs. Nothing he'd said or done had given Kelsey any indication he was interested in her. She wondered what kind of explanation he would come up with if she confronted him about it. Not that she could, because then he'd know she had been snooping through his photographs.

Numb inside and cursing herself for being so goddamn foolish, Kelsey popped the card from the slot and replaced it in her pocket. The couple behind her let out a shriek of laughter. The girl had her arm around the guy, pulling him in and teasing him over the images on their screen.

With tears prickling in her eyes, Kelsey collected up the photograph and took the envelope from her pocket, then realized she was handling it without the gloves.

"Shit!" She hurriedly folded the photograph printout. Those images had knocked her off-balance. All she could see was Maria's perfect face and gleaming white teeth grinning at her, the whore.

Suddenly, she was furious. Her cheeks flashed hot and a shot of rage scorched through her. She hated slutty Maria Puentez for forcing herself on Matt; she hated Matt for letting her, and she hated Lionel for … well, for being the asshole that he was. But most of all, she was furious with herself—furious for being so stupid she didn't even see what was going on; furious for being dumb enough to handle the envelope without the gloves. With her mouth pressed into a thin line, and fighting back the tears, she shoved the folded print into the envelope so savagely it tore it down the side. She ripped it out, unfolding the note so she could refold it with the photograph, when her eye caught the words. When she unfolded it, the first line she saw was:

"… do not have the money by 3pm tomorrow, the kid dies …"

"Three? What?" She said it loud enough that the couple behind her went quiet and the girl whispered something in the guy's ear. Kelsey swiveled around with her back to them and read the note through again.

Matt had lied to her. Okay, he had probably told her they would give them the twenty-four hours just to shut her up, but that wasn't the point. Now, she found herself wondering what else she didn't know about. Of all the years they had been together, they had always been on the same side—watching each other's back. It was only since Lionel had come back into his life that this had started. Now she felt like a kid who finds out that nothing her mother ever told her was true. She felt like a fool. She hadn't seen what had been right in front of her the whole time—Lionel had torn Matt away from her.

Hollow inside, and using fingers too numb to work properly, she unfolded the photograph, lining it up with the note so she could refold the pages into the envelope. Then she caught a glimpse of the picture again—those tired, swollen eyes, the innocent expression, the questioning face staring from the photograph, trustingly holding the foldout as she'd been told to.

But Kelsey now knew what she had to do.

She roughly folded the sheets of paper and stuffed them back into the envelope. It didn't matter about fingerprints or identification or whatever. The witness the police found had probably already identified her. Now, she had to think; she had to come up with her own plan. A glance at her watch told her the deadline was seventeen hours away. She didn't want to wait that long. For now she would play along with the boys; do whatever Matt wanted. He had to trust her. But, when the time came and the opportunity arose, she would take Holly. And she'd run.

CHAPTER ELEVEN
DAY ONE: 11:21 PM—KELSEY

The Roadster was still parked in the driveway outside the McClaines' house, but someone had put the top up. Kelsey parked the SUV two doors down, cut the ignition, killed the lights, and slid down in the seat with her arms folded. From here she could just see the house. Lights shone out across the enormous front yard, highlighting a row of ornamental trees in the front garden that cast elongated shadows across the lawn. Beyond the downstairs windows she could see the pale glow of an interior light somewhere inside the house. She glanced at her watch and settled back to wait.

After three minutes, a late model Crown Victoria cruised by. It couldn't have been more obvious that it was a cop car if it had the precinct lettered across the side and blue and red lights on the roof. Kelsey wondered why they didn't just send a black and white. The car slowed past the house, then sped up and disappeared around the corner. She checked her watch again and unwrapped a stick of gum and stuck it in her mouth. Hugging herself against the cold, she slid a little further down in the seat again and waited. Five minutes later the car reappeared, cruising slowly past the house, then accelerating to the corner again.

The instant it was gone, Kelsey got out of the car, locking it with the key so the automatic lock wouldn't bleep, and crossed the street. Chewing rapidly on the gum, she hurried down the side of the house and in through a side gate, closing it quietly behind her.

An enormous pool and barbecue area stretched across the back of the property. She moved quickly through the shadows to the rear of the house and dropped into a crouch by a set of French doors. From here, she checked the area for security cameras. Sure enough, she spotted one mounted to her left that was panning across the yard from right to left and back, covering as far as the back of the pool area; a second above her head, securing the remaining area.

The camera above her head had probably caught her as she entered the gate.

"Shit."

If it did, it was too late. She removed the gloves and the glass cutter from her jacket pocket, and the wad of gum from her mouth. She pressed the gum onto the window next to the latch, forming it into a peak in the center. With a steady hand, she traced an arc around it with the glass cutter. It wasn't the perfect solution, but it worked. The biggest problem was if you left saliva on the glass. Leaving saliva behind would score you first place on the suspect list in three minutes flat.

But none of that mattered now.

Kelsey used the butt of the cutter to tap the outer edge of the hand-hole and removed the glass using the gum as a grip. She checked her watch. In one minute the cop would cruise past. Then she'd have to go like hell. The alarm would sound ten seconds after she got inside. From then on, she had five minutes to get up the stairs, get the eye cream, grab Holly's toy lion and get back to the car. It would be touch and go, but it was possible. She watched the second-hand on her watch come around …

… three, two, one …

At the distant sound of a car speeding up, she tapped the glass out, stuck her hand through the hole and unlocked the door. She pushed it open and was halfway across the vast dining area before she noticed that the alarm hadn't gone off. She paused, looking all around—nothing.

Cautiously, she tiptoed to the nearest door, pressed herself in close by the doorframe and peered out into a hallway. There was no sign of movement. She moved on into the house, tiptoeing toward the front. And stopped. She could hear water running. At first she thought someone had left a faucet turned on. But when she came to a wide hallway at the front of the house, she found an expansive entranceway featuring an entire wall of slate with water cascading down it. Kelsey reversed up three steps so she could view it in its entirety. She couldn't believe anyone would have a wall of water in their house. She had lived in places where the water flowed freely down the walls, but it wasn't intentional.

"The rich. What the hell next?" When she turned to move on, she noticed a marble hallstand set with a crystal bowl. Inside the bowl was a set of keys. She hesitated, hand hovering over them, then picked them up. The key ring had a Mercedes badge attached. "Well, I'll be damned," she said and put them back. She took two steps, reversed, retrieved the keys and tucked them into her pocket.

The next doorway on her left opened into a vast marble-floored foyer where an enormous stairway curved in two directions to the second floor. She stepped across, feeling like Alice in Wonderland, and let out a low whistle that echoed faintly in the expansive area.

Where to now?

The bedrooms were probably on the second floor, so she headed straight up the stairs, pausing briefly to peer over the side and wonder what it would be like to live in a place like this.

The first door on the left was a bedroom. So was the next. The third was obviously the McClaines' own room. A king-sized bed stood beneath a four-poster frame that was draped with heavy burgundy-colored fabric. To her left stood a large, mirrored dressing table, with a matching wooden dresser positioned on either side of it. To her right were twin doors leading to two large walk-in closets. Kelsey stepped across to the nearest closet and flipped on the lights to find row upon row of men's suits. In the second were racks of dresses down one side, pants and suits on the other. A blue silk cocktail dress had been hung on the back of the door as if someone had been trying it on. Kelsey lifted the hem, feeling the fabric smooth and silky between her fingers, and wondered what it would be like to dress in clothes like this instead of wearing jeans every day. Out of nowhere, the image of Maria Puentez flashed into her mind. She cast the fabric aside like she'd been stung, switched off the light and closed the door. She didn't have time for screwing around. The alarm might not have activated, but Holly was still alone with Matt and Lionel. She had to get back. She flipped off the bedroom light and went straight to the bathroom.

At the very back of the bathroom cabinet, she found a small bottle of Tobramycin complete with eye dropper. The directions for use read, "one drop three times a day to the affected eye," and it was in Holly's name so she figured that was what she was looking for. After inspecting the rest of the medicines and finding nothing else useful, she tucked the bottle into her pocket, closed the cabinet and went in search of Holly's bedroom.

Five doorways down, at the very rear of the house, she found it. The bed was made with a Dora the Explorer motif comforter, matching curtains at the windows. Toys of various sorts were placed with care on shelves that Holly would never have been able to reach, while a toy box sat with a pile of clothes flung on top.

And there, sitting on the pillow in pride of place, was a ragged lion a little larger than her fist. It had one button eye and a thread of cotton where the other should have been. She walked straight over and picked it up. "Lilly Lion, I presume." And that's when she heard it ...

... the distant clunk of the front door.

"Shit."

She stuffed the lion into her jacket pocket. Trust her to be pissing around in the parents' room when she should have got what she came for and gone. She tiptoed to the window. This side of the house looked out over the pool. It was a sheer drop onto the tiled barbecue area beneath. With no ledges or frames to climb on, exiting that way was a sure invitation to a broken ankle and the noise would wake the entire neighborhood.

She exited Holly's room and paused. Someone was moving around downstairs. She did a running tiptoe into the next doorway along and leaned out. The hallway was dim, darkened doorways set along it. She crept toward the top of the stairs and dropped into a crouch, scanning the area downstairs. In the living room just off the left she spotted someone, a woman. Kelsey duck-walked to a point just behind the railing and bent her head low. The instant she came into view, Kelsey recognized her; knew the curve of her cheek, the angular shape of her slim frame; the tousled hair wrenched back from her face.

Shit. Kelsey checked the time. The woman took several bottles from the liquor cabinet and tucked them into a large canvas bag beside her. Then she moved out of sight.

Kelsey leaned to survey the foyer. She'd never get out without being seen, and there was no way she could leave by the rear of the house.

She retraced her steps, searching the hallway for options when she heard footsteps on the stairs and her heart did a barrel-roll.

In desperation, she darted back to the McClaines' bedroom, crossed straight to the closet and stepped inside. That woman would never dare come in here. She just wouldn't …

… but Kelsey had no sooner pushed the door closed, when the light snapped on, and through the gap she saw Sienna Alvarez, the nanny, sweep into the room.

Kelsey hunkered down with her eye to the crack, tracking her as she moved from drawer to drawer, pulling them out, selecting items and depositing them into the bag. At the faint sound of movement in the hallway outside, Sienna froze and her eyes cut to the doorway.

Kelsey could just see the edge of the bedroom door through the crack. Sienna stood rock solid still, eyes wide on the door. So did Kelsey. The door moved a little and Sienna gasped.

Someone thumped the bedroom door from the other side and it flew open. Sienna folded over with her hand on her chest, saying,

"*Ay dis mio*, you frighten me. Why are you here?"

Through the gap, Kelsey saw a guy move into the room—black leather jacket, dirty jeans, long stringy hair. He stepped across with his back to Kelsey so she put her hand on the door and gently narrowed the crack. The hinge let out the softest whine and the guy's head jerked around, hollow eyes searching the room, and Kelsey recognized him immediately.

Deitz. He had the skeletal features and the eroded teeth of a regular drug user. Kelsey only knew Deitz in passing. But Matt knew him. So did Lionel—merciless, cruel, lacking anything approaching a conscience, Deitz was his dealer.

So what the hell was he doing here? And how did Sienna know him?

Deitz silently scanned the room. When he came to the closet, his eyes locked on it. "Who's there?"

Kelsey pulled her head back. Panic and fear drove a thousand tiny needles into her flesh. A bolt of adrenaline shot up her spine like molten steel and her pulse hammered at her temples. She blew out a long slow breath and tried to relax.

"There is no one here," Sienna said. "I been here ten minutes. I see no one."

A silence stretched. He broke it, saying, "What about Kelsey? You see her? Her car's outside."

So it was Deitz following her. Why?

"I tell you, there is no one here. Just me." Sienna's tone had developed an edge. She went to say something else but stopped midway like he'd hushed her. Kelsey heard movement—the soft rustle and squeak of Deitz's jacket. It stopped and she realized he was inches from her, on the other side of the door.

Sweat flashed on her forehead and chin. She inched back from the door and held her breath. Outside, the silence echoed. Not a movement; not a whisper.

She eased out another breath, wondering if they'd left the room, when the light snapped on and Deitz punched the door open. It swung hard enough to hit Kelsey on the knee and spring back, and the stink of stale cigarettes and sweat wafted into the closet with him. Kelsey was standing right behind him now, frozen in place behind the door with her face squeezed and her muscles burning. Still with his back to her, he reached up and parted a few hangers.

"So when does Lionel give me my money?" Sienna called after him.

Kelsey felt her jaw drop. *Lionel's paying her?*

Deitz threw a look back over his shoulder. If he'd glanced to his right, he'd have seen Kelsey. She didn't flinch, didn't breathe, just watched as he bent down, picked up a shoe, turned it in his hand like it was something hateful, and threw it back.

"Well?" said Sienna. "When does he pay me? I done what he say and now I wan' my money."

Deitz let his hand slide down the edge of the door as he stepped out into the bedroom again. The light went off and the door closed. Kelsey wilted inside the closet and heaved out a silent breath.

"How much did he say?" Deitz was asking.

"*Ten. Thousand. Dollars,*" Sienna replied, emphasizing each word so he heard it right.

Kelsey also heard it. So, Sienna had sold Holly out, the bitch. A little kid. *Jesus!* Kelsey clenched her mouth shut and squeezed her eyes closed. She wanted to punch something. If she got the chance, maybe she would.

Deitz let out an amused snort. "Ten grand. Just for goin' to visit your mom, huh? Holy shit."

"Not just to visit my mother," Sienna replied like he'd offended her. "He tell me to call the driver, tell him go late to the school. I done that, too. Now tell him I wan' my money."

This was Holly's nanny—the person who was supposed to watch over her, care for her. Kelsey felt every muscle tighten, lips pressing in a hard line, breaths coming long and slow. When she looked down, both her fists were clenched.

Deitz was saying, "You'll get your money when Lionel's ready. Not before."

"You tell him," Sienna insisted. "He don't give me my money, I go to the police. I tell them everything."

"Yeah, we thought about that." The reply was so soft, Kelsey almost missed it. She leaned closer to the door, straining to hear more. But a muffled grunt was followed by the sounds of slapping and groping and the rustle of clothing. Kelsey rocked her head back, mouth open. She couldn't believe it—they were making out and here she was stuck in the closet. She stood there with her stomach churning and her fists squeezed. After a while, she glanced down at her watch, aware of how much time she'd been away, when she heard a thunk—like someone falling against the dresser. It was followed by hurried footsteps back down the stairs. Then nothing.

She frowned and pressed her ear to the door again. Still nothing. After another long silence, she eased the door open and peeped out.

The first thing she saw was Sienna slumped awkwardly against the dresser.

Kelsey flew across and dropped at her side. She reached out, not knowing whether to shake her, give her mouth-to-mouth or what.

"Sienna! Can you hear me?" She drew her back by the shoulder. But the girl's head lolled back and Kelsey saw the marks on her neck and the tiny specks of blood in her eyes.

Sienna was dead.

"Oh, Holy shit." She dropped the girl like something contagious and scrambled backwards. "Holy fucking shit."

She jumped to her feet and stepped wide. *Think. Think!*

She had to get out. She had to get back to Holly. Then she had to tell Matt what she'd seen and convince him to take Holly home. And she had to do it now.

CHAPTER TWELVE
DAY ONE: 11:39 PM—ELIZABETH

Delaney drove while Elizabeth sat in the back seat of the car, staring out the window like a petulant teen dragged home from a party by an angry parent. In front of her, Officer Wallace sat in the passenger seat, answering radio calls and snapping out instructions and locations, then listening to their incomprehensible replies. Why she couldn't have taken her car to the press conference was beyond her. It was a plain and sensible Ford Fusion Hybrid—nothing extravagant, nothing that would incense Richard's precious voters. If she had been allowed to take her car, she could have gone home as soon as the press conference was over. She wouldn't have had to suffer the pitying looks of hangers-on pretending they cared, when all they wanted was something to report in their papers, or tell their friends over cocktails. The very thought of them disgusted her. They didn't have the tact to keep their stupid questions to themselves. Instead they insisted on making comments they weren't qualified to and expected her to lap it up.

Would she have felt differently if Holly had been born a normal, healthy child? Would her desperation to find her be any deeper?

Maybe she'd never know. From that first day, there was no joy, no burst of new-motherly excitement and wonder at the birth of her child. That had been replaced by an all-consuming shroud of hopelessness and despair. Even when her own mother had died, there was pain, there was grief; but time took that away. Time healed the wounds and allowed them to close over.

This pain was different. These wounds had never healed. They had stayed with her, weighing her down like a burden strapped to her back. Every morning she had woken to find the pain and anguish waiting for her, dragging her down and bending her at the waist like a woman twice her age.

Now, those chains were broken—the severed ends left raw and unfinished. Yet still there remained an invisible thread, an unbreakable connection that stretched through distance and time, bonding her to her child. Elizabeth wondered once again how she would ever live with herself again, regardless of the outcome.

As if sensing her anguish, Delaney caught her eye in the rearview mirror. "Are you all right, Mrs. McClaine?"

She pulled in a ragged breath and folded her arms across her chest. "Yes, I'm fine. Can you tell me what's happening with the investigation?"

"We've put an APB out on the vehicle that was used in the kidnapping," he told her. "The witness didn't get the license plate but she managed to identify it as a blue Ford Explorer. Probably an older model."

"And you've heard nothing? Not one person has seen it? I find that hard to believe."

His sharp look in the rearview mirror told her she'd crossed a line. "These things take time, Mrs. McClaine," he replied.

Elizabeth bit her lip. "I'm sorry. I didn't mean to … I'm sure you're doing everything you can." Feeling uncomfortable, she turned her attention to the window where a blur of scenery rushed by. Every time she thought about the interviews Alice had set up for her, her stomach clenched. First the hospital, and then the school—both visits in the company of the du Plessis woman. Why she had to go along with a reporter, she had no idea. All in the name of Alice Cressley's election campaign. A surge of resentment flashed through her. That woman didn't care that their little daughter was being held somewhere by people who would do her harm if their demands weren't met. She probably wouldn't even notice if Richard vanished in a puff of smoke. She would continue on her campaign regardless, working like a spider spinning a web that had been damaged beyond repair—still adding to it, forming silken ties that went nowhere and had no use.

When did I last hold her? Elizabeth thought. The realization struck her so unexpectedly, she heard herself gasp. She glanced up to find Delaney's questioning gaze on her again.

"Are you sure you're all right, Mrs. McClaine?"

She laced her fingers in her lap, squeezing them until her knuckles ached. "I'm fine. Do you know who these people are who have taken my daughter? Would they … would they hurt her?"

Delaney turned into Belle Vue Drive, directing Wallace's attention to the rear lights of a vehicle turning right at the end of the street. He slowed, ducking his head as both officers watched it disappear from view. Wallace picked up the radio and made a call while Delaney accelerated gently and swung the car into the driveway to bring it to a stop. He pulled the key from the ignition, then turned around, leaning his elbow across the back of the seat while he addressed Elizabeth. "Well, we know the woman who took Holly is

Kelsey Terrasone. She calls herself Kelsey Money after her mother's de facto husband, although in fact, there's no record of her ever being adopted," he said, dusting something from the front of his shirt. "Officer Wallace here has been following up her associations with Matthew Subritzski, and his brother Lionel. Lionel was recently released from prison." He lifted one shoulder. "We thought they could be involved but three people have come forward claiming they were with them at the time of the kidnapping. Matthew Subritzski's certainly had his share of problems, but no arrests in the past year. I wish I could say the same of Miss Terrasone. She's been in and out of trouble with the law for most of her life. We believe either she's working with someone who's off the radar, or she's working alone."

"Is it possible she took Holly because she just wants a child of her own? Maybe she just wants to love her and care for her …" she began, but Delaney was already shaking his head.

"It's unlikely. The ransom demand suggests money is the motive."

The dull ache of disappointment sat heavy in the pit of her stomach. The thought of someone wanting to care for Holly so badly that they would steal her away from her family, somehow offered her a glimmer of hope—a heartfelt, if somewhat distant, possibility that the child would finally be loved the way she deserved. The way Elizabeth had never been able to. Now, to find that her little child was only seen by those around her as a meal ticket brought Elizabeth a sudden pang of sadness and regret.

"Do you have *any* idea where they could be?" she asked, then realized how ridiculous the question was. As if he'd be sitting there talking to her when he knew where her daughter was.

"I'm afraid we're still working on that, Mrs. McClaine. But rest assured, we will find them."

She hunched her shoulders and hugged herself. For all her bravado and her desperation to find her child, that old sense of powerlessness was already leaching back. "Is she dangerous, Mr. Delaney? This girl, would she hurt her?" Noting his hesitation, she added, "You can tell me. I need to know the worst. I need to be prepared."

"I think we have to try and stay positive. Chances are Holly is safe, and she'll be home soon."

Elizabeth stared at him, barely daring to breathe. "But what if we don't find her? What if …" That overwhelming sense of loss hit her again, stealing away the words.

"It's late, Mrs. McClaine. You've had a hell of a day. No doubt you'll have another tomorrow. I suggest you get some rest."

She plucked her keys from her purse. "Thank you."

"I'll see you safely inside."

As soon as they got to the door, Elizabeth hit the remote for the alarm, then looked up.

Delaney noticed her surprised expression and followed her gaze. "Is something wrong?"

"The alarm wasn't set."

"Perhaps you forgot."

"Perhaps."

Inside the house, Elizabeth flicked on the lights and placed her keys in the crystal bowl in front of the water feature. "Thank you," she said to Delaney. She couldn't wait for him to leave. All she wanted was a drink. One solid hit of vodka and she would feel better. Maybe she'd take the bottle up to bed with her. Who was there to object?

"Do you mind if I use your bathroom?" he asked a little awkwardly, obviously embarrassed.

"Of course. There's one right down the hallway there," she said, pointing towards the downstairs bathroom at the rear of the house. *And then please go*, she thought but didn't say. She watched him tentatively moving down the hallway, then went straight into the living room and pulled open the liquor cabinet doors, stopped and blinked. It was almost empty. She frowned and turned as if someone in the room might be playing a joke on her and watching for her reaction. Then she turned her attention back to the empty shelves.

Delaney leaned briefly in through the doorway. "Thank you, Mrs. McClaine. I'll see myself … is something wrong?"

"The liquor cabinet. I had three bottles of vodka in here. They're gone." She crouched low to look in the back of the cabinet. "So is the scotch. And the bourbon. Who could have taken it?"

"Would your husband have removed it?"

"No. He was with me." She cast a look towards the stairs, then across to the front windows. "Someone's been here."

"Stay here," he said, and went back to the foyer. After searching the rooms leading directly off the foyer, he started up the stairs. "Is anybody up there?" he called as he made his way up.

Elizabeth stood at the foot of the staircase, watching him. When she glanced back towards the front door, she spotted a white envelope lying on the floor, just to the left of the door. She went across, scooped it up, opened it and read the message. "Mr. Delaney! Detective!" she cried out. "They've been here. They left the letter. Mr. Delaney?"

A moment later, he appeared at the top of the stairs and descended them quickly, his face ashen, his expression grim. Immediately she knew something was wrong, something upstairs. She moved towards him, looking up.

"Don't go up there," he said, wrenching his phone from his pocket. "And don't touch anything."

She started for the stairs again. "Why? What's happened?" As she reached the foot of the stairs, he reached out and placed a restraining hand on her arm, stopping her.

"Please. Just wait." He hit a key on his phone, put it to his ear and paused while it rang. "This is Detective Warren Delaney," he said and gave his police ID number. "I need a crime scene unit at 243 Belle Vue ..." and he spelled the street name out, assigning each letter its respective radio code. Then he stalked around the room, barking out instructions and massaging his forehead with his fingers before finally hanging up. "I'm afraid there's been an incident upstairs, Mrs. McClaine," he said, slipping the phone back into his pocket. "You can't stay here. You'll have to find somewhere else to stay tonight."

"But ... this is my home. What's happened?" she said and looked upstairs.

"A woman appears to have been assaulted in one of the upstairs bedrooms. I believe it's Miss Alvarez."

"Sienna? But what's she doing here? What did she say?"

"Does she have a key to the house?"

"Yes, but ... is she all right? Perhaps I should call an ambulance."

"She's dead, Mrs. McClaine. I'm sorry."

"What? Oh my God," Elizabeth said, just as the front door opened and Officer Wallace strode in. He glanced at Elizabeth, then took Delaney aside and told him something that made Delaney look up sharply.

"Mrs. McClaine," Delaney said, gently taking her arm and steering her toward the living room. "Why don't you come in here and sit down."

"I can't believe it. Who would want to kill her?" she was saying, still looking back up the stairs.

Delaney noticed the envelope in Elizabeth's hand. "Where was that?"

She looked down at the envelope in surprise, and handed it to him. "Over there. Just behind the door. I have to call Richard." She pulled her phone from her bag with trembling hands and hit his number. Behind her, Delaney and Wallace carefully opened the note, then slipped it into a plastic bag and sealed it.

Richard answered her call sounding tired and edgy. She told him in hushed tones that Sienna was dead, that they had to find somewhere else to stay.

"Dear God, Richard, what are we going to do?" she asked him in a strained whisper. "We're broke, our daughter's been stolen, and now this." And she burst into tears.

He heaved a weary sigh. "I'll book us into a hotel."

"Can we afford it?" she blurted out, and glanced back at the officers in case they had heard.

"It sounds like we don't have a lot of choice. I'll write it off as a campaign expense, but—"

"But what?"

"Just get back here as soon as you can," he said and hung up.

*****

Elizabeth and Delaney sat facing each other in the exact positions they had sat in not eight hours earlier, except this time, Officer Wallace stood at the door like a sentry while they waited for the crime scene unit. So much had happened—Holly kidnapped, Sienna dead. Not to mention they were now broke and, dear God, could it get any worse? If the day had been long, Elizabeth could see the night stretching out in front of her like a never-ending slide into oblivion, an impending plummet that she could not avoid, and would probably never escape from.

And worse yet, the only drink in the house was now marked as police evidence.

CHAPTER THIRTEEN
DAY TWO: 12:10 AM—KELSEY

The party was in full swing by the time Kelsey got back. She heard the music the second she turned the corner, then saw the lights brightening the neighborhood from the end of the street. Now cars lined either side of the roadway while people milled around, and groups of laughing, raucous party-goers collected in bunches out in front of the party house and spilled out onto the street.

"Shit." She drove slowly along the length of the street, wondering who the hell Matt had rented a place like this from. Downtown Cleveland, Ohio, on a Saturday night, you could understand. But this was Shit City back streets on a Thursday—and after midnight, if you don't mind, and all you could see was car after car parked up and down the street and a friggin' Mardi Gras in full swing.

She inched the SUV along the car-lined street, slowing almost to a stop every now and then to allow clutches of muscled-up guys and slutty-looking girls to part like the Red Sea so she could maneuver the car on through. A few taps on the hood, raps on the roof as she passed. Avoiding them but otherwise ignoring them, she swung the car into the driveway and cut the engine. She quickly collected up the paper bag containing the toy lion and the eye drops, then got out and hurried toward the house.

"Hey you," shouted a guy from across the street. When she turned, he called, "You wan' some of this?" and he grabbed his crotch while the girls around him threw their heads back and laughed like a bunch of friggin' hyenas.

"Thanks, I'm trying to give it up," she called and they all laughed even louder. She could still hear them as she mounted the stairs and pushed her way in through the front door.

A single bulb illuminated the room, its thin watery light pulsing as images jumped and flashed across the TV. Matt was perched on the edge of the living room sofa while Lionel lounged back in his chair with his feet on the coffee table in the exact same position as he was when she left, so she knew she'd have to pick her time to talk to Matt. The second they turned towards her, she felt the tension. Matt muted the TV and got to his feet. His mouth was a light line.

"Where have you been?" he said.

"At the house. I went by the Giant Eagle on Biddulph Avenue because that was the nearest twenty-four-hour—"

"You've been gone almost two fuckin' hours."

"Yeah well, y'know, it takes time. I took all the backstreets like you said. And I had to get the photo and then get over to the house, and ..." They were both glaring at her. "What?"

Matt casually opened his palms. "Anything happen along the way?"

Her gaze went from Matt to Lionel and back. This wasn't the time. "No. Nothing. I got the photos, I dropped the letter—"

"—and you killed the fuckin' nanny!" he yelled, and pointed back to somewhere behind him.

"No! What? No."

"Look. Look at the TV, you stupid bitch." He grabbed her by the back of the neck and propelled her toward the TV. His face was scarlet, eyes blazing. "Look at it. Look at the news." On the screen a female anchor with perfect teeth and perfect hair reeled off facts as a red band of text trailed the words, "Nanny found slain," across the bottom.

"It's all over the goddamn news, on every channel. The nanny got beaten to death in the house. What the hell happened?" he demanded, and he shoved her away.

She turned to him. "Matt, I swear it wasn't me—" she began but he slapped her so hard and so fast, she stopped mid-sentence and put her hand to her cheek.

"You went inside. I told you not to piss around. I told you to just take the letter." He slapped her again. "Just drop the letter, that's all you had to do." And he slapped her even harder. "And you go and kill the fuckin' nanny."

Her face stung, her eyes watered. "No. It wasn't like that. Yeah, I went inside but while I was there—"

He snatched the paper bag out of her hand. "And what's this?"

Her face was throbbing, her left ear ringing. "It's just …"

But before she could say anything else he had reached in and pulled the toy lion out of the bag and then the medication. He hurled the tiny bottle of eye drops so hard it hit the wall with a crack and the top snapped off. Then his attention was on the toy lion, turning it in his hands, glaring in rage-fueled astonishment from her to the toy and back again. "For this?"

"It's her lion. She was asking for it—but I swear I didn't kill …"

Teeth clenched, jaw muscles working, Matt gripped the lion in both hands, and started pulling and wrenching at it.

"Oh God, please Matt, don't do that," she begged. She grabbed hold of his arm but he turned away from her, savagely twisting and tearing at the toy, ripping its head off, pulling out stuffing and tossing it aside.

"Oh come on. Please, Matt, she loves that thing," she said, but it was too late. Stuffing was flying and Matt was furiously kicking it across the floor. Finally he threw the limp remains across the room.

"You didn't have to do that," she said, dropping to one knee, trying to collect up the stuffing and the torn remains, and one button eye that lay on the floor staring up at her.

"And you," Matt growled between clenched teeth as he grabbed her by the hair and dragged her to her feet, "you are …"

He raised his hand to hit her again but a squeal from the stairway stopped him short. They both turned to see Holly standing at the top of the stairs, peering over the railing at them, and sobbing "Ninny, Ninny," as she snatched at the air.

Lionel leapt angrily from his seat. "Jesus, fuck. I'll go. Get back up there, you little shit," he yelled, and started for the stairs.

"Leave her alone," Kelsey called after him, but Matt shoved her so hard, she went reeling backwards and fell on her ass. "Matt, no wait." She scrambled to her feet. "Matt, will you listen to me," she begged but all she could hear was Holly screaming. All she wanted to do was run up there to help her. "Matt, listen, just listen." Finally, he turned to her. "Let me go up to her. I can make her shut up."

"*I* can make her shut up."

Kelsey knew what she had to do when Matt was like this. Arguing didn't work. She had to find reason and she had to do it soon. Holly's cries reverberated through the house, mingling with the shouts of laughter and revelry outside. "Okay, you're right. I shouldn't have gone inside. That was dumb."

"It was more than dumb. You're a fuckin' idiot. I don't even know why we brought you along."

"You're right, you're right. I am, I'm dumb. I shouldn't have gone in. But if we don't shut her up, someone out there will hear. And what if they call the cops, huh? What if the cops turn up?" His glare was hard on her, but he was listening. "I'll go up. I'll shut her up, we'll be fine. Nothing's changed. Okay, the nanny's dead. I didn't do it, but what difference does it make? They don't know about you and Li. Just me. There's only me in the frame. I'm the only one they know about. Just let me go up to her."

He was still glaring, still pissed, but somewhere in there, the thought processes were kicking in.

"You and Li are in the clear," she told him again.

The door upstairs opened and Lionel appeared at the top of the stairs. "She's shit herself. It stinks up here."

"It's okay. I'll change her. Let me do it. I'll keep her quiet." She reached out her hand, touched it gently to Matt's face. "Hey, baby, remember? Blue skies and crystal clear water. Far as the eye can see. Just the three of us, and all the money we could ever want? That's why we're doing this, right? And Lionel—we'll get him into rehab, remember? Once he's clean and we've got the money, we're outta here. We're home free."

Calmer now, he reached up and removed her hand and turned away from her, searching the room as if he had forgotten where he was. But the snarl had gone, the fury abated.

Lionel stood at the top of the stairs, leaning on the railing. "I can tape her yap shut, that's no problem. It's the stink that's the problem."

"Don't tape her mouth." Kelsey realized it came out a little too sharp and changed her tone. "Listen, we don't have to. She trusts me. She'll be quiet if I tell her to."

Matt dropped his head into his hands, scrubbed at his face. "Jesus," he sighed. He looked tired. He was handsome, he was smart. He had been her rock. That rock was now crumbling, debris sliding in drifts down the cliff-face like an avalanche in the mountains. Deep in the heart of that chaos, a dark rumbling resounded. A tremor that only Kelsey could hear. It had grown louder and louder, gathering momentum as it shifted and crashed. At first, she had ignored it. But now she knew exactly what it was, and what had caused it.

Right now, that didn't matter. Whatever they'd once had was gone. Was it Maria Puentez? Was that the final strike? She didn't know, didn't care. All she cared about was getting to Holly.

"Matt, let me go. I'll get her cleaned up."

Too tired to argue, too exhausted to think, he shook her off and waved her away. "Go. Do whatever you have to. Just keep her quiet."

"You got it." She went straight for the stairs. Halfway up, she stepped back to let Lionel pass. As they crossed, their eyes met briefly and he gave her a smirk and a wink. He skipped to the bottom and turned briefly to grin back up at her. Then he went back to his chair.

*****

In the upstairs room, Holly was crouched on the bed clutching the filthy comforter to her mouth and sobbing as she peered over it. She lowered the comforter as soon as Kelsey appeared at the door and reached for her.

"Hey, hey." Kelsey crossed quickly to the bed and sat on the edge, stroking her hair back off her face and thumbing the tears from her cheeks. "Are you okay? Did he hurt you?"

Holly's eyes were puffy and red, her face wet with tears. A trail of clear mucus streamed from her nose down the scar to lips that were red and sticky. Tears swelled and wobbled, then splashed down her cheeks as she snuffled and sobbed. "Nine-a," Holly hiccupped. "Ah ho," she said, and jutted a lip.

"Yeah. He is an asshole. Let's get that face cleaned up." When she dug into her pocket in search of a tissue, the first thing she came up with was the keys to the Mercedes. "Ah, not those." She stuck them back, located the tissue and gently wiped Holly's nose and mouth. "How about we get those panties changed, huh? You don't wanna sit in shitty panties."

Holly blinked up at her and squeezed her nose. "Poo."

Kelsey smiled. "Yeah, they're a little stinky. Let's get 'em changed."

She took the child's hand, feeling it small and soft and warm in her own, and helped her from the confines of the covers. Kneeling in front of her, she removed the soiled panties, and found her mouth tightening at the stench. "Boy, you really did fill 'em up."

Kelsey went to the bathroom, dropped the panties into the toilet and tore a length of tissue from the roll. She dampened it, then returned. "This is all I got. I don't have any wipes or nothing. This'll have to do."

As she wiped and patted the child dry, Holly put out a tentative finger, touching it to the swelling on Kelsey's face where Matt had struck her. Instinctively, Kelsey ducked her head away. "Don't worry about that. That's nothin'. I hit it, that's all." When she looked up, there was doubt in Holly's eyes. "I fell down, oopty oop."

"Oopny oop. Ah fah down."

"That's right, all fall down, oopty oop." Kelsey pulled up the clean panties and bundled the child back into the bed. Sitting on the edge, she leaned close and brushed a stray wisp of hair back from Holly's eyes. "Now listen," she whispered. "You gotta be real quiet. I'm gonna take you home to your mommy and daddy …"

"… aangh …"

"Shh, no I gotta. I'm sorry. I shouldn't have even brought you here. But I have to think about how I'm gonna do it. If you make a big noise, it'll piss Lionel off and that's gonna make it even harder, y'hear?"

Holly sat up, eyes locked on Kelsey. She took Kelsey's face in her little hands and leaned in close. "Ah po' 'em bo'," she said, carefully molding the words. "Ah—pop—'em—bo'."

Kelsey held her gaze a moment. The words had registered but it was as though she could not absorb them. She took Holly's hands in hers, held them enclosed in her own, and leaned her face in close to the child's. "Nobody's poppin' nobody," she said. "Who said that? Lionel? He an asshole."

"Mah'."

Kelsey sat back. It was a knife in her chest. She shifted her focus, plumping and fussing with the comforter. "Well, you ignore him. Nobody's getting popped, you or me. And Matt's being stupid saying something like that. I'm takin' you home."

Holly's face crumpled. "Snay wah Nangsie Mommy."

Kelsey huffed out a breath. She wanted to say, "Yes. You can stay with me. I'll take care of you and keep you safe …" But from somewhere deep down, in a place she'd almost forgotten, the image of her own mother swam into her mind's eye—her long blond hair, the sound of her laughter, the touch of her hand …

She shuddered and pushed the images away. "No. I told you, you can't stay with me. God," she said as she tucked the child down again. "Now, listen to me, are you listening?" She leaned down close, taking the child's face in her hands. "I am taking you home. But if something goes wrong, if something happens and you end up leaving this room without me … are you listening?" Holly nodded up, wide-eyed and still. "If you ever leave this room without me, I will find you. You hear? I *will* find you."

"'a fine' meh."

"It's a promise."

"What are you doing?"

Kelsey turned in fright to find Matt standing in the doorway. "Just tucking her in. She's gonna be quiet now, aren't you?"

Holly nodded and slithered down under the comforter.

Matt took one step into the room, glared down at the kid. "Get downstairs," he told Kelsey. "You been up here too long."

There was no anger, no threat. It was a demand. Kelsey wondered if he'd heard what she'd been telling Holly. She had to assume he hadn't. At the door, she turned, jabbed a finger in Holly's direction, and said, "Remember what I said. If you leave this room, I *will* find you." Then she closed the door and followed Matt downstairs.

CHAPTER FOURTEEN
DAY TWO: 1:49 AM—ELIZABETH

Elizabeth stood at the window and stared fourteen stories down to the street below. Car lights swept this way and that and neon signs flashed in silence beyond the glass. Every now and then she could see the blue and red flashes of a police car speeding through the night. She wondered if whoever they were rushing to felt as numb and as empty as she did. Delaney had called in the forensics and backups and scene-of-crime crews and God only knew who else. Right at this moment they were probably crawling all over the house—her house—dragging Richard's and her lives out into harsh white lights, throwing their darkest secrets and most private possessions into public view. All so they could determine who had killed Sienna Alvarez.

She and Delaney had left the house with police cars parked at odd angles and lights blazing up and down their beautiful street. They had driven her to the high-rise hotel Richard had booked downtown, and Delaney had escorted her to a room where the mini-bar had been stripped dry. After impressing on her that he would return to his office and work through the night to find their daughter, he told her to get a good night's sleep. Then he left.

As if she would rest. As if she would be tucked up in a strange bed, sleeping away the trauma of the day while her daughter was in the hands of a stranger who had murdered their nanny and ruined their lives. She lifted her eyes to the horizon. What on earth did people think went on in her head? Did they think she was callous? Thoughtless? Stupid, perhaps?

"Poor Sienna," she muttered to no one in particular as she watched yet another police car speed the length of the street below and vanish into the maze of buildings.

Richard was sitting on the bed, his tie loosely coiled next to him, exhaustion creasing his face. "Hmm? Yes. Poor Sienna."

"Detective Delaney said there were fingerprints everywhere. He said it's probably the same woman. She didn't even try to get rid of the evidence. She obviously doesn't care. What kind of person does this? What kind of a monster steals a child from her family and murders a girl like Sienna?"

Richard rubbed his hands together, as if he was cold. "I wish I had something to drink."

"If Alice hadn't stripped the bar you would have," she told him and returned her gaze to the window. "I could do with a stiff martini myself," she muttered, ignoring the look he flashed her in the reflected glass. "Holly loved Sienna. She'll miss her terribly."

"Yes, because you'd know." He said it so quietly, Elizabeth almost missed it.

She turned, frowning at him. "Excuse me?"

He paused, underpinning the moment. "I said, 'You'd know, wouldn't you?' Oh, for God's sake, Elizabeth, don't look so aghast.

It's not like you're at home every day to see them together. Well, is it?"

"What are you accusing me of?"

"I'm not accusing you of anything. When were you ever there to do anything? You were always at your charities or your luncheons—"

"Working for *your* campaign."

"You call being drunk on your ass working? And if you're not making a fool of yourself—of me—at your luncheons," he said, getting to his feet, "you're passed out on the bed. Oh! Which seems to be your second favorite pastime these days."

"Oh, go on. Let's get the knife right in there. Like you're anyone to talk."

"Please, don't act like you're surprised. It's a wonder you even recognize the kid—"

"The kid? That 'kid'—that little lost girl," Elizabeth said, pointing off to the window, "is our daughter. Or have you forgotten?"

"Back to that old tune again," he said. "You know what? The minute Holly came along, our lives were flipped upside down. You started acting like she's the only person in the world. You lost all perspective. Nothing else mattered. But guess what, *I'm* still here."

"You? Holly has Down syndrome. She has a cleft palate, in case that's conveniently slipped your mind. She has *special needs*, for chrissakes. And that's not just a label you plaster on people. And since when was this about you?"

"Me?" he said, jabbing himself in the chest. "How could I ever think it was about me? I never saw you. You spent every minute with her—dragging her from one doctor to the next, hoping they could change her into something you wanted."

Elizabeth felt a barb of truth hit her in the chest. "How dare you."

"And me? I might as well have been dead, for all you cared. You never touched me, you never came near me. Do you remember the last time we had sex, Elizabeth? Do you?"

Elizabeth felt her face twist into a bitter sneer. "Well, I know about me, Richard. But I don't know about you. How is Pamela Jacobs these days?"

The shock instantly registered in his face. "I … well, I …"

"Yes, that's right. I know all about your nasty little affair."

"Yes. That's right. I was the bad guy. But think about this, Elizabeth. What choice did you leave me?"

"What choice? *What choice*?" she shrieked. "You ran straight into the arms of your secretary. Well, how clichéd. Did you tell her your wife doesn't understand you?"

"It wasn't like that."

"And what about the DNA tests? What about the paternity tests you had done, hmm? What about those?"

He said nothing. The color had washed from his face and his mouth opened and closed, forming words without sound.

"That's right. All your hard work provided ample money to pay for the best private detective I could find. And what were you going to do, *dearest darling*?" she said, using the words Pamela had used in the voice message she had found. "The minute you could prove she wasn't yours, you were going to run off and leave us, isn't that right? But you ran into one big, fat problem, didn't you? The tests came back positive. Oh God, Richard, I would love to have seen the look on your face. I can just imagine your expression when you realized how much alimony and child support you were up for. It must have been a pretty penny because soon you came running home to become the loving husband again—minus the loving part, of course." He made a dismissive noise and turned away, but she went on. "You talk about me. *You* ran out on *us.* When we needed you—*really needed you*, you weren't there. And you're still running, Richard. The only difference is now you're holed up in your office instead of in some seedy hotel with Pamela … oh no, that's right. You did it in *our house*, in *my bed*."

"What the hell would you know? I had to work. I had to earn a living." His voice was low, bitter. "God knows, I had to keep you in booze, didn't I?"

Elizabeth was about to launch back in when a sharp rap at the door made both of them turn. They exchanged a glance, and Elizabeth went to the door. "Who is it?"

"It's me. Open up," Alice called from outside the door.

Elizabeth turned the latch and the instant the door gave way, Alice pushed her way in.

"What the hell are you two doing? We've got half the press in the state sitting right outside the door and you two are at each other's throats like a couple of stray cats. What are you yelling about?" Her fiery gaze shifted from Elizabeth to Richard and back.

"Nothing," said Elizabeth. "We were just talking."

Richard stepped across and placed a hand on Elizabeth's shoulder. "We're fine. We're just very tired. This has been an ordeal for both of us."

"Well, keep it down, for God's sake. You'll have every paper in the state writing up divorce stories before we know it. Is there any news? Do they have any idea who these people are that took your daughter?"

Elizabeth twisted out of his grasp and went back to the window. "The police tell us it's the same woman. She left fingerprints everywhere. And there was the second letter telling us they've given us until three o'clock tomorrow afternoon."

Alice heaved out a sigh. "Well, three hours is better than nothing. It gives you a little more time to come up with the money. Speaking of which, have you seen the campaign contributions? We're up to almost three million. That's in a matter of hours. Maybe we should have thought of this sooner." She bent to square off a stack of papers on the coffee table, then handed them to Richard. "These are the breakdowns of the Columbus debate. Take a look over them, see where we scored. Oh, and we have an extra slot on prime time TV at six-fifteen tomorrow morning so I want you two looking ... well, I want you there. These slots are boosting our ratings. We're up twelve points—*twelve points*, Richard. That's in a matter of hours. At this rate we can forget the second term—we'll go straight for the White House."

And there it was—like something emerging from the mists of chaos and confusion; a truth that had materialized into something only Elizabeth recognized. She turned slowly, eyes narrowing on Alice Cressley. "You," she said in the barest whisper. "It was you."

Alice blinked. "Me? What about me?"

"It was you," Elizabeth said again. "You're the one who took our daughter."

"What?"

"Elizabeth," Richard said. "Don't be ridiculous."

But she was slowly advancing on Alice. "You set all of this up to boost your pathetic ratings. This is a campaign stunt—a sham. You organized these monsters to steal our child."

"Oh, please," Alice groaned at the ceiling.

"You took my baby from me," Elizabeth shouted. "You stole her away."

Alice pressed her fingers to her eyes. "Oh, for chrissakes, somebody give her a drink. And keep her away from me," she said, and took a step back.

With her fists bunched, lips drawn back in terror and rage, Elizabeth flew at the woman. "You did this, you did this. Don't try to deny it," she said, until Richard grabbed her and yanked her back. "How could you?" she wailed and burst into tears.

"Sobriety really is doing you no favors, Elizabeth. Dear God, I thought you were a bad enough drunk. I was well wide of the mark."

"Tell us what you've done with her," Elizabeth demanded. "What did you do with my baby?"

"I didn't do anything with her, you stupid woman. Listen to me. If I had organized this, believe me, I would have done a far better job. For one," she said, counting points off with her fingers, "I would not have sent a goddamned letter. I would have called. To hell with the fact your number's unlisted, who knows how many people would have it. I surely wouldn't. Secondly, I would not put your daughter through this. What kind of a person do you think I am? Do you honestly think I could do this to a little girl? Your opinion of me must be so far down the sewers it's halfway to Japan. Thirdly, I would not have asked for ten million. It's a ridiculous amount. Where would I put it? What would I do with it? Banking security systems in the United States would have flagged that amount the instant it left your account and hit mine, and I'd have had the CIA blasting holes in my front door before I could call out 'Who's there?' Fourth, if I was going to kidnap anyone—anyone at all—I would not hire a pack of imbeciles such as these people obviously are. I would have hired people who actually had a brain cell between them. Not idiots who run around breaking into houses and killing innocent people, and leaving their fingerprints all over the evidence." She regarded first Elizabeth and then Richard. They said nothing. "And finally," she added quietly, "I would have kidnapped the child of people who actually had money. Not people who are down to their last dime."

Even Richard gasped.

"Oh, for chrissakes," Alice groaned. "Do you think I don't follow the stock market? Do you think I can't read a newspaper? I've seen how much this campaign has cost. I see how many contracts are going your way and how many you're losing because of Ray Townsend and his political cheap tricks. I also know you just laid off every one of your employees at both the Painesville airport construction site, as well as that new shopping mall in Beachwood—though why on earth they need another shopping mall is anybody's guess. Do you honestly think I don't notice these things? You must think I'm stupid."

There was a deathly silence for some moments. Then Richard finally asked the question that had obviously occurred to both of them. "So, why are you doing this? If you knew our position, why did you continue on with this campaign—with the ...?" He gestured weakly around them, then dropped his hand.

"Because despite my bitch gland being bigger than both of your brains put together, I would actually like to see this child come home. Although, God only knows, after seeing the two of you scrapping like a couple of spoiled kids, there's a chance she's better off where she is." She pulled in a long, tired breath. "And, despite everything, I believe we have a serious chance at the White House. And I believe in my heart, that I can get you there. Well, don't look at me like that. Everybody needs a purpose," she added and sat down.

"I'm exhausted," said Elizabeth.

Alice got up and collected her briefcase and paused at the door. "Maybe you should stop searching for enemies in your own camp and get some sleep. You've got two hours with Diana du Plessis tomorrow. She's enough to test the patience of God himself, and even then," she added pointedly, "given ten minutes with her, even He would probably smite her. Good night, Richard. Elizabeth."

And she left.

CHAPTER FIFTEEN
DAY TWO: 3:58 AM—KELSEY

Kelsey had followed Matt back to the living room downstairs, where she sat watching Lionel opening up his stash to have "just another little taste."

She had seen this routine so many times she knew it by heart. First, he tied the band around his arm, tightening it with his teeth while he prepared the needle like it was some kind of surgical instrument. It was a ritual he carried out as if the act itself was integral to the high. She watched him slip the needle under the skin, drawing, finding nothing, then repeating it over and over.

Half the guy's veins had collapsed. It was a miracle he could get anything into them at all. At one point she was so engrossed watching this jackass with his tubes and his contraptions, going through his shitty ritualistic procedures not six feet from her, she suddenly became aware of the scowl that had crept across her face.

As though sensing her revulsion, Lionel's bleary gaze turned on her. "What are you lookin' at?"

Kelsey simply shook her head, as if to say, "Nothing." Because that's exactly what she was looking at—an empty shell. Whatever soul he may have once possessed had been eaten away by drugs, until there was nothing but a black hole that sucked in everything around it and pulverized it into more nothingness. If this bottomless pit of expectation was in pain, he had brought it all on himself, through need and greed and his pursuit of self-gratification. And yet this empty remnant of a human being would think nothing of taking Holly's life—a little girl who carried her own burden without complaint; an innocent child who gave out love without question and demanded nothing in return.

Kelsey had never liked Lionel. But watching him now, injecting chemicals into his veins like pouring gas into a never-ending tank, she wondered yet again how Matt could have ever seen him as a hero. And somehow, in that moment, something in her mind clarified and locked into place. Lionel had no intention of going into rehab, and never did. It was just another lie so he could get what he wanted—no matter what the cost to those around him.

Truth was, Kelsey didn't care. If she'd found Lionel spread-eagle in the street on the brink of death, she would simply have stepped across him and continued on her way without a backward look. That was how little he meant to her.

When he'd finally released the tourniquet and flopped back in the chair with the same stupid look of satisfaction on his face, Matt spoke.

"Okay, listen up. There's a couple of changes I made to the plan."

Kelsey had known Matt since she was fifteen and he was seventeen. From the day she met him it took hellfire and a tornado to make him change any of his plans. So this was unusual.

"Now, this is the deal," he told them, hunching forward in his seat. "Instead of staying here tomorrow morning until eight like we were going to, we're heading out at six. I got us another place to hole up in."

"Where? Why?" Kelsey asked.

"Because now we've got another twenty-four hours to kill, that's why. We can't risk being here all that time, so we gotta move. 'Specially with that goddamned party going on over there." He jerked a thumb over his shoulder. "Half of fuckin' Cleveland's over there. We can't risk the kid being seen. It only takes one nosey asshole and the whole thing goes to shit. So, we head out at six. Clear?"

"Yeah, sure," she said. So he was still pretending they were giving the parents another day. For some reason that small betrayal—that minuscule blip in his otherwise solid façade angered her more than she would have expected. "So, where's this place we're going?" she asked again.

"Why? What does it matter?"

"I was wondering, is all."

"Who's planning this?"

"You are."

He gave her a long, searching look. "Six o'clock tomorrow morning. Just be ready."

And that was that. She promised him she would keep Holly quiet until he called her at six, then she went to bed. Upstairs, she lay next to that small body, pulling her close, smelling the scent of her, feeling the softness of her hair. For almost an hour she lay there, holding her, listening to the child's gentle breathing, until she fell into a fitful sleep.

At four o'clock on the dot, Kelsey opened her eyes. It was time to move.

"Hey," she whispered in Holly's ear. The child groaned softly, snuffled, then nestled down and went quiet again. "Holly. C'mon, wake up." Kelsey shook her gently by the shoulder. "C'mon, baby, we don't have all night. We gotta get up."

Holly's little feet pushed down the bed, her back flexing as her thin little body stretched out to its full length, arms reaching high above her head, tensing and shuddering. She yawned wide and ground her fists into her eyes.

"Now, shh," Kelsey told her in a voice she herself could barely hear. "We gotta be real quiet."

Holly blinked up at her and put her finger to her lips.

"That's right. I'm taking you home to your Mommy and Da …"

"Angh! Angh!"

"Shh no, shut up," Kelsey hissed, and clapped a hand over the child's mouth. "You gotta be quiet."

She pulled the cover back and waited until Holly scooted to the edge of the bed. Kelsey crouched down next to her, slipping the child's shoes on and whispering, "I'm sorry, but you gotta be real quiet now, okay?" Holly said nothing, just blinked at her in the dim light while Kelsey tucked and straightened the clothes she had dressed her in the night before. At last, Kelsey took her hand, lifted her own shoes, and the two of them trod lightly towards the door.

Kelsey leaned out the door, peering along the landing, when Holly said, "Go poddy."

"What …?" Kelsey whispered. "Oh, shit." She was about to tell her she'd have to wait but Holly was clutching herself and jiggling. "Yeah, yeah, okay, but shh." She gently placed her shoes down, checked the stairs below, then led Holly to the bathroom where she quietly closed the door and lifted Holly onto the toilet. When she'd finished, Kelsey pulled up her panties, straightened her clothing, and cautiously cracked the door. From somewhere in the darkness downstairs she could hear Lionel's soft snoring. He must have fallen asleep in the chair while Matt had retired to the bedroom at the rear of the house.

Her heart picked up a beat. "Dammit," she whispered. She thought they were both sleeping in the rear bedroom. This was never going to be easy. But Lionel was one more element she hadn't counted on. She reached for Holly's hand, and turned just in time to see her reaching for the flush.

"No," she whispered and pulled her back. Heart pounding, and holding Holly's hand in hers, Kelsey turned back to the doorway again.

Downstairs, the sounds had turned from snoring to deep breathing. Kelsey hoisted Holly into her arms. Clutching her shoes in one hand, she moved warily to the top step, and waited. The party across the road had died down. The silence left behind filled the house like something tangible. She put a tentative toe on the second step, then started down the stairs. On the third one down, the creak of wood cut the air and Lionel sucked in a deep breath. Kelsey froze. He smacked his lips a couple of times, moved in the chair, and let it out. She leaned close to Holly's ear, and said, "Shhh." For some moments, they clung together in the dark, waiting. When Lionel's breathing returned to a soft snore again, Kelsey took the next step, then the next, moving quickly and quietly to the bottom. At the foot of the stairs, she paused again, listening for movement. There was nothing but Lionel's snores. Hugging the child close, she crept to the front door, placed her hand on the knob, and gently turned it. Without the slightest noise, the door eased open and a shaft of moonlight sliced into the room.

Holly's arms clung tight around her neck, legs locked around her. Kelsey checked behind her once more, then stepped across the threshold and spotted the car. That's when it hit her. She'd forgotten the damned car keys.

Cursing under her breath, she placed Holly on the front porch. "Wait here." She placed her shoes by the open door, turned and stepped quietly back into the room.

The last place she'd seen the keys was where she had dropped them on the coffee table the night before. They were still there when she went upstairs earlier that night. Narrow blades of moonlight cut through the gaps in the curtains, picking out shapes in the darkness—the sofa, the coffee table, the TV. Barefoot, she moved six careful steps across the living room.

Not three feet away Lionel lay back in the chair, hands dangling, feet still up on the coffee table, still asleep. Kelsey turned briefly to where Holly was silhouetted in the doorway, quietly peering into the darkened room.

Kelsey reached down and tamped the flat of her hand across the table top, searching for the keys. Her eyes had adjusted enough that she could make out a glass and the ashtray. She found the keys just beyond. She lifted them with a faint clink, and Lionel shifted. She waited with her heart in her mouth. After a few moments, the long, slow breathing resumed and he lay motionless. Gripping the keys in her palm to prevent them jingling, Kelsey backtracked to the door.

As soon as she had eased the door closed again, Kelsey let out a breath. Tension had tightened the muscles across the back of her neck into stiff cords. She rolled her shoulders briefly, then took Holly's hand and walked to the car. With one eye on the house, she eased open the passenger door, lifted Holly into the seat, and buckled her in. Instead of closing the door, she eased it back to the point where it touched the frame. Closing it, no matter how carefully, would echo around the neighborhood. This way Holly would be secure in the safety belt until they got around the corner into the next street. Then she'd close the door properly.

Kelsey quickly rounded the car and opened the driver's door. For the briefest while, she paused to give the house one last look. Now, for the first time, she realized just how far she had come. She had set one foot across an invisible line. When Matt realized what she'd done, there would be no turning back. Some small part of her was urging her to run back—to fall into his arms and cling to the safety she'd always known. She wanted to tell him she was sorry and that she would never betray him. But something stronger had emerged—a curiosity, a hunger, a need to find her own blue skies and crystal clear waters. And stranger still, it was only now that she realized it had been the photographs of Maria Puentez and Matt that had given her the strength to break out; to take the child and leave.

Kelsey hoisted herself into the driver's seat and pulled the door towards her without closing it. Holly sat next to her, watching her every move. Kelsey smiled down at her, touched her on the nose, then slipped the key into the ignition and twisted it.

It clicked.

She turned it again. No ignition, no spark; just a click, and the car remained lifeless. She tried again and again, each time easing her foot on the gas, but each time the result was the same hollow click.

"Fuck."

Dropping her head in frustration, she pulled on the hood release which activated with a faint thunk. She pushed her door open once more, got out, and went around the car to lift the hood. In the faint moonlight, she could clearly see the battery lead dangling free of the terminal. "Oh, shit …"

"Having battery problems?" said a voice behind her.

She caught a glimpse of Matt, saw his fist …

… then nothing.

CHAPTER SIXTEEN
DAY TWO: …

The throbbing in Kelsey's face hit her even before she reached full consciousness. It echoed through her head like a gong, dragging her through a fog of oblivion and back to reality. At last, she realized she was sitting on a chair. The edge of the wooden seat bit into the backs of her knees. Her hands were secured to the back. She figured the restraints were cable ties because the bindings were thin plastic strips, rigid and sharp enough to cut into her skin. She also knew her face was a mess because her eyes refused to open. After some moments of lifting her head and raising her eyebrows to force her eyelids apart, she eventually stretched her mouth wide, leaned her head right back and her right eye cracked open. Then the left. The instant they split apart, she looked down. Cords of sticky blood and saliva had trailed from her nose and mouth and pooled in her lap where it had partially dried.

She didn't know how many times Matt had hit her. She went down on the first and never even saw the rest. Now, here she was in this dingy kitchen of the house, tied to a chair, hands behind her back, shins bound to the legs, and no idea of the time.

"Matt," she called out. Her voice was a dry croak. "Matt!"

Nothing.

She was alone in the house. She suspected as much. They'd be long gone.

How dumb was she? How could she have possibly thought she'd outsmart Matt? He was the one with the brains. He was the one who looked after her—looked after everyone. Goddamn it, she hadn't even taken her shoes with her. From where she sat she could see them still sitting over by the front door where she had left them. A sudden and overwhelming feeling of worthlessness and stupidity washed over her—a feeling of such despair that a sob welled up from her very core, and burst from her throat. Her face tightened and throbbed as wave after wave of anguish hit her. But just as she was about to give herself up to it, to let the tide of desolation crash over her and wash her away, her eye caught something glinting on the living room floor. She blinked back the tears and realized what it was. It was the single button eye of Holly's Lilly Lion. She had picked it up after it was torn from the toy and cast aside. She must have dropped it when Matt slapped her.

Kelsey had let Holly down. She had let them take her.

But she had made a promise. She had told Holly that if they were parted, Kelsey would find her. And that was one promise she wasn't going to break.

Slivers of pre-dawn light were slicing between the kitchen curtains. She figured it must have been around five a.m. That meant she still had ten hours. She had no idea where they would have gone, but she knew exactly where to start looking.

The kitchen contained nothing obvious that she might cut her bonds on. But the kitchen utensil drawer might. First she had to get to it. She tried leaning forward and duck-walking, but instead of moving, the chair wobbled and threatened to fall over. So she sat down again and began rocking it, creating enough momentum to inch her toward the drawer. As soon as she was almost within reach of it, she squeezed her eyes shut, bracing herself for impact. She threw her weight back and forth until her center of gravity moved to the rear legs … teetered … then toppled backwards. She landed on her back with both hands jammed beneath her. Easing herself up on her hands, she moved around until the toes of her right foot were level with the handle of the second drawer down. Inching forward, she hooked her toe up under the handle, then she hand-walked herself backwards, slowly pulling the drawer out.

Three times her foot slipped. Three times she cursed and tried again. All she thought about was Holly. She kept telling herself they'd be dumb to kill her before the money was transferred, that the parents would want to know their child was alive before they handed over the money. That didn't mean they wouldn't hurt Holly. And it didn't mean they'd give her back alive.

Knowing it only made Kelsey more determined.

Finally, she dragged the drawer out far enough to feel the weight of the contents shift. With one last pull, it fell on the floor with a crash of steel and knives and forks and God only knew what else. Among it all she spotted a carving knife. She swiveled around on the chair, rocking until she tipped sideways onto an assortment of sharpening steels, soup ladles and can-openers. Straining against the ties, her fingers found the knife. She turned it, angling it around until she felt the handle in her palm. Slipping the blade under the tie, she sawed back and forth until the plastic strip snapped apart. Using her free hand she collected the knife and slashed the ties on her other wrist and ankles.

At last, she dragged herself to her feet, wincing at the bruising to her ribs, the stiffness in her shoulders. She rolled her neck. Her entire body was stiff and sore.

The bathroom cabinet contained several tubes of ointment, some baby talc and a blister pack of Tylenol. She threw three tablets down, washing them back with a couple handfuls of water, then splashed water on her face. A brief assessment in the mirror told her that her right eye was bulging and turning black, her nose a swollen, bloodied mess. When blood began snaking down her upper lip she tore off a strip of toilet tissue and rammed a wad of paper up each nostril. Then she limped to the front door, put on her shoes and left.

Outside twenty or so cars still lined the street. Their owners were probably lying in a drug and alcohol-induced stupor inside the house. She walked from car to car, ducking her head to look into each until she crossed the street and came to a black '67 four-door Chevy Impala in pristine condition. The chrome-work shone like it had just come out of the shop, and the rims on the tires practically sparkled. Dangling on a chain from the rearview mirror was a tiny Saint Christopher.

On the downside, the Saint Christopher spelled trouble. That minor adornment marked it as a gang car. On the upside, the thing was parked three doors from the party house and some idiot had left the right rear passenger door unlocked. She pulled the door open, released the lock on the driver's door, and got in.

"Hey!" some guy yelled from the front steps of the party house. Before she knew it, he was coming at her like a bull with its ass on fire. "Hey, *chola* muthafuckin' bitch, get outta that car. Hey, Frankie, someone's stealin' your ride," he yelled over his shoulder, and next thing, guys were pouring out of the house, pulling on pants and jackets, and running towards her.

"Shit." She ran her fingers back and forth under the dash searching for the ignition wires but she wouldn't have time.

She heard someone yell, "Hey, bitch, that's my car," and figured it was Frankie.

"Oh, no." She slapped down the driver's visor to find nothing. "No, no, no." She hit the door lock with the side of her fist just as a bunch of pissed-off Latino guys in gang colors surrounded the car like a nest of angry hornets. They wrenched on the doors, slapped at the windshield, and yelled at the windows with faces twisted in rage. Now the car was rocking and swaying. Any second someone would smash a window.

In desperation she slapped down the passenger's visor and a key slid into the passenger's seat along with the registration papers. She plunged the key into the ignition and twisted it. The engine grumbled into life just as a fist came through the driver's window in a shower of glass and reached for her. She dodged the hand, threw the car into drive and hit the gas. A big guy who'd climbed up on the hood bounced off and rolled into the road while others kicked and punched the panels, swearing and yelling threats as the car lurched forward. She cut a path through twenty or so guys with scarlet faces and the rage meter set on "Overload."

She pulled away, feeling the car speed up as they released their grip one by one. In the rearview mirror she could see them scrambling, running to cars and jumping in, and in a chorus of screeching tires they started after her.

She hit the first corner, laying the car hard into it but the suspension was spongy, the steering rangy. The car fishtailed on the first bend and she almost lost the back end into a stationary truck on her right. She straightened, checked the mirror. All she could see was a train of cars right behind her.

She hit the gas and took the next bend, heading straight out onto the turnpike with the car swaying side to side like a fairground ride. She hit the Ohio Turnpike Connector and barreled down I-80. Behind her, Frankie and half the local gang, the L21s, were trailing her. A Ford Explorer pulled up on her left and a gun came up over the sill. She stamped her foot on the brake, heard the pop of the gun and the tink of the bullet hitting the car on her right. She slowed then sped up, trying to maneuver away, but the Explorer swerved, crunching into her and grinding the two cars together like a pair of angry bison wrestling for position. Again, she stamped on the brake and the cars on either side shot forward. She spun the wheel into a right-hand turn and rocketed up the next off-ramp to the *tink, tink* of bullets hitting the trunk.

The rear window shattered and she ducked. Barely able to see the road ahead, she hit the gas and slalomed left and right to keep them from pulling alongside her but the suspension was shot and the car swayed like a hula girl and the rear end kept drifting. She veered left, saw a Chevy lose it and one-eighty into a tree. She swung onto East 31st, straightened and hit the gas again.

That's when she heard the distant whine of police sirens. She threw a right, then a left to find two police units angling in across the road up ahead to form a block.

Decision time: She could run it, or she could stop. If she stopped, they would take her in. She'd be locked up in a cell for the next ten hours while they printed out her rap sheet and questioned her. By that time, Holly could be dead.

But this car would never outrun the cops or the L21s. She didn't even know how she'd gotten this far.

Decision time.

She slowed. Think, think. If this was Matt …

… it wasn't. This was her decision.

She slowed to a crawl. Flashing lights appeared in the rearview mirror, lights flashing up ahead.

One by one she could see the L21s pulling over behind her, cops getting out of their cars and running over to them as they stopped. She rolled to within a few feet of the block and hit the brake. She cursed the L21s, cursed the cops, cursed Matt. Most of all, she cursed herself. How dumb could she be?

She cut the ignition and sat with her head down, staring into the dried blood crusted in the lap of her jeans while a cop ambled over. He knocked on the driver's window with the knuckle of his forefinger and called, "Ma'am, would you mind stepping out of the car?"

She released the door, pushed it open, eyes pinned to the dash, hand to the tattoo on her neck.

He leaned down and said, "I said, would you mind …" but paused when he spotted the bruising to her face. Then he said, "Are you okay, ma'am?"

"Yeah."

"Stay there. Is this your car?"

"No."

"Whose car is it?"

Face down, tear-filled eyes not meeting his eyes. "My boyfriend's."

The cop jerked a thumb over his shoulder. "Is that him?"

Kelsey lifted her head, blinked away tears. In the rearview mirror she could see the L21s surrounded by cops. They were jabbing fingers in her direction and yelling threats about how she'd never get away because they'd find her and they'd fuckin' kill her. Out in front was the owner of the car, Frankie. A cop cuffed him, then dragged him away to a waiting police car. "Yeah, that's him."

"Nice guy."

"Yeah."

"You got registration papers for the car?"

She reached across, handed the papers to him. He took a few seconds to go over them, turning them, turning them again. "And this is Francis Rodrigo Duarte's car?"

"Yeah, the asshole."

"You mind telling me where you were headed to?"

Kelsey hesitated. This could go two ways. "A shelter. For battered women," she said in a hushed voice.

"A shelter?"

"Yeah."

A second cop walked over and joined the first. "What have you got here?"

"Girlfriend taken a beating. She's on her way to a shelter."

The second cop also bent to look into the car. "Are you okay, ma'am?"

"I'm … I'm okay. I just need to get to the shelter. I called them. They're expecting me."

"Would you like us to call 911, ma'am? Maybe get some paramedics out here?"

"No," she said, a little too quickly. "No, I'm fine. Please, I have to go."

The cops stepped away from the car, talking in hushed tones. Back down the road one of the L21s lashed out and two cops jumped him and wrestled him to the ground while insults were traded and the situation threatened to flash out of control.

The two cops reached some kind of agreement and the first one stepped back to her. "Listen, I'm gonna let you go, but I want you to go straight to the shelter and as soon as you're safe, I want you to surrender the car, you understand?"

"Yeah."

"Once you're at the shelter, you call the nearest police department and arrange for someone to bring the car in. Okay?"

"Yeah," said Kelsey. Hardly daring to breathe, she turned the key in the ignition, checked the side mirror and slowly cruised off.

Someone was watching over her.

CHAPTER SEVENTEEN
DAY TWO: 5:32 AM—ELIZABETH

Ironically, Elizabeth awoke feeling better than she had felt in months—maybe years. No hangover, no parched mouth, no throbbing head. Despite a lack of sleep, she felt alert, and energized. She assumed she must have dozed for perhaps as much as an hour because the night she expected to stretch on forever seemed to have come to an abrupt halt when she opened her eyes. Now morning light spilled into the room, picking out the clothes and bags and cases she and Richard had hurriedly packed the previous night.

But almost as soon as she had brushed the sleep from her eyes, the memories of the previous day flooded back, and all at once, she felt exhausted again.

Richard was already up and in the shower. Elizabeth didn't want to move. She wanted to pull the covers over her head like a child and go back to her all-too-brief sleep. At least that had relieved the pain of reality, regardless of how fleetingly.

The sounds of pattering water in the bathroom ceased, the shower door clunked closed, and Richard came into the room with his hair slicked to his head and his shoulders slouched. She had never seen him look so old. From where she lay beneath the covers she watched him for a moment, studying his reflection in the mirror as he combed and patted, preened and dabbed, finally slapping cologne to his cheeks. His gaze crossed to her just as a waft of spicy fragrance she didn't recognize hit the air.

"It's time you got up. We're on at six-fifteen," he said, and drew a part in his hair that was so sharp, he looked as if he might fall in two.

Reluctantly, Elizabeth got up, showered and was dressed by 5:49 am. She was just putting the final touches to her makeup when two sharp raps sounded on the door. The second Richard opened it, Alice swept in, wearing an azure-colored skirt and jacket in much the same style as she had worn the previous day, and clapping her hands like a high school football coach.

"Okay, people, this is what we have on today ..." But on seeing Elizabeth, she paused, looked her up and down, and said, "What's the matter?"

"Nothing. I'm fine, Mrs. Cressley. And you?"

Alice hesitated a beat. "I'm also fine. Thank you for asking. Nice choice of color," she said, and dipped her head at Elizabeth's peach-colored silk jacket and skirt.

Elizabeth sat on the edge of the sofa and slipped on her low-heeled leather shoes.

"Are we all ready for today?" asked Alice. Without waiting for a reply, she opened her briefcase and took out a file. "So, this is what I want from you both. First we—"

"Do you have to go through this again?" Elizabeth interrupted. "We already know what we have to do, Mrs. Cressley. After all, we only did it a few hours ago."

"I have no doubt about that," she replied. "But there are a couple of items I need to ensure you have correct. *If* you don't mind."

Elizabeth sucked in her cheeks, pursed her mouth, and stepped across to the mirror to check her makeup.

Alice licked her finger and dealt the pages from the file into three piles on the coffee table. "First of all," she said, addressing her comments only to Richard, as though Elizabeth had left the room. "I want you to start by thanking the people of America for their support and their love. Anyone whose love and support you don't have by now, believe me, you don't want it. Then, I want you to use the words, 'Please bring Holly home.' It's the catch-phrase we're using in the press releases. Tomorrow morning three of the biggest newspapers in the state will be running, '*Bring Holly McClaine Home*' across the front page. That means we'll have your name right there in prime position on every morning paper. Then I want you to go on to say, 'If anyone sees our little girl, et cetera, et cetera, and then we'll flash the photograph of her ..."

"Oh, God," Elizabeth groaned and pressed her fingers to her eyes.

Alice paused with the last page in her hand. "Excuse me?"

"I said, 'Oh, God.' Would you like me to repeat it?"

"You don't need to repeat it, Elizabeth. I heard it the first time. I was giving you the opportunity to adjust your attitude." She thumped the page down on one of the piles.

"My attitude is perfectly well-adjusted the way it is, Mrs. Cressley. Some bastard has stolen my daughter and you want us to go on national television and beg for them to give her back?"

Alice took one step toward Elizabeth. "That's exactly what you'll do, Mrs. McClaine. And do you know why? Because the moment you make demands, the moment you start issuing threats, they'll take it out on your daughter. Is that what you want?"

Elizabeth turned back to the mirror. An icy silence spanned the next four seconds. Alice was about to continue when another soft rap sounded at the door. "Oh, for chrissake, what now?" she groaned to the heavens. "Will somebody get that? Richard, the door."

As if desperate to escape the tension in the room, Richard quickly crossed to the door and opened it.

"Oh," said a girl's voice from out in the hallway. "I'm sorry, I was told the room was ready to make up."

Elizabeth joined Richard at the door where a girl dressed in a white hotel uniform and lace-edged cap stood beside a large trolley loaded with towels, cleaning equipment and replacement shampoo and soap packs. Behind her, clutches of tired-looking reporters looked hopefully towards the door.

Alice crossed to the door and peered out. "Who called for room service? This is ridiculous. I'll be speaking with the hotel management about this."

"It doesn't matter," Elizabeth said and quickly closed the door. "Just let her do her job."

"Fine. Come back in ten," Alice told the girl. She closed the door and checked her watch. "It's almost six. Elizabeth, you're meeting with Diana du Plessis at seven-forty-five; then I want you at the hospital by eight-thirty. You can discuss the format of the interview on the way. Just make sure she understands her brief. See that she doesn't go off on a tangent. I don't want a story that comes out like some Liberal Democrat dissertation. It's asking a lot, I know, but I live in hope. Also, remember there's a march set to move downtown at seven-thirty, so traffic will be rerouted and the streets will be gridlocked. You may want to leave a few minutes early. Are you ready?"

The moment they opened the door, a wall of reporters pressed forward, snapping photographs and shoving microphones in their faces as they moved down the hallway. Four bodyguards closed in around Richard, Alice and Elizabeth, shepherding them to the elevator and fending off reporters. When the elevator doors opened, the bodyguards stood aside and Elizabeth stepped into the car, followed by Alice. Richard paused in the doorway and raised his hands, thanking everyone for their support but asking that they please be patient, and telling them that any questions they had were to be presented during the interview.

Downstairs, the conference room was already packed. Reporters and TV crews scurried left and right with cables and cameras, looking like a reenactment of the previous day in Alice's temporary campaign headquarters. The only difference was now the numbers had swelled by more than half again. The din of people talking across each other died down as Elizabeth and Richard entered. The hush turned to an echoing silence as they walked the length of the room and took their places at the front, this time seated behind a bench with a row of microphones lined up before them.

Elizabeth placed her purse on the floor and leaned her elbows on the wooden surface, hands clasped at her mouth while she scanned the room. Sitting in the second row she could see Diana du Plessis. She gave her a taut smile, which was returned with a measure of warmth she hadn't expected. Elizabeth was not looking forward to spending any time with the woman. She would have preferred to go back to the hotel room and have a bottle of vodka sent up while Richard handled the interviews and questions. After all, this was his domain, not hers.

Still scanning the attendant throngs, she spotted Detective Delaney entering through the main door. He raised his head and looked around. When he spotted Alice, he cut his way through the crowds towards her. As soon as he was within reach, he tapped her on the shoulder and she spun around.

Elizabeth watched as the two of them then fell into a guarded and serious-looking discussion, each mirroring the other with one arm across their waists, fingers to their lips as they spoke. Every now and then they glanced across at Elizabeth and Richard, then continued on. At one point Delaney said something that caused Alice to shake her head briefly and touch her fingers to the corners of her eyes. After a second, she looked up and nodded understanding.

"I wonder what's going on over there," Elizabeth said.

Richard lifted his head and followed her gaze. "Maybe there's some news."

"If the look on his face is anything to go by, it can't be good news."

Blake appeared at Richard's side. "We're almost ready."

Richard straightened his tie, pulled his shoulders back, and placed one hand across the other in front of him, angling his head in preparation for the camera.

"I'm going over there," Elizabeth said and went to get up.

Richard immediately grabbed her by the arm and yanked her back into her seat and held her there. "Stay where you are. We're on in one minute."

Delaney and Alice were now looking their way.

"No, I'm going over there. Let go of me," she said. But he pulled her back down with such force that she knocked over the chair and stumbled backwards. "Let go of me," she said as she floundered to her feet again.

He grabbed her arm again. "Elizabeth."

"I want to know what's happened. Let go of me," she said, hearing her voice echo across the suddenly silent room over the now fully functional sound system. When she turned, every eye in the place was on her. She ignored them and moved out from behind the bench while Richard stood, trying to stop her. "Mr. Delaney," she called. "What's happened? Is there news about my daughter?"

The entire room turned to him. He looked momentarily shocked, then gathered himself, saying, "We have no comment at this point in time."

She paused halfway across to him. "Then why …? What were you talking about?" Even to Elizabeth, she sounded like she'd lost her senses.

Richard stepped in behind her. "Elizabeth, come and sit down." He placed his arm protectively around her shoulders and drew her in. "They'll tell us if there's any news."

The room fell into silence as everyone appeared to go back to whatever they had been doing. But Elizabeth knew they were still watching her, waiting for her "Britney moment"—the one that would catapult her name into the headlines worldwide. She held her breath and pressed her lips together, fighting back the rising tide of emotion. To her surprise, Richard enveloped her in his arms, pulling her in close. "Are you okay?" he whispered.

Tears filled her eyes. She nodded.

"Then pull yourself together. Half the country is watching us. We can't afford to fall apart here. Understand?"

"Yes, I'm fine," she said, and pushed away.

"Excuse me, everyone," Richard called out across the crowds. "I'm sorry, but my wife is unwell. As you can imagine, this has taken a terrible toll on her. Mr. Ressnick will escort her back to our room and I will continue the interview alone." He looked to Elizabeth for her approval. She nodded, and he handed her into Blake's care.

She rode the elevator with Blake to the fourteenth floor. The entire way, Blake never offered one word of solace to her; he never even looked at her. At one point, Elizabeth scrutinized him out of the corner of her eye. Almost as tall as Richard, Blake maintained a cool façade. Elizabeth knew that icy exterior went right to the bone. His YSL suit and tie were elegant, his white shirt crisp; his hair flopped rakishly to one side across his forehead. The only telltale sign of anxiety was the way he kept touching his phone. As if he might lose it and miss something crucial to the campaign.

Elizabeth wondered whether Blake had given even a fleeting thought for Holly—a child that wasn't his—a child rendered unsightly by the scar on her face. To him she would be simply an impediment to his campaign—to his career. Her life would be of little consequence. Outside his own personal aspirations and this election, nothing existed to him.

When they got to the room, Elizabeth thanked him in a cool voice, opened the door, and watched him return to the elevator.

In the quiet of the empty room, she sat on the bed and took off her shoes. She wondered yet again what kind of person she was, tried to see herself from outside her own skin. How could a mother distance herself from her own child the way she had? What kind of person would feel the loss of her child like a yawning void in her chest, and yet be paralyzed at the thought of her return? If this was some kind of test that God had set, she was patently unworthy of the task. Hadn't she proved so time and time again?

Richard had his career. What did Elizabeth have? In her anger, she had systematically pushed away everyone and everything she had once loved. Now she had nothing: no one she could confide in, no one she could turn to. Perhaps Alice was right—maybe Holly was better off without her.

She went to the door and peered out to find an empty hallway. She returned to the elevator and rode it to the top floor. On the twenty-fifth floor, she exited the car and walked to the end of the hallway where she found a door with the words "Roof—Authorized Personnel Only" stenciled in black lettering across it. She tried the handle, and to her surprise it opened. She climbed the fifteen steps to the top, then opened a door and stepped out onto a vast area of white concrete that formed the roof of the hotel. A low barrier ran around the periphery, enclosing the external vents of air-conditioning units that squatted here and there like a miniature walled city.

Elizabeth gazed up into the bright blue of the sky, blinking against the glare of the late autumn sun and feeling a glimmer of warmth from the concrete under her bare feet. Up here everything was still and quiet. There were no problems, no decisions. Everything was calm, clear. From far below she could hear the distant hum of traffic, and every now and then the ducts from the air-conditioning units belched out a whoosh of air.

Slowly, she walked across the surface of the roof and felt an unexpected surge of peace flow through her. Far off on the horizon, she could see a blue haze of the distant hills. It was as if they represented a freedom she could almost touch, but not quite. Drinking in the silence, reveling in the escape from the prying eyes and questions, she stepped up onto the barrier, feeling the smoothness of the concrete under her feet. She leaned to look out over the edge. From twenty-five floors up, the cars moved silently along the street like toys. People flooded the intersections as they crossed the street, then vanished and went on with their lives. Smiling down on the scene, she watched the comings and goings, wondering who would even miss her …

"It's a beautiful view up here," said a voice behind her.

Elizabeth didn't turn around. This woman, whoever she was, had shattered her peace. Instead she straightened, eyes still on the street below. "Yes. And quiet."

"It's surprising how far you can see across the city," said Diana du Plessis. She had moved alongside Elizabeth, her hand shielding her eyes against the glare as she also gazed out towards the distant hills. She didn't even seem to have noticed that Elizabeth was standing on top of the barrier with her toes curled over the edge.

"And the breeze is wonderful. So fresh after that crowded room," she said and smiled up at her. When Elizabeth said nothing, she continued, "When I was a child I used to visit my grandmother who lived on a farm. I used to climb the trees across the meadow. One day, I climbed so high I couldn't get down. Up until then, my only thought was to climb higher and higher, intent on how far I could see. And then, for some strange reason, my focus changed from how far I could see, to how far I could fall. I think that was one of those moments when reality chips away at the child and the adult steps in. Somehow, what you gain in safety, you lose in your sense of wonder. I'm still not so sure it's such a great trade-off."

"Oh really," Elizabeth said. Even to her, she couldn't have sounded less interested.

"It must be very difficult for you, but you know—"

"If you're going to tell me that God only sets upon us burdens He knows we can bear, you can save your breath. I've heard that one more times than I can count," said Elizabeth. She turned her face up, staring into the broad blue stretch of the sky. But that moment of peace was gone, stolen by this interfering woman.

"Believe me, Mrs. McClaine, I wasn't going to say anything of the sort. I've seen plenty of people with greater burdens than they can bear and it's no use blaming God. I've interviewed people crushed under weights you wouldn't believe, and those who hand out such platitudes are offering them for their own benefit, not for the victims."

Elizabeth turned and regarded Diana du Plessis for a second. Then she stepped down off the edge.

"The other saying I can't stand," said Diana, leaning to her in a conspiratorial manner, "is, 'It could have been worse,'"

The bark of laughter that sprang from Elizabeth's lips surprised even her. "People tell me, 'It could have been worse,' and I say, 'Yes, but it could have been better.' But they still insist it could have been worse. Why do they do that? How would they know?"

"They don't. And you know something?"

Elizabeth angled her head, waiting to see what she would say next.

"They don't have to. They never did and maybe they never will. They offer you the words they think you want to hear—or, at least, the words they think they should say, and then they go home and forget. But when you go home, you take it all with you."

Elizabeth eyed her with suspicion. Was this some technique reporters use to coerce their subjects into giving away their darkest secrets? Would she awaken tomorrow to find the blackness that tainted her soul spread across the morning's first edition?

As if recognizing the look, Diana smiled. "You're skeptical. I don't blame you. I'm a reporter, after all. I'm here to get a story. I make no apologies for that. But I'm not interested in blame or how the police are doing with the investigation, I'm more interested in what you're going through."

"That's very kind," Elizabeth told her without emotion. She didn't think it was kind at all. The woman was there to do a job. She'd freely admitted it herself. This was money to her—end of story.

"I understand more than you think. Not so long ago I wrote a story on a woman whose daughter was born with Aicardi Syndrome."

"Oh, really," Elizabeth replied in the same dull tone. "I must confess, I don't know what that is."

Diana hugged her purse in under her arm. "No, of course not. It's not common. When the mother told me about her daughter, she said she was the most wonderful child. She was so good, slept like an angel, never cried ..." Again her smile broadened. "That alone should have been a warning, but of course, being a first child, she had no idea. Lauren. That was her daughter's name. Her beautiful little Lauren."

Elizabeth wasn't the slightest bit interested in yet another person's pain. It's what she lived with night and day. It's all she'd heard about in all the support groups and Mothers Coping with Down Syndrome groups and God only knew what else. One depressing story after the next. And rather than benefiting from the experiences of these people, Elizabeth had always left their company feeling overwhelmed and powerless.

"When Maggie first went to the doctor," Diana continued on, "well ... that's when it all started. MRIs, EEGs, CT scans. She once told me that one minute you're a mother, the next you're a walking encyclopedia of medical terms." She clutched her purse in front of her, smiled again. "I'm sure you've heard all this before."

"Yes," said Elizabeth. "That's very sad." But a voice in her head was saying, *Here we go*. Whatever this reporter had intended, all she'd managed to do was annoy Elizabeth. However sad the story, her own pain would be diminished in the face of someone else's, turning it into another form of "It could have been worse."

Perhaps sensing she had lost the connection between them, Diana glanced at her watch and quietly said, "I think we should go. We're due at the hospital in forty-five minutes and the traffic's dreadful." She turned towards the door, then paused and added, "But I think we'd better find your shoes first."

CHAPTER EIGHTEEN
DAY TWO: 6:17 AM—KELSEY

Kelsey found Maria Puentez's house sitting two doors from the corner of Washington Avenue in a run-down backstreet in Lorain. She pulled the Impala to the curb, shut off the engine, and surveyed the street.

Much like the place she had stayed in the previous night, Maria's house was a clapboard single-family residence with a covered porch. This one, however, was painted a dirty pale pink that somehow made the house look even more run-down than it really was. A slatted railing ran the length of the verandah with a gap in the middle where four steps led up to the front door. Out front, a rusted blue Ford Taurus sat on the crumbling driveway like an exhausted animal waiting to die.

The place looked deserted. Kelsey got out, locked the Impala and paused briefly to scan the street. This was still L21 territory. The last thing she needed was another run-in with Frankie. She had been lucky so far. Pushing that luck wouldn't be smart.

She tucked the car key into her pocket and walked quickly up the driveway, ducking her head briefly to check the front seat of the

Taurus. A pair of turquoise shoes with spike heels sat on the passenger's seat. That alone told her she had the right place.

Still with one eye to the street, Kelsey headed down the side of the house and stood on tiptoes to peep through the windows. There were no signs of life inside. Casually checking out the houses on either side in case a neighbor was watching, she went to the back door and tried the handle. It was locked. A neighborhood like this, she'd have been surprised if it wasn't, but she had to try.

She returned to the front of the house, quietly moved up the front steps and cupped her hands to the window. The interior was in darkness but she could make out the shapes of furniture and the highlighted outline of a door leading to the rear of the house. After checking the street again and finding no one around, she reached across and tried the door handle. No surprise, it was also locked. Four glass panels were set two up, two down in the top half of the door, and behind them hung a grubby lace curtain. She took her glass-cutter out of her pocket, etched a circle in the glass panel above the handle, then tapped the disc she had cut. It let out a soft crack, then fell inwards onto the floor and shattered on the wood floor.

Kelsey froze. After a silence of around five seconds, a woman's voice from somewhere inside the house called out, "Who's there?"

Kelsey put her hand through the hole in the glass and reached around to find the key had been removed and she couldn't unlock it. Sighing heavily, she stood back, took careful aim at a point just below the lock, and kicked the door. The entire quarter of glass she had cut the circle from shattered and fell out, while cracks radiated throughout the panes next to and above it. But the door held fast.

"Who is it? Who's out there?" the voice called. She now recognized it as Maria's. She sounded frightened. She was probably alone in the house. Kelsey stood back, took aim at the door and kicked again. This time two panes of glass shattered and fell onto the floor with a splintering crash and Maria screamed. But the door remained solidly in place.

"Jesus H.," Kelsey groaned. She couldn't have made more noise if she had brought a shotgun and blasted the windows out. Standing back, she gave the door a third kick and the latch finally gave and the door wobbled inwards, sending the final pane crashing to the floor with the others. She stepped inside with glass crunching beneath her shoes, and looked around. The place stank of stale cigarette smoke and overly sweet perfume.

She was just moving toward the rear of the house when Maria appeared, framed in a doorway, flinging a heavy robe around her shoulders and hugging it to her waist. Her hair was tousled, her makeup smudged into two black smears down her cheeks. Eyes still puffy with sleep, she looked first to the door, then the glass on the floor. "What the fuck are you doing?" she shrieked. She recoiled briefly at the sight of Kelsey's bruised face, then gathered herself. "Get out. Get the fuck out of my house," she yelled and pointed at the door.

Kelsey stayed where she was. "Is this your place?"

Maria ignored her and swept across to inspect the damage to the door. "What? Are you fucking loco? Look what you done! You broke the fucking door."

Kelsey crossed to the bedroom Maria had emerged from, opened it and leaned in. "Ange told me where to find you. You live here?" she asked her in disgust and closed the door.

"When did Ange tell you this?"

"Ten minutes ago when I called her." Kelsey crossed to a bookshelf, took down a book that turned out to be something written in Spanish, then put it back.

"Ange got no right telling you shit! Now, get out!" Maria shouted and pointed to the door again.

"Tell me where Matt is."

"What? You smash my door and you think I'm gonna tell you where Matt is? You are fucking crazy."

"Hey. I got an idea. How about you call him, tell him how I'm gonna knock all those beautiful teeth of yours clear down your throat, and ask him to get over here and protect you. Sound like a plan?"

"You are crazy in the head. And you know what? They gonna lock you up and throw away the key. The police know you took that kid. They don't know nothing about Matt." She pursed her mouth and hugged the robe in tighter. "Me and him will walk away free with ten million dollars. And you know why? Because you are too stupid to know when to leave, is why."

Kelsey shifted her weight. "Just tell me where he is, Maria, then I can get the hell out of here."

"What if Matt don't want you to find him? What if you're not part of the plan no more? You think of that? Huh?"

"All I want is the kid."

"Well, Matt and me are together now. He don't need you no more." Maria jutted her chin in defiance, as if that was the real reason for Kelsey's visit. "You are just a … dyke," she said and gestured dismissively. "You're a crazy person—fighting and stealing and shit. Matt wants a woman that treats him right. And when we got all that money, we'll have blue sky and water, far as—"

"—crystal clear … actually," Kelsey interrupted. "The water. It's crystal clear water. You're gonna steal someone else's dream, get it right."

"Fuck you. Go away and don't ever come back."

"Fine, congratulations, Matt's all yours and you're welcome to him. But I'm not leaving till you tell me where he is. And if you don't, I'll have to start smashing your house up. And listen, I'm really hoping you hold out a little, because after I'm done with the house, I'm starting on you." Kelsey stuck her hands on her hips and gave the place a once over. "Although," she added thoughtfully, "I don't know if smashing this place up is gonna make any difference. This place is a worse shit-heap than the last place we were in."

"Hey, watch your filthy mouth. This is my mother's house," Maria said.

Kelsey stepped in so close to Maria, they were toe to toe, almost touching. Maria stood her ground, staring back, chin high …

… until Kelsey spun her into a headlock so fast, all Maria had time to do was gasp. With one arm levered against Maria's throat, Kelsey put her lips to her ear and said, "Now, tell me where Matt is or I'll forget about trashing the house and Matt'll come home to find he's dating a corpse." She tightened her hold a notch, adding, "And remember, I have nothing to lose here."

"He's …" Maria croaked out, so Kelsey loosened the lock. Maria swallowed and hissed, "He's taking her to a construction site. Lemme go."

Kelsey released her and gave her a shove that sent Maria stumbling across the floor. "Where? Which construction site?"

Maria gathered herself slowly, pouting and clutching at her throat like she should be hospitalized. "I don't know. All I know, it's a big construction site somewhere."

"Why did they go there? What's there?"

"I don't know—buildings and shit, how would I know?"

"Dammit," said Kelsey. "And they're at this construction site now, right? Is that what you're saying?"

Maria shook her head, still swallowing hard and holding her throat to emphasize her pain. Which was also pissing Kelsey off. She moved toward her and Maria retreated, yelling,

"He went to make some arrangements with the bank transfers."

"At the bank? What bank?"

"I don' fucking know!"

Kelsey took the Impala key from her pocket and tossed it on the coffee table.

Maria eyed it like it was something dangerous. "What's that?"

"It's a car key. What does it look like? It's for the car outside."

Maria hesitated, then sidestepped around her, moving to the window with one eye on Kelsey. She drew the curtain aside and looked out to the street, then turned with a confused frown. "You mean that car?" she asked, thumbing towards the Impala.

"Yeah. It's yours. It's a little damaged, but let's call it a gift. I'm taking your car."

"You want *my* car in exchange for *that* car?"

"You got a problem with that?"

"Why do you want my car?"

Kelsey couldn't believe it. Talk about your gift horses. "Because my car handles like a whore in a mud-wrestling match. It reminds me of you."

"Yeah, well," said Maria, searching for a witty retort, "my car handles like a … like a piece of shit. And that reminds me of you."

There was a tense moment as the two women regarded each other. Kelsey shifted, head tilted. "So, do we have a deal, or don't we?"

Maria pulled the robe in around her waist. "Yeah, we got a deal." She swooped on the key and tucked it down between her breasts. Smug little grin on her face. "Actually," she said, "my car is stolen and there is no key."

"Actually, so's mine," said Kelsey. "And I don't need one."

And she turned and walked out.

CHAPTER NINETEEN
DAY TWO: 7:45 AM—ELIZABETH

By the time Elizabeth and Diana du Plessis were riding the elevator back to their floor, the press conference downstairs had broken up and half the journalists had trailed Richard upstairs like a swarm of angry wasps. Now there was a crowd of them camped outside the door, waiting for that inside scoop, that million-dollar photograph. So, as soon as the elevator doors opened, cameramen, reporters and television crews rushed the two women, swamping them in a crush of bodies, shoving microphones at them, and calling for comments as they carried them along on a wave of humanity.

When they reached the room, Elizabeth swiped her key card and the second the door opened, both she and Diana fell into the room, groaning with relief as they pushed the door closed.

Richard turned from where he was sitting at the desk, then quickly got to his feet. "Are you all right?"

Diana had one palm flat to her chest, the other clutching her purse. "The paparazzi are definitely in town, Mr. McClaine."

Across the room, Alice swung around on them, holding the phone she'd been talking on away from her ear. "Where the hell have you two been? You're due at the hospital in forty-five minutes. Dear God, the woman'll be cured before you get there … no, not you," she barked into the phone. "I'm talking to Elizabeth … yes, she's here. Well, how would I know?" she snapped at the caller. "Yes, she's only just walked in." She held the phone away from her ear again, saying, "Well, what are you waiting for? Go, get moving. It'll take you fifteen minutes just to get to the car. Richard!" He looked up from where he was going through files with a peeved look. "We've got a meeting with Blake in ten. Get your tie on, and get yourself organized. Are you there, Blake?" she said back into the phone.

Elizabeth collected her shoes, leaving Alice issuing orders left and right like a drill sergeant while she and Diana went back to the elevator. Even in the escort of four burly security guards they were jostled by reporters and camera crews, first to the elevator, then to a waiting taxi.

When the car doors thunked shut, the cab inched its way through the crowds, while all around them, lights flashed and cameras rolled and people yelled for them to look this way and that. Diana let out another long sigh of relief. "Oh, my goodness. Mrs. Cressley takes no prisoners, does she?"

"No, she does not," said Elizabeth. She was watching the furor outside with a mix of horror and curiosity as hands and bodies pressed to the windows as people crushed in on them.

"And she certainly knows how to put on a performance," Diana said, turning to look out the rear window.

"I have no idea where all these people came from," said Elizabeth. "I can't even think what they want."

As the car finally turned in to the street and sped up, Diana visibly relaxed. "We should have brought my car. It's a nondescript little, gray box that nobody ever notices. I sometimes think it has a cloaking device. People ask me why I don't get something bigger, but I like it." She tucked her purse at her feet and smiled across at Elizabeth. "It's not an easy road, is it?"

The comment surprised her. "I'm sorry, Miss du Plessis, I'm not sure I know which road you mean."

"Please, call me Diana," she said, settling back with her hands clasped in her lap. "I was saying, I know the road you're on. I've seen people who have walked that road. It can be a very lonely place."

"I suppose it can be. I never thought about it." Elizabeth returned her attention to the view out the window. Whatever road she was on, and however lonely it may have been, was none of this woman's business and she wanted to keep it that way. She had learned early on that she was, indeed, walking this path on her own because everyone else—including Richard—had run for the hills and left her to it.

Every now and then, she had caught herself lost in this sullen reverie. Looking back, she couldn't believe how much she had changed over the years. These days she barely recognized the person she once was. She was gazing sightlessly at the world, watching it skim by, when she realized Diana was speaking again. "I'm sorry, you were saying …?"

"I was asking where you and Richard met," Diana replied.

Elizabeth now noticed she had a notepad positioned on her lap and a pen poised over it. At least she could handle this part of it. She must have done it a million times before—answering with the same stock answers she always used. With the hint of a smile, she said, "At Harvard. We were both studying economics. We never really spoke for a long time. And then we both found ourselves pitched against each other in a debate." Her smile broadened at the memory. "I was independent and outspoken in those days. Probably a little too feisty for some people's taste. And probably a little naïve, as well," she said, narrowing her eyes at the realization of just how naïve she had been. "I fell into politics in college. I had an insatiable hunger to change the world and I didn't care who I went up against to forward my beliefs. I headed up political drives and instigated rallies against pollution, abortion, poverty; you name it. I challenged anyone and everyone who'd sit still long enough hear me out."

Elizabeth's smile was genuine now. It was directed at a point a couple of feet in front of her, where she could see the scenes playing out as if she were right there; still vital, still burning with a raw energy that seemed to fuel itself. "Then, one day, at an end-of-year dinner, we sat next to each other. He was young and ambitious. And *so* handsome," she said and glanced across at Diana, who was also smiling. She turned her gaze back to the window, frowning in wonder as those memories rushed her one after the other, reaching out and touching her, then vanishing like the wind whistling through her fingers.

She drew in a breath and stiffened in her seat, modifying her voice back to her standard, flat interview mode. "Three years later we married. At the time Richard's father was keen for him to follow in his footsteps, building up a separate arm of the construction business. So his political career suffered a rather longer-than-expected hiatus. Then we moved to Chicago and everything changed. Everything he touched turned to gold. He was incredible—invincible." The words had come out so low she could barely hear them. She cleared her voice, and continued on. "He threw everything he had into the business, and with Richard's passion, and his eye for detail, there was no stopping him. The business thrived; we found ourselves moving in all the right circles, making a raft of supportive friends. Then eventually, Richard decided to step back into the political arena."

How many years were they treading those boards before the shades came down? she suddenly wondered. Too many. The days and months had simply flown past. Now look where she was.

"You left having a family until quite late," Diana said.

Right then, Elizabeth saw her agenda. It was as if the woman had swept a magician's black cloth back to reveal her nasty little trap, and now it was sitting right there in the spotlight, waiting for Elizabeth to blunder into. This was where Elizabeth had to keep her guard up. Something could so easily slip, and that blackness she kept locked up in her heart could leak out into the light of day. It wasn't an issue if she kept calm. She'd done this God knew how many times with half a bottle of vodka under her belt. All she had to do was stick to the script.

"When I turned thirty-nine, we decided to start a family. We knew the odds, but of course, it never seems real. How many women now are still having babies later in life? The newspapers are always full of celebrities who start families as late as their mid-forties. But after two years we were beginning to think we'd missed our chance. We were in the early stages of in-vitro fertilization when I discovered I was pregnant."

"You must have been delighted."

"We were." A smile formed as the memory sharpened. She had rushed home and straight into Richard's arms. She could still see the tears forming in his eyes at the news. He had lifted her from the floor and swung her around, and they had both joked about how *that* wasn't going to happen for too much longer because she'd be like a whale in no time, and they fell apart laughing.

Right then and there they made a pact: It didn't matter if it was a girl or a boy, as long as the baby was healthy and had all its fingers and toes and could one day go to Harvard—well, where else?

Naturally, he or she would eventually take the helm at the company, leaving Richard to follow his career in politics and Elizabeth to prepare the way for a clutch of grandchildren.

Over the next days, weeks, months of her pregnancy, Elizabeth found herself overcome with emotions she had never dreamed possible. Emotions that ranged from abject terror about the future for her child, to a sense of attachment that burned so deeply, it was as if this child—her child—had become the very ground beneath her feet, the sky above her world and the air she breathed. At times like this she had become so overwhelmed by her love for this child, she had wondered in despair how she would ever live her own life again.

It wasn't until she felt that first flutter, that infinitesimally small movement, that she truly realized her most desperate wishes had been granted; that this was not an elaborate ruse set up so they could pretend at normality. She really was to have her own child.

Without thinking, she had called Richard at his office, excitedly demanding that he leave work this minute and come home. By the time he got there, his panic had risen to a point where every tragic scenario he had imagined on his way home was etched into his face, and he looked like a man ten years older.

It was only when she took his hand and laid it flat to her belly and he felt the faintest movement from deep within, did his expression soften. At the tiniest twitch of his child, it was as if the troubles of the world had dissolved, and in that instant she saw the man she'd known in Harvard; the man she'd known in lives past; the man she would know forevermore. And she knew how truly blessed they were.

The birth stole all of that away. At the first sight of the child it was like looking into the face of an imposter who had been slyly substituted in the crib while her own beautiful, golden-haired child had been stolen away. That was the first time she had wondered if

God was punishing her for wanting something so very much. It was not the last.

Over the days and months that followed the birth, a black shroud descended upon Elizabeth, blocking out the sun, stifling any light and happiness once present in her life. They seemed to leach out into the air and dissipate like smoke in the wind. This was a place she referred to as "the Darklands," a place she could neither understand nor escape. Even now those memories struck cold in her chest, like a metal pick hitting icy ground.

Lost for any further words, Elizabeth let her gaze drop into her lap and opened her purse as if searching for something. "What else would you like to know?"

Diana had been watching her. As if sensing the tension, she smiled. "So you were forty-one when you conceived? Did you consider having tests done?"

"No," Elizabeth replied, wondering again what the hell business it was of hers whether she'd had tests or not. She was beginning to think this reporter intended to put out a story that made her out to be some kind of naïve idiot. Either that or some overindulged scatterbrain who didn't know which side her bread was buttered on. "Of course, being an avid pro-life advocate, it was my belief that there was little point to taking tests, so I refused them. I was fully prepared to welcome this child into our family regardless of ..." her throat constricted, causing her to swallow involuntarily, "... regardless of any ... problems she might have."

Oh, how the mighty have fallen, she thought and returned her gaze to the window.

She could feel Diana regarding her quizzically. How could she understand the road Elizabeth was on? Who was she to question the decisions she had made when she didn't even understand them herself? Once upon a time she had had the world at her feet. Now it seemed that whole world had turned its back on her and left her floundering in those Darklands. And if things weren't already bad enough, here they were broke, their little daughter stolen away and held for a ransom they couldn't pay, and their marriage nothing but the shriveled skin of something that was once alive and vital. Elizabeth wondered yet again how much further she could fall, and whether she should have simply jumped from the hotel roof when she had the chance.

"Oh, look, I can see the hospital just up ahead," Diana said, sitting forward on the seat and looking out over the driver's shoulder. When she glanced back at Elizabeth, she almost did a double take. "Are you all right, Mrs. McClaine?"

"I'm fine," Elizabeth said again, and dug her nails into the palm of her hand, noting as she said it just how many times those words had slipped her lips. "I hope Mrs. Patterson likes the flowers I sent over." At last she might have a chance to speak to Audrey Patterson, to find out what she'd told the police. Audrey had seen the kidnapper, spoken to her. She must have seen whoever the girl was working with. *What if it was Sienna*? she thought and suddenly felt ill.

The taxi cruised to a stop outside the main doors of the hospital and the driver got out, holding the door for each of them. Once their entourage had guided them in through the front doors and through the lobby, they rode the elevator to the fifth floor amid a clutch of reporters, and now, escorted by the charge nurse, they made their way to room 512. A second nurse, who had been waiting for them, raised a hand and asked for absolute quiet. To Elizabeth, this was just more of the hoopla—more grandstanding for the media. In her mind's eye she could see Audrey Patterson sitting up in bed, waving to the cameramen like the Queen of England, surrounded by gifts.

"Are you ready?" asked Diana.

"Of course," she replied, turning to give the press a curt nod and switching on the disposable smile she kept for such occasions. In a blaze of photo flashes, the nurse pushed the door open and she and Diana stepped through.

Inside the air was cool and the blinds were drawn against the morning sun. Once the door closed, the lighting was so subdued that Elizabeth first thought they had stumbled into the wrong room. The woman lying in the bed wasn't even recognizable as Audrey Patterson. Bandages crisscrossed her chest and arms and her hair had been shaved from one side of her head to reveal a line of angry stitches across her scalp. Her face was swollen and grazed, her left leg suspended above the bed in traction. Through a gap in the covers, Elizabeth could see what looked like a gauze adhesive tape stretched across her right hip and thigh, holding together flesh that resembled something from a butcher's shop window. All around her machines bleeped and hummed. Elizabeth flinched, then turned to Diana. "But … I knew that … well, I don't understand …"

The nurse went to the bed, checking drips and lines and saline levels. "She gained consciousness at five this morning but she's heavily sedated," she told them in a hushed tone. She leaned over Audrey and said, "Are you comfortable, Audrey? You have visitors."

Elizabeth lowered herself into a chair. She could feel the shock coursing through her veins and robbing her of speech. She knew the woman was ill, but she had no idea of the extent of her injuries. It wasn't until now that she looked across and noticed the young woman sitting opposite her. Perhaps in her mid-twenties, the girl had short blond hair and startling blue eyes. She wore a simple cotton dress, hair pulled into a ponytail, no makeup.

"Mrs. McClaine, Miss du Plessis," she whispered, smiling and nodding at each of them in greeting. "I'm Amy Cartwright. I'm Mrs. Patterson's personal assistant over at the school."

"I'm pleased to meet you," Diana whispered back. "How is she?"

Amy drew a faltering breath and two lines formed between her eyebrows, making her appear suddenly ten years older. For a moment, her lip trembled and she looked as though she might burst into tears. "She's lucky to be alive. They're doing some skin grafts as soon as she's strong enough, but … I think she'll be here a while."

"But …" Elizabeth could feel her fingers teasing at the leather of her purse, trying to ground herself. Nothing made sense. "I had no idea. How did this happen?" she asked, looking from Amy to the nurse.

"She was trying to stop the kidnappers. Witnesses said she wouldn't let go." Amy angled her head in loving admiration toward the woman in the bed. "Isn't that just like Audrey? She kept hanging on to the car and eventually they sped up and she got dragged along the blacktop. That's why she lost so much skin. And how she broke her leg."

"Oh my God," said Elizabeth. She was frozen in her chair, barely able to think. "Has she said anything? Anything at all about who did this?" Elizabeth asked, only to receive an incredulous look from Amy. Of course she hadn't. The woman had almost died.

Amy frowned as if the question was ludicrous. "No, but I'm sure once she's awake she will. Audrey would go to any lengths for any of the students at the school. But Holly …" she said, and shook her head. "She's her favorite." She clasped her hands tightly in her lap and dropped her gaze to them, fighting back the tears. "And doesn't Holly just know it? If ever there was a teacher's pet, it's her. Oh God,

I hope they find her soon." She put her hand to her mouth and folded over as her face crumpled.

"Yes," said Elizabeth. "The police are doing everything they can."

Amy gathered herself, sniffing and dabbing a handkerchief first to each of her eyes, then to her nose. "She loves people. Holly, I mean. She adores people."

"Yes, she loves … loved Sienna, too," Elizabeth said as the memory of her last exchange with the nanny scorched into her mind—the bitterness in the girl's eyes, her only concern being how she'd pay for her car. That still clanged somewhere inside, not to mention the question of where she'd really been that day. "Sienna was our nanny. She was …" She couldn't even bring herself to say the words.

"Oh, yes, I heard," Amy said and bit her lip. "I heard she was murdered. I'm so terribly sorry."

"Yes," said Elizabeth. "Holly will miss her."

A noticeable silence stretched out. "Yes, I'm sure she will," Amy said in a tone that implied she wouldn't.

Elizabeth looked up sharply. The girl held her gaze briefly, then looked away.

"Is there something I should know?"

Amy froze for a second. "Well, I don't want to speak ill of the dead or anything," she said, picking at something on her lap to avoid Elizabeth's gaze. "But Miss Alvarez probably wasn't …" Having said this much, she looked as though she regretted saying anything at all. She wrung her hands together, struggling to find the words. "At least, we didn't feel that she was the most suitable nanny for a child with disabilities. Or …" she added quietly, "maybe for any child—although that was only our opinion," she said all at once. "But when we tried to talk to you about it, you never replied to our messages."

She chewed her lip and looked away, apparently realizing that it had come out sounding like an accusation.

Elizabeth smiled and shifted in her chair. She looked from Amy to Diana and back, feeling as though this was some kind of sick joke and she was supposed to see the punch line. "Messages? What messages?"

"We sent you a stack of messages, Mrs. McClaine. We even left voice mail asking you to contact us. We never heard anything back so Audrey came over maybe a dozen times to see you. When you weren't home she left messages with Miss Alvarez." She shrugged and shook her head. "She obviously didn't pass them on."

"No," said Elizabeth. "Obviously." Feeling foolish and angry with Sienna, she sat rigid and dug her nails all the deeper into her palm. Then again, maybe if she had been there none of this would have happened. Maybe Holly would still be at home …

"Perhaps we should go," said Diana. "We don't want to tire Mrs. Patterson. And we have the school visit yet."

"Yes, of course." Elizabeth hesitated for a moment, then stepped across and leaned over Audrey Patterson. "Mrs. Patterson, can you hear me? Can she hear me?" she asked the nurse.

"Perhaps. As I said, she's heavily sedated."

Elizabeth leaned low, and quietly said, "Thank you. I know I don't …" But tears began to well in her eyes and she sat down again, searching her handbag for a tissue until Diana reached across with one. "Thank you, I'll be fine," she said and dabbed her eyes.

"I know she'd say Holly was worth every second and every scratch," Amy said. "You're so lucky to have her, Mrs. McClaine. I only hope she comes home soon."

"So do I," she replied. And for the first time, she realized she really meant it.

CHAPTER TWENTY
DAY TWO: 8:16 AM—KELSEY

Maria was right; the car did handle like a piece of shit. Kelsey couldn't understand anyone stealing a car like this. The engine was running on three of its four cylinders and whereas the Impala's suspension was spongy, the suspension in this thing was nonexistent. At a guess she'd say the struts and the shocks were all shot and judging from the screeching sounds coming from the front wheels every time she turned a corner, at least two of the CV joints were screwed. It had one thing going for it, though—it was still mobile. All it had to do was get to Stacy's Gym. Then it could fall apart in the dirt.

She nursed the car along the backstreets until she got to Brookpark. At least in this neighborhood she didn't have to worry about the L21s. This was outside their territory. This was Crims territory. She had no beef with them. Her biggest concern here was the cops. A car like this would get taken off the road in two seconds flat. Kelsey figured Maria hadn't taken it out of her driveway from the time it landed in front of her house. Kelsey counted herself lucky the battery wasn't dead.

Around a dozen cars were parked in the lot outside Stacy's Gym when she got there. The place was primarily a backstreet training facility for would-be boxers and kids off the street; in fact, for anyone that wanted to try his luck. Or hers. Stacy's clientele ran from semi-professional fighters all the way to street-fighters and gang members. This day and age, it didn't pay to be fussy where your dollars came from. So, Stacy's clients tended to come in before it got too busy, and by eleven there were usually a half-dozen or so waiting to step into the ring. She checked her watch—it was nearly eight-twenty. She shouldered her way through the front door and squinted into the gloom.

It took a few seconds for her eyes to adjust to the lighting. The place was dim and dingy and stank of sweat and grease and testosterone all mixed together with a measure of desperation. Two fighters were going toe to toe under the glare of harsh white lighting of the ring while their respective trainers watched on and yelled instructions, jabbing and hooking the air from the sidelines. Same old, she thought as she walked straight past them and crossed to the weight training area that was gated-off to her right.

Until now she had gone pretty much unnoticed. It wasn't until she jumped the gate and moved quickly down the rows of machines and benches, searching the faces either side, that she felt attention slowly turning on her, like she was crossing into foreign territory, walking on someone else's soil. A week ago these guys would have been calling out to her, making jokes or tossing a friendly taunt her way.

Not now. The expressions told her she had broken some unwritten law and she was no longer welcome in their midst.

"Tough shit," she thought. All she wanted was to find someone who knew where Delmar lived, then she'd get out. That's when she spotted Jackie the Snake—one of the few people who knew Delmar well enough to know where he hung out.

Jackie was lying on his back pressing weights when she moved up alongside him. He glanced up at her, but said nothing, just kept easing the bar up and down, exhaling loudly with each press as she walked around him with one eye on the rest of the room.

"Hey, Jack," she said and crouched beside him. A dozen or so guys were pretending to ignore them, making a point of not looking their way. She could see right through them, the big dumbasses. She chewed on her lip, then said, "Hey, I'm looking for Matt. You know where he is?"

The strain had raised the veins on Jackie's forehead and neck. She could see them engorged and pulsing just below the skin. Jackie reached back, replaced the bar on the stand and lay there for a few seconds, sucking in air. When he got his breath back, he said, "Fuck off, Kelse. I got nothing to say to you," and he lifted the bar again.

She'd never been any friend of Jackie's, but even so.

"Listen, I don't …"

"I said, fuck off," he said, the intense pressure of the weights forcing the words out in short bursts.

She gave it a second, not knowing exactly how to take it from there, so she said, "Y'know, I just need to find Matt. If you know where he is or …" she lifted one shoulder, "y'know, maybe where Delmar is or whatever."

She waited while Jackie did another ten reps then replaced the bar back on the rack and sat up. He reached across for his towel, ignoring her while he wiped the sweat from his forehead and neck.

She straightened, determined to stick with the casual approach. "Because, I think him and Li were going to pay Delmar a visit and I missed the address." Another shrug. "You know me—I wasn't listening and ah … you know how it is."

He gave her a sideways glance, took a deep, irritated breath and tossed the towel back on the floor. Then he lay back and lifted the bar again.

His attitude was pissing her off. She didn't have time for this screwing around. "So, do you know or not? Like, where he lives? Delmar, I mean …"

"Yeah, I know where he lives. Go look him up in the phone book," Jackie said, and started pumping the bar again.

"I doubt he's in the phone book." She gave him a forced grin. "Probably doesn't even have a phone." She waited, felt her grin turn sour. She wanted to punch him in the mouth. "And, I'm in kind of a hurry here."

His eyes came up to her. He replaced the bar with a burst of breath, and said, "Lionel owes me money. You give me the money, I'll tell you where Delmar lives."

"I don't have any money."

"Then you won't get the kid." And he lifted the weights, pumping them up, down, up, down.

Kelsey wasn't too sure how to play this. The smug look on his face said Jackie knew he had the upper hand—which he did—and he was making the most of it.

"You know about the kid? Like, where they've got her?" she asked as he came to the last rep.

"Suck my dick." Exhausted, he spat out a breath and reached back to ease the weights back onto the cradle. Kelsey grabbed the bar and jerked it back across his chest with such speed he had no time to react. Straddling him, she pressed down, bearing all her weight onto the bar, squeezing every last bit of air out of his lungs. Leaning down with her face in his, she said, "Tell me where Delmar is and quit screwing me around or so help me I will kill you."

Jackie's eyes flew open. His face was scarlet and swelling, his eyes bulging as he struggled under the collective weight of Kelsey and the bar. Spit and sweat flew as he gasped for breath, but she leaned even harder on the bar and grabbed him by the hair. "Tell me where Delmar is, Jackie, or God help you, I'll wring the fuckin' life out of you." But before he could wheeze out an answer, someone grabbed her by the back of the shirt and dragged her off and threw her on the floor. When she looked up Stacy was standing over her—three hundred pounds of tattooed muscle and an attitude you didn't want to mess with.

"What the hell are you doing, Kelse? You're gonna kill him," he said, gesturing towards Jackie who had sat up with the help of a couple of guys who'd rushed over. Now he was now doubled over and clutching his chest.

"You crazy bitch," Jackie yelled at her. "You could'a killed me."

"Next time I will, you asshole," she said.

"You wouldn't last two seconds," he said.

She lunged at him again, but Stacy grabbed her, wrenched her around and started dragging her back across the gym. "I'm looking for Delmar," she yelled as he half-dragged, half-carried her toward the door. "I just want to know where he lives," she called out. "Just tell me!"

"Come out here." Stacy opened the front door and hauled her out onto the steps, closing the door behind them.

"Let go'a me," she said and yanked her arm loose. "You didn't have to drag me out. I just want to find Delmar. That's all. Then I would'a left straight away."

"You nearly killed one of my clients," he said, pointing back to the door.

She dusted herself off and straightened her clothing. "He deserved it. And he's like, six months behind with his gym fees so why would you care?"

"Because that's my business, not yours. Now, is this about this kid?"

Kelsey's eyebrows shot up. "Does the whole goddamn world know?"

Stacy stuck his hands on his hips, dropped his head for a second. "Stay out of it, Kelse," he said. "Go home and get that eye cleaned up. There's a whole mess of shit just about to go down and you don't wanna be caught up in it."

Her fingers went to the swelling on her face. She had almost forgotten it. "Why? What's happened? What do you know about all this?"

"Just go. Keep your head down and don't come back." Stacy turned for the door but she grabbed the back of his shirt and tugged. A guy that size, you don't swing around by the shirt. He paused and turned, and for a second she thought he was going to hit her.

Her hands went up in surrender, as she stepped back. "Whoa. Now, hold on there, Stace. All I want is the kid, that's all. Whatever Matt's doing, I don't even care."

"You think he's gonna just hand over the kid and walk away with nothing? That kid's worth a lot of money."

"Was there some kind of broadcast I didn't know about?"

He scanned the street briefly. When his eyes came back to her, she saw something like empathy in them. He looked like he was wrestling with the question of how much he should tell her. "Listen; let's just say Lionel's got a big mouth."

"Lionel? When was he here?"

"Take my advice, Kelse. Just go home, leave 'em to it? There's nothing there for you."

"I can't. Where's Lionel now?"

He folded his arms across his chest, dropped his gaze to his feet. "I dunno."

"C'mon, man, level with me here. I'm working blind." When he just stared at her, she said, "Just tell me."

"Lionel's got some deal going on. He's buying in smack."

"So, tell me something new," she said.

"I'm talking serious quantities here, Kelse. Way I hear it, he's setting up deals with the L21s, the S-Hoods and the Brookliners—fuck knows who else. He's stitching together some kind of dealer network. You go getting into that kind of shit, you're digging your own grave."

"Jesus," she said and let her gaze wander while it sank in. "So what kind of money's he talking?"

"Ten million."

She snorted. Okay, she already knew Lionel had no intention of going into rehab. That had been Matt's idea all along. But now it looked like the douche bag had earmarked the whole ransom for his drug deals. It had her wondering what his own dealer would make of it. "I see," she said, because suddenly the whole picture became very clear and frighteningly complex.

"There's a whole bunch of people hurting out there, Kelse. That kind of money in Cleveland right now, well …" He stared off down the street. "A lot of people want a piece of it."

"Jesus," she said again. And there was Holly right in the middle. "Fuck." She felt her shoulders wilt at the enormity of it. "I gotta find her, Stace, c'mon, gimme a break. Please."

Out in the lot, a car pulled in and parked. A guy got out, took out his bag and headed their way. He hesitated briefly when he saw the two of them, then pushed past Stacy.

"Greg," Stacy said by way of greeting. "I'll be right in."

The guy said nothing but when he had gone, Kelsey said, "At least tell me where Matt is. If I can find Matt …"

"Why the hell are you doing this? Why can't you just leave it alone?"

She looked straight up into Stacy's eyes and said, "Because they'll kill her."

He shrugged. He had no answers.

"Please. I can't let that happen. I made her a promise. I said I'd find her. If there's anything you can tell me, anything …"

Stacy seemed torn. Face squeezed in deliberation, he looked up and down the street like he was searching for someone to come and help him out. Then he said, "What's Delmar got to do with all this?"

"He's set up a bank transfer to Somalia. The money gets wired out of the country and a minute later it comes back."

Stacey's eyebrows went up. "That's gotta be the dumbest idea I ever heard."

"You and me both." He was still deliberating, still hesitating, so she said, "Stace, I don't give a shit about the money. He can have it. The 21s can have it; the whole fuckin' world can have it. I don't care. I just need to find her." She looked up to find his gaze but he was looking everywhere but at her. "She's just a little kid, Stace. A scared little kid. I got her into this. Let me get her out."

At last he turned to her. He grimaced, like the decision he'd just come to was killing him. But he said, "Delmar's got a place over on Pollard Street. I don't know the number. It's purple is all I know."

Kelsey was already backing towards the car. "Thanks, Stace. I owe you."

"Pay me by not coming back," he called after her.

CHAPTER TWENTY ONE
DAY TWO: 9:03 AM—ELIZABETH

Elizabeth and Diana du Plessis were just leaving the hospital when Richard called. The schedule had changed. The appointment at the school had been pushed back to ten-thirty, and Elizabeth was to return to the hotel immediately for a "briefing." What this "briefing" was about, Elizabeth had no idea. But she was more relieved than she would have cared to admit.

All the way back to the hotel, Diana sat with her little recorder in her lap, asking questions; Elizabeth replying with her practiced answers—all delivered in her standard monotone, accompanied by a thinly applied smile. She was sure the woman could see the hairline cracks forming in her responses. It was only a matter of time before one of those cracks widened and Diana would see straight into the roiling pit of emotions beneath. All she wanted to do was escape before this woman tricked her into saying something she'd regret. And as exhausted and run-down as she was, that wouldn't take much.

After ten minutes of questioning, Diana closed the notebook, clicked the pen, and sat with her hands folded. Elizabeth felt the muscles across the back of her shoulders relax. Then Diana hit her with another question. This one hit her harder than she'd have expected.

"Are you able to tell me how Holly is physically?" Diana asked. "I know Down syndrome often comes with accompanying problems—heart defects, thyroid problems. Does Holly have any particular health issues you can tell me about?"

Elizabeth rallied. She could do this. "Well, of course she has a cleft palate. Which isn't necessarily associated with Down syndrome. Holly had the initial surgery to correct the palate, but of course," she said, running her thumb along the leather handle of her purse, mentally fending off the panic attack she could feel welling, "everything went wrong and the final surgery was postponed. She'll be under the best surgeon to complete it when she's strong enough." She turned a smile on Diana that she hoped said, "So take that." If her words had conveyed such a sentiment, the woman simply ignored it. She sat poised, waiting for more.

When the silence stretched, Elizabeth added, "Oh, and there was the chest problem." Diana said nothing, just tipped her head, signaling for her to continue. "There was a time when she was hugging herself, pulling her arms into her chest like this," she said, crossing her forearms to her chest just as she had seen Holly do so many times. "I thought she was in pain, but the doctor who examined her said there was nothing wrong." She smiled and lifted her chin—point to her. If Diana du Plessis thought she could outdo Elizabeth in a bout of mental sparring so she could prove Elizabeth was a lousy mother, she'd have to think again. Elizabeth mentally added a strike in her own favor.

"Tell me, Elizabeth, did you ever …" Diana began, but Elizabeth cut her off, saying:

"I'm sorry. Will you excuse me? I just remembered I have to call someone—a ... friend," she explained and hooked her phone out of her bag.

"Of course," Diana replied, but Elizabeth could feel the woman watching as she opened the phone and scrolled through the menu, searching for someone—*anyone*—she could call.

First up was:

Abby Montgomery—Not in a million years. She was once Elizabeth's closest friend. Elizabeth hadn't spoken to her since Abby's wedding two years ago. Abby had searched far and wide among her friends' children for a flower girl. Holly wasn't asked. Elizabeth was more wounded than she let on.

Alice Cressley—Obviously not.

Blake Ressnick—Ditto.

Caulder Jackson—Oh, yes, hilarious. Calder was the private investigator Elizabeth had enlisted when Richard had his dirty little affair. She doubted she could look him in the eye again. Especially after everything he'd told her, and she had still chosen to do nothing.

Dr. Felicity Sevenada—The therapist Elizabeth had consulted five years ago when depression threatened to drive her over the edge. Richard had forbidden her to see her again. He said that people without money got on just fine, and so would they. And with his political aspirations, a shrink was the last skeleton he could afford to have found in the closet.

Diana's presence was like a crow on her shoulder. She wasn't watching her directly but she may as well have been. Elizabeth turned toward the window and scrolled on.

Emily Pearson-Grange—dear God, no. How could Elizabeth forget the tantrum her daughter Sharya had thrown when she discovered Holly at her sleepover—screaming at her mother that she "didn't invite that ugly kid" and stomping off and locking herself in her room until Elizabeth had taken Holly and gone.

Kap Gordon—Good lord, why did she even have his number?

Lydia—No thanks. She was depressed enough without speaking to Richard's bitch of a mother.

Mom. Oh, God. She had forgotten the number was still there. The instant she saw it, her chin crumpled and her breath caught because more than anything in the world she wanted to call her and hear her voice. She still couldn't believe she was gone. When she noticed Diana cut her a quizzical look, she covered her mouth and pretended to cough.

Nancy Davidson-Reed. Never! Nancy was also once a friend. Until her darling son, Harley, first clapped eyes on baby Holly where Elizabeth had propped her up on Nancy's living room floor. Harley's eyes had grown into saucers. Then he yelled for his brothers and sisters to come and see the "funny-looking kid," and he doubled over laughing and pointing. Elizabeth had told Harley that "that wasn't a very nice thing to say." Nancy told Elizabeth that Harley was "only four, for goodness' sake," and "not to be so sensitive." Elizabeth told Nancy that Harley may be only four, but Nancy was not. She also told her that maybe she should teach her child some manners. Upon which, she'd snatched Holly up and left without a backward glance. She hadn't spoken to her since.

Richard. No.

"I'm sure the number's here somewhere," she said, still winding back through what seemed like a past life—or at least the bits she hadn't deleted.

Sienna. She stared at the name, barely able to believe the girl was dead, then went to the next entry.

Stephanie Compton. Head of the mothers' support group. Good old Stephanie. She carried her burden like some kind of shield—using it to fend off negative vibes so she could embrace only the positive. In the face of such vitality, Elizabeth never had the courage to air her problems, much less her feelings. So she had abandoned the support groups. They could offer her nothing, and in return, she had nothing to give.

Finally, the menu brought her back to Abby again. Did she have one friend left in the world?

Elizabeth offered Diana a grim smile. "I'll call her later." She slipped the phone into her purse, noticing with relief that they were just pulling up in front of the hotel. A slightly thinner crowd had gathered outside, but almost immediately, it was obvious something had changed.

Whereas the people who had waved them off not an hour before had been calling messages of support and love, these were waving placards with pictures of Holly and the words, "How could you?" and "Richard McClaine would sell his own daughter" scrawled across them. As soon as the car drew in, they rushed forward, yelling and chanting slogans and slapping at the windows, causing the driver to slow to a crawl.

"Oh, my goodness," said Diana. "This could turn into a rough ride."

"What are they doing?" asked Elizabeth. "Why are they so angry?"

"This will be the beginning of Ray Townsend's response to Richard's campaign. I knew things would get ugly, but I didn't think it would happen this soon." She was about to say something else, when her phone rang. She lifted her purse, fished the phone out, saying, "Would you excuse me, Elizabeth?" and hit the answer button. After a few yes's and no's, she cut the connection. "I'm afraid

I'm going to have to leave you here, Elizabeth. I have another meeting, but I'll see you at the school at ten-thirty."

"Fine," said Elizabeth, who was only listening with half an ear. She was more concerned with how she was going to get out of the car with all these people around. When the car finally stopped in front of the doors, the crowd closed in, pushing and jostling and shouting. Four bodyguards immediately moved forward, surrounding the door to form a barrier while she stepped out.

"Ten-thirty," Diana called from the car. "Don't forget." The car door slammed and she was gone.

Flanked by security, Elizabeth was jostled in through the front doors of the hotel, leaving the shouts and jeers of the surrounding crowd outside. How the hell she would ever get away from all these people was anyone's guess. At this rate, she'd never escape them long enough to find Holly, and time was running out.

As they entered the lobby the guards stepped away and ushered her to the elevators, then to her room. As she slipped in the door, Richard peered quickly out over her shoulder, pulled her in, and closed it behind her. He was hurriedly tying his tie and smoothing his hair, preparing for another press conference.

"How was the hospital visit?" he asked her as he slid the tie up to the collar and checked his look in the mirror.

She tossed her purse onto the sofa. "Fine. What the hell is going on?"

Blake was over by the window with a cell phone clamped between his shoulder and his ear while he zipped from screen to screen on his iPad. Alice, on the other hand, stood in the center of the room with the fingers of one hand pressed to her mouth while she flicked from channel to channel with the TV remote. The sour expression on her face solidified as she paused to watch a news item in which hard-faced redhead was interviewing a panel of three women and two men. The camera angled in on a young black woman who was pounding the desk top with the side of her fist and saying:

"... and all I can say is, this is blatant abuse of position. Richard McClaine is using his own child as a political pawn ..."

Alice dropped her face into her left hand and groaned, "Oh, for chrissake, someone shoot me." When she flicked channels to the *Morning Show*, the same charade was being played out. "And someone shoot *her*," she groaned and jabbed the remote at the TV. It flicked to yet another channel where a protest rally had spread across several city streets. "Dear God, we'll have the running of the bulls next," she said and savagely hit the off button.

"What's going on?" Elizabeth asked. "What's all this about?"

Alice answered, saying, "Townsend fired David Rattley—his campaign manager of six years, if you can believe it. Now he's hired Jacinda Hayes and she's come out firing with all her guns set on nuclear. If we don't make some ground in the next two hours, she'll have us buried by the end of the day."

"That's ridiculous," said Elizabeth. "Nobody fires their campaign manager days before the election."

"Try telling Ray Townsend," Alice said and threw the remote on the sofa where it bounced onto the floor. "Seems like he's the only one that doesn't know that."

Blake pocketed his phone. "Townsend's ratings just surged. He's up six points already, and climbing."

Alice rocked her head back and groaned again. "Jesus Christ."

Richard said nothing. The haunted look on his face said it all.

"So what happens now?" Elizabeth asked. "What about Holly? You said the police called. What did they say?" Noting the quick exchange of looks between Alice and Richard, she said, "What's happened? Tell me for chrissake, I'm her mother. I have a right to know."

Then it hit her—perhaps Holly was already dead. Here she'd been wasting time with schools and hospitals, and all the while, her daughter was being brutally murdered. The thought unleashed such a surge of fear and anger, she felt suddenly faint. "Well?" she demanded of each of them in the room. "Tell me, goddammit!"

Richard scrubbed at his cheeks, obviously frustrated. "Delaney was on his way over, but he got called away."

"Why? What did he say? Richard, what's happened?"

He hesitated a second. "There was an incident. Over in Lorain…"

"An incident?" said Elizabeth. She wanted to shake him. "What kind of incident? Have they found her? Is she all right?"

"Apparently there was some kind of gang brawl—"

"—a gang brawl? What the hell has a gang brawl got to do with Holly? Why is Delaney going to gang brawls when he's … oh God," she said as the implication struck her cold. "Don't tell me she's been murdered by a gang. Tell me she's …"

Richard threw both hands up. "Calm down. Nothing's happened. He said a car was stolen and one of the neighbors saw two people putting a small blond child into a Ford SUV. It may be Holly. Delaney's gone over to check it out."

"When? What time was this?"

"A few minutes ago."

"I'm going to find her," Elizabeth said and snatched up her purse.

"How?" asked Richard, stepping across to cut her off. "Where would you even start? And that's assuming you get two feet out the door."

"I don't know but I have to try," she said.

Alice stepped across and cut her off. "Sit down, you're not going anywhere. Richard's right. The second you're out that door, the rumor mill will crank into action and we'll be fighting fires we don't need to. Let Richard and me figure this out."

"That's what we've been doing," Elizabeth said. "And has that brought my daughter home? It hasn't done anything. Even your precious ratings are dropping now."

Across the room, Blake was silent, but his glare sent needles into her flesh.

Alice was on her feet. "And what good have you been? Moping around like second runner-up on prom night. Everything's too hard, everything's a problem—"

"Will you all *shut up*," Richard cut in. "This isn't getting us anywhere. For chrissakes, bitching at each other isn't helping." Just then, his phone rang. He hooked it out of his pocket to answer it, but Elizabeth snatched it out of his hand, twisting away from him as she hit the answer button. "He'll call you back," she told the caller and hung up. Then she tossed the phone on the table.

Richard pushed past her and grabbed the phone. "What the hell are you doing?" he said as he raked through the menu to find who the caller was.

"I'm not done. You're right," she said to Alice. "I haven't been a great mother, if that's what you're waiting for. I haven't committed myself to this plan of yours. But what about you? This has become all about your election. News flash, Richard. This is about our daughter's life. Do you even give a shit about her?" Elizabeth asked him. "Does anybody here actually care whether my daughter lives or dies?" she shouted, looking from him to Blake and Alice, both of whom looked away.

Richard grabbed her elbow and spun her around. "Will you excuse us?" he said and steered her to the adjacent room. "Let's talk in here," he said to Elizabeth and pulled her inside. When the door was closed, he turned on her. "What the hell are you trying to do? Ruin me?"

"I'm trying to get our daughter back. Something that seems to have slipped to the bottom of your priority list."

"Keep your voice down, for chrissakes." Even the rage couldn't mask his exhaustion. His jaw clenched for a moment, then he said, "Do you think I've forgotten about her?"

"Yes, I do. You're so busy propping up your lousy campaign you can't even think straight. You're a lousy husband, a lousy father, and now you're a lousy politician ..."

"Shut up," he said and slapped her hard across the face. Immediately, his eyes widened and he stepped back, aghast.

"I'm sorry. I didn't mean to ..." Richard stammered. "But this isn't the time or the place."

She put her hand to her face. "You never loved her."

For the longest time, he said nothing. Just stood there, staring down at his hands. When he finally spoke, it was a whisper. "It wasn't that I didn't love her. But from the minute she came into our lives, everything changed. Everything got so goddamned hard. You threw yourself into your charities and your luncheons. I never saw you. You have no idea what Holly's birth did to my mother."

"You're blaming Holly because your mother is a selfish bitch?"

"I'm blaming her because you changed." His expression hardened. It was as if he had been holding the words back for so long he'd forgotten they were there. "One day I had everything. I had a wife and a job I loved. Suddenly, I woke up with a woman I didn't know, and a life I hated. My God, there were days I could have ..."

His eyes went briefly to his hands, but when they came up to meet hers, the anguish had been replaced by something deep and cold. "The only thing holding me here was my work. It certainly wasn't you. Now will you get out of my way and let me get on with my campaign? Or are you planning on destroying that, too?"

And there it was. All that hatred, all that anger, all that disappointment was out in the open. But everything Elizabeth saw in her husband—all that venom, all that rage—were merely a reflection of her own and she knew it. Like Mr. Rochester's mad wife in *Jane Eyre*, a hidden presence remained locked up in that dark place where she hoped it would lay quiet and let her find happiness. But under pressure, it escaped and turned against her.

"I have a press meeting," he said. "Put some ice on your face. I'm ... I'm sorry," he said again and turned to leave.

"Talk to me, Richard," she said quietly. "Tell me you love her—tell me you hate her, tell me any damned thing, I don't care. Just talk to me." Suddenly, tears welled and splashed onto her cheeks.

He paused to stare down at her, perhaps not knowing what to say or do. "We'll talk about this later. Right now I need to get back and prop up this show before Townsend wipes us out completely." She withdrew her hand and he opened the door. Just before he left, he said, "I have a press meeting in twenty minutes and you're meeting Diana du Plessis in five. We'll meet back here afterwards." And he walked out, leaving her feeling drained.

Almost as soon as she was alone again, it was as if the exchange had never even taken place. The poison had been expelled; the Band Aid back on the wound. But, along with a clanging emptiness and exhaustion, came a wash of relief. Releasing some of that demon—that self-hatred—meant she could function again, even if she was running on empty.

One day soon, she knew she would have to pick this up, and roll it all out once more. When that day came, she would have to find a way to address and exorcize these demons or she would live like this for the rest of her life. And if her stint on the roof was anything to go by, that time wasn't far away.

CHAPTER TWENTY TWO
DAY TWO: 9:48 AM—KELSEY

Kelsey got back in the car and headed for Pollard Street where Delmar lived. She had no idea what she would do when she got there. Maybe once she had some idea of the setup, she'd come up with a plan.

She nursed the Taurus across town, avoiding the main streets where she might pick up police attention. After forty-nine minutes, she turned into Pollard Street and did a slow drive-through, cruising cautiously along the entire street while she searched the houses on either side. Matt had only known Delmar six months. He had met him a month after Delmar had entered the country under refugee status from Somalia. Six months, that's all. She still couldn't believe Matt would trust someone he'd known such a short time with ten million dollars. Then again, if Delmar cheated him, she wouldn't want to be within fifty miles of Delmar's ass when Matt caught up with him. So, taking that into account, maybe six months was enough.

As it turned out, Pollard Street had three houses painted various shades of purple, all run-down, and all within a few doors of each other. Only one had a blue Ford SUV sitting in the driveway.

Kelsey did a U-turn at the end of the street and drove past the house again, slowing to search the place for signs of life. The SUV looked empty. So did the house. That didn't mean anything. None of the houses in this street looked lived in. They were all in various states of disrepair, with grass in the front yard you could get lost in, and windows smashed from both inside and out. Every one of these places looked like it would fall down under a good storm.

She rolled to the next intersection and turned left onto Kramer. Twenty or so yards down Kramer, she pulled to the curb, mulling over what she should do next. It was doubtful they'd leave the child in the car while they went inside. So she was probably in there with them. And the only way Kelsey would get into the house without being seen was to come in through the back.

She got out of the car and walked back to the corner. After checking Pollard was all clear, she returned to where she'd left the car and hopped the wire fence at the corner house. She trotted through a yard strewn with broken toys, a rusted bicycle and an empty sandbox, then hopped the fence on the opposite side, but just as her feet hit the ground a woman sitting on the back steps and smoking a cigarette spotted her and got to her feet.

"Hey, you get outta my yard!" she yelled.

Kelsey called, "I'm sorry, okay. I'm going," and she sprinted across the yard and hopped the next one. No sooner had she cleared this fence when she heard the rattle of chain and she knew it was a dog before it even appeared around the corner. She caught a flash of black, heard the whiz of the chain unraveling and an incensed Rottweiler came straight at her. She jumped the next fence like a steeplechaser, stopping only long enough to watch the dog lunge and spring back on the end of the chain.

"Stupid dog," she said and dropped into a crouch. After a second, she did a duck-and-run across to the next fence, jumped and kept going. At the third fence she jumped and found herself standing on a pile of garbage that was stacked up to the top of the fence in the back yard of the last purple house she had seen. She scrambled down and hid behind a ragged-looking shrub while she looked the place over.

It was a run-down, three-story clapboard place with a veranda running across the front and ten miles of shit piled up front and back. Half the windows were broken and boarded up and the grass hadn't been cut in forever. So, no different than any of the other houses on this street. A place like this, Delmar must have been living pretty much rent free since he got here. And judging by the size of the house, chances were he didn't live alone. She crept through the undergrowth until she was a few feet from the back door. The place was huge. Three floors plus a basement was a lot of house to have to get into and sneak through unnoticed. She was wondering what to do when a broken basement window caught her eye. She scurried along the side of the house, pulled the window open, and slid feetfirst into the darkness below.

The first thing her feet hit was an old table. It wobbled under her weight, but once she got her balance, she carefully lowered herself onto it, then jumped to the floor. The place smelled of earth and mold, the only light filtering in through the dirty windows. She squeezed through a gap between two stacks of boxes and headed for the stairway that led up to the ground floor. On the first step, she paused to listen.

At first she heard nothing, just the resounding silence of the house. But as she moved up the stairs, she picked up a faint rasping sound. At the basement door, she put her ear to the wood panel and listened.

Nothing but the distant rasping.

It sounded like two pieces of rusted metal grinding against each other. She gently eased the handle down and cracked the door. The hinges whined softly so she paused again. The rasping was coming from upstairs. Other than that, nothing. A narrow, high-ceilinged hallway ran from the front of the house to the back. She moved quietly along, moving from doorway to doorway, peering in each until she reached the living room. She pressed her back in beside the doorway and angled a look inside. Still nothing, so she went in.

The place stunk of marijuana and damp. A threadbare sofa and a couple of battered chairs were arranged around a low table that was cluttered with pipes and spoons and various drug paraphernalia. Kelsey moved quickly across to the front window and looked out. The car was still in the driveway. But now the rasping sound upstairs had changed rhythm. Instead of a steady one, two, it missed a beat every now and then and she recognized the sound of irregular breathing.

"Shit." She moved quickly out into the hallway where a flight of stairs ran steeply to the second floor. From here she could see no one, hear no movement. She took the stairs cautiously, dropping into a crouch as she reached the top. Finding nothing and no one, she straightened and tiptoed down a second hallway that ran from front to rear with doors leading off to either side, peering into room after room as she moved along. When she came to the third room on the left she drew back, pushed open the door and peered in. In the middle of an otherwise empty room Delmar lay flat on his back, staring up at the ceiling with his hands clutched to his stomach and gasping for air like a drowning man.

"Oh, my God, Delmar," she said and dashed in. But before she was even halfway across to him she saw the pool of blood surrounding him and flinched. His face was gray, eyes fixed on the ceiling above.

"Delmar, can you hear me? What happened?" she said and carefully lifted back his sodden shirt. Beneath was a mess of blackened blood pooled in a crater that was once his stomach. "Oh. Shit," she said and swallowed hard. It looked like he'd been shot in the back and the cartridge had exploded outwards. "I'll call nine-one-one," she said. "Just … you'll be fine," she told him and pulled out her phone and dialed. When the operator answered, she said, "There's been a shooting, Pollard Street, I don't know the number but it's a big purple place with a … blue Taurus outside." And she hung up. Matt and Lionel were gone. She figured she could take the SUV and replace it in the driveway with the Taurus. At least she'd have a reliable vehicle.

"Delmar," she said, leaning close to him, "listen to me. Can you hear me? Were Matt and Lionel here? Did they do this?"

No reply. Just short and sharp breaths like pistons, eyes riveted on a point above him, like he was clinging onto something that was slipping through his grasp. "Delmar. I need to know if they had a kid with them. Did they have a little girl with them?"

The rasping slowed. Delmar turned his gaze on her, locked it there for no more than a couple of seconds, then he fell silent. His face grew still while the life drained from his eyes.

"Shit. Delmar," she yelled and shook him by the shoulders but it was too late and she knew it. Now she had to get out of there. But when she got to her feet and carefully stepped back from his lifeless body, the toe of her shoe had touched the edge of the pool and now she was tracking blood across the floor. "Oh, man," she muttered. "How could I be so dumb?"

She quickly went to the rear of the house in search of a bathroom so she could clean the blood off her shoes, peering into one room then the next. At the back of the house, she found it, but when she pushed open the door the first thing she saw was a woman—probably Delmar's wife—propped drunkenly up against the toilet bowl, arms and legs thrown wide and a bullet hole in the side of her head. She also had a phone in her hand. Kelsey figured she was probably calling for help when they caught up with her, and almost at the exact moment she realized that the police were probably on their way, she heard the sound of cars and the slamming of doors from out front.

"Oh, no. Please God, no." She quickly exited the bathroom and went straight to the front of the house, angling herself in next to one of the front windows so she could and peek out. Three cops were just getting out of a cruiser that was parked hard up behind the SUV, while a second cruiser pulled into the driveway behind it. Cops were jumping out of the second car, and within seconds she heard the sound of the front door crashing open and the pounding of boots as cops poured in and fanned out.

She turned to head for the rear of the house but the pounding of footsteps on the stairs told her she was sprung. She hadn't even made the last doorway when a voice behind her yelled, "Police. Freeze."

Kelsey stopped short, clasped her hands on top of her head and called, "Don't shoot, I'm unarmed." She turned slowly to find herself looking straight down the barrel of a Remington 870 police shotgun and a young cop in a vest behind it. They came expecting trouble. Chances of her convincing them they'd missed it were zero and she knew it.

"Down on the floor," he said and took his cuffs from the back of his belt. "Got one here," he called and three other cops came up the stairs behind him and began a systematic search of the upstairs rooms.

Kelsey dropped to her knees and lay facedown on the filthy wood floor with her hands behind her back. "They're gone," she said, but she may as well have saved her breath.

"All clear down here," someone yelled from downstairs while two more cops came up the stairs.

"One down in here," yelled a cop from the room Delmar was in.

"Another one here," called the second cop from the bathroom.

"Somebody's been busy," said a third cop, aiming the comment at Kelsey.

"I didn't do it," she said.

"Yeah, I never get tired of hearing that," the cop with the Remington said as he snapped the cuffs on her. He hooked her under one arm and hoisted her to her feet. He paused for a second to look over her swollen eye. "At least they got a little of their own back," he said and shoved her towards the stairway.

"I didn't do it," she said again, and wondered why she bothered.

"No sign of the weapon," one of the cops called.

"Where's the weapon?" the shotgun cop asked her and gave her another shove.

"I just told you I didn't do it. They were like this when I got here. I'm the one that called nine-one-one."

"What a saint," said one of the other cops.

The first cop took her by the arm, reciting her rights as he guided her downstairs to the car, leaving the others to do another sweep of the house. From out here she could hear them radioing in call-codes and tearing the place apart. Kelsey knew the drill. This was like a rerun of the bust at Jesse Milano's auto shop almost two years ago. Only this time she really didn't do it. And this time she had to figure a way out.

The cop angled in past her, opened the car door and put his hand on her head to push her into the car, but just as she bent to get in, she spotted the black Lincoln out of the rear window. It cruised slowly past with the passenger's window half down and just as it came parallel with them, a barrel came up over the sill, and she yelled, "Get down." But two shots rang out and the cop went down.

The Lincoln took off and she dropped to the ground. But the screech of tires from the end of the street told her they were coming back. She rolled and leapt to her feet in one movement, then ran. She barely made the corner of the house when a shotgun blast took a chunk out of the fence right next to her. She dived, rolled again, and was back on her feet. She tore down the side of the house, mounted the pile of shit and jumped the fence into the adjacent yard. By the time she got to the second fence, a cop was behind her, yelling for her to stop. She dove into the next yard but the cuffs were restricting her. Now she was going over fences like a drunken high jumper, throwing one leg over and rolling over the fence then stumbling to her feet and going for the next one. By the fourth yard, three cops were yelling for her to stop and hopping fences right behind her. A shot rang out and went wide. A second whistled so close to her ear that she heard it pass by. Every yard they were gaining and just as she hit the ground in the fifth, she felt a hand grab her by the back of the shirt. Then she saw the dog barreling towards them. It went straight for the cop while she rolled out of his grip, leapt to her feet and kept running. By now the woman in the corner yard had wandered across to the fence to see what the commotion was. The second she saw Kelsey her eyes flew open. "What the hell's goin' on?"

"Hold your fire," yelled one of the cops as Kelsey jumped the fence into her yard saying, "Sorry, ma'am, can't stop." Then she ran for the street.

"You there! You come inna' my yard, I'm gonna break your head," the woman yelled at the cops, but they paid her no attention because it sounded like they already had their hands full trying to get the dog off their buddy. Kelsey didn't even look back. Just as she got back to the Taurus, she heard a shot and figured the cops had solved the dog problem. She went to the driver's door and squatted so she could step through the cuffs so at least now her hands were in front of her. She ripped open the door, jumped into the car, touched the wires together and drove off just as the last two cops came over the final fence. By the time she hit the first corner sirens were sounding off in the distance. Her first instinct was to hit the gas but she knew she'd never outrun them. Twenty yards along, she swerved into a driveway with several junkers angled up in the front yard, and pulled the Taurus in behind them. She cut the engine and ducked down just as two police cruisers and a car flashed by, lights blazing, sirens screaming. She stayed there for five full minutes waiting for her heart to quit pounding and her hands to stop trembling. Finally a guy came out of the house, ducked his head into the car, and said, "Hey. They're gone. Now, would you mind getting outta my yard?"

She sat up. "Thanks." His eyes went to the cuffs and he made a face that said, "Good luck with that, lady." Then he went back inside.

Kelsey blew out a breath. She couldn't believe she had gotten away. Now all she had to do was get these cuffs off and find Holly. It was already 10:27 am. And all the time she'd started out with was rapidly running out.

CHAPTER TWENTY THREE
DAY TWO: 10:35 AM—ELIZABETH

No one would ever have suspected the scene that had played out outside the Special Children's Center less than twenty-four hours before. While normally the street was quiet, now cars lined the roadway and people walked their children up to the front doors, perhaps fearing their own child might suffer the same fate as the McClaines'.

Even after everything she knew, Elizabeth found it somehow absurd that Audrey Patterson could be lying so ill while the world she had ruled over less than a day before had simply picked up and gone on without her.

The car pulled to a halt in front of the school and Elizabeth got out on legs so weak, she could barely stand. A small crowd had gathered around the front entrance where a woman she recognized as the head teacher, Laura Miles, stood at the front door, smiling and greeting people as they arrived. Elizabeth walked towards her, noticing the teacher's smile ice over. In that instant, Elizabeth saw a flash of hostility and knew exactly how this was going to play out.

So far, there was no sign of Diana du Plessis. Elizabeth immediately felt a mix of relief and distress. On the one hand, she was terrified of the direction the questions had been heading on her last meeting with the woman. On the other hand, using Diana du Plessis as a buffer between herself and Audrey Patterson's sainted world would serve her better than she'd fare on her own.

"Mrs. McClaine, I'm so glad you could make it," Laura Miles said smoothly as Elizabeth approached with her entourage of bodyguards huddled around her.

"Thank you. It's wonderful to be here again," she lied, and pulled on a tight smile. "I don't suppose Miss du Plessis …" she said hopefully, looking back over her shoulder to avoid the woman's frosty gaze.

"Yes, she's inside," she replied. "Do come in."

Elizabeth followed Laura Miles into the inner sanctum of the Special Children's Center. The room they now found themselves in was wide and bright. Paintings and murals adorned the walls and low tables were scattered with blocks and toys. To all intents it looked like any preschool might. Several children were already lined up along one table playing with puzzles and toys, but as Elizabeth's gaze went from one to the next, that old familiar panic began to emerge. Now she could feel her heart pounding, the blood pulsing at her temples, and the muscles in her neck and face tightening. Her smile had begun to ache. She drew a deep breath, trying to ease the knots away but everything inside her told her to run.

"Elizabeth," Diana called from the other end of the room where she was admiring a wall painting. "I'm so glad you made it." And she started towards her.

"Yes, so am I," Elizabeth replied uneasily. Only now, she saw the woman had brought along a photographer who was also approaching, camera angled, and preparing to shoot. "I'm sorry if I'm a little late. The traffic's terrible," she said and turned away from the lens.

"Since we're all here," said Laura, "let's begin. First I think it would be nice if you meet some of Holly's friends."

"Yes, wonderful," said Elizabeth in a tone that, even to her, sounded like an ice shelf breaking free and sliding into the sub-zero waters below. Regardless, she followed her across to the clique of children at the first table.

Diana, Elizabeth now noted, had fallen in behind them, apparently satisfied to remain a passive observer while the photographer moved around them, catching the moment in a flurry of flashes and clicks. Elizabeth wished she could say something, do something that would draw Diana back into the fray. That way she could step back and let the reporter take the brunt of what she now felt was gearing up to be a veiled attack.

Laura had dropped to one knee beside a boy in a wheelchair. "This is Darcy," she said, gently touching the child's hand. "Darcy is Holly's closest friend."

Elizabeth stepped a little closer and smiled. "Hello, Darcy," she said self-consciously and clutched her purse all the tighter. Darcy threw his head back, arms and legs stiffening as he jerked uncontrollably, hands grasping awkwardly at the air as the spasms racked his withered limbs, twisting and contorting his features.

Elizabeth actually flinched. She didn't want to be there. She wanted to make an excuse and leave. She wanted to be somewhere where people were normal and did the expected, and spoke with words she could understand. She wanted to be where she could bury all this and pretend it didn't exist because she felt as though she was wading through quicksand and any minute she'd be swallowed up.

"That's right, Darcy," Laura was saying to the child, "this is Holly's mommy."

Elizabeth smiled. Again she dug her nails into the palm of her hand while they watched the child convulse, gripped by spasms as he struggled to form a single word. When he finally succeeded, the word, "Mom … me," came out and he grinned and waved his arms in excitement.

"That's right, Holly's mommy," said Laura, touching him tenderly on the cheek and smoothing back his hair. "Don't worry, we'll see Holly soon. He and Holly do everything together. He misses her so much," she told Elizabeth as the boy whooped and rocked his chair in response. Another little girl had drifted across from one of the tables. She moved in close to Laura and tugged on her blouse.

"Yes, Ellie?" she said and dropped to one knee. "I'm listening. What would you like to know?"

The child looked to Elizabeth, then whispered into Laura's ear.

Laura drew the child into her arms. "Well, Holly's away for a little while," she said quietly. "But she'll be back real soon."

The child gazed briefly up at Elizabeth, then went back to her seat, leaving Elizabeth feeling as though she were to blame for Holly's disappearance. Maybe she was. Maybe if she had been a better parent, she'd still be here with her friends. Maybe if she hadn't left her in the permanent care of a nanny she now knew was only interested in the money, her daughter would still be safe, because, if she had given her nothing else, she would have at least given a damn. And all at once, everything seemed that little bit less bearable, and her instinct to flee and find a drink clicked into a higher gear.

They worked their way across the room in chilly politeness, inspecting art and sculptures while the photographer snapped enthusiastically at everything that moved. Behind them, more children were arriving: children in wheelchairs, children twisted and deformed, children hobbling on walking sticks, children with splints and calipers on buckled legs. Children whose bodies twitched and convulsed involuntarily as they tried to do what everybody else took for granted.

This was the world Elizabeth had done everything in her power to avoid. The pain she had suffered even thinking about it had been so insufferable she had thrown up every barrier she could to hold it at bay. Now, looking back, she was beginning to realize just how successful those barriers had been. Standing here in the room she had only visited on one single occasion since Holly first started at the school, it was frighteningly apparent just how little she really knew her daughter. In the past three years, she had had virtually no contact with her. She had spent almost every moment of her time setting up her charities, attending luncheons and dinners and parties, all held by influential people like the Chestertons—*Oh, my God, the Chestertons*, she thought at once. They hadn't even contacted her, and there was no way they hadn't heard about Holly. For that matter, who of their so-called friends had they heard from? Did any of them care? The very thought drove a knife of resentment through her.

Elizabeth drew back her sleeve, preparing to announce that she had other engagements, but Laura cut her off, saying, "Oh, and I thought you'd like to see Holly's work folder." It was as though this was the coup de grace, the knockout blow the woman had been saving for last. She lifted a large manila folder onto the table, opened it and stood back. Like it was a bomb, waiting to go off. "We try to give the children a range of stimulating projects to work on," she said with a smile. "I think you'll be surprised at how gifted Holly is."

"Yes, of course I'd love to see them," Elizabeth said. She had now been at the school a total of seven minutes. She could hardly feign a headache and leave already, regardless of how much she wanted to. Especially since everyone was now watching her with a veneer of thinly disguised animosity mixed with a measure of expectation. She stepped across to the file. But the instant Elizabeth began to shuffle through the pages, something extraordinary happened, something she never would have expected. As she flicked from painting to painting, she began to notice forms emerging from the brushstrokes. At one point she paused and frowned down at these crude spatters of paint; swirls and dashes of brilliant color; purples and blues mixed with reds and greens all dashed together into shapes and angles. When she leaned in closely to study one of the pages, she suddenly realized what she was looking at. "These are people," she said in surprise. "Are these people?"

"This one here," said Laura as she riffled through the pile and selected another page, "is you. You see? She's given you yellow hair and a blue dress, and this brown square is your purse. Down here she's written an 'M' for Mommy."

"An 'M'? For ...?" Realizing how astounded she must have appeared, she cleared her throat and touched her fingertips to the edge of the painting.

"If you're looking for the rest of the alphabet," Laura said, "we haven't quite got that far. She can write an 'M' for Mommy, and a 'D' for Daddy." And she pointed out a second letter that was scrawled in the corner of yet other painting that had the same yellow-haired figure next to a taller one, a smaller one between them.

"And this is her?" Elizabeth asked. Something in the pit of her stomach fell so hard she felt the jolt. It was little wonder these people despised her. They saw this child every day—working with her, loving her, while her mother was off hiding in a bottle or at some "important" event she couldn't possibly tear herself away from.

Mortification and self-hatred bolted through her: that same self-loathing that had followed her every living day like an accusing ghost.

Laura was sliding painting after painting past her. "This one is her. But most of her paintings are of you. Let me show you another one," she said, but Elizabeth wasn't listening. Looking over these strokes and scrawls that seem to have found lives in the confines of these pages, Elizabeth felt something from a past life reach out with pale and transparent fingers, stretching across the miles. Somewhere, deep in the Darklands, something had awakened. Suddenly, she caught the barest glimpse of something she had thought she would never see—her child.

"I had no ..." She bit her lip, almost too afraid to say anything more in case it broke that fragile moment as she shuffled through the pages once more.

"They're very nice," she whispered in a voice only she could hear. Threads of images began to knit together and find form. And one by one, those images meshed and merged into something that seemed to have been eluding her all these years—this was really her child. From that very first day, she had viewed Holly as some kind of imposter, a child sent to deny her the child she should have had. These pictures had broken a spell. It was as if a light had flickered on to reveal the world as it really was. And her daughter had appeared right in front of her.

"How did you know these figures are of me?" Elizabeth asked. "They could be ..." She almost said *Sienna* and stopped herself. "Well, they could be anyone."

"She told me they were you," said the teacher.

Elizabeth frowned.

"The sign language we've been teaching her. You ... knew she signed ..."

"Of course. Of course I did," Elizabeth lied and turned her attention back to the pictures. But now she could see Diana du Plessis moving in and she felt her defenses go up like a ten-foot fence around a tiny, vulnerable settlement on some far-flung prairie, because this was the fatal blow, and she wasn't prepared for it. One of those cracks had been wrenched apart to reveal a vulnerable, newly beating heart beneath.

"You've probably seen her using this sign," Laura said as she placed the thumb of her open hand to her chin. "It's the sign for 'Mommy.'"

"I see," she said. Of course she recognized the gesture. How many times had she seen Holly do that and ignored her? In fact, somewhere in the back of her mind she remembered telling her to stop doing it because it was aggravating her. She had told Sienna to take the child to the park or her room or wherever that was out of Elizabeth's sight because just being in her presence intensified her feelings of discomfort and failure.

Six long years of sadness were already weighing heavily on her when one of the young teachers crossed her fists over her chest, and added, "Oh, and this is the sign for 'Love.' Then again, you've probably seen that a million times—though I doubt you'd have known it."

Elizabeth cut an angry look to her, but Laura stepped between them, saying, "Thank you, Belinda, that'll be all."

Elizabeth straightened, head high. "For your information, young lady, I did know that." She didn't dare look at Diana du Plessis. Instead she turned her attention back to the paintings and lifted a couple so she wouldn't have to face her.

Belinda jutted her chin. "Is this the first time you've ever been here?"

Elizabeth felt her bravado falter. "Of course not. I'm sorry, I missed your name. Miss …?"

"Fischer. Belinda Fischer. I've been Holly's teacher aide for the past six months. I'm amazed I never met you before."

Laura touched her on the shoulder. "Why don't you go and see to the other children, Belinda?" If her tone was meant to admonish, it flew straight over the young teacher's head because Belinda stood her ground.

"Do you have any idea why your daughter comes here, Mrs. McClaine? What she does …?"

Laura cut her off. "I said that's enough, Belinda. Why don't you go and help Ellie?"

Belinda glared from Laura to Elizabeth. "I don't care who you are or how much money you have, you're a lousy mother." And she walked away.

"Well, I really …" Elizabeth felt as if her temples had been crushed. Her hands trembled and her breath caught in her throat.

"I'm so sorry, Mrs. McClaine," said Laura. "Please understand, this has been very hard for us, too."

"Yes. I'm sure." Elizabeth turned, fumbling in her purse as if she was searching for something.

Laura gestured to a door leading to the play area outside. "Why don't we move on to the activities out here? I think we could all do with some fresh air."

Now, all Elizabeth wanted to do was get out and go home to hide because the tightness in her chest was suffocating her. Feeling genuinely nauseous now, she touched her fingers to her forehead and said, "I'm sorry, Mrs. Miles, I feel rather unwell. May I have a glass of water?"

"Oh, of course. Sit down," she said, searching around them for someone to bring a glass. Elizabeth sank into a nearby chair and massaged her temples.

Meanwhile, Diana had moved in again, bending at the knee and placing a hand on her arm. "Are you all right, Elizabeth?"

"I'm fine. I didn't sleep well last night," she replied.

"Of course. You've been through a terrible ordeal." When a young woman appeared with the water, Diana took the glass and handed it to Elizabeth, who put it to her lips and sipped. For some while, she sat staring into the bottom of the glass, mentally fending off the sensation of internal collapse and searching for an excuse to leave. The ringing of her cell phone broke the tension. She dredged it out of her purse to find Richard's name flashing on the display. She immediately got to her feet, excused herself, and stepped away while she answered.

"Elizabeth," he said in an urgent tone, "you need to get back right away. The police called. They've had an anonymous tip-off. They think they know where Holly is."

If Richard had been there, she would have kissed him.

CHAPTER TWENTY FOUR
DAY TWO: 11:07 AM—KELSEY

Jesse Milano had made a tidy sum in the seven years he ran the chop shop. Which was just as well, because the day he turned forty-two, he was busted and his whole distribution network came tumbling down, and it took almost every penny he had accumulated to hire his fancy-ass lawyer to keep him out of prison. The standing joke after that was that, of the two—Jesse and his lawyer—it was hard to tell which of the two was the greater criminal. Most agreed it was the lawyer, but at the end of the day, Jesse was still a free man. He may have been well and truly screwed over, but he never let a bad word pass his lips about it.

The auto shop he had built up since his all-too-expensive brush with the justice system was three doors down from an Asian market in Old Chinatown where the rents were cheap and business was steady. Kelsey did a slow drive-by, checking out the wide garage door that was rolled right up to reveal a single bay service area and workshop inside. When she doubled back and parked across the street, she spotted him. Dressed in his customary dark blue coveralls, he was turning something that might have been an alternator in his hand as he moved around a white Honda Civic that was up on the hoist. After checking the rearview mirror and giving the street a thorough scan, she figured she was good for at least ten minutes so she pulled the car into the workshop forecourt and cut the engine.

Jesse immediately looked up and pushed his wire-rimmed eyeglasses up onto his forehead, eyeing the jackass who'd just parked right in front of the Do Not Park sign. He reached up, plucked the glasses off his head and strode forward, gearing up to give the ignorant son-of-a-bitch a piece of his mind. But when Kelsey emerged from the car, his you-gotta-be-shitting-me expression softened and gave way to a half-grin.

"Kelse," he said and nodded in greeting. "Long time, no see."

"Yeah, long time." Instead of going to him, she stood with the car door open and her foot on the sill so she could keep an eye on the street behind her. It was a ploy to keep the bruising on her face out of his line of sight because she knew exactly what he'd say. With her head angled as if something in the street had caught her attention she pushed the door closed, then she stepped into the workshop, still with the bruised side of her face turned away.

It felt like yesterday. All the tools and used parts and old tires and piles of shit, all laid out with that old familiar smell of hot grease and sump oil and sweat and bad coffee. He'd even brought along all the grease-laden photographs in boxy black frames that had lined the walls in the last place, each showing Jesse posing alongside a series of the fifteen vintage cars he had lovingly restored before the lawyer took them and a stack of cash into the bargain. She smiled as she moved from one frame to the next, studying each of the photographs until she got to one of herself with Jesse and Matt, all huddled together and grinning into the camera. She broke away from it and turned to take in the rest of the place. The shop might have been smaller than his last outfit, but it was like coming home.

"Hey, this is nice," she said, looking all around and nodding in approval. When she turned back to him, his gaze zeroed straight in on her swollen eye, then went to her broken nose and down to the blood-encrusted stains on the front of her clothes, and his demeanor did a shift. She dropped a self-conscious gaze to the sticky, half-dried blood on her jeans and her shirt, and thought, *Here we go. Same story, different shop.*

"So, what brings you here?" Jesse asked, his tone a little chillier.

"I need a favor." She smiled and raised her hands to show him the cuffs—as if he hadn't already noticed them, for chrissakes.

"I see." Jesse stuck his glasses back on the top of his head while his attention slid across to the car she had pulled up in. "Is this what you're driving these days? Things must be looking up."

She glanced back at the Taurus, pile of junk that it was. "Yeah. I traded it with Maria Puentez."

"A trade, huh? What'd she get?"

"A '67 Chevy Impala with a Saint Christopher hanging from the rearview mirror."

He nodded without enthusiasm. "And does she know whose car that is?"

"Give her time," Kelsey said, and grinned wide.

"Did she deserve that?"

Now she felt like shit. "Probably not," she admitted, and wished she'd gone somewhere else. Like there *was* a "somewhere else."

Jesse switched his attention back to the alternator he'd been working on, turning it in his hands for a moment. Having apparently come to some kind of decision, he reached across and deposited the alternator on the worktop, then leaned back with his butt perched on the corner of the bench, folding his arms while he regarded her.

"Yeah, so," she said and shifted uneasily, "I, ah ... I can't stay long. Y'know, stuff goin' on—well," she added and lifted the cuffs, like this was some hilarious situation she'd found herself in and surely he could see the fix she was in. When he still said nothing, just sat there eyeballing her, she said, "And besides, I ah ... I got things I gotta do. Y'know," and she nodded and bit her lip, and shifted her weight.

In lieu of a reply Jesse reached across and hit a button that was set on the wall next to the office doorway. Behind her the garage door clattered down, drawing a line of shadow across the workshop like the rapid descent of daylight in a time-lapse sunset. When it finally touched the floor and stopped, they were plunged into a wash of dull gray and shadows. Now, the only sources of light were a cracked and filthy window to the left and a strip light hanging over the pit. "So ... is there anything you can do for me?" she asked cautiously. "Y'know, I was thinking bolt cutters, or something like that might do it."

Jesse narrowed his eyes on her, then eased himself off the bench. "I got better than bolt cutters," he said and sauntered across to a cabinet that was strewn with tools and nuts and bolts at the rear of the shop. He stood with his hands on his hips, a deep-rutted frown creasing his face as he searched the shelves above. "I just gotta remember where I put it."

She hung back, feeling a little vulnerable now, what with his attitude change and the cuffs—not to mention feeling crappy about how she had pulled a fast one on Maria, even though the bitch deserved it for what she'd done. She shot a furtive glance back at the door, wondering how the hell she'd get back to the car in a hurry if she needed to, when Jesse came back with bunched-up coveralls tucked under his arm and what looked like a set of keys. "Found it," he said and held up a ring of maybe fifty tiny keys hooked over his finger.

"What's that?"

"Well, this," he said, handing her the coveralls, "is the only change of clothes I can offer you. They might have a spot of grease here and there but they'll be cleaner than yours. And these," he added, lifting the keys, "could be what you're looking for. I got them off a guy I supplied with a '62 Caddy back in the day. He said I'd find a use for 'em one day," he said, pulling his eyeglasses down and giving her a pointed look over the top of them. "And here was me thinkin' he lied."

"Well, just as well I came along, huh?" she said and grinned.

He squinted down at the keys in his hand, selected one and tried it in the cuff. It didn't fit so he tried the next, then the next, while she watched. She was thinking the bolt cutters would have been faster. "So, I'm guessing he didn't tell you which keys are which, huh?"

"Patience, Kelse. Freedom has its price," he said and tried another. There was an awkward silence while he kept selecting and trying keys. Finally, he looked up and said, "So, what's with the eye?" Like it was something and nothing. Like he didn't care.

When she looked up this time, their eyes met. "Nothin'."

"Looks like a pretty painful nothin' if you ask me." He selected another key and tried it.

"It's just … y'know …"

"Yeah, I do know. I'm guessing it's just the same old shit, Kelse. The same old shit, and how many times do you have to wind up like this, huh?"

"I'm not. It's over."

This time when he peered at her over the top of his glasses, his expression softened. "That's good to hear. You're not one of the boys, Kelse. God knows you tried hard enough. Your mom could have told you—"

"Leave her out of it," she said sharply. "She's dead and gone and I'm glad."

He leveled a stare at her until she broke eye contact, dropping her focus to the cuffs. "I don't believe that," he said softly. "She knew he was bad news. She would have told you he never did you any favors."

"Yeah, well."

"And while I'm on a roll here, I'm going to tell you something else," he said and picked out yet another key.

She pulled in a long breath and thought, *Here it comes.*

"You've got twice the brains Matt ever had and he never forgave you for it. You hear me? I don't know how many times he took credit that wasn't his. And when shit went down, you were the one under the bus." Then he added, "And that's all I'm saying on the subject," and went back to the keys. "She knew that, too," he added softly.

She bit her lip and shook her head. What did he know? How many times had she heard this before? God, it was the old broken record.

"That's not true. You just don't know how smart he is. No one does. And you don't know what he's been through. He had it tough when he was a kid."

"Oh, boo hoo."

"Yeah, well, he did."

He must have spotted the look on her face because he shrugged, tried another key and said, "You think he's Mr. Terrific, you go right ahead. I'm not gonna argue. But how many times are you going to wake up looking like you went three rounds with Tyson, huh?"

"I just told you—"

"But no, you never listen. You go your own way and next thing, it's happened all over again," he continued on, like she hadn't spoken. "He cut you out from the crowd, lost you all your friends, chipped away at your confidence. When I first met you, you were …" He paused for a moment, then shook his head in frustration because hadn't he just said he wasn't going through all that again? And now look. "Anyhow, I'm glad to hear you're rid of him. She would have been, too." He stuck another key into the cuff, turned it. Nothing. Selected another. "Maybe now you can get out, make a new start. Jesus, Kelse, you could do anything you want—*any*thing …"

"How many keys to go?" she asked.

He paused. "About a thousand," he said and tried the one in his hand. Another of those silences descended; him still trying keys, her pretending there was a wall between them. Then he said, "I had the cops in here earlier."

She looked up so sharply her mouth dropped open.

He caught the expression. "What, you think they're too stupid to look me up?" He angled his head and narrowed his eyes at her. "They said you were wanted for a double homicide over by Lorain."

"It wasn't me," she said. "That was Lionel. He killed Delmar *and* his wife. Jesus," she said. Jesus, was right. Just the memory of that poor woman made her sick to her stomach.

"Well, that's not what the police said."

"Yeah, well, they're wrong. It wasn't me."

He let it hang for a while, then he said, "They also said you killed a girl—Richard McClaine's nanny."

She huffed and rolled her eyes. "That wasn't me, *either*. Turns out she knew Lionel. He owed her money. He was going to pay her ten grand to stay out of the way when the kidnapping happened."

"You got proof?"

"Well, she's dead and Lionel doesn't have to pay her. Coincidence? I don't think so." Their eyes met. "And I didn't kill her."

Jesse shrugged. "I'm just telling you what the police said. They also said they've got fingerprints, fibers, the whole nine yards. And it all points to you."

"Yeah well, whatever. They can have whatever they want. It *still* wasn't me."

"And what's this about this kid? I don't know why you want to get mixed up in Matt's shit for. Why don't you just walk away? Give yourself up while you've got the chance."

"Why doesn't anyone get it?" She snatched the keys from his hand, shook one out, tried to insert it, before giving up in frustration and shoving them back at him. "Nobody else gets it." When he just looked at her, she said, "I gotta get her home. She's just a little kid. She's lost and she needs her mom."

Jesse shuffled through the keys, trying to identify where he'd left off and adjusting his glasses like they were the problem. In the end he simply selected one from the middle and tried it. "Well, the way I hear it, her mom's a drunk."

"So? Maybe she doesn't care. Maybe she loves her mom anyway. Maybe she's all she's got." Just then, the key turned with a satisfying click and the cuff sprang apart. "Man, I gotta get me a set of those," she said, watching as he inserted the tiny key into the second bracelet with the same effect as the cuff fell away. She massaged her wrists.

"I'm kind of hoping you won't need them again." Jesse returned the keys to the drawer, then turned to her, arms folded as he perched on the corner of the bench. "Jesus H., I worry about you, Kelse."

She gave him a half-grin. "You don't have to. I'm okay. You mind if I change?"

"That was the idea of the coveralls."

She ducked into the office and closed the door. In here the desk was littered with invoices and pens and assorted office equipment. A mug captioned "Kiss the boss" anchored down a bunch of grease-covered Post-it notes and hand-scrawled messages alongside a G-clamp that was holding a stack of invoices from cascading onto the floor.

Hanging on the wall above all this was a dirty square of mirror with a crack across the corner. She moved across to it, angling her head to look over the damage to her face. The bridge of her nose was swollen and spread wide, and her eye was puffed up from the brow right down to her cheek. She touched her fingers to it and winced. Already the area was turning black.

She peeled off her jeans and tee-shirt, then pulled on the blue coveralls, noting a smear of grease just above the knee and a greasy strip of rag in the pocket that made her wonder whose they were. When she pulled the narrow straps up over the shoulders and found it a little too revealing, she slipped them down to the waist and pulled her tee-shirt on again. With the bib front pulled up, the blood stain was hidden, so she figured it was the best of both worlds. Just as she picked up her jeans to retrieve her phone and her four dollars change from the night before, she felt something in the pocket. It was the button eye from Holly's Lilly Lion. She turned it in her fingers for a moment, then tucked it into the pocket of the coverall along with the phone, the Roadster key and the coins. After taking a minute to brush herself down and check her face again, she noticed a cap on the desk with "Jesse's Autoshop" embroidered along the peak. She tried it on.

"You okay in there?" Jesse called from the other side of the door.

"Yeah." She opened the door and stepped out, still shrugging into the coveralls while she adjusted the cap.

"They fit okay?" he said.

"A little roomy, but that's fine. Thanks."

She went to take the cap off, but he said, "Keep it. It's good advertising." And grinned, probably seeing the irony of having a person on the run promoting his auto shop. "So where to now?" he asked.

"I don't know," she said and looked him right in the eye. "I gotta find her, Jess. I don't even know why. Something inside me just …" She took off the cap and ran a hand through her hair. He waited, head cocked while she shook her head at the stupidity of the whole situation and turned the cap in her hands. "It's like, sometimes you gotta do something right. Y'know?"

"And you gotta do a whole lot of wrong to do it?"

"It's not like that. I just have to find her. Something inside says I have to bring her home." She looked up at him. "I put her there. I did this. I have to make it right."

"And if you don't? If you just walked away? Left it to the police?"

"I can't do that. If I just walk away, it's like … I lose a little bit of me, y'know? And I lost enough of that already."

He nodded once, like he understood. She knew he didn't. She was just opening her mouth to try and explain—to try and reason it through so he'd understand, even though she didn't really understand it herself—when her phone rang and broke the moment. She dredged it out of her back pocket to find Matt's name flashing on the screen. Standing there, staring at the phone, she froze. From the look on Jesse's face, he had guessed who was calling.

"Don't answer," he said.

She wasn't going to. She stood glaring at it, but out of nowhere a stab of panic hit her. Something could be wrong. He could be hurt or he could need her or any goddamned thing. Before she knew it, she'd hit the answer key and now she was standing there with the line open and her mind scrambling for words.

Jesse simply shook his head and went back to his bench while she turned her back to him, stuck the cap in her back pocket and lifted the phone to her ear. "Hey."

"Hey," Matt said.

Silence stretched out for almost ten seconds. It felt more like a day and a half. Finally, his voice came through in a whisper, and he said, "I'm sorry, Kelse. I am so sorry." When she said nothing, he went on, "I don't know what got into me. I'm just plain no good. I'm just bad, that's all." And she wanted to tell him too damn right he was no good. He was bad right down to the soles of his shoes. But all at once he pulled in a ragged breath and something in her chest tightened as he sobbed into the phone.

Now she didn't know what to do. She bit her lip because she wanted to yell at him, to tell him he'd hurt her so bad, and then hang up. But it was breaking her heart to hear him. Matt—her big, strong, handsome, so-fucking-cocksure-of-himself Matt. Now here he was on the other end of the line, breaking his heart and crying like a little kid. And all because of her.

"That's not true," she said without emotion, because she didn't know what the hell else to say. She didn't want to listen to this.

She was about to hang up, when he said, "Kelse? Are you there?" Vulnerability and pain seeped through in his voice.

Beyond all reason, she wanted to reach out and touch him. She wanted to help him but at the same time she wanted to end the call. As much as she wanted to hang up and turn her back on him, she couldn't while he was falling apart like this. Cutting him down like that would hurt him even more than he was already hurting, and she couldn't do that. Not after all they'd been through together.

"You hit me," she said at last. "You fucking hit me, Matt. It really hurt." And she touched her fingers to her swollen face as if he could see it and understand that her pain wasn't just physical.

"I know, I know. Jesus, I'm so sorry." His voice was so strained he could barely hear him. He pulled in another ragged breath. "It's all that shit, y'know? That's when it started …"

"Yeah," she said a little impatiently because she knew what was coming and the sorrow inside her subsided.

"It was when I saw my mother die," he told her. "Overdosed, just like that, right in front of us. Me and Li, just standing there while she died. That does something to a kid …"

"Yeah. Yeah, I know." Like she wouldn't know, for chrissakes. He always did this: rolled out the same old story when he knew how her own mother had died and how it had shadowed her ever after.

"Eight years old …" he whimpered.

"I thought you were six …" she said, a little abruptly because the ages kept changing and just lately, she'd begun to wonder whether the story was really true, or maybe something he made up to manipulate her with.

"Yeah, well *I* was six, but Li was eight. And you know what that does, Kelse. I know you do."

"Yeah, I do know," she said quickly. Another silence hung between them. She glanced back at Jesse, who had his back to her while he worked on something, making it obvious he was ignoring her. "Listen, I gotta …"

"Wait!" he said. "I need you."

It was so unexpected, she felt her breath catch. "No, you don't."

"You left me, Kelse. Why did you leave me?" he said, sounding hurt and confused all at once. "You just turned around and walked away. How could you do that? After all we had together. You could'a just stabbed me right in the heart, it wouldn't have hurt any less."

"I told you I had to take the kid home."

"But …" There was a pause, then he said, "But that's exactly what we were doing. Wasn't that the plan?"

She hesitated. "Yeah, but …"

"And I told you as soon as we got the money, we were out of there. All of us. You, me and Lionel. It was so damn easy. And everything was going exactly the way I said, wasn't it? Huh?"

"Yeah, but …"

"And then you just walked away."

"I know, but …" Now she was confused. Yes, she'd left them to take Holly home, but he was right—if they'd waited for the money, they could have taken her straight home. But that raised the other issue …

"You lied to me about when the deadline was."

"I know," he said as if he was finally telling her the truth but it was killing him. "I know, Kelse, and I'm sorry. But sometimes when you're the one in charge, y'know, when you're the one with everybody else depending on you, you have to make the decisions. You gotta be the one that sets out the rules, right? And sometimes not everybody likes those rules. And you didn't like 'em, did you? So what was I supposed to do?"

She didn't know what to say. He was right. He was the one planning everything; the one making the decisions. She was the one turning against them. Now she was in two minds. She felt like she was making an issue out of nothing and she didn't know what to do.

"Where is she now?"

"She's fine. And she'll stay that way till we get her home. But there's something else ..."

"What? What's happened?" she said.

"Lionel's gone."

"What do you mean 'gone'? Gone where?"

"I don't know. He just up and left. I've decided to ... y'know," he sucked in a breath, blew it out, "... take the kid back home."

"Are you serious?"

"Of course. I just said it, didn't I? This whole thing is turning to shit. And Lionel lied to me," he said.

"Yeah, about the money and that drug deal he's putting together," she said.

A clanging silence followed. Then he said, "Yeah. I ah ... I didn't know you knew about that."

She could hear the sledgehammer shock in his voice. "Yeah," she said, trying to imagine the scene at the other end of the line. "I heard about it from one of the guys."

"Anyway, the thing is ... I need you back."

She fell silent while a thousand emotions hit her all at once. She wanted to believe him more than anything. She wanted to fall into his arms and hear him say he loved her. She wanted everything to be true. She knew it wasn't. "Where is she? I want to talk to her."

"Huh ...?"

"I want to talk to her. Put her on."

"Well ..." There was a moment where the line sounded like he'd put his hand over the mouthpiece, oblivious to the fact that she could still hear a whispered debate going on even if she couldn't hear the actual words. Lionel was probably standing right next to him, the lying shit. "Here," he said, and the next thing she heard was the adenoidal breathing she knew was Holly, and she found herself smiling.

"Hey, baby. Is that you, Holly?"

For a second there was nothing but the breathing. Then she heard Matt say, "Well, go on, say somethin'."

And a tiny voice said, "Nangsie Mommy."

And she said, "Yeah, it's me, baby. Listen, sweetheart, I'm comin'. Don't you forget it," and the breathing ceased and Matt was back.

"See, she's fine."

"Who were you talking to?"

"No one. I was talking to her. She keeps asking for you. I need you, Kelse," he said. "Fuck, *she* needs you. You're the only one that can talk to her. I can't understand a word she says. You know what I'm like. I'm just no good with kids, y'know? And that's what you're good at, right?"

"Well, I don't …"

"You absolutely are. I mean, look how you talk to people. Look how you always talk 'em around. That's what you're so great at. That's why I need you. That's why I love you so much," he said softly, and let it hang between them. "Just come back to me, Kelse. And everything will be just the way we always wanted. You'll see. I'll take care of us. Just like I always did. It'll be perfect. Come back and we'll take the kid home and then we're gone. We'll find our own blue sky and crystal clear water …"

She could see it right now. Lazing back in one of those inflatable rings and floating on water you could see forever in. He had been her rock. He had been her everything. Right from when they were kids too stupid to know shit from clay, he had been there for her.

"I miss you," he whispered. "I need you."

"Where?"

"So you'll come?" he asked hopefully.

"Tell me where. I'll think about it."

"There's an empty building over on Collingwood. Used to be an old fertilizer company or some such. Meet us inside."

"I'll think about it," she said again.

"I need you, Kelse. Be there." And he hung up.

She put the phone back in her pocket and turned to find Jesse still working at whatever and ignoring her. Hearing Matt's voice had moved her. It brought back memories of all those times he'd said sorry, all the promises that it would never happen again, that he'd change. He once said he would always look after her, and now look. Another of those little stones came loose and tumbled into that echoing canyon inside her. This time, she knew why.

If she was going to save Holly, she had to move fast. She'd meet up with them. But this time she'd be the one with the plan.

"I guess I'll get out of your hair," she called to Jesse, who had moved to the far end of the shop. Without even turning around, he reached across and hit the button to the roller door, then went back to whatever he was doing. The garage door rumbled behind her and the harsh rays of daylight flooded in as it went up. "Thanks. Y'know … for everything," she called, but it was as if she'd never even spoken. So she turned and left.

She had no idea what Matt had in mind. But at least now she knew where to find them. The deadline for the ransom was in three-and-a-half hours, and Collingwood was a half-hour's drive away. She got back into the car and hit the road.

Holly was still alive. Kelsey had to find her before Matt and Lionel figured out she didn't have to be.

CHAPTER TWENTY FIVE
DAY TWO: 11:32 AM—ELIZABETH

Elizabeth leaned forward from the rear seat of the taxi and peered through the windshield ahead. All she could see was a UPS van in front. Behind them was a baby blue Chrysler in which a thirty-something guy in a suit was drumming his fingers on the steering wheel and shaking his head in frustration.

"Excuse me," she said to their driver, "what's taking so long? Can't you go another way?" They had been gridlocked in the same spot for the past six minutes, during which she must have checked her watch every twenty seconds and she'd called Richard twice.

The driver was slumped in his seat, one knee up, elbow rested on the frame of his open window. He shifted his gaze up to the rearview mirror and said, "What do you want me to do, lady? Drive over the top of the cars in front? Go up on the sidewalk and run people down? Sheesh."

"I expect you to drive the damned car," she told him. "Not to plow us into a traffic jam and make us sit here—"

"—Elizabeth," Diana said, leaning forward and touching her gently on the arm. "The traffic is like this everywhere. There's a march heading downtown. We'll get there. We just have to be a little patient."

Elizabeth sat back again with her mouth set in a thin line and her gaze directed out the window. When she spotted a liquor store, she thought, *Maybe if I could just ...*

"What did the police say?" Diana asked suddenly, breaking the moment.

In total, Elizabeth had made four phone calls to Richard since they had left the school. None of which had got her any of the information she wanted. "Apparently, an anonymous call came in. Someone saying they knew where the woman who took Holly is. They didn't say anything about Holly. I hope Detective Delaney can tell us more when we get there. God, I hope it's not a hoax."

"Prepare yourself for the worst," said Diana.

Elizabeth coughed out a bitter laugh. "The worst? How could this situation get any worse?"

"While we're sitting here, why don't you tell me a little about when Holly was born?" Diana said gently. "What do you first remember?"

Elizabeth's first instinct was to roll her eyes and say something sarcastic. But the image of that little face leapt into her mind: the sweet, plump little cheeks, the pink fists bunched under her chin, her lip ...

For the first time Elizabeth had no idea what to say. The lambasting Belinda had given her still echoed, still ached. It had stolen something away from her.

"I can't even explain," she said, suddenly feeling as though the air had been punched out of her. "When I found out I was pregnant, I was so excited. And then ..." Her gaze shifted to the window where it locked on something out on the street.

"And then, when she was born, you were thrown."

"Yes."

"And disappointed."

Elizabeth's lips parted but nothing came out.

"Elizabeth?"

"Well, of course, it was traumatic."

"Your life was changing in ways you never expected."

"Yes."

"And you blamed her for it."

"No!" Elizabeth said, but the bolt of emotion hit her so hard tears sprang to her eyes and her resolve crashed to the floor. "I never blamed her," she said and pressed her clenched fist to her mouth. "I never, never blamed her." She drew a couple of desperate breaths and tore at the tissue in her hand. "I loved her. I always loved her." Her lower lip trembled while she fought against the pain that was now gripping her. "It was God that I blamed. It was all those people who looked down on us with pity that I blamed. I hated them and the tired old clichés they tossed my way like chicken feed while they went back to their own perfect lives and forgot all about us. I hated the fact that they could all walk away and desert me. I hated people with their ... their perfect children and their perfect lives. I hated our so-called friends who threw dinner parties that Holly wasn't invited to, and I hated Richard for letting that happen. I hated people who told me that it was time I learned to accept and move on. Huh! What the hell would they know? Maybe they should have been telling a person who's clinically depressed to 'turn that frown upside down' or tell a paraplegic to get up and walk. Dear God. These people were supposed to be my friends." She swiped away the tears with the heel of her hand. "They turned their backs on me and I don't blame them. I'm a lousy wife and I'm a lousy mother. Maybe she's better off without a failure like me. I couldn't fix her, God knows, I couldn't even fix myself," she said as fresh tears sprang to cut streaks down her face and drip onto her hands.

For some moments she sat motionless, fighting to regain control, until finally, she sucked in a deep breath and sat back, pale and drained and exhausted. She teased out the tissue and dabbed at her eyes, glancing up just in time to catch the amused eye of the taxi driver in the rearview mirror before he quickly looked away. "Did you get all that?" she fired at him. "Well, lucky you. Now you'll have something to tell all your friends and laugh about over a beer tonight. As for you," she said to Diana, "now you've got something you can write in your article. *Elizabeth McClaine Breaks Down, Admits Complete and Utter Failure as a Mother*. It's what you've been waiting for, isn't it? Following me around like a hyena waiting for a wounded animal to fall. Well, I've fallen. Do your worst."

Diana remained silent, just sat watching her. "Do you really think you're a failure?"

Elizabeth's face crumpled briefly. "I'm not sitting here listening to this." She snatched up her bag and after a quick glance front and rear, she opened the door and got out.

"Hey," the driver yelled. "You can't get out here."

Behind her, she could hear Diana calling after her, but she was already weaving her way through the traffic like a shipwreck survivor wading to shore. Diana called again. She ignored the woman. Just strode down the street, bumping into pedestrians who turned furtive glances her way or watched openly as she thundered past. When she glanced back, she spotted Diana hurrying after her, calling, "Wait, Elizabeth."

A young man passing held up his iPhone and snapped a couple of pictures as she went by. Right out in the open. Not even the decency to try to hide the fact. She didn't care. She checked her watch then turned the corner and ran straight into a rally that was marching down the main road carrying banners that read, "The Politicians Have Homes. What About Us?" and, "First my job, then my house! What's next?" and "My kids can't eat tax breaks."

Elizabeth stopped short. "Oh, my God." If the crowds outside the hotel weren't bad enough, she had no idea what would happen if this lot spotted her.

"This way," Diana said and grabbed her elbow, steering her towards a nearby alley. No sooner had they cleared the main street, than they were stepping across boxes and the belongings of people who were obviously living there. "Excuse us," Diana said repeatedly as they made their way through the lives of these destitute people, heading for the corner and the next street.

"Who are all these people?" Elizabeth asked, looking back in horror.

"Elizabeth! Listen to me. These are people who have lost their jobs, their homes, everything. You could not have gotten out of the car in a worse place."

"But ..."

"But nothing. Can't you see what's going on around you? You're a politician's wife, for God's sake. You're the one that's supposed to be helping these people. How long is it since you actually had your feet on the ground?" she shouted over the noise of another march descending on them from the western end of the street they were on. She grabbed Elizabeth and pulled her quickly across the street and around another corner, only to find an opposing march of people waving pennants and flags and pictures supporting Ray Townsend. The demonstrators swept toward them, cutting off any escape in that direction, so Diana maneuvered her around, meaning to head back to the alley, when her phone rang.

She hooked it out, answering, "Yes, hello!" as they quickly retraced their steps and ducked down a side street. Down here were the back doors of restaurants and Dumpsters, between which clusters people sat with their lives packed in boxes and bags around them.

There were even more people in this alley than the last. These weren't the drug addicts and derelicts Elizabeth had grown used to seeing. These were families—people with children, the newly dispossessed still grappling with their circumstances and finding themselves ill-equipped to cope. "My God," she said, looking around her. "How many of these people are there …?"

"Yes, I do understand, but can't you just …" Diana pleaded into the phone. "Isn't there anything you can do? Please …" Finally, she hung up and said, "Elizabeth, listen to me."

Shocked by her surroundings, Elizabeth turned slowly to face her. She felt like a refugee in some strange country.

"Remember when I left you earlier?" Diana was saying. "When I told you I had a meeting?" Elizabeth nodded. "The thing is, I went to meet some contacts to see if I could find any information."

"Do these people live here?"

"Listen to me. Elizabeth! I have information. About Holly."

"What information?" she said at once.

"The kind the police don't get. My contact just called me back. Are you listening?" she said and actually shook her.

"Yes, yes," said Elizabeth. "I'm listening." Although her gaze had shifted back to a child who was sitting on a filthy rug against the graffiti-covered wall, staring up at her.

"We have names. Holly's kidnappers are a Matthew Subritzski and his brother Lionel. The girl that was with them is Kelsey Money."

"Yes, but we already knew that."

"Well, it turns out that Lionel Subritzski was in prison up until three weeks ago for dealing drugs. Now suddenly, Lionel's setting up some very big drug deals."

"So ...?"

"We're talking ten-million-dollar drug deals."

"The ransom money ...?"

"And that's not all. The Subritzski brothers ditched Kelsey Money."

"But what difference does that make? Somebody still has Holly."

"The police received an anonymous call saying that *she* has your daughter. That this Kelsey Money murdered six people and now she's hiding out at some abandoned factory where *she's* setting up these drug deals with a known drug dealer named Wayne Clemmons."

"Well, that's good news," Elizabeth said, then saw the look on her face. "It's a lie, isn't it?"

"I'm afraid so. Kelsey Money didn't murder these people and she doesn't deal in drugs. My contact says that when things got ugly, she tried to bring Holly home. The Subritzskis caught her and beat her up. Then they ran out on her and took Holly. Now she's trying to find them so she can bring Holly back home. It was Matthew and Lionel Subritzski who were responsible for the deaths of those people, Elizabeth," she said solemnly. "Holly is in terrible danger. They don't intend to let her go home alive."

"Oh, my God," gasped Elizabeth, oblivious now to her surroundings.

Behind them, a man had gotten to his feet and was advancing slowly on them, head angled in curiosity. "Hey, you're Elizabeth McClaine," he was saying.

Diana was watching him over her shoulder. She took Elizabeth's arm and drew her a little further down the alley. "We can't stay here," she said. "We have to get back."

But Elizabeth stopped and jerked her arm loose. "These men have nothing to lose, do they?"

Diana spotted another man advancing on them, his eyes narrowed in a curious glare. She angled Elizabeth around and dragged her on. "It's worse than that. The Subritzskis have alibis and now the police are only looking for this Kelsey Money."

"Did somebody say 'McClaine'?" yet another man was saying. He was now also getting to his feet and cutting off their exit. "Are you Elizabeth McClaine? Your husband lost me my job. So thanks a bunch," he yelled at them.

Diana steered her around them. "This way," she said, towing her past the men and to the end of the alley.

"I lost my job and my house because of your asshole husband," the first man yelled and now a woman pointed at them and shrieked, "You think your fancy tax policies for the rich are gonna help me? You can all rot in hell."

Diana gave them a brief backward glance and shoved Elizabeth around the corner into the next street. "These people out here are hurt and angry. Come this way."

"No. I can't. I have to find my daughter," Elizabeth said and stepped back out of Diana's grasp.

"Leave it to the police, Elizabeth. We'll tell them …"

"Like hell. When little Christobel Hopkiss was kidnapped and murdered last year the police couldn't find her. Six days they searched. She'd been dead since day two. I'm damned if I'm letting that happen to Holly." And she went to storm off, but Diana grabbed her again.

"Not that way," she said and gave their surroundings a searching glance. "Come with me. I know a place."

They doubled back to the main street with their heads furtively bowed and fell into the flow of marchers. One block down Diana pulled Elizabeth into a doorway, opened the door, and they both fell into the reception area of a small, shabby office. Diana went directly to a middle-aged woman sitting at the desk and said, "Excuse me, I wonder if Chad Summers is here."

"May I say who wants to see him?" the woman asked, slipping Elizabeth a suspicious look. Up on the wall a TV was running a live feed from the march, echoing the same noise they could hear from the street. The camera panned across to a young black woman with a microphone who spoke in urgent tones as she pointed off to her right.

When Elizabeth turned back, a young man had appeared from the offices behind them. He had long dreadlocks tied back in a clump, and wisps of patchy hair on his face. His shirt and jeans hung loosely over a thin frame. He went straight to Diana, who took his hand in both of hers. His questioning gaze crossed to Elizabeth, then back to Diana.

"Diana," he said.

"Chad, we need your help."

CHAPTER TWENTY SIX
DAY TWO: 11:28 AM—KELSEY

The Taurus went through gas like water through a sewer pipe. The tank was a little over half full when Kelsey left Maria's; now it was almost empty. Three blocks from Collingwood, she swung into a gas station, got out and dug what little money she had from her pocket. It was just as she was crossing the forecourt, counting out the four dollars in coins for the gas she'd pumped that she glanced back over her shoulder to see a police cruiser swerve smoothly into the forecourt and pull up behind the Taurus. Without missing a beat she walked straight into the gas station and pulled the cap down hard, pretending to shop as she watched one of the cops get out of the car and walk alongside the Taurus. He bent briefly to look in the windows, then circled the car and signaled the other cop, who lifted his radio and called it in. The first cop gave his partner a nod, then directed his attention to automatic glass doors Kelsey had just walked in through. The second cop got out of the car and joined him. After a brief discussion, they both headed for the door.

Kelsey's initial reaction was to run. Fat chance. She'd get about six steps and they'd be on her. When they stepped inside and surveyed the store, she moved to a door at the rear, then made a bee-line for the restroom out back, intending to slip out the window. But when she got there, the only accessible windows were nailed shut, so she went from stall to stall, looking for a second option, but locking herself in one of them wouldn't work because the cops would simply come in and knock the goddamn door down. If she stayed where she was, though, she'd be cornered. So head down, cap low, and her heart in her mouth, she calmly walked straight back into the store.

The two cops were standing at the counter pointing to the Taurus. The guy behind the counter peered across and shook his head, then indicated the surveillance camera up behind him. Kelsey moved down the magazine aisle toward the back of the store, pretending to search for something on the shelves as the cops turned to give the half-dozen customers in the store a once-over. After another brief discussion, one peeled off towards the restrooms, leaving the other at the counter, scanning the store with his thumbs tucked into his belt.

From where she had ducked down behind a stand, she could just see him. When his partner called something and he strode across towards the restrooms, she hooked a pair of sunglasses from a stand, picked off the price tag and shoved them on her face. Then she walked quickly to the exit. Just as the door swept open, the guy behind the counter yelled out, "Hey, you!"

She paused, sweat flashing across her forehead, and glanced back. The guy was pointing at a strung-out-looking girl who was backing away from the cops, protesting her innocence and clutching at the huge "belly" in front of her that was now spilling assorted stolen items onto the floor.

Kelsey went out the door like her heels were on fire and headed straight across the forecourt, feeling like the eyes of the world were on her. Now she had to do something decisive. One mistake now and the cops would pick her out in two seconds flat. In a snap decision, she walked straight across to a red late-model Honda Accord that was parked at a pump and facing the street. She ripped open the rear passenger door, got in and pulled the door closed. Then she dropped down behind the front seats and held her breath.

Two seconds later a plump woman somewhere in her late thirties opened the driver's door, juggling a bunch of purchases as she dropped heavily into the driver's seat, saying, "Okay, I got you a Snickers bar and a Coke, but you may not have them until after you visit the hygienist … What?" she said sharply. A girl of around eleven or twelve and with tight red curls and a smattering of freckles sat up in the front passenger's seat, thumbing towards the rear of the car. "We got company."

"What?" the woman said and immediately turned in her seat. "Oh, my …"

"I got a gun pointed straight at your back, lady," Kelsey told her. "Just hit the ignition, nice and easy, then drive straight out and head left."

"Who are you?" asked the woman, flashing a look in the rearview mirror as she started the car. "You're that woman I've seen on TV. Kelsey something-or-other. The police are looking for you."

"Shut up and drive unless you want me to blow a hole the size of Texas in your back."

The kid twisted around in her seat and peered over. "She doesn't have a gun."

"I do, and I'll shoot."

"What have you done with that child?" the woman demanded as she guided the car out of the forecourt and turned left. Kelsey felt the car speed up so she lifted her head. The woman had both hands gripping the wheel, knuckles taut. "Tammy, will you sit around?" she snapped at the kid. "You want her to kill me?"

"Mom, she doesn't have a gun," the girl insisted. "She's just lying there."

Kelsey sat up. "Just keep driving," she said and scowled at the kid. "I mightn't have a gun, but I could strangle your mother to death from right where I'm sitting. You want that?"

"Oh, yeah, that'd be smart. You kill my mom, and she drives straight into a truck and kills all of us," the girl said and rolled her eyes.

"Would not," Kelsey said, and glared at her.

"Whoa," said Tammy, who had twisted right around to kneel on her seat, "what happened to your eye? Did your boyfriend do that?"

"No." She looked away. "I walked into a door."

"Tammy! Sit around and don't engage," her mother snapped while she shot Kelsey another look in the mirror. "She's dangerous. The TV reports said not to approach her."

"A door?" Tammy was saying, "I'm eleven years old, even I don't believe that."

"Will you sit around and quit your yap, young lady? Let's just do as she says and get her out of our car. Where am I going to?" she asked Kelsey while Tammy slid down in her seat again.

"Take a left up here. I'll tell you when to stop."

Tammy smiled back at Kelsey again. "I'm Tammy, by the way."

"Well, gee, I'd never have guessed," Kelsey replied.

"And this is my mom, Rona," she said, and waved dismissively at her mother. "Did you really kill all those people?" she asked, obviously impressed.

"All what people?"

"They said on the TV you killed six people."

"Six? I didn't kill six people. I didn't kill anyone. Jeez," she sighed. In her mind's eye, she could still see the dead nanny. Was she really naïve enough to think Lionel would hand her ten grand? Just for disappearing for a few hours? She looked off out the window and wondered how everything had come to this. "Turn right up here."

"Where are we going?" Rona asked again.

"Go straight ahead then turn right again." Kelsey's plan was to circle around and approach the abandoned fertilizer factory from the rear. She'd find Holly and Matt, and assess the situation when she got there. Maybe if she could just see him, talk to him, she could convince him to let Holly go. Was it a good plan? Who knew? It was the only one she had. "Just keep going," she said.

"So how many people *did* you kill?" Tammy asked, like it was less remarkable now.

"I told you, I didn't kill anybody," she said. Rona was still eyeing her. "And I don't have the kid," she told her.

"Then where is she? She must be terrified, the poor child."

"I keep tellin' everybody, I'm trying to find her. She's with … some people. I'm the one looking for her. I'm the one tryin' to get her home."

"But you're the one that snatched her, right?" said Tammy. "I know because you got that tattoo on your neck," she said, pointing. "They showed that on the TV, too."

Kelsey clapped her hand to the tattoo and spotted the woman's accusing gaze in the mirror again. "Yeah, well okay. I did that. But I shouldn't have." The kid was still staring at her. "I did a bad thing, okay? Now I have to find her and get her home."

"Why don't you turn yourself in to the police and let them find her?" Rona said. Seemed she was feeling a little braver now, speaking to Kelsey like she was one of the kids and she'd started a fight with her sister during a road trip.

"I can't go to the cops. They won't believe me. And the guys that took her are …" She slipped a look at Tammy, who was gazing wide-eyed at her. "Well, they could hurt her. I can't let that happen. Turn right up here and slow down." They cruised along a wide dusty street and came to a stop outside a chain-link fence. Razor wire ran along the top and signs warning of the penalties for trespassing were dotted along at intervals above a line of straggly bushes that had sprung up along its length. "Shit," she muttered when she saw it.

"You think she's here?" Rona asked in concern as she also looked the place over.

"That's what he said," Kelsey replied as she turned in her seat to look back down the empty street. Something felt wrong.

Rona was also looking up and down the street. "You'll never get in from here. I'll drop you around front." And she went to start up the car again.

"No!" Kelsey said and touched her on the shoulder. "No, stay here. This is good."

"This is the perfect place for a setup," said Tammy.

This time her mother gave her a look.

"What? I watch TV, don't I?"

"Matt wouldn't do that," Kelsey said.

"Oh, yeah," said Tammy. "And is that the same guy that wouldn't smack you in the face?"

"Look, I told you …" Kelsey started, but Rona butted in, saying, "All right, that's enough, the both of you. Now, I don't know why the police can't help you, but if you think that child is here and you think you can find her and get her home safely, maybe you better go look."

"We'll wait here for you," Tammy offered, then caught her mother's expression. "Oh, c'mon. Who needs a hygienist when you've got a wanted *criminal* in your car?"

"Hey!" said Kelsey. "I'm not a wanted criminal. I'm just …" She shook her head and let it go. She was stalling and she knew it. And she still had no real plan.

"Is there someone I can call?" Rona offered. "Or maybe I can take you someplace else."

"No, I'm good. Thanks for the ride," she said and opened the door and got out before she lost her nerve. Rona and Tammy gave her a wave then took off. Kelsey stood on the side of the street with her hands tucked into the pockets of the coveralls and watched the car round the corner and disappear. Then she turned to the abandoned factory fifty yards or so beyond the fence.

She hoped Holly was here. Kelsey had no car, no money and less than three hours to find her.

But someone was still watching over her. And that gave her hope.

CHAPTER TWENTY SEVEN
DAY TWO: 12:09 PM—ELIZABETH

The most Chad could offer Elizabeth and Diana was an old coat each by way of disguise and an escort back to the hotel. As it turned out, their final destination was only three blocks from where Elizabeth had gotten out of the car.

Chad and Diana had briefly discussed some issue in hushed voices and cryptic terms, all the while slipping furtive glances in Elizabeth's direction while she pretended not to hear. In fact, she wasn't the slightest bit interested in what their business was. She had tried repeatedly to call Richard to tell him what she knew, but he was either ignoring her attempts or he'd left his phone behind—something which, knowing Richard, seemed extremely unlikely. Now all she wanted to do was get back to the hotel.

Chad accompanied them as they walked one block over, but when they turned the corner, they found themselves confronted by a wall of humanity. The protest march had now moved east from the downtown area. It traveled along like a single entity, with people waving placards and shouting slogans into any television cameras that got close enough.

Chad grabbed each of them by the arm and tugged them back out of sight. They retraced their steps, then turned down a side street to emerge behind the rally on a virtually empty street. By the time they reached the hotel where Chad parted with them, it was twelve-twenty.

The moment one of the security officers spotted Elizabeth and Diana cutting their way through the semicircle of journalists outside the hotel, he spoke into his radio and five armed guards dashed forward to surround them. Together they moved toward the hotel and in through the front doors with the guards fending off journalists who crushed forward, filling empty space like sand falling into holes. All around them, microphones and cell phones and cameras were shoved at them while people called out questions like, "Is there any word on your daughter, Mrs. McClaine?" and "Is your husband still proceeding with his run for the Senate?"

Inside the lobby the guards moved in formation, heads swiveling for potential threats, as they guided the two women to the elevator and someone pressed the button. When the doors slid open, Elizabeth moved forward with the guards. But when she turned, Diana was standing outside the elevator car. "I'll leave you here. My car's in the parking garage two floors down."

Elizabeth placed her hands on the doors to prevent them closing. "You're not coming up?" The question surprised even her.

Diana hesitated a moment, then leaned into the elevator car and threw her arms around Elizabeth, drawing her into a hug. "I'm sorry. I have some pressing matters to attend to." She pulled back, squeezing Elizabeth's hands in hers, and saying, "If there's anything I can do, just say the word. I mean it." Then she pressed her card into Elizabeth's hand, pausing to hold it a little longer.

Then the doors slid closed.

Feeling somehow abandoned, Elizabeth rode the elevator straight to the fourteenth floor where, still enclosed within a small space made by the six armed guards, the doors opened and a second wave of journalists lurched towards them. Two of the guards stepped forward, shepherding her down the hallway to her door while the others closed in around her. She hurriedly slid the passkey through the slot and slipped quickly into the room to find almost as many people inside as there were out in the hallway, all sitting or standing around with surprised expressions. As soon as she closed the door, Richard looked up from where he was perched on the edge of the sofa, studying a pile of reports that were stacked up on the coffee table. On seeing her, his manner became immediately guarded, as if he'd been caught doing something he shouldn't.

"Elizabeth," he said and got to his feet. He dashed a guilty glance across the towers of paperwork, then quickly bent to close a file. "How was the school?"

"Interesting." She placed her purse and phone on the coffee table, and surveyed the room. Alice and Blake were in a huddle over by the windows, while Richard's speech writer, his treasurer, their head of security, and chief of staff, were all seated around the room. On the periphery were a couple of young men Elizabeth didn't recognize. Judging by the line-up, she figured Richard had assembled a council of war and they were now in the midst of thrashing out new strategies, poring over tactics, gauging the political temperature and analyzing the way forward from here. As she moved into the room, she noticed a disorderly stack of newspapers on the corner of the coffee table. The top one was folded so that all she could see of the headline was, " … aine in Meltdown." When she picked it up and shook it open, the whole line read: "Elizabeth McClaine in Meltdown." It showed a picture someone had taken of her the previous night with her eyes half closed and her mouth misshapen. It was obvious she'd been just about to speak but the effect was damning. She looked dreadful. Worse, she looked drunk.

"Ignore them," said Richard, reaching across and taking the paper from her. But the one beneath read: "Your Money or Your Child: Richard McClaine's Choice?" and below that another read: "How Far Can Elizabeth McClaine Drag Her Husband Down?"

Richard gathered up the papers and folded and refolded them, saying, "They're garbage. Ignore them." What was in those pages had no doubt brought about this meeting, and Richard's campaign team was now sitting in steely silence, avoiding her gaze. The only one with enough spine to level a critical eye on her was Alice, who stood with her back to the window, arms folded and the corners of her mouth pulled down.

"What's going on?" Elizabeth asked, despite the fact it was obvious.

"What do you think is going on?" Alice replied immediately. "We're in the middle of a strategy meeting is what's going on. And now you're holding us up."

"Thank you, Alice," Richard said abruptly. "I'll handle this."

"Excuse me, Richard," said Blake, drawing his attention for a moment. "I'll get that press statement out. I know this is a difficult time, but we need to move fast. Townsend's heading back to Columbus today. I think he's planning an announcement about—"

"—Yes, yes," Richard replied. "You do that."

Everyone else dropped their eyes to their shoes or fumbled with briefcases and papers, looking discomforted and embarrassed.

Elizabeth ignored the atmosphere along with the newspaper headlines. "Where's Detective Delaney?"

"He's on his way," Richard replied as he gathered and squared up reports and pages of statistics.

"Will you all excuse us?" Elizabeth said. "I'd like to speak to my husband in private. Can we talk in here?" she asked Richard, and gestured towards the bedroom. After searching the faces around him, he restacked the handful of papers onto the table then followed her.

As soon the door was closed, she rounded on him. "What the hell are you doing?"

"I'm trying to stitch together a strategy to get us out of this goddamned slide we're in. Townsend's shitting all over me and I can't do a goddamned thing to respond. If I don't get out there and get us back on track we'll be in a freefall situation we won't recover from."

"Your *daughter* is being held captive by some murderer and you're discussing popularity points and margins of error?" she said, incredulous. "I don't believe it."

"Do you even know what's happening in this country? Do you know what the hell I'm trying to achieve here? This nation needs me. These people are depending on me. I have a responsibility to them."

"And what about the responsibility to your daughter?" she hissed. "What about your own child? Or is this a case of the good of the many over the good of the one?"

Richard dropped his head in sheer exasperation. When he looked up again, all she could see was raw determination, the savage resolve of a man she barely knew. "What the hell do you expect? This is what I do." He paused, breathing long and deep, struggling to regain his composure. When his words came, they were slow and measured. "You have no idea how much I've sunk into this campaign: the blood, the sweat, and yes, the money. I put my business on hold—"

"—which is collapsing—"

"Through no fault of my own. Do you … do you have any idea what it's taken to get this far?"

"*Your child,*" she said, "*has been stolen.* Is this all you can do? Does she mean nothing to you?" She spread both hands wide. "Richard, she's your daughter—*our* daughter. She's the only daughter we'll ever have. Hate me if you want. I don't care. And Christ knows I wouldn't blame you. You're right. I haven't been there for you. I haven't been there for her." Her voice was low, firm, but there was fire in her eyes and she knew it. "Richard, she's our little girl. She's our baby. We have to do something *now.* Before it's too late and we've lost her forever."

For the longest time he said nothing. Then he whispered, "What can I do? This is all I know."

And there it was. It was as if the truth deep within him had finally welled up and surfaced like the body of a drowned man, once thought lost. She wanted to reach out to him, to reassure him that he wasn't alone, that she knew exactly how he felt because she'd felt like that for the past six long years. But as she stepped towards him and placed her hand on his arm, there was a sharp rap at the door and Alice called.

"Richard! Delaney's here."

Richard took a long, relieved breath and gently removed her hand from his arm. Once again, the moment had passed, and the husband she'd once known was gone.

"We'll be right there," he called. "Listen to me," he said to Elizabeth. "Let the police find Holly. That's their job. They know what they're doing."

"And what if they don't, Richard? What if they're wrong and Holly's the next to turn up dead six days after she went missing?"

Delaney stood just inside the door with his hands clasped in front of him as he ran a calculating eye over Richard's staff, each of whom was now packing away papers into briefcases in a stony silence. As soon as the last of them had departed, nodding and mumbling their goodbyes, Alice closed the door and Delaney shifted his attention back to Elizabeth and Richard, his expression unreadable.

"Please, take a seat," Richard told him.

Delaney gestured Elizabeth to a chair, waited until she was sitting stiffly with her hands clasped on her knees, then took a seat opposite her on the sofa. "I know this has been very difficult for you both, and I know you're anxious, so I'll keep this brief."

"Have you found her?" asked Elizabeth.

Alice pointedly massaged her forehead. "You think he'd be sitting here with that face if he had?"

"Do you mind, Mrs. Cressley?" he said, causing Alice to roll her eyes and mumble.

"For chrissakes, just get on with it, will you?" And she turned her attention back to the window.

"We have made some progress," he told them. "It appears Miss Alvarez was the one who canceled Holly's car."

"Meaning what?" said Richard. "That she was involved?"

"It looks that way," Delaney said.

"I knew it," Elizabeth whispered. The image of that girl sprang into her mind—smiling in their faces while she took their money and stole away her little daughter—and she hated her. Then she remembered Sienna was dead, murdered in their home, and a wave of guilt struck her for even thinking that way.

"And what about Holly?" Richard was asking. "Is there any news?"

"About an hour ago we got an anonymous call telling us that Kelsey Money has your daughter. And that's what we suspected all along. We think she and Sienna Alvarez set this up together. But the good news is it sounds like Holly is alive and well."

"Well, that is good news." Richard let out a relieved breath. "Thank God."

"So where are they?" Elizabeth asked flatly.

Delaney looked up, perhaps surprised by her tone. "We have a location for an abandoned factory where she's being kept, Mrs. McClaine."

"With this Kelsey Money, I suppose." When Delaney nodded, she said, "And you believe it?"

The detective tipped his head, perhaps expecting the question. "Mrs. McClaine, we follow up any and every lead we get. I sent a car straight over there to search the place, but they found nothing. She could be on her way there now, so I sent two officers back to keep the place under surveillance until we know one way or the other."

One way or the other. Obviously implying that at three o'clock, they would have their answer. Holly would be found alive—or she'd be dead.

Elizabeth got to her feet. "And what if I told you that this Money girl doesn't have our daughter? What if I told you that the Subritzski brothers have Holly?"

"Where did you hear that?" Richard asked her.

Delaney's quizzical gaze was asking the same thing.

"It doesn't matter. What I want to know is, are the police investigating the Subritzski brothers or not? Because if you're not, I want to know why."

"I don't believe it," Alice muttered and squeezed the bridge of her nose. "She goes from 'couldn't-give-a-damn' to 'Mother of the Year' over lunch."

Delaney frowned and heaved a sigh. "I can assure you that we will be speaking to the Subritzski brothers. Their relationship with Kelsey Money obviously implicates them by association. Believe me, Mrs. McClaine, we leave no stones unturned. Especially when we're talking about a child's life. But both these men have rock solid alibis. We're convinced Kelsey Money was working with Miss Alvarez. She murdered her in some kind of disagreement, and now she's the one who has your daughter." With that, he got to his feet and drew his hands heavily down his face. He looked worn out. As if the immensity of the situation had suddenly overwhelmed him. "Try not to worry. We're doing everything we can. Of course, if we had unlimited resources ..." he added pointedly and shrugged. It was a thinly veiled barb at one of Richard's speeches that suggested spending on law enforcement should be put under the spotlight. "Anyway, I'll keep you informed."

"Thank you, Detective. We know you're doing everything you can." Richard stood to escort Delaney to the door. "If you need anything further, please let us know immediately."

Elizabeth lifted her hands and dropped them. "Is that it?" Both men turned as if they'd forgotten her. "Is that all you've got? You've been searching for my daughter for almost twenty-four hours and that's all you've come up with? An anonymous call that anyone could have made? A couple of alibis that were probably paid for?"

"Mrs. McClaine, I've already told you, we have a number of avenues we're already investigating. There's a procedure we have to follow with these cases."

"Procedure be damned. I just told you—"

"Elizabeth," Richard interrupted. "The police know what they're doing. They'll tell us as soon as they know anything."

"I'm sorry I can't bring you better news, Mrs. McClaine. But we will," Delaney said. Then he left.

Behind them Alice had the TV on, flicking from channel to channel on which every news item was accompanied by the rhythmic thrum of the chanting crowds. She paused on a headshot of a young woman shouting into a microphone:

"... The rally has now moved into the central city and police are preparing for the worst." A wall of people surged behind her, shouting slogans and almost drowning her out. She put one finger to her ear and shouted, *"This city is angry and opposition to this bill is not dying down anytime soon. And while Richard McClaine remains absent from the helm ..."*

On the next channel was a young male reporter yelling:

"... The streets of Cleveland have come to a complete standstill. While placard waving voters send their message to the world, six-year-old Holly McClaine still remains ..."

And the next ...

"... election day draws near, police have no further leads on the whereabouts of six-year-old Holly McClaine. With only a matter of hours to the kidnappers' deadline, the question on everybody's lips: Is it already ... too late?"

"How can the police possibly carry out a thorough investigation with all this going on?" Elizabeth grumbled.

Richard said nothing, just watched the items without expression. He looked dazed.

Alice snapped her fingers and pointed at him. "We support Dave Craney's bill to increase spending on law enforcement," she said. "We go out there and tell the people that *this must not happen again.* That *law-abiding Americans will not stand for this. Not on your watch ..."*

"Don't be ridiculous," Richard told her. "My campaign platform is based on tax initiatives to increase business and stimulate the economy. It's about finance. That's my background. Besides, we haven't done the figures."

"Oh, phooey," she said and waved his objections aside. "We make the figures fit. It's a matter of simple manipulation ..."

"I'm not fudging the figures and I'm not making promises I can't keep." She went to say something but he cut her off, saying, "And that's an end to it."

"Oh, for God's sake," Elizabeth growled, and picked up the phone. "I can't believe you two. Yes," she said as soon as the operator answered. "I want room service and I want it right now. Send me a room attendant who's around five feet six, blond and around a hundred and twenty pounds. And tell her to bring her cart. Have you got that?"

"Terrific," said Alice, raising her hands briefly and dropping them. "And now the mother finally loses it."

"What are you doing?" Richard asked her.

Elizabeth ended the call saying, "Thank you. As quickly as you can," then hung up and immediately prodded in the numbers from the card still crushed in her hand.

"Put the phone down," he said and went to take it from her.

She twisted out of his reach and the second the phone picked up, she said, "Hello, Diana, it's me. I need your help," then hung up and dialed again.

"What are you doing?" Richard asked again.

"I'm finding our daughter, that's what I'm doing," she said and put the phone to her ear.

"The police said to leave it to them. Who are you calling?" He reached for the phone but she turned away out of his grasp.

As soon as the phone picked up, she said, "Hello, it's me, Elizabeth. Are you in your office?" She nodded once and said, "Good. Wait there, I'm coming over." She ended the call and put the receiver back into the cradle.

"Who was that?" Richard demanded, pointing to the discarded phone.

Elizabeth scooped up a notepad and pen from the coffee table and tucked them into her purse. "The police in this city can hardly maintain any sanity on the street out there. I'm damned if I'm sitting around waiting until my daughter is murdered."

"Delaney told us to leave it to them. They're doing everything they can."

She cut him a glare. "Is that what they told the parents of little Christobel Hopkiss? That they were doing everything they can? I'm finding our daughter, and if you're not going to help, get out of my way."

He opened his mouth to speak, but almost at once there was a knock at the door. When Alice opened it a girl in a hotel uniform stood framed in the doorway with her cart, peering in while the reporters behind her lifted their heads to see what was happening. "You called for room service?" the girl asked.

"In here," said Elizabeth, practically shoving Alice aside so the girl could get into the room. Beyond her, the waiting journalists were moving forward like a pack sensing blood. The second the door was shut again, Elizabeth said, "Is this the only uniform you have?"

The girl's astonished gaze crossed from Elizabeth to Richard and back. "I'm afraid so. But I—"

"Then go to the bedroom and strip," said Elizabeth. "Let me see if your shoes fit first," she added, kicking off her own.

"What …?"

"Now," said Elizabeth. "Please, I don't have time to argue. You can choose anything you want from my wardrobe—anything at all. Just give me your uniform."

The girl moved into the bedroom and, still shooting Elizabeth bewildered glances, she stripped off her skirt and blouse. After a brief search through the closet, she selected a Marc Jacobs silk blouse and skirt which she slipped into, while Elizabeth put on the uniform. It was a little baggy around the waist but it didn't matter.

"Oh, it's a disguise," said the girl. "So the press won't jump all over you."

"That's right. And thank you," she said. "I'm sorry if I was sharp, but I really am in a hurry."

"That's totally cool," the girl replied. "Are you sure it's okay for me to wear these? I'll bring them straight back tomorrow."

"Keep them. And don't worry about the uniform," Elizabeth told her. "I'll call your boss and square it with her."

After adjusting the headwear into place, Elizabeth went back to the living area where she snatched up her purse and cell phone from the table, and tucked them down behind a stack of towels on the lower rack of the cart. She wrestled the door open, holding it open with one foot and ignoring Richard's hissed orders to "stop being ridiculous and get back here," as she reversed out of the room with her head down, drawing the cart along with her. Just as she thought, the pack of reporters outside fell back and waited while she maneuvered the cart through the doorway, peering over her shoulder in annoyance as they tried to get a sneak-peek into the room. Finally, they fell back, parting for her to push the cart towards the elevator. With a trembling hand, she pressed the button and the instant the doors opened she pushed the cart inside and hit the button for the parking garage.

Two heart-pounding minutes later, the doors opened and she looked out into the dim expanse of the parking garage. At first she hesitated, wondering whether she should have specified the floor and meeting place. But after no more than a few seconds of frantic searching, a silver Nissan Micra rounded the corner and Diana pulled up alongside her.

"Perfect timing," said Elizabeth as Diana got out.

"Are you sure you know what you're doing?" she asked.

"Never more so," said Elizabeth. "And when I'm done here," she said, getting into the car and snapping the seatbelt into place, "I'm coming back to help those people out there." And she threw the car into gear and took off.

CHAPTER TWENTY EIGHT
12:09 PM—KELSEY

Dark thunderclouds had been rolling in from the north. They had given way and now the sun was cracking through the clouds, brightening the landscape. *Cleveland,* Kelsey thought. *You don't like the weather? Wait a minute.*

The abandoned factory on Collingwood was a two-story structure clad in dirty beige-colored aluminum siding, and with three enormous silos that sprouted from the roof. Graffiti had been scrawled across every available surface. The place sprawled across an entire block from Appleby Road on the left, to Stretham Avenue on the right, all surrounded by a high, razor-wire-topped fence. Up until two years ago, this had been the home of Ferti-Chem, manufacturers and exporters of agricultural and industrial compounds, with over five hundred employees. The last downturn had seen the place closed down and now the only visitors here trashed the place and left their mark everywhere in spray paint.

The rear entrance into the building was via a flight of steel stairs that led from the center of the parking lot up to a small landing where a broken door leaned drunkenly on one hinge.

Keeping one eye on the street, Kelsey followed the fence along to within a few feet of the corner. She was beginning to think she'd have to walk around to the front after all, when she spotted a small depression in the ground and the signs of a gap under the fence. When she dropped to one knee she found the fence had been cut and pulled back into place. She eased back one side of the wire, dropped to her belly and slid through.

On the other side, she did a duck-and-run across to a spot under the stairs where she hunkered down behind a stack of broken crates. Apart from the distant hum of cars from the freeway a few blocks away, there were no obvious signs of life. It was as if these three entire blocks had become invisible to the rest of the city. It was the perfect place to keep Holly—no neighbors, few passing cars and a great view of approaching traffic from every side.

She swung out of her hiding place and took the stairs two at a time to the top and with another quick scan across the lot, she pushed her way in past the broken door and stepped inside.

The first room looked like the cafeteria. A counter stretched along one wall with a sink and a gap where the dishwasher might have once sat. Broken tables and chairs had been overturned and the dirty linoleum floor was littered with files that had been wrenched apart, their contents stripped out and flung around. The place looked as if a violent storm had swept through.

She crossed to the door on the far side of the room and carefully cracked it. Outside was a wide, dimly lit hallway with offices dotted along. All she could hear was the occasional sound of creaking metal, as though the bones of the old building were beginning to ache. The place must have been a sweatbox in summer. Even now with the windows all smashed out the air was heavy and stale. She followed the hallway along the rear of the building. About twenty feet along she came to a door with a sign lettered out in red on the upper glass panel. It read:

Warehouse Personnel Only—Protective headwear must be worn at all times

Now she didn't know what to do. The place was much bigger than she'd imagined. It was the perfect place to disappear. It was also the perfect place to get ambushed. To make matters worse, she couldn't decide whether Matt would stay on the ground floor where he could make his escape, or whether he'd come up to the second floor where he could keep an eye on the front entrance. And, running all over the building looking for him was out of the question.

She dug her phone out of the back pocket of her coveralls and hit Matt's speed-dial but it went straight to voice mail. She was just beginning to think this was one big waste of time, when she heard the creak and clunk of a distant door.

She froze on the spot.

Shoving her phone back in her pocket, she tiptoed back along the hallway until she came to the top of the stairway. Again, she paused, listening.

"Matt?" she called tentatively.

Nothing.

She turned full circle, listening. "Matt, is that you?"

Silence. She was beginning to wonder if she'd imagined it, when the sound of footsteps sent her heart into overdrive. She spun around, hesitated, then ducked into one of the empty offices where she gently pushed the door closed, and slid down with her back to the wall and an ear to the crack. Almost at once, the footsteps came thumping along the hallway and stopped outside the door.

"Jesus Christ," a guy's voice yelled. "Where are you?"

"I'm right here," came a muffled reply. Kelsey figured the second person had been on the ground floor, because this was immediately followed by a door closing, then the footsteps thundering up on the stairs. Before she knew it, they were right outside the door. She turned to look to give the room a once-over. It was completely bare—not a stick of furniture. She leaned hard against the door and held her breath. So much for Matt's promises. Jesus, even Tammy had seen this was a setup. How could she be stupid enough to think he'd be here? Why didn't she ever learn? Now here she was, trapped in a room with nowhere to hide and barely two hours to find Holly.

"Anything?" This was the first guy. Kelsey recognized the voice but couldn't put a face to it.

"Nothing down there. What'd I tell you?"

"This is bullshit. "

"You sure this is the place?"

"That's what he said. He said she'd be here, with the kid. Told me she'd come in the front way but there's no cars or nothin'."

"Lionel's full of shit. Always was. I don't know why you even listen to him."

"So, what do we do now?"

"Go back, I guess. Where's Luke?"

"He's comin'."

"Okay, we'll do one more run. This time you check downstairs, I'll stay up here."

"Why? You think I'm too stupid to know if I seen her?"

Irritation grated in the second guy's tone. "Because she might'a been hiding, is why. So just do it, okay?"

The thud of footsteps receded downstairs, and the guy outside the door muttered, "And fuck you, too."

Silence followed. She sat listening, but now she didn't know whether the first guy had moved off or if he was still outside the door. She glanced at her watch. Time was slipping by. She put her ear to the crack, but all she could hear was the echo of the empty building, the creak of metal, and the distant whisper of wind in the roof.

After almost a minute of silence, she eased back to her feet and cracked the door. The few feet she could see was empty, so she cautiously pulled the door open and peered out.

The entire length of the hallway was empty. She had no idea where the guy had gone. Hugging the wall, she crept back toward the rear of the building, pausing beside office doorways, stealing glances inside, before moving on. At the end of the hallway, she turned right and retraced her steps until she reached the cafeteria.

The door was closed.

Did she close it? She couldn't remember. She stood in front of it, trying to decide. When she leaned her ear to it, she heard nothing. She curled her fingers around the handle, and eased the door open. A thin, wraith-like guy stood right in front of her, staring at her with his eyes wide and mouth open.

"Fuck!" he yelled and reached into the back of his jeans. "Fuck, fuck." He pulled out a gun, but he fumbled and almost dropped it.

Kelsey put her shoulder down and charged him, ramming him in the midriff and driving him backwards until he toppled over an overturned table and she went over with him. They wrestled back and forth, hands grabbing for the gun, until someone behind them yelled, "Gotcha, you bitch. Now, get off'a him."

She released her grip on the guy's jacket and raised her hands, fingers spread. The guy on the floor shoved her aside and she rolled off him and onto her back to find Wayne Clemmons standing over her with a gun pointed at her head. "You bitch," he said and cocked the hammer. "I am gonna take great pleasure in shooting your sorry ass. Get outta the way, Luke."

Luke scrambled to his feet and stepped wide. Wayne ran his tongue across his lips and blinked hard. He looked strung out. His gun hand trembled and sweat trickled from his hairline.

"No, wait! Wayne, it's me, Kelsey," she yelled.

"I know who you are," he said, and blinked hard and licked his lips. "This is for Stick," he said and closed one eye to sight along the barrel.

She threw out her hand. "What? I don't know what you're talking about. What do you mean, 'This is for Stick?' Wayne, stop!" she yelled.

Behind him the door flew open and a third guy in a beaten-up black leather jacket burst in. She recognized him at once—Melvin something. Another of Lionel's contacts. He looked her over, nodded, and said, "Good, you got her. Where's the kid?" he asked Kelsey.

She got slowly to her feet. "I don't know. I'm looking for her."

Melvin briefly considered her reply, then said, "Shoot her."

"No! Wait. You shoot me you won't get the money!" she said at once.

He placed a hand on Wayne's arm and angled his gaze on her. "Go on."

"I don't have the kid, Matt does. He said he'd be here with her. That's what he told me." Some unspoken communications ran between them, so she added, "I don't want the money. You can have it. I just want the kid."

"I'm still listening," Melvin said.

Wayne snapped a look at him. "And what about Stick? Doesn't anybody care that she killed my brother?" he said, jabbing the gun at Kelsey.

"I what? No, why would I kill Stick?"

"Will you *shut up* about Stick?" Melvin snapped and gave the fronts of his jacket a tug of frustration. "We got enough problems already." He turned his attention back to Kelsey.

"You mean Stick's *dead*?" she asked Wayne, incredulous.

Melvin ignored her. "So why did Matt say he'd be here? And what's this shit about giving the kid swimming lessons?"

"Swimming lessons?" She was struggling to keep up. "What, like in a pool or something?"

"Lionel said 'a high dive.'" Wayne corrected. "Then something about 'the big swim.'"

Melvin did a palm up. "Swimming lessons, diving lessons, whatever. I don't give a shit. Just tell us how we get the money."

"First up, I didn't kill Stick, I swear," she told Wayne. "They told the cops I killed, like, six people or something, and I didn't. I got over to Delmar's and he was already dead. Him *and* his wife. I mean, shit, why would I kill Delmar? I liked the guy."

"So, what about Maria?" asked Wayne. "What about her and her mom? Did you like them?"

Kelsey's jaw dropped. "They killed Maria? *And* her mom? Why? When?"

"This morning. Around ten," Wayne said.

Kelsey felt sick. At the time she was at Delmar's, Matt and Lionel must have taken Delmar's car over to Maria's. Maybe Maria had called him, told him Kelsey had been there. Who knew? "So, who was the sixth one got killed?"

"Deitz," said Melvin.

"Deitz?," she whispered. So Lionel must have got rid of him as soon as the nanny had been dealt with. Seemed like he wasn't going to let anyone stand in the way of his drug ring. Who else had he got rid of that no one knew about?

Melvin snapped her out of her thoughts, asking, "So why did Matt want to meet you?"

She turned the corners of her mouth down and shook her head. "I don't know. He called me an hour ago, said he'd be here."

Wayne dropped the gun to his side and stalked across to the window, muttering. "This is bullshit. This is fuckin' bullshit."

"So why didn't you ask him what it was about?" Melvin asked flatly.

She could feel the suspicion, the distrust. The air was electric with it. If she was going to lie to him, it better be good. If they caught her out, they'd kill her. She figured her best bet was to level with them. "Listen, I don't know what Matt's got planned. He told me to be here is all I know. But I know Matt. I know how he works. If I was him ..." she began, and took a moment to put herself in Matt's shoes. *Think, think!* She knew him better than anyone, knew how he thought. She focused on a point right into front of her and let the scene unfold before her. For a start Matt would probably ...

"... set up a fall-guy for the kidnapping. Pfft. That's a no-brainer," she muttered. It was no coincidence that he and Lionel had stayed out of sight in the car and she was the only one identified. How could she have realized this late in the piece that she *was* that fall-guy? "He'd do the same for the shootings. He'd make sure I got the blame for those, too—maybe an anonymous call to the cops. That way they're still in the clear, and the fall-guy—that's me—would be even deeper in the shit. After that, he'd call you guys up because ..." They were watching her, waiting for one wrong word, so she said, "Well, he told you I killed Stick, didn't he? So then he'd tell you where to find me because he knew you'd come after me." The realization hit her like a fist. *Would Matt really do that? Would he really throw her to the sharks?* She couldn't think about that now. "So," she reasoned, thinking through the sequence of events, searching for the obvious outcome, "as soon as he knew we were all out here, like, in the same place, then I guess he'd call ..." She looked up. "We need to get out."

"We're not going anywhere," said Melvin. "I say we wait for Matt. When he gets here, we'll get this shit straightened out."

"Seriously, we need to go. Now," she insisted. They weren't listening.

Melvin spun her around and shoved her. "He'll come in from the front. Let's go."

It was pointless arguing. Kelsey walked to the front of the building, shaking her head, with the three of them following. She tried putting herself in Matt's shoes again, wondering what he'd do. With a gun in her back and nowhere to run, her chances of escape were zero. Now it was only a matter of time before Melvin shot her. Or Wayne flipped out and shot her. The time to act was now.

She tried running different scenarios through her head—making a break for it down the stairway; spinning around and knocking Wayne's gun aside; diving through an open doorway and barricading herself in. But every setup ended with her getting shot. By the time they got to the first of the front offices, her head was spinning.

Like everywhere else, the front offices were also strewn with broken desks and chairs and all kinds of crap in between. But the wide span of unbroken windows looked directly out across the parking lot.

Melvin jabbed his gun at a tangle of chairs. "Sit down."

She righted one of the few that wasn't broken and sat on it.

One by one, the others did the same, positioning themselves where each could clearly see each other. From their sullen attitudes and furtive glances Kelsey figured there was something bad going on among them. Sitting around with this kind of tension was like putting a match to a fuse. Either Wayne would pick a fight with one of the others, and someone would end up dead, or they'd turn on her and she'd wind up dead. Seemed like every situation, ever since this whole mess started, wound up the same way.

And because of her, Holly was stuck in the middle of it.

She dipped her hand into the back pocket of her coveralls and found the button eye from the toy lion. It was brown glass with a circle of black in the middle. On the back was a shank with a single thread looped through. She turned it in her fingers, wondering if Holly knew that she'd keep her promise, that she'd keep looking for her no matter what. Or if she'd think Kelsey had given up and abandoned her.

Out of nowhere, Kelsey's mother's face swam into her mind's eye. Wavy blond hair falling around her shoulders, the curve of her mouth when she smiled. A smile like that could light up Times Square. It didn't happen often enough. When it did, the sun and moon shone out of her.

Melvin was watching her. "What are you grinning at?"

She put the button eye back in her pocket and leaned back with her arms folded across her chest. "Nothin'."

She had two hours and nine minutes to find Holly. Two hours and nine minutes to put everything right. All she had to do was come up with a plan.

But the sound of tires on the gravel outside beat her to it.

CHAPTER TWENTY NINE
DAY TWO 12:59 PM

Elizabeth parked the Micra in a parking building on St Clair in the downtown district, and walked a block back to the office building she had last visited four years ago. Inside the lobby, she checked the board listing the tenants. His name was ninth from the top. He was still in the same office, on the same floor. Last time she was here, her world was crashing down around her. Déjà vu, she thought.

When the elevator opened, she stepped inside with her head down, avoiding eye contact with the other passengers. At level six she got out and walked quickly down the hallway, checking off office numbers until she came to Suite 609. She knocked once and entered.

The small reception area had a sign affixed to the wall that read, "Caulder Jackson Private Investigations." Directly below it, a woman sat behind a broad black desk that was set with phone, a computer and a nameplate with "Valerie" lettered on it. Somewhere in her mid-forties, Valerie had dark hair wound into a severe knot at the back and heavy-looking designer eyeglasses that didn't suit her. She looked up just as Elizabeth closed the door. "May I help you?"

Elizabeth tucked her keys into her purse. "I'm here to see Caulder. I called twenty minutes ago. He's expecting me."

Valerie frowned and switched her attention to the computer screen, then clicked her mouse. "I'm sorry, I don't have an appointment marked for you, Mrs. …?"

"McClaine—Elizabeth McClaine," she told her, looking towards Caulder's closed door just behind her. "I don't have an appointment. I just told you, I called him directly. Look, I'm in a hurry. Just tell him I'm here …"

"I'm sorry, he's with someone at the moment. But he does have a two o'clock tomorrow, if that's convenient."

"Oh, for God's sake, I don't have time for this," Elizabeth said irritably and rounded the desk.

Valerie spun her chair. "Hey, whoa! You can't go in there," she said, and leapt up just as Elizabeth threw Caulder's office door open and strode in.

Caulder Jackson looked up in surprise, while the girl sitting on the other side of his desk turned in fright. Obviously embarrassed, the girl quickly turned away and began dabbing at her tear-reddened eyes with a wad of compacted tissue she had scrunched up in her hand. Caulder immediately got up, circled his desk and placed a reassuring hand on the girl's shoulder.

"Will you excuse me a moment, Leah? Elizabeth," he said, and moved self-consciously across to her. "When I said come over, I didn't mean now."

"Holly's been kidnapped," she told him without preamble.

"Well, yes, I heard." He shot a quick glance back to his client, who was now sitting rigid and staring into her lap. "I'm sorry, Leah, I won't be a moment," he said and guided Elizabeth across to the door.

"I need your help. She's been taken by two men—" she said and opened her purse.

"—whoa, Elizabeth, I'm sorry but I don't have the authority to get involved in something like this. I thought I made that clear on the phone."

She was scrambling through the contents of her purse, searching for something to write on. "I've got their names. Here, I'll write them down," she said and produced a notebook and pen from her purse.

He placed a firm hand on her arm. "Elizabeth, listen to me. This is a job for the police, not for me. They have the resources, the records, background information that I don't have access to. What can I do?"

"Don't tell me you don't have access," she said sharply enough to make Leah turn around. "You have plenty of access ..."

"Not this kind."

They eyed each other for a moment, then she said, "The police aren't doing enough. I can pay, if that's what you're worried about—"

"—that's not what I—"

"I don't have pictures or addresses or anything but ..."

Caulder grabbed her by the shoulders, turning her to face him. "Elizabeth, you're not listening. I know nothing about the case. I need time to get all the background facts, talk to the police, call up my contacts."

"There is no time."

"Why don't you come back tomorrow and—"

"I can't! Tomorrow's too late," she said, and broke away from him. This time Leah moved in her chair and Elizabeth lowered her voice again. "I don't need you to find them. All I need is the word on the street, that's all I'm asking."

"But whose word? Who do you think I'm going to ask?"

"I don't care who the hell you have to ask. Pay them if you have to. Someone out there knows where my daughter is. They're hiding her somewhere. I need to know where."

Caulder glanced back at Leah, who was sitting with her head slightly inclined—obviously listening. He shook his head slowly and sighed heavily. "Give me the names."

Elizabeth scratched down the names Diana had given her. "She has just over two hours," she told him as she tore the page from the notebook and pressed it into his hand. "They're going to kill her." This time she met his gaze straight on. "All I need is somewhere to start looking, that's all. I'll do the rest."

Caulder opened his mouth to object again, but wound up simply shaking his head.

"Lionel Subritzski was released from prison three weeks ago."

He opened out the square of paper and looked the names over. "Which prison?"

"I don't know. He's a drug addict. I assume he's getting drugs from somewhere. That could be a start." She watched him fold the square of paper. "Caulder, I have to try. I'm her mother. I'm all she has. Please." She placed her hand on his arm, held it there a moment.

"I'll see what I can come up with."

"Thank you," she said and left.

She had one more unannounced visit to make. It wasn't one she was looking forward to. But by the time she was finished, she was hoping she'd have some answers.

And the ten million dollars.

*****

At the sound of the car pulling into the lot out front, Kelsey took her feet off the desk and sat up. Wayne also sat forward and shrugged into his jacket while Luke and Melvin straightened and looked toward the windows. The sound of car doors opening and closing was followed by gravel crunching underfoot as at least two people moved across the lot.

Luke got to his feet, lifting his head and leaning towards the windows to look out front. "That'll be him. About fuckin' time."

He got up but Melvin hissed, "Wait," and waved him back. "Let her go."

Kelsey also got to her feet. "Yeah, I'll go." She lifted her head and sidled across to look out.

The second she saw them, her heart flipped.

On the other side of the lot was a dark blue Impala that these three had obviously driven up in, and now it had two cops bent over peering into it. She pulled back just as the cops turned to give the building a once-over.

"Yeah, it's them," she told Melvin. "Listen, here's an idea." Her heart was in her mouth, praying they wouldn't look out and see the cops. "Why don't you stay in back while I'll go talk to him?"

Melvin took out his gun and checked the chamber. "We'll all go."

"What if the kid sees you and screams her lungs out?" she asked.

He looked up. "I'll shoot her."

"You shoot her," Kelsey said, "you get nothing."

They stood, eyes locked, challenging. Then Melvin turned to Luke and Wayne. "You two stay here. Cover us out front."

It wasn't what she would have planned. Then again, what was?

They headed down the hallway and when they came to the door leading to the ground floor, Melvin nodded at the stairs, then followed her down.

Shelving and machinery sat haphazardly around the downstairs area, turning the entire ground floor into an enormous maze. It must have been ten degrees cooler down here, and the air stank of rust and oil and chemicals. Kelsey felt like she was underground. The three massive silos stood lined up on the left side of the building like giant sentries left there to guard the area. She wondered how the hell she'd get out alive.

With the gun in her back, she moved cautiously between machines and shelves, wondering what she'd do if she ran into the cops. They had gone no further than ten feet, when she heard a voice up ahead say:

"You find anything?"

Kelsey and Melvin both stopped short, and dropped into a crouch. From off to their left, another voice answered, "Nothing. I'll check down here, you look upstairs."

Two guys. The cops she'd seen. Kelsey felt sweat prickle. Plan time.

Melvin tugged at the back of her coveralls and gave her a suspicious look.

"That's him, that's Matt," she whispered. "Stay down. Let me go talk to him."

Melvin pressed the gun to her temple and mouthed, "Back."

Kelsey stayed firm.

Melvin cocked the hammer. Then he hesitated. He leaned in close and whispered, "Who's with him?"

"Lionel."

He waited, deliberating. "One wrong word …" And he showed her the gun. She nodded, let go her breath, and crept toward the cops. Ten feet or so along, she looked back. Melvin was crouched low in the shadows, watching her like a rat in a corner. He waved her on.

When she caught a glimpse of movement between two shelves, she hesitated. This could go very bad, very quick. Melvin was still watching her so she inched toward a gap in the shelving and called, "Hey, Matt, I'm over here."

"Who's there? Don't move," the cop said. She could see his gun panning, trying to get a bead on her location as he picked his way between machinery and shelves and crates.

When she looked back this time, Melvin's expression had hardened and the gun was pointed straight at her. Had he figured it out?

She put her hand up to him, then called, "Yeah, that's it, Matt, I'm right here. Just keep comin'." Melvin's eyes narrowed on her. He looked ready to run.

"Where are you?" the cop called.

"You got something?" the other cop called from some distance off to the left.

"Yeah. Over this way," the first replied.

She felt a hand on her shoulder and turned in fright. Melvin was right behind her. "What the hell are you doing?" he hissed.

"I'm calling Matt over here where you can see him. I'm over here. A little more to the right," she called to the cop.

"What the fuck …?" Melvin said. He grabbed her by the hair and pressed the gun hard to her temple. Tension twisted his features and tightened his finger on the trigger.

"You shoot me, you get nothing," she said. "And he'll probably kill you into the bargain." Melvin lowered the gun. Kelsey's heart skipped a beat. "Let me go talk to him."

"Come out slowly and put your hands where I can see them," the cop called.

Melvin leaned over and whispered, "That's not Matt. You think I'm fuckin' stupid?"

But before she could answer, the cop stepped out in front of them and raised his gun. Melvin's eyes flew open. He yelled, "Fuck!" and fired.

Kelsey dived aside, and the cop yelled,

"Freeze!" and also fired.

She scrambled into a gap between two work benches while shots went in all directions. The second cop was yelling, "Jacobs! Where are you?"

She did a duck-and-run for the door just as Luke and Wayne came barreling down the stairs, yelling and shooting. All around her, shots rang out and bullets pinged off the shelves and thudded into walls.

When the second cop scurried straight past her, Kelsey got up and ran. She weaved between machines, jumped over crates and sprinted straight for the door. Shells zinged past her, pinged off metal and thunked into wooden crates. She didn't look back. Just as she got to the last silo, she felt a hot flash rip through her thigh and she knew she'd been hit. She clapped her hand over it, fighting back the pain lancing down her leg, and hobbled for the car. Behind her was the cop yelling for his buddy, then calling, "This is Quebec Forty-two, we have an officer down. I repeat, officer down."

As soon as she got to the car, she dropped and checked the wound. She clamped her hand over it again, pulled the door of the Impala open and hauled herself into the driver's seat. Her thigh throbbed, heat rolled through her flesh in waves and blood saturated the coveralls down to the knee. Breath held, lips pressed hard, she rocked against the pain, then grabbed the two wires dangling from beneath the steering column. When she tapped them together, the car sprang into life, but just as she threw the car into reverse, she heard the cop behind her yell:

"Police! Put your hands where I can see them and step out of the car."

She could see him advancing from the building, gun held high, aiming at her. She released the brake and slammed her foot on the gas. The car shot back so fast, it kicked up a shower of gravel and spun ninety-degrees, missing the cop by a foot, and came to a halt facing the road. She threw the car into drive and lay sideways across the seat with her foot to the floor as she careened out of the driveway with the *tink tink* of bullets hitting the trunk. The rear window shattered as she spun into the street, and as soon as she hit the corner, she sat up.

She threw a right and kept her foot to the floor until she'd driven three blocks. After checking the mirror again, she pulled into an alley and cut the engine. Searing hot waves radiated from her thigh. Her entire body trembled. Shock was setting in. With a sense of dread, she inspected the damage to her thigh. The leg of the coverall had a hole three inches across ripped through it. He'd probably just winged her. That didn't make it hurt any less. Or bleed any less. She opened the glove compartment to find a small pack of tissues. Squeezing her eyes shut to fight back a sudden wave of nausea, she wadded the tissues up and pressed them into the wound. Then she remembered the rag in her pocket. She pulled it out and knotted it around her leg to secure the tissues in place. Sticky blood had seeped hot and wet beneath her, and now it was cooling, thick and tacky.

"Jeez, Mom, if this is your idea of watching over me, try keeping your eye on the ball."

Once again, she touched the wires together, started the car, then backed out of the alley and drove. That's when she noticed the St.

Christopher dangling from the rearview mirror. Different car, same friggin' gang. Now on top of everything else, she had to ditch her ride before the L21s caught up with her again.

Then it came to her. Her guardian angel might have blinked, but Kelsey knew exactly what she had to do. Groping in the side pocket of the coveralls, she located the key to the Benz and turned it in her fingers. She tucked it into the front pocket next to her heart and swung the wheel. At the end of the street, she turned right and headed north. She had just over an hour to find Holly.

But at least she knew her next move. And when she found Matt, she'd have something to bargain with.

CHAPTER THIRTY
DAY TWO: 1:22 PM

Road repairs on the edge of the city had slowed Elizabeth. She pulled into the driveway into Edgewater Drive in the up-market district of Lakewood ten minutes later than she had estimated. Now she was panicking. She got out of the car and walked quickly up the front steps of the expansive home her mother-in-law referred to as "quaint."

Lydia McClaine opened the door almost immediately. Dressed in her usual flowing chiffon and full makeup, she looked like she was just stepping out to a dinner party. Despite her obvious surprise, she forced a tight smile and gestured Elizabeth inside.

"Elizabeth, how nice to see you," she said as her gaze went straight to the hotel uniform Elizabeth was wearing.

"I'm sorry, this isn't a social call, Lydia," Elizabeth said. "Is Charles here?"

"He's in his office, but he's just taken a phone call. Come through. I'm making some tea."

"Thank you, I don't have time. How long will Charles be?"

Lydia turned a cool look on her. "I couldn't say. Tell me, what's happening about Holly. Have the police found her yet?"

"Not yet." Elizabeth checked her watch, then glanced down the hallway towards Charles's office. "I'm sorry, Lydia, I need to speak to him now." And she started for the door.

Lydia followed, saying, "You can't go in there. He's on the phone ..."

Elizabeth wouldn't have cared if he was in the bath. She threw the door open to find her father-in-law standing by the window, holding the phone to his ear and gazing out across the lawn.

He glanced back, hesitated, then said to his caller, "I'll have to call you back," and he hung up. "Elizabeth," he said, replacing the phone on the cradle as she strode toward him. "What a surprise. How are you holding up? Tell me what's happening."

Panic hit her like a train. All the way over, she had deliberated how she should broach the subject. At first, she had planned to beg him. But this was their granddaughter. Since the day she was born, they'd practically dismissed her. Then, she was going to tell him it was his duty, goddamn it; that Holly was his grandchild—his only grandchild—and he and Lydia hadn't done so much as pick up the phone to ask how she and Richard were coping, or what they could do to help. They didn't live on the other side of the world, for chrissake. They lived not ten miles away.

"I need ten million dollars," she blurted out all at once.

"Don't be ridiculous," said Lydia, who then looked to her husband. "Charles, tell her it's out of the question."

Charles looked like he'd been hit with a bucket of ice. He lowered himself into his chair. "Well, that's a lot of money, Elizabeth."

"It's the ransom. The kidnappers are demanding ten million."

"Well, they're not getting it," said Lydia. "Go back and tell them they can go to hell."

"You don't tell these people to go to hell," Elizabeth shouted. "They're holding my daughter hostage. They'll kill her. Is that what you want?"

"Calm down," said Charles. "Let's discuss this sensibly. Lydia, how about some tea?"

Elizabeth slammed her purse down on his desk. "I don't want tea. I need this money to save my daughter's life."

She knew all along this wasn't going to be easy. The whole drive over she'd mapped out a plan, an appeal. She knew she may not convince Lydia, but she had to convince Charles. That was her only hope. But with the delay in traffic, now here she was shouting the odds and making demands and Charles was sitting agape, staring at her like she'd just suggested they run off together.

"Elizabeth," he said, and gestured to a chair opposite him. "Is that what they're asking for? Dear God, I had no idea."

"Charles, I'd love to sit here and have tea and whatever the hell else, but I'm asking for that money because these kidnappers have given us until three o'clock this afternoon and if I don't do something soon, they're going to kill her."

His mouth dropped open. "But … that's less than two hours away." He checked his watch against the clock on the wall, and added, "It's *an hour and a half*, Elizabeth. You don't even know where she is."

Elizabeth planted both hands on the cherry wood surface. "I'm painfully aware of the time constrictions, Charles, and you're right, I don't know where they're holding her. But I do know that if they don't get the money, they'll kill her. Please …"

"And how do you know they won't kill her anyway?" Lydia asked.

An unexpected flash of rage ripped through Elizabeth. She straightened. "Is it the money? Is that the problem here? Because if you're worried you won't get it back, I'll underwrite it personally. I'll take out a loan if I have to—whatever it takes. Would that make you happier?"

"Elizabeth, calm down ..." said Charles.

"Because I would have thought your granddaughter would mean more—"

"Sit down," he interrupted. "You've got me all wrong."

"I don't have time—"

"Sit down!" he shouted.

She slid into the chair with her hands folded on her lap and bit her lip. She wanted to cry.

"Now, tell me what you need—"

Elizabeth looked up in surprise, while Lydia did a double take and put her hand to her chest like she was having a coronary. "Oh, for God's sakes. You're not handing her over more money ...?"

Elizabeth leapt to her feet. "What do you mean 'more money'?" she demanded. "What money have you already given us?"

There was no love lost between Elizabeth and her mother-in-law. Elizabeth had come from a one-parent family, and Lydia had never let her forget it. She hadn't even come to her mother's funeral. That was something Elizabeth would never forgive her for.

Lydia placed the flat of her palm on her chest. "Pardon me, Elizabeth," she scoffed. "But you come in here asking—no, not even asking—*demanding* ten million dollars ..."

"—to rescue *your granddaughter*—"

"—and you have the audacity to stand there and expect us to hand it over after everything you've done? After everything you've put Richard through?"

Charles turned a look of long-suffering patience on his wife. "Lydia, that's enough. Please, just go and make some tea. I'll handle this."

"What *I've* done?" Elizabeth said, advancing on this shrew of a woman. "Oh, I'm sorry, I forgot you never got over the fact that Richard married me instead of that sour-faced orangutan you tried to set him up with. That's what this is about, isn't it?"

"Oh come now, dear. Devinia Astley-Smythe was light-years ahead of you. She had class. If Richard had married her, he could have made something of himself ..."

Charles jumped to his feet and rounded his desk. "Lydia. I said that's enough. Elizabeth, sit down," he said and pointed to a chair.

"In case you hadn't noticed," Elizabeth sneered past him, "Richard did make something of himself. But he did it with me."

"*You*? You're not in Richard's world. You're not in his universe," Lydia called over her shoulder as Charles took her by the arm, steering her out of the office. "At least Devinia wasn't a drunk. She didn't grow up in the Boondocks, scratching through life on what? Scholarships ...? Ha!"

"Lydia, this is not the time," Charles growled and maneuvered her across to the door.

He almost had her out but she pushed past him saying, "And you! You spent every dime he had on that monstrosity of a house and gave him what? A Mongol for a child? You ruined his life ..."

"Shut up!" Charles hissed and physically pushed her out into the hallway. "Get out. Leave us alone."

"How dare you," Lydia snarled at her husband. "Ten million dollars, indeed. If you give this woman one dime, I'm leaving."

"That's your choice," he told her and slammed the door.

When he turned again his face was ashen. He stood with his hand on his chest for a moment, then looked up. "Don't listen to her. She's as worried as we all are. Now," he said, rounding his desk and dropping heavily into his chair. "Where were we? Oh, yes." When he looked up this time, his blue eyes were suddenly leaden. He looked as though he'd aged five years in the last five minutes. "I called my broker this morning and liquidated some stocks, so that's given us just over three million. I'm waiting on word from my banker on some debentures ..." When he saw the look on Elizabeth's face, his eyebrows rose and he sat back, regarding her. "Yes, all right," he said, sighing heavily as if she'd beaten a confession out of him. "Richard called me last night. He asked for five million for the ransom. He didn't mention the total amount, so I can only guess he was trying to come up with the rest himself. As a matter of fact, that was him on the phone when you arrived. He knew you'd come here, even though he told you not to. He asked me not to say anything to you. I don't suppose he knew you'd come steaming in here like the fifth battalion, demanding action. But if that's what you had to do, I guess that's okay."

"You were already giving us the money?"

"Of course. I'm her grandfather. What did you think I'd do? Say no?"

She wanted to say she was sorry. She wanted to thank him. She wanted to cry. She wasn't sorry; she didn't see why she should have to thank him because he was her grandfather, and dammit all, she didn't have time to cry. She glanced at the clock on the wall. "We've got just over an hour, and I've no idea where she is. All I can do is to pay these bastards, and pray they'll give her back. Alive."

"It's been very hard for you, Elizabeth," he said. "Holly's condition, your depression. I wish we'd done more. And I wish we'd done it sooner. I'm so sorry."

Tears welled in her eyes. "It's been hard for all of us. It was bad enough, but it's only since she's been missing, I've realized how hard it's been for Holly. I have a lot of making up to do."

"There's something else."

She felt her lips pressing into a thin line, wondering what was coming.

"Maybe it's not my place to tell you this ..."

"Just say it," she said and straightened in the chair.

"When I last spoke to him, Richard told me something I think you should know. He said that when you left, for the first time in a very long time, he got a glimpse of the feisty, determined woman he married." He smiled sadly. "Even wearing a hotel worker's uniform, she made him proud."

The tears broke and splashed down her cheeks. "He said that?"

"Would I lie?"

She pulled in a ragged breath and blinked the tears back. Crying would have to wait.

Charles got up and rounded his desk. "I'll call you when the money is ready. Let me know which account to transfer it to."

She stood, clutching her purse like it was a life preserver, tears distorting her view of the floor. "I'll let you know." She walked straight to the door and opened it. When she turned, she saw the worry etched into his face. "Thank you," she said and left.

Elizabeth had just reversed the Micra out of the driveway, heading for the city again, when an unfamiliar phone-ring sounded in the car. At first she thought it was Diana's phone, and that she'd forgotten to take it, but after a brief search she found it in her own purse. She pulled over, groped through the contents and came up with a phone identical to hers. The caller had blocked the number, so she hit the answer key and cautiously put it to her ear.

"Where the fuck is our money?" yelled some guy on the other end. "We heard nothing from you, you asshole, now what? You were supposed to call an hour ago. You want this kid buried in her old man's construction site?"

Elizabeth didn't even breathe. A thousand thoughts and images scrambled through her brain: the money; a construction site; her baby. And the phone in her hand—which she must have picked up in the hotel room. That meant the call was for someone else who had been in that meeting. Now here she was, sitting with an open line to what sounded like one of the kidnappers. She didn't know what to say.

When she finally spoke, her words came out a whisper. "Please, don't hurt her."

Silence.

"Please, you'll get your money. We need more time. Please …"

"You got until three. Three o'clock on the dot she's doing backstroke in cement," he said, and hung up.

"No, please," shouted Elizabeth, but he was already gone.

She knew exactly what she had to do. She had to alert the police, then she had to figure out what the hell he was talking about. To do that, she had to know whose phone she was holding. She scrolled through the menu and found numbers for Richard, Alice Cressley, Lynette Cross, Kap Gordon, Stanley Prentice, and a few others she knew; many she didn't. There was one name missing. Just to be sure, she scrolled back to Richard's number and hit the send key. It rang four times and he picked up:

"Yes, what is it?" said Richard. He sounded harassed.

"Richard, it's me."

She imagined him sitting up in surprise. "Elizabeth ...?"

"I picked up the wrong phone."

"The wrong phone? What do you mean you picked up—?"

"Back at the hotel room. During your meeting. I put my purse on the table and when I picked it up, I picked up someone else's phone instead of mine."

Richard sighed. "Well, that'll explain why he's not picking up."

"Why who's not picking up, Richard? Whose phone have I got?"

There was a brief silence, then Richard said, "Why? What's happened?"

"I just got a call on this phone from someone demanding to know where his money is. A man. I think it was one of the kidnappers. He said, and I quote: 'You want her buried in her old man's construction site.' Then he said something about swimming in the cement."

"Jesus Christ. The Beachwood construction site. It has to be. They were laying the foundations when I put the crew off. That'll be what he's talking about."

"Whose phone is this, Richard? Tell me who the bastard is that took our daughter."

"It's Blake Ressnick's," he said.

CHAPTER THIRTY ONE
DAY TWO: 1:49 PM

For the third time in the past two days, Kelsey slowed to cruise past the same house, ducking her head and scanning from left to right. The yellow crime scene tape had been removed, but the doors and windows were shut tight. There were no obvious signs of life. The car, however, was still in the driveway.

She parked the Impala two doors down and trotted back to the house, checking the street as she turned into the driveway, and walked quickly towards the house.

As she approached the Roadster, she hit the key in her pocket. The lights flashed and the alarm let out two low bleeps as the locks thunked. She pulled the door open, slipped into the driver's seat and pulled the door closed while she inspected the dash. Everything just the way she remembered.

Black leather interior. The smell took her straight back to Jesse's shop. She wondered briefly if the blood would stain the upholstery. Not that there was anything she could do about it. Next to her on the passenger's seat was a thick envelope with a wad of papers folded inside. She ignored them and checked her phone. Nothing. She thought Matt might have called by now. Her plan had been to talk to him, try and figure out where he was. Now her only option was to go back to the house they'd stayed in the previous night. It was doubtful they'd left any clues, but it's all she had.

The instant she hit the starter, the car rumbled into life. She did a snap review of the dash and controls, put it into gear, and reversed out. On the street, she put it in drive and eased her foot down on the accelerator. The bucket seat picked her up and hugged her while the computers checked settings, adjusted seats, and activated the airconditioning. She drove to the end of the street, trying to imagine what Matt would do. Last night's safe house was at least twenty minutes away, maybe more in this traffic. Just as she turned into Remington, a metallic voice from the GPS said, "Good afternoon, Richard. You are now leaving ..." at which point a man's recorded voice interjected with, "Home," and the automated voice continued with, "at 243 Belle Vue Drive, Bay Village. Where would you like to go today, Richard?"

Kelsey almost ran off the road. Either the guy that owned the car had somehow personalized the thing to death, or he'd removed the standard system and replaced it with this thing because there was no way the last car sounded like this. "Ah, nowhere—forget it," she told the system as she searched for the off switch.

"I'm sorry, Richard, please repeat your destination."

She turned out of Remington flicking switches and pressing buttons. She pulled to a stop at the lights and the system repeated the message.

"Shut the hell up and let me think," she said. The voice was breaking her concentration and pissing her off. The obvious route was straight down East Erie to Lake Road.

Simple, wouldn't you think?

But when the voice began repeating the same line over and over, she pounded buttons and stabbed switches and twisted stalks—anything to find the off switch. She was so focused searching the dash to turn off the GPS that when the light turned green, a gray Micra cut in ahead of her and when she swerved to avoid it, a cascade of papers slid from the folder onto the floor. Now she'd missed the turn.

"And screw you, too!" she yelled after the car as it veered off down the road. She was about to take off, when the GPS started up again. Then she had a thought.

She pulled to the shoulder of the road and studied the controls. When she hit a button marked "My Maps," she scrolled through and found a list of street addresses. The Belle Vue address was the last one, the one before, an address in Bay Village. It was the next one that sparked something in her memory—an address out in Painesville. That's when she spotted the words, "East Flight Airport and Control Tower" on one of the pages. As she reached down and picked it up, the driver behind her leaned on his horn. She ignored him.

Matt's last job was laying foundations for the runway of a new airport out Painesville way. Then he'd been laid off. That was the East Flight Airport construction site. The guy behind her was pounding the horn and yelling out the window.

"Try driving around me, asshole," she called over her shoulder. At the bottom of the plans and schedules and schematics, she came to a series of drawings of the control tower. "Oh no, oh God no." Panic gripped her chest.

But all she could see ahead of her was a bank of traffic. Her only alternative was to turn off and go back in the direction she'd come from. That meant even more time she didn't have. Sweat beaded on her upper lip and her thigh burned like a torch. Her first instinct was to swerve up onto the sidewalk and hit the gas. But the last thing she needed was an accident or a cop pulling her over, so she clenched her teeth and followed the traffic at a sedate twenty miles per hour to the next on-ramp. The second she hit the freeway north, she put her foot down.

All around her, the leather seat gathered her up and catapulted her through space like a rocket. The pain of her broken nose diminished; the white-hot iron in her thigh faded and all she could see in her mind's eye was Holly. She blinked sweat away and slalomed through traffic like it wasn't there. Horns tooted behind her; the road stretched out in front. She took the car up to a hundred and held her course while cars parted around her like the Red Sea. At one point she looked down to find she'd cranked it up to a hundred and forty. She looked up to find the traffic ahead had slowed at the northbound exit, so she maneuvered in and out for some way, and eventually, everything came to a halt. She searched for an opening, looking front and back, then realized she was stuck behind the same shitty little Micra that had cut her off earlier. Well, the damn thing wasn't going to cut her off again, so she inched up the exit with the front bumper almost touching the Micra, determined to swerve around it the first chance she got. Sitting right there behind the car, she could clearly see the driver—a woman—peering at her in the rearview mirror. Then she turned and waved at her. Kelsey didn't know anyone who would drive a car like that. But the woman waved again, this time signaling Kelsey to pull over.

"Yeah, lady, because this would be the perfect place for it," she said and leaned on the horn, hoping the stupid woman would drive the friggin' car instead of sitting there holding up traffic. When the woman inched forward, Kelsey pulled out and swung past her, showing the woman her middle finger and yelling, "Learn to drive, lady," despite the deeply tinted windows in the Mercedes that would prevent it from being seen. She hit the gas and shot across two lanes on the northbound freeway with her teeth in her lip to ward off the pain.

That's when, she heard the first siren.

*****

Richard had told Elizabeth he'd call Delaney immediately. His advice to Elizabeth was to leave everything to the police.

She'd replied, "Screw that. I'm bringing my daughter home or I'll die trying." She also told him that leaving it to the police was exactly what they'd done since the moment Holly had been kidnapped, and if it weren't for her own efforts, they'd be burying her regardless of what the police did. Now that she knew where these bastards had her child, there was no way she was sitting back and doing nothing.

She'd been heading to Beachwood along the Clark Freeway when the traffic had come to a standstill and a Roadster had barreled up behind her. Dark-tinted windows obscured her view of the driver, but she would have bet anything it was Richard's car. Turning in her seat, she'd waved and tooted, but the driver ignored her. At the first opportunity, the Roadster swerved around her and hurtled up the exit onto I-90 leaving her on 490. The plates confirmed it was Richard's car.

Frustrated, Elizabeth picked up her phone, hit Richard's speed-dial and the moment he picked up she said, "Richard, it's me. What the hell are you doing? I was right in front of you in the gray Micra."

"What …?"

She hesitated, then said, "Where are you?"

"I'm in my office, waiting for Alice. Soon as she gets here I'm headed over to Beachwood. Why?"

"*Dammit.* I think your car was right behind me. I only got a glimpse of the plate, but I'm sure it was yours."

"My car? My Roadster? Who's driving it?"

"With those windows? You are kidding, aren't you? Call Delaney. Have the police follow it. Tell him to use the internal GPS tracking system."

"I'm on it." There was a moment's hesitation, then he asked, "Are you okay?"

The concern in his voice caught her by surprise. "I'm fine. I'm headed out to Beachwood. Soon as Alice picks you up, meet me out there." She waited a beat, then said, "Your father told me you called him."

"I asked him not to. I should have called him sooner. I'm sorry—"

"It doesn't matter now. We'll get her back, Richard. We have to."

"Please be careful," he said. "These people are dangerous. I can't lose either of you."

"You won't," she said and hung up. Almost at once, the phone rang again. She picked it up, glanced at the screen, hit the answer key. "Caulder, how did you get this number?"

"I'm a private detective, Elizabeth."

"I'm impressed."

"You should be."

"You have something for me?" she asked. The phone bleeped. She checked the screen to find the battery indicator flashing low.

"I did some digging, came up with some information."

"Give it to me."

"The two that have Holly are Matthew Subritzski, and his brother Lionel."

"I told you that."

"Lionel Subritzski came out of prison six weeks ago."

The phone bleeped again. "... something I don't know, Caulder ..."

"Don't screw around with these people, Elizabeth. Leave them to the police. They're unpredictable and dangerous. They'll manipulate any situation for their own means."

"Thanks for the concern. Is that all?"

"No. Lionel's been doing some deals since he's been out. He's setting up a drug network with two local gangs. But Lionel's got a big mouth."

"So what does that mean?"

"At least two local gangs know that Holly is now worth ten million. We're not the only ones looking for her."

"Oh my God. Did you find out where they're holding her?" The phone bleeped another warning. "My phone's low, Caulder ...!"

"Matthew Subritzski was last known to be working on a construction site. He was laying cement."

"Yes, yes, out at Beachwood," she said, wondering why he was giving her information she already had when her phone was just about to die.

"No. He wasn't employed at Beachwood. He was working at an airport."

The words hit her like a fist. The construction site at Painesville—the East Flight airport. "We've got the wrong ..." she began, but the line went dead. "Caulder! Are you there ...?" She looked at the blank screen, then cast it aside.

The fastest way to Painesville was on I-271 North, then jump onto 2 going east. It was at least another half-hour's drive. She swung northbound at the next turn and put her foot down. And prayed she'd make it in time.

*****

Kelsey had four cop cars behind her, each weaving in and out of traffic, trying to come up alongside her. If she slowed, they'd barricade her in and bring her to a rolling stop. They had to catch her first. And if they wanted to chase her, let them. The more the better. When she turned up to the construction site with a million cops right behind her, Matt wouldn't do anything stupid … well, that's what she hoped.

She checked the rearview mirror then checked her speed. She was going at 120 … 130 … 140 … with cops weaving in and out, trying to keep up with her; commuters up ahead pulling over at the sound of sirens so the cops could cut through. Kelsey slowed a little, let the patrol cars catch up, then took off again; slowed, took off. It was working …

Until the chopper banked overhead.

Man, what a day. She had eighteen minutes to get to Painesville—eighteen minutes to find Matt and somehow convince him to hand Holly over. She could just see the look on his face when she turned up with half the cops in the state right behind her. She couldn't wait to see Holly, to see her safe. Seventeen minutes. At this speed she knew she'd do it easily.

Until she glanced in the rearview mirror.

The cop directly behind her slowed, then veered across two lanes to peel off heading south. She slowed to see a second cop follow, then a third and fourth.

She pulled to the shoulder and turned in her seat to watch them. "What the f…? Where are you going? What are you doing?"

Then, the chopper banked and soared off ahead of them.

She leaned forward over the steering wheel to watch it angle and roar off to the south while the patrol cars screamed off down the adjacent exit, lights flashing, sirens wailing. "You're supposed to be following me, you morons," she yelled, but all she could do was watch them go.

Now she was alone. The clock on the dash told her she had sixteen minutes to get to Painesville, and she'd be turning up on her own. She had no weapon and no one watching her back. But she did have the car, and that gave her something to negotiate with. The situation wasn't what she'd have asked for, but it's what she had. So she pulled out and hit the road again.

Weaving in and out of traffic now, she kept checking the rearview mirror, searching for someone—anyone that might still be pursuing her. All she could see was a bunch of pissed-off motorists that she'd left behind who were now catching up. Wondering if there was something she'd missed, something she should have known that could explain the cops' departure, she searched the dash and switched on the radio. It was tuned to a news station on which a woman was saying:

"… full story. Holly McClaine, daughter of Senate candidate, Richard McClaine, was abducted by an armed woman yesterday afternoon, and is now being held hostage at a Beachwood construction site. Police are closing in…"

"No! It's not Beachwood, you dummies. Where the hell did you get Beachwood from? It's …" She shook her head. No point in yelling at the radio. There was only one other hope. She pulled out her phone, hit Matt's number. It rang four times while she held her breath. She was sure he'd ignore it, sure she was wasting her time. Then the line opened.

"Matt? Listen to me. You don't want to do this. She's a little kid. You wanna end up on death row? And for what? Let me take her, Matt. Let me take her home. Please." She waited. Silence. She clenched her teeth and said, "I know you can hear me. Talk to me, Matt." Then she heard the soft snort of laughter and her hatred flared. "Where is he?"

"Matt's kind'a busy," said Lionel. "Told me he can't be disturbed."

"Please don't hurt her. Take the money. Take anything you want, just don't hurt her."

"'Take the money'? You're telling us what we can do now?"

"Just let me have the child. Just give her to me, and I'll take her home."

"No problem. You can have her." For a second Kelsey's heart leapt, then he said, "Just make sure you bring a shovel. Oh, and a big plastic bag."

And the line went dead.

Keeping one eye on the road, one eye on the phone, she hit the keypad again. This time she dialed 911.

The second the operator picked up she said, "I just heard a news report on the radio. I need to talk to someone."

"Ma'am, can you tell me which service you require?" the operator said.

One hand on the wheel, checking the road, the mirrors while she ducked and dived through traffic. "*Police.* It's about the kid—the McClaine kid."

She waited a moment, then a voice said, "Ma'am, do you have information regarding the missing child?"

"It said on the radio she's at Beachwood. She's not at Beachwood."

"May I ask your name, caller?"

"Who gives a shit who I am!" she yelled into the phone. "I'm giving you information here, so shut up and listen ..." She looked up just in time to see brake lights. A truck and trailer unit was drifting sideways across lanes and the Dodge truck in front of her came to a screeching halt so she slammed her foot on the brake. Tires squealed, her head snapped forward and she lost the phone. She jerked the wheel and nicked the rear of the truck as the momentum swung her around like a fairground ride. There was a thump, and something impacted to her left. She heard the crash of glass, felt metal compacting into metal ... and finally she came to a halt ...

CHAPTER THIRTY TWO
2:47 PM

Kelsey opened her eyes. Her vision was blurred, her head swam and the airbag was hard against her chest. Some guy appeared at her window, tapping on the glass and yelling, "Are you okay?"

"I'm …" She cast a quick look around. "I'm fine." The seat belt was tight across her chest so she hit the release, pushed the seat back and sucked in a breath. Metal screeched as Kelsey pushed her door open. A white-hot flash of pain went down her side as she swung out of the car seat and her thigh throbbed as she limped around to assess the damage. The front of the Mercedes was a little bent, but the left front corner was crushed, the headlight smashed and the front bumper skewed. It was undrivable.

All around her cars were pointing this way and that in one big crush of metal while bewildered people wandered through the stink of gasoline and burnt rubber and drivers barked out demands and orders, searching for sense in the chaos and noise. Somewhere to the rear, a horn sounded one long, continuous note. People walked around the wreckage they'd just stepped out of, checking with others and using phones to call for help while up ahead the truck that had jackknifed and caused all this sat bent in half with its cab folded around to meet its trailer. Somewhere a woman was crying and men's voices were urging her to stay calm. And behind all this, the gridlock of cars was building as more traffic slowed and came to a stop.

To the south, the freeway looked like an apocalypse had taken place, as though something had picked up all the cars and dropped them in a heap all around her. Up ahead to the north, past the folded-up rig and a pileup of smashed cars, lay four vast and empty lanes of freeway.

She limped around, squeezed past the truck to inspect the front of the Mercedes and spotted a little silver Camaro convertible sitting off to the right. It had spun maybe ninety degrees and was now wedged between a Honda Civic and the Dodge truck in front, with a Nissan angled in behind. The Camaro had a few dents and the passenger's door was crumpled. Otherwise, it looked okay. Better yet, the airbags hadn't deployed, and the keys were dangling from the ignition.

The Dodge driver was a man in his fifties wearing jeans, a plaid shirt and windbreaker. He was wandering around evaluating the damage to his truck and shaking his head.

"You okay?" she called out to him.

He stalked around to meet her. "Was that you in the Mercedes?" he asked, pointing.

"I'm sorry," she said.

"You came from nowhere, you dumb bitch," he yelled. "Look what you done. You could'a killed me." Then he spotted the blood down the side of her leg and flinched.

"I have to get out of here," she said, more to herself than to him.

"Nobody's going anywhere," he told her. "And I want your insurance details."

She looked back over the tangle of cars. "Yeah, sure," she said, but she didn't have time for negotiations and blame. While he strode around the truck, telling her how he'd just bought the thing, and groaning at every newly discovered scratch or dent like it was a physical assault, she hobbled around the Camaro, checking the position of each car blocking it in.

Another guy trotted up behind her, pointing to the Mercedes and saying, "Excuse me, is this your car?" Kelsey ignored him. She figured if she could move the truck three feet to the right and reverse the Camaro enough, she could get it out. She circled the truck and peered in the driver's window. The keys were in the ignition, so she hauled the door open and hoisted herself into the driver's seat.

The Dodge guy, who'd gone over to exchange details with the Honda guy, turned at the sound of the truck starting up. "Hey, what the hell are you doing?"

When he charged across, she hit the lock.

"Are you crazy? Get outta my truck …" he yelled, pounding the door with the flat of both hands.

"I'm just moving it," she told him.

She put it in reverse with him still hitting the door and yelling, "You can't do that. You're gonna hit—"

Metal groaned and screeched as the truck inched back, then something clunked to the ground. She pressed her foot to the gas and there was another shriek of bending metal from the Honda, the driver of which was also yelling. When she threw the truck into drive and pressed her foot to the pedal again, the truck lurched and the Honda's front bumper popped and clattered onto the road. Now a small crowd had gathered around her, shouting and pointing as she shunted the Honda sideways. She didn't know if she'd moved it three feet but it would have to do.

By the time she cut the engine again, people had closed in around her, yelling abuse and threatening her with everything they could think of. The Nissan guy squeezed past his car and the instant she released the lock he ripped the door open. "I'll have you know I'm an attorney and I'm suing you for every scratch …"

"Go ahead," she said as she hobbled back to the Camaro. He grabbed her arm and swung her around, but she pulled back and landed him a roundhouse that sent him reeling.

She slid into the seat of the Camaro and hit the ignition just as another guy yelled, "Hey! What are you doing in my car?"

She threw the Camaro in reverse and three people jumped out of the way as she eased back and hit the Nissan. "Nope, not quite three feet," she said, then put the car into drive. She twisted the wheel and pulled out, nudging the rear of the Dodge again, while some guy banged his fist on the side of the car and another jotted down her plates. "Good luck with that," she muttered and turned the car north.

On the open road, she floored it. She had six minutes to get to Painesville and save Holly. There was no way she would make it.

But she had to try.

*****

At almost the same time as Kelsey was plowing into the Dodge, Elizabeth hit on an idea. She pulled the Micra to the side of the road, lifted the hood, and stood to the side, gazing hopefully up and down the street. Less than a minute later, a late model Explorer pulled up and a man in his sixties got out. Dressed in a thick wool-lined jacket and Indians peak cap, he ambled towards her. "You got some trouble?"

"Do you have a phone?" she asked.

"I can take a look if you want. I know a thing or two about engines. It's usually something small."

"I need a phone. Please."

"I got one in the car."

He retrieved the phone and gave it to her. While she punched in Richard's number, the man angled his head, regarding her and said, "Anyone ever tell you, you got a remarkable resemblance to Elizabeth McClaine?"

"My husband used to," she told him distractedly. "He hasn't in a while. Richard," she said as soon as he answered the call. "It's me. She's not at Beachwood. They've got her at Painesville. It's the Painesville construction site. Tell Delaney. We've got …" she checked her watch. "Oh God, Richard, we've got five minutes," and her breath caught in her throat. The man was frowning at her, as though still trying to decide if it was her. "Never mind how I know," she told Richard when he asked, "just tell Delaney. I'm on my way there now." And she hung up.

"Is this about your little girl?" the man asked. "The one that was kidnapped?"

Tears pricked in her eyes and her throat tightened. "Yes. I have to get to Painesville."

"Get in the truck," he said. "I'll take you there."

"But my car …"

"We'll call someone. Let me get you to Painesville to your little girl," he said and opened the passenger's door for her. "You just worry about calling the police."

CHAPTER THIRTY THREE
2:58 PM

Kelsey found the construction site at the end of a short side street off the main road. A vast area of churned-up earth stood like an open wound in the landscape. In the middle, buildings sat in an expanse of surrounding concrete like a raft in a swamp. Leading off to the right, a long tongue of blacktop was pegged out with upright markers from which tape flapped like bedraggled streamers in the wind. And at the far end, a control tower stood maybe a hundred or so feet high. Surrounded by a network of scaffolding, it looked like the skeleton of some medieval fortress.

She rolled slowly past signs warning off trespassers, then turned into the parking lot with the crunch of gravel under the tires. Friday afternoon she'd have expected the place to be crawling with construction workers. Not now. The place was deserted.

She got out of the car and surveyed the buildings. Wind whistled around scaffolding and torn building paper flapped from the unfinished walls. Dust swirled and snack wrappers and plastic drink bottles skittered across the ground. No signs of life. Just wasteland.

Cleveland, the comeback city, she thought. *Some comeback.*

With the throbbing in her thigh sending heat waves up and down her leg, and the swelling stiffening her knee, she gritted her teeth and headed for the front entrance. In lieu of doors, heavy plastic screens were draped across the opening. Inside the floor was bare concrete covered in drywall dust and boot prints. Empty crates and boxes of nails and lengths of metal were stacked on makeshift workbenches while, overhead, electrical wire snaked across the open ceilings and down the walls to terminate in coils and tangles on the floor.

Kelsey hobbled across the enormous open area of the main terminal, looking all around. All she could hear was the wind howling around the corners of the building and the echo of empty space inside. She figured she had the wrong place after all.

"Shit!" she said and turned full circle, taking the whole of the place in. "Shit, shit, shit." Furious with herself for getting it wrong, angry with Matt for making this so friggin' hard, pissed with Lionel for everything else, she started back towards the car. She was wondering what the hell she should do, where she should go next, when a gust of wind picked up the plastic screen covering a doorway at the far end of the building and she caught a glimpse of a car. She stopped short, then limped across to it. With her back pressed close in beside the opening, she leaned briefly and peeped out. A green Toyota Land Cruiser sat in a parking lot at the base of the control tower.

She waited a beat, then leaned out again, this time peering up at the tower. A concrete structure, it was surrounded by a framework of steel rods and planks that made up the cage-work of scaffolding. At the top was the viewing platform. From here, all Kelsey could see was the underside of the deck. If they were here, that was the only place they could be. She turned to head on down the corridor that connected the main terminal with the control tower when she heard the echo of footsteps, then a voice.

"Pick up your phone, asshole," he yelled. "Jesus Christ." Lionel, the douche bag. She stepped out into the open. He was just tucking the phone into his pocket when he looked up. "Oh, not you an' all."

"Yeah, me an' all." When he pulled a gun from the back of his jeans and aimed it at her, she said, "What's happened, Lionel? Did you lose the money?"

"Fuck you. We got the money."

She snorted. "If you had the money, you'd be long gone by now. You're probably down here trying to talk to your contact because Matt doesn't know about all your drug deals and shit. Am I right?"

He snorted. "Still the same smart-mouth bitch you always were. We should'a got rid of you when we had the chance."

"Maybe you should have. Wouldn't have made a difference. You're screwed whatever you do from here on in." She inched towards him. He raised the gun and sighted her down the barrel, finger stroking the trigger, so she stopped. "Lionel, it doesn't have to end like this. Give her to me and I'll give you plenty of time to get away."

"Well, you're too late. By ten minutes. Just ten minutes!" He shrugged theatrically and grinned. "What a shame."

She wanted to hit him, throttle him, punch him out. She also wanted Holly back. She took a step closer, and said, "Get out of my way."

He grinned. "I already told you. She's dead. Pulled the trigger myself."

"Bullshit."

He reached into his jacket, pulled out a crumpled up bundle of fabric and tossed it on the floor. She bent and picked it up. It was the blue sweater Kelsey had dressed Holly in not twenty-four hours earlier. She shook it out. Blackened bloodstains radiated from a tear across the middle and her heart stopped.

"How could you do this? How could you hurt a little girl …?"

Lionel snorted and looked around like he was addressing an audience. "Have you seen the time? Anyone would'a thought her parents cared more. I certainly did. We told them she had until three o'clock. We couldn't have made it clearer. Shit, even you knew she had until three o'clock, and yet here you are at—" he checked his watch. "—seven minutes after. So is this our fault? No, it's yours."

Tears pricked at her eyes. One broke and ran down her cheek as she clutched the little sweater close to her heart, and wondered who she hated most—Lionel, or herself. She had made a promise for Holly to cling to. And she'd failed her. Oh, sure, she could fight, strip a car, drive better than any of the guys she knew. What the hell use was any of that when all she ever did was fail anyone who put their faith in her, or destroy those who crossed her? Look at the nanny. Look at Maria, Maria's mother.

What about her own mother, for chrissakes? All gone, and just because of her. Vic was right, she was useless. Dumb as a sack of hammers and no use to anyone.

"I hate you," she whispered. Despair had reached into her chest and drained the very essence of her. When she looked up, Lionel was watching her, grinning, enjoying the moment. He raised the gun and took aim, but at the sound of a car pulling into the lot out front, he hesitated. He backtracked a couple of steps and peered out a window across the lot. His expression shifted briefly. When he regained his composure, some of the confidence was gone.

Curious, Kelsey stepped back to an opening and looked out across the lot. A red Dodge Caliber sat next to the Camaro. The doors opened and three muscled-up black guys in long leather coats and jeans stepped out. They each paused to survey the area, then sauntered across to the Camaro. The tallest opened the driver's door, bent and touched the seat. He examined what Kelsey knew would be blood on his fingers, and said something. At once their collective attention turned to the terminal and each drew out a gun.

"I hope they fuckin' kill you," Kelsey told him. That's how she felt. It wouldn't make a damn bit of difference to him, but she felt better saying it.

Lionel tipped his head in defiance and lifted the gun again. "Ain't gonna happen. But you won't be around to find out, anyway. You'll be takin' that big cement swim with the kid while me an' Matt will be heading out for those blue skies and crystal clear waters with a cool ten mill in our pockets. Who'd'a thought, huh?"

He thumbed back the hammer, ready. At the sound of a second car entering the lot, his attention wavered. He glanced outside and this time the grin vanished and the gun dropped a fraction, so Kelsey put her head down and charged him. He cracked off two shots, but he was too late and they missed her and pinged off the floor. She caught him in the midriff with her shoulder and drove him back so hard they both hit the wall with a crash and the gun flew out of his hand and skittered wide. Kelsey stumbled over him, rolled and got straight back to her feet, but Lionel was already coming at her. He threw a right and missed, spun on his toes and followed it up with a couple of jabs. She responded with a left hook that glanced off his jaw but it knocked him off balance, so she followed it up with a combination left and right that dropped him on his ass. He put a hand to his mouth, then looked up at her and grinned.

The sound of footsteps on gravel was getting closer, so she had to finish this fast. Lionel got to his feet and fell into stance. She shadowed him a few steps, bouncing unsteadily on her toes, looking for an opening. Concentration—that was the key. Out of nowhere the image of Holly flashed across her mind—the innocence, the trust. She hit him hard and he went backwards. Driven by determination, by anger, she launched herself at him. With her head down and her teeth clenched, she pounded his face, his gut, anything she could reach. When he folded over, she grabbed his shirt and drove her forehead full in his face and heard bone crack. Breathing hard from the exertion, she bent with her hands on her knees, watching him flounder back and fall on his ass with blood spurting from his nose.

"Yeah, hurts like a bitch, don't it?" She straightened and wiped blood from her brow with the back of her hand.

He went to get up but she stepped in again, hit him with a kick in the side that toppled him over sideways. "And that one's from Holly, you asshole," she said and bent again, to fend off the pain radiating through her.

Lionel's face squeezed up in pain, arms holding his ribs while he lay grunting and gasping for air.

"Yeah, I know," she told him. "Ain't exactly Queensberry rules, but hey, you started it." Blood gushed from his nose, his face was pale, and he could barely breathe. Why wasn't she surprised when he simply looked up at her with that stupid grin again? "Where's Matt?" she said.

But before he could answer a squeal echoed from the door of the control tower. "Holly! Is that you, baby?" she called. She went to move, but the sound of slow clapping from the far end of the corridor stopped her short and made her turn.

Three black guys were standing across the doorway, two with guns aimed straight at her. "What do you want?" she snapped.

"We got no business with you. We're here for the kid," he said, and tipped his head. "But we'll cut you a deal. We'll just take the money instead." He turned his attention on Lionel, who was now on his feet, leaning heavily on the wall with his sleeve pressed to his nose. She opened her mouth to tell him they could have Lionel, when the throb of a car sound-system at full throttle pulsed across the lot, and another car pulled in. All five of them looked to the windows.

"How the hell many people did you blab to?" Kelsey asked Lionel. "It's like Saturday night downtown around here."

Lionel gave her a smug little smile. "It's called finding the highest bidder."

"Highest bidder? Highest bidder for what?" she said, but before he could answer, the black guy snapped off two shots that just about made her heart jump out of her chest. A bloody hole opened up in Lionel's forehead and he slid down the wall to sit staring blankly at a point right in front of him.

"An' this," the guy who'd shot him said, "is called cuttin' out the middleman." When Kelsey turned a look on him, he simply shrugged and said, "You got somethin' you wanna say?"

"No."

Out in the lot, four Hispanic guys had climbed out of a dark blue Escalade and were now also checking out the Camaro. Like a TV rerun, they also drew out their guns and directed their attention at the terminal.

"But," she said, tipping her head toward the lot, "I think they may have."

As if to underline her words, the sound of a chopper rumbled overhead and banked towards the runway.

"What the fuck …" said one of the guys, raising his palms in exaggerated wonder. "Downtown nuthin'. We got the whole of fuckin' Cleveland out here?"

From the top of the stairs behind her she heard clatter of footsteps. They were followed by another scream, then Matt yelling, "Get back here, you little shit."

Then silence. She went for the door to the tower, but Matt's voice echoed down. "All of you stay back or I'll kill her."

The first guy grinned wide, regarded his associates, then checked his gun. "I can work with that. Outta my way," he said to Kelsey.

"I'm not movin'," she said and stood square in front of the stairs with her fists clenched. "You want her, you'll have to go through me." She glared at them, heart thumping and wondering what the hell they'd do next.

She was just opening her mouth to bargain with the guy, when the crack of gunfire echoed off the walls and he fell forward, arms wide, a halo of blood across the floor. The other two dived for cover and dropped into a crouch, guns out, eyes sweeping the terminal.

Outside the sound of sirens wailed and a stream of police cars streaked into the lot and across to the tower. Following them were three mobile television units with people jumping out, shouting orders and fighting for position before the vehicles had come to a halt. And all at once it really did seem like half of Cleveland had turned up.

Kelsey swooped, grabbed Lionel's gun and ran for the stairs. She knew Matt, knew what could happen if he panicked. Didn't matter how many cops were outside, it could still end badly. And after all she'd been through, all she'd done, she could not fail now.

Gingerly, she placed her foot on the first step and gazed up. Her heart was thudding in her chest, her head pounding. Anyone else might have thought she was nuts. Jesus, if anyone had told her what she'd go through, *she* would have thought she was nuts. But this was the home stretch. When she got to the top, she'd have one last battle.

But Matt would be the toughest of all.

CHAPTER THIRTY FOUR
3:07 PM

Elizabeth undid her seat belt, opened the door and jumped from the car before it stopped moving. She lifted her head, searching the area, and spotted a group of policemen who were stationed in a semicircle formation on the periphery of an ever-growing crowd, herding journalists and television reporters back as even more trucks and cars poured in through the gates behind them. So, she headed for them.

Overhead a helicopter banked, whipping up swirling gusts of dust and cold air that made people snatch at their hats and duck their heads. Way over in the center of the gathering crowd, Elizabeth spotted Delaney. He was directing traffic this way and that and snapping out orders while policemen ran here and there trying to hold back the surging crowd. Elizabeth had no idea how he'd got there so quickly. She had no idea how any of these people had got there. She didn't care. She pushed through the crowd toward him.

"Detective Delaney," she shouted, waving him over as she shouldered her way past bystanders and reporters and television crews. "Mr. Delaney, over here. What's happening? Is there any news?"

He waved her back. "Mrs. McClaine, please stay back. We have everything under control." Suddenly, the radio in his hand squawked into life. She inched closer, finally falling in beside him as a metallic voice from his radio crackled into life. "We have a clear shot, sir."

"Wait for the green light," he snapped into the handset, and raised his eyes to the control tower.

"Where is she? Where's Holly?" Elizabeth demanded and followed his line of sight up to the tower. One hand went to her chest. "Oh, God, tell me she's not up there."

Delaney signaled for her to follow him. She trailed him through the crowd, but just as they cleared the huddles of onlookers, she glanced back and spotted Blake cutting through the sea of heads with his eyes riveted to the top of the tower.

"Detective," she shouted, grabbing the back of his jacket, "that's the man who planned all this. Please, go and arrest him now."

"Where?" said Delaney.

"Over there," she shouted and pointed. "Blake Ressnick. He's responsible for my daughter's kidnapping and I want him arrested right now."

"Mrs. McClaine, we know who took your daughter. It was Kelsey Money. She was working with Matthew Subritzski and his brother Lionel. They're up there now. We have all the evidence we need."

"So do I. Please, I'll explain. But don't let him leave."

He lifted his head, directing his gaze across the heads of TV reporters and sound crews to where she had indicated. Blake Ressnick was pushing past clutches of bikers who regarded him with open amusement as he made his way towards the front line where half a dozen or so cars were parked in formation and several policemen were shepherding people back from the base of the tower.

Elizabeth was yelling over Delaney's shoulder as she trailed him through the crowd. "Blake was behind it all along. I picked up his phone," she said and squeezed past another group of spectators. "The kidnappers called me on it, asking where the money was. They thought I was Blake. Dear God," she said in frustration, "where the hell did all these people come from?"

"I have no idea," he said, exasperation leaching into his voice. His radio crackled and a voice said, "Third sniper in position, sir."

"Snipers?" Elizabeth shoved her way through and stepped in front of him. "My daughter's up there. You can't let anyone—"

"Mrs. McClaine, please stay back. My officers have orders to shoot as soon as they have a clear shot, but not before. Mr. Ressnick," he called, then cut his way through to him. "I'm afraid I'm going to have to ask you to come with me."

Blake regarded him, then shifted his attention briefly to Elizabeth and back. "What's this about?"

"You know very damn well what it's about," Elizabeth said. "You did this. You took my daughter—"

"Mrs. McClaine, step back and let me do my job." Delaney turned to Blake, gesturing toward the edge of the crowd. "Mr. Ressnick, *if* you don't mind."

"I was trying to help. I was trying to get her back," Blake told Elizabeth.

"You didn't try hard enough," Elizabeth shouted after him as Delaney took him by the elbow and steered him across to where two policemen were standing. She watched him hand Blake over. One of the officers snapped a pair of handcuffs on him and read him his rights while Delaney lifted his radio again and listened to whatever message was coming in. He made a brief reply and turned his focus to where two officers were escorting a group of gang members from the main terminal, then he switched his attention back to the control tower. On receiving the next message, he was suddenly on the move again, pushing urgently through the crowds toward the semicircle of police cars near the base of the tower.

A huge crowd had gathered behind the cars at the base of the tower, all watching the point high above where the viewing platform jutted out. Elizabeth shielded her eyes and looked up as a man came into view. An excited murmur ran across the crowd, and when he turned she realized he had Holly in his arms. He leaned out and shouted something, but his words were lost over the rising sound from those on the ground.

Panic gripped Elizabeth. "The hell with this," she said as she cut through collections of people standing there gazing up at it like it was some kind of circus act, waiting for the police to … what? Talk this guy down? Even Elizabeth knew there were only two outcomes here.

And she wasn't waiting to find out which it would be.

CHAPTER THIRTY FIVE

Instinct told Kelsey to run, to take the stairs two at a time until she reached the top. Her gut told her otherwise. Once upon a time, she'd have said that she knew Matt, knew what he'd do in any given circumstance. Right now, after all that had happened, she wasn't so sure. Cautiously, she followed the stairs higher and higher, both hands on the gun, her shoulder to the outer wall, until gray light filled the stairwell and she knew she was near the top.

As soon as she cleared the top step, she saw him. She tucked the gun into the back pocket of her coveralls and gingerly stepped out into the open. The surrounding walls were shrouded with plastic drop sheets that blew in the cold wind like the lungs of the tower, but directly opposite her was a yawning void where an enormous floor-to-ceiling window would eventually fit. It spanned almost a third of the circular wall area and looked out over the runway and for miles beyond. Even from where she stood, the view stole her breath and left her dizzy.

Matt stood just off to her right, watching her. His face was washed of color, sweat glistening on his forehead. A patch of blackened blood saturated a tear in the right shoulder of his shirt. His arm was tucked in close. She guessed he'd been shot and the arm was either cracked or broken. As if reading her thoughts, his eyes dropped to the wound, as he pulled Holly in close. When she took another step forward, his hand went straight to Holly's throat. "You come any closer, I'll break her neck."

"Nangsie …" Holly whimpered and reached for her but Matt pulled her back and tightened his grip.

Kelsey stopped in her tracks, then took one step back. She had no idea what to say. Eventually, she asked, "Are you okay?"

His eyebrows knit together. "No, I'm not fucking okay. I got shot. How the hell do you think I am?" There was defiance in the set of his mouth, in the jut of his chin. But his eyes betrayed him and Kelsey saw fear.

"I can see you're hurt." A wave of emotions hit her so unexpectedly, she felt her breath go. This was Matt: the man who'd taken care of her when her mother died, the man she'd depended on. For the past ten years he had been the only man she'd loved.

Still loved, in some small way.

"It's okay," she told him. "I'm here now. We can work this out. Just put her down and let me take a look at your shoulder."

"Don't come near me."

"Just … put her down. I can help you."

He turned away and peered over the edge to where the crowds were still gathering below. He seemed unsure, as if he'd been thrown into a play and he didn't know the lines. "Where'd they all come from, Kelse? They weren't supposed to be here."

She smiled, shrugged. "I don't think any of us was supposed to be here, babe."

A smile stretched across his face. "Remember the time we went to the Grand Canyon? Drove all that way just because you wanted to see the Grand Canyon. Couldn't shut you up till you saw it."

She smiled, dipped her head then looked up. "Yeah. You said it was just a big hole in the ground. You said you didn't know what all the fuss was about."

His expression softened. His eyes went to a point on the floor just in front of him while the memories came flooding. "That was so cool. Man, that place was deep," he whispered. "Miles and miles of land just carved away over millions of years."

"Yeah."

"And here's us ..."

"And here's us," she said and nodded. "We can get out of this, Matt. Both of us—all of us."

When his eyes came up to meet hers, the smile was gone. She'd seen that same shift a thousand times. Why could she still never see it coming? "That's what you did to me," he said. "You kept grinding me down, and grinding me down till there was nothing left."

She said nothing. She'd heard all this before. There was no correct answer. Whatever happened, whatever it was about, it was still her fault.

"I was never good enough for you, was I? Nothing I did was right. Nothing I gave you was enough." When she still said nothing, he straightened, angled his head. "Where's Li?"

"He's ah ..." she said and looked away. "He's downstairs. He's hurt—but he's ah ... he's fine," she added and tried to smile. "Lemme take a look at that shoulder. It looks bad."

"Li?" he called toward the stairs. "Li, get up here, man." When there was no reply, his eyes came back to her. "I know what you're doing."

She shrugged. "Me? I'm not doing anything. I'm trying to help you." Her voice was casual, calm. But acting was never her forte. Neither was lying to Matt and no matter how hard she tried, she could not meet his gaze. Holly's eyes were on her, her little brow crumpled, eyes questioning. "Let me take her. Please. And I'll ..." she began, but he swung the child up under one arm and stepped to the very edge. "Whoa, wait!" The heel of his left shoe was right over the edge. She reached out, as if she could stop him.

When a horrified gasp echoed up from the crowd, he turned to look down at them and the toes of both shoes went over the line. He leaned out, gazing so precariously down that Kelsey gasped in a breath and held it. Still reaching for him, fingers stretched, she took a single step forward.

Matt seemed oblivious to the drop. He adjusted his grip on Holly, and leaned out further over the edge. "Listen up," he yelled, "because I'm not saying this twice. I want one million in used notes in a case. Then I want a plane with enough fuel for ten hours' flight. Anyone comes within a hundred feet of me, the kid dies."

From somewhere below, an amplified voice called up:

"Mr. Subritzski, please step back from the edge. You have a phone. Pick up and let's talk. We can work this out."

Kelsey slowly sidestepped around, following the curve of the platform. She had to get closer, had to be ready.

"You heard me!" Matt was yelling. "Or so help me, I will drop her. You think I won't ...?" He snatched up a handful of Holly's sweatshirt and hoisted her up and out over the edge, holding her at arm's length.

Kelsey's heart flipped. "Matt, please," she said and shuffled closer.

Below, the crowd moved restlessly.

"Mr. Subritzski," the cop said through the bullhorn. "Think about this. If you harm the child, there's no turning back. We have options here. Please, pick up your phone and let's talk."

"I told you what I want," he yelled.

Trembling now, Kelsey inched toward them—hand out, fingers stretched. She felt as if any sudden movement would tip the platform, and they'd all go over the edge.

"Mr. Subritzski, I want to bring you all down safely," the cop was calling.

"Matt," she said gently, "please don't do this. They have snipers. They'll have a fix on you."

His eyes cut to her. "Stay back. Over there." He nodded toward the doorway. "You're on their side, go be with them. You were never on my side." He leaned out and shouted, "I told you what I want. If I don't get it, the kid takes a dive. Jesus," he muttered, staring down into the masses below, "are they stupid or what?"

Kelsey could see Holly's sweatshirt sliding up. The waistband had risen to just under her arms. Any minute now she'd slip straight through it and fall. "Nangsie Mommy," she cried out.

Kelsey gritted her teeth and eased forward. "It's okay, baby, just be still."

"Shut up, shut up, shut up," Matt was mumbling. His arm was beginning to sag. Holly had already dropped six inches. Kelsey knew this script so well, that even with his back turned she could see his mounting anger and frustration.

"What the fuck are you all looking at?" he spat out in defiance. When he shifted position and raised the child in his grip, Kelsey saw it coming. She flew to the edge and dived just as Matt released his grip. Kelsey grabbed Holly's hand in hers while the screams of the crowd filled the air. Kelsey locked her grip on the child's hand. With her muscles burning, tendons straining, she steadied herself, then began to pull her up.

"Fine," said Matt from somewhere behind her. "You can both go."

Kelsey closed her eyes, concentrating on that one thing—on hauling Holly up and into the safety of her arms. When Matt's first kick hit in her thigh, her body swiveled and her knee went over the edge. She gripped the edge with her free hand and kept lifting, drawing Holly up. The second kick got her in the small of the back and her hip crossed the line and the gun slid from her pocket and went over the edge. She watched it fall into the crowd and disappear. Now she was clinging grimly to the platform with one hand, the child dangling in the grip of the other.

"Matt," she yelled. "C'mon, help me here. *Please*." She could feel her center of gravity shifting, her weight tipping. Sweat beaded on her forehead and dampened her palm. The little hand began slipping through hers, but she held tight and fought to stay her ground. When she looked out, all she could see was open fields. Below, the upturned faces of the people on the ground. Still she clung on, desperate, determined—then she caught the look in Holly's eyes and the child smiled up at her, her eyes full of trust. Right then she knew there was no turning back. Right then she knew she could not fail.

The little hand was blue, squeezed so tight in her own she could feel the bones crushed together. She was waiting for Matt to land the final kick, sure she was just about to go over when she heard a woman yell, "Get away from them, you bastard," and Matt moved away.

From somewhere over by the stairs Kelsey heard Matt curse, the sound of a scuffle, and a woman cried out. Kelsey felt every blow landing, heard the sound of her tumbling down the stairs and Matt going after her. If Kelsey could have helped her, she would have. Right now, all her energy was going into hanging on to this child.

Gritting her teeth and using every last ounce of her strength, Kelsey eased herself to her knees. Squeezing even tighter on the child's hand, she dead-lifted the weight and felt her coming up. As she appeared over the edge, Kelsey got to her feet and pulled her in to safety.

The child gazed up at her with red-rimmed eyes and grinned. "Nangsie Mommy. Nuvs Nangsie Mommy." Kelsey scooped the child up in her arms and held her so close she thought her heart would melt.

The swelling in her face ached. Her thigh felt like it was on fire. Kelsey didn't care. She pulled back to look into the child's eyes and she smiled. "I told you I'd come. I told you," she said, then hugged her again.

The sound of footsteps made her turn. She caught a glimpse of Matt just in time to throw Holly to safety. He came at her like a train and hit her hard. She went stumbling back. For a second her knees went from under her, but he grabbed her and swung her around until she hit the scaffolding and fell to the floor.

Holly screamed, but Kelsey said, "Stay back, baby, he's not going to hurt us. I won't let him." Her body ached, her head throbbed. But she got to her feet and fell into stance, bouncing, ducking, guard up and ready.

Matt tipped his head, cracking the vertebrae in his neck, and frowned like he couldn't believe she'd even consider this. He came at her again, threw a left cross that took out her guard and knocked her stumbling sideways.

"Is that it?" he said and shrugged. "Is that the best you got? Y'know, your left shoulder always drops. You wanna watch that."

And he stepped in and hit her cheek so hard her head snapped back and she hit the floor and saw stars. She blinked them away, got up again. Finding her stance, blinking hard, she pulled in a breath and waited for her head to stop spinning. Her legs trembled, her focus faded in and out, and her ears were ringing.

Matt stalked her, following her every move. She was bent and bruised and ready to fall down, but she stumbled left, stumbled left, forcing him to lead with the broken arm and wrong-footing him. Whatever happened, she had to stay out of his reach until she came up with something.

His confidence was back. He dropped his guard, walked casually after her, tracking her like it was a game. "You have never beaten me yet. I don't know why you think you can now. Even with one arm, I'll knock you right into the middle of next week," he said and shrugged. He did a shoulder roll, and stood back to regard her. "Oh, come on, let's see what you've really got."

She tried skipping around him, bouncing on her toes but her knees gave out and she almost fell, so she moved to his left, drawing him in. He followed her, frowning in amusement and shaking his head like he couldn't believe how dumb she could be. Every time he made a move, she jerked away and moved to his left. He turned, chuckled like it was a joke.

Holly was watching, her little hands clutched at her mouth, eyes wide. She made to move, but Kelsey yelled, "Get back. Go sit ..." and Matt landed her a hook to the eye that sent her reeling backwards and sat her on her ass. Any minute that eye would close over—she could feel it. Her face already felt like she had two layers of hellfire laid across it. Her body was stiff, joints swelling. She was tired beyond anything she'd felt before. But she eased herself to her feet and fell into stance. Pain lanced through her limbs. She sucked in air and tried to bounce on her toes and almost fell.

"What the hell is that?" he said. "You done already? You're pathetic. All this is your fault, you know."

He threw a jab and she stumbled to the left. Again, he followed, muttering, "You just can't do what you're told, can you?" She stepped again and this time when he turned, she dropped her shoulder and charged, ramming her shoulder into him, driving him back. He staggered, shoved her away, laughing, so she put her head down and rushed him again. He pushed her off, looking down at her like she was ten kinds of stupid. She caught her breath, and when she charged him the third time, his left foot slipped off the edge. His eyes flew open and his left hand snatched at her. She felt his fingers slip across her wrist and he went over. There was a collective scream from the crowd below and the garbled voice of a cop yelling something through the bullhorn. When she dropped to her knees and leaned over Matt was right below, clinging to the scaffolding with one hand and dangling in midair with his feet kicking.

He looked up at her, eyes filled with terror. "Kelse, help me."

This was the only man she'd ever loved. He had made mistakes but hell, who hadn't? In times past she had looked deep into his eyes, into his soul, and she'd always known that somewhere inside, there was a good person. She reached down and grasped his hand. For the longest time, she knelt there, wondering what to do. Off in the distance the sound of the crowd and the cop on the bullhorn turned into white noise. She felt movement and Holly crouched next to her, looking over the edge. No expression, just staring.

"Stay back, baby," she told her. "Go sit over by the stairs."

"Kelse," Matt was pleading. Tears and regret flooded his eyes. "Please. I'm so sorry. Help me." She let her gaze range out across the crowds, across to the police, and off into the thunderclouds that were gathering in the distance. Any time now, it would rain.

Below, the silence was almost something tangible. Off to the right, she spotted a sniper crouched behind a car. To the left was another. She dropped to her belly and latched onto Matt's wrist, and he whispered, "That's it, that's my girl. Just pull me up. I can't use my right arm. Just ..."

She wrapped her fingers tight, feeling the warmth of his skin. When she'd pulled him to safety, then what? Matt would never survive in a prison. As long as she'd known him, he'd been a free spirit. Looking back, she knew that spirit had survived at her own expense. Did that matter? You did what you had to for someone you love.

He was begging her, pleading with her. But frustration edged his voice now. "Help me, Kelse. Fuckin' help me ..." What choice did she have? She adjusted her grip, but just as she took the weight, his hand slipped through hers and she watched in horror as the crowd gasped and Matt plummeted to the ground with a crack. A hundred feet below, she could see him lying there, staring into the sky, and she knew he was dead.

A knot twisted in her chest. Could she have saved him? Did she try hard enough? Below the crowd moved in on him but the police pushed them back again. Almost at once, the attention of the crowd shifted to her. Right there in the silence, she saw accusation.

"I didn't ... I tried to help him," she called. It was no use. Even she could see that.

When she got to her feet, Holly nestled in next to her, also peering down.

"Come here, baby, come away from the edge." Kelsey lifted the child into her arms, hugging her close.

When she heard movement behind her, she turned. The woman standing at the top of the stairs was Holly's mother, Elizabeth McClaine. Their eyes met and Elizabeth kneeled, arms reaching, calling for her child. Kelsey placed a kiss on the tip of the child's nose and gently lowered her to her feet. Holly hesitated, fingers in her mouth, one arm clasped around Kelsey's legs.

"Go on, go to your mom," Kelsey said, and after a moment, the child shambled across and fell into her mother's arms.

The bruising on Elizabeth McClaine's face showed every blow Matt had landed. She drew her child in, enclosing her in a relieved embrace. Then she looked up. "Miss Money—Kelsey …?"

Kelsey clasped her hands tightly to her lips. "I'm … I'm sorry. I'm so very sorry."

"It's okay. It's all okay now. You brought my daughter back to me." Tears glistened in Elizabeth's eyes, then broke to streak her cheeks. She dashed them away. "And for that—I thank you." When the sound of footsteps clattered up the stairs behind her, she threw up her hand and shouted, "Wait. Stay back."

The squawk of police radios and the murmur of the crowd echoed up from below.

So little time. So much to say. Kelsey dropped her head briefly. She swallowed hard and looked Elizabeth McClaine straight in the eye. "I was wrong. I should never have …" and she gestured helplessly. "If I could take it all back—"

"It's all right, Kelsey. Everything's going to be all right. Come, we'll get you fixed up, find you a doctor, get you some help …"

Kelsey smiled. Behind her she could hear the cop on the bullhorn yelling "put down your weapon," but she ignored him because she had one more thing to do. She slipped her hand into her pocket for the Roadster key. "I'm so sorry," she said and held it out to Elizabeth

McClaine. She wanted to tell her she was sorry for taking it, for wrecking their car and their lives, but Elizabeth shouted, "No!"

The world behind Kelsey went deadly silent, and in that instant she knew the sniper hadn't seen a key, he'd seen a gun, and in the distance she caught the crack of a single shot. She felt something slam into her back and the front of her coveralls exploded in a shower of red, and she knew she'd been hit. Elizabeth's mouth was moving, her face distorted by a soundless scream as she drew Holly into her arms. Spatters of red flecked her face, her hair and the plastic screening behind. Holly also blinked up at her, her cheeks and hair striped red …

… then violent, searing pain.

Kelsey clamped her arms across her chest, clutching at her life's blood. Her surroundings wavered. When she looked up, Holly clamped her little arms across her chest, and mouthed the words Kelsey knew were, "Nuvs Nangsie Mommy."

"I love you too, baby," Kelsey whispered, but her words were red mist that was swept away in the wind. The world shimmered, and from somewhere among the murmurs and the sobs of the crowd below, she heard a voice. The words sharpened against the din, and she caught the sound of her name.

When she turned, the brilliance of the sun's light stabbed her eyes. She blinked against the glare, but when she opened them and lifted her face, all she could see was a sky so blue it ached. It stretched out for forever while the warmth of the sun touched softly on her skin. When the voice stirred her from the moment, she blinked and leaned over to look down.

And there she was. Blond hair flung back, lips painted red and stretched wide in laughter, dimples creasing her cheeks. She lounged back in the swim ring, painted toenails showing peeks of red beneath the surface, hands swirling lazily at her sides, cast there in the acres of crystal clear water that shimmered and sparkled as far as the eye could see.

At the sound of her laughter chiming out across the endless oceans, Kelsey smiled. "Mom?" she whispered. "Mom."

"Kelsey," her mother called, paddling around so she could see her. She smiled up and waved. "Come on in, baby, the water's fine."

"I love you, Mom."

Still smiling, tears filling her eyes, Kelsey stepped forward. She had never seen her mother look so beautiful.

She wanted to tell her. She wanted her to know how much she'd missed her, how much she'd needed her, when she heard the distant sound of a sigh; felt light flood her body …

… then nothing.

EPILOGUE
FOUR MONTHS LATER

The winter had been a harsh one. January had drawn a heavy blanket of white across the whole of Cleveland. It formed solid banks down the sides of streets. It encrusted windows, blocked walks, piled up against doors. February and March were no better.

April brought the thaw. Snow melted under the clearing skies and the cleansing showers of spring washed it away. The first buds and green shoots appeared on otherwise naked trees, and daffodils burst yellow into gardens again.

Elizabeth zipped up the front of Holly's coat and pulled the woolen collar high around her neck.

"Now, listen to me—are you listening? I want you to go find your bag," she told her in clear, measured words.

Holly gazed up, mouth open, eyes blank.

"I know you can understand me, young lady. Go find your bag. He'll be here soon." The child raised her open hand and tapped her thumb to her forehead. "That's right—Daddy," said Elizabeth. "Now off you go."

As Holly tottered away down the hallway, Elizabeth folded her arms and watched her. There was no knowing if she would return with the bag. Chances were she would be sidetracked and ten minutes later Elizabeth would find her lying on the floor playing with her new toy lion.

Smiling at the thought now, she pressed her lips together, still waiting.

So often these days, she found herself wondering how much Holly remembered. How much was she able to comprehend? For Elizabeth, it was a lifetime ago and yesterday all at once. The sight of the girl, Kelsey, standing on the edge of the world with her chest a bloodied, gaping wound still haunted her. She still awoke in the night calling her name, reaching for her.

What she remembered most vividly, though, was the girl's smile. Elizabeth had lunged, trying to reach her, desperate to save her, but she knew no matter what she said or did, it was already too late. As if obeying a greater power, Kelsey had spread her arms, leaned into the wind, and let herself fall …

The sound of the doorbell jolted Elizabeth back to the present. She touched her fingers to the corners of her eyes and went straight to the front door.

Out on the stoop, Richard turned, his breath clouding as he rubbed his hands together for warmth. He blew into his gloves. "Who said spring was here?" he said and smiled. "Is she ready?"

"She's getting her bag. Come on in."

He stepped into the house behind her and looked around. "I still think you need a bigger place."

She followed his gaze around the tiny house. "It suits us. And there are no stairs. Holly baby," she called, "Daddy's here! You will look after her …" she began, then stopped herself.

He smiled. "You know I will." There was an awkward silence, then he said, "I still think you should run for office."

"It's early. I've got a long time ahead and right now Holly comes first. And when I'm not with her, the charities and work for the homeless are my next priority. Maybe one day things will change. How's the company coming along?"

He tipped his head. "Still struggling a little. We'll come back."

To her surprise, Holly appeared at the end of the hallway lugging an enormous bag.

"What have you got in there?" asked Richard as he went to meet her.

"Ninny Nion."

"Oh, that Lilly Lion. She must have gotten awfully big since I was here last," he said. He lifted the bag from her with one hand, and took the child's hand in the other. Then he turned to Elizabeth. "I miss you both."

Her gaze dropped briefly. "I need time."

"How about tomorrow?" He smiled.

She also smiled. "More time than that."

He hoisted the bag then shuffled Holly out the door in front of him. Just as he was about to leave, he turned, and looked her straight in the eye. "I'll be waiting."

"I know you will," she said and closed the door.

The End

Read an excerpt from the next in the
McClaine and Delaney series of thrillers by Catherine Lea

CHILD OF THE STATE

PROLOGUE

CARRINGWAY WOMEN'S PRISON, OHIO—AMY

Amy knew she should have gone to Stacy the second she'd opened the box. All night she'd lain there in her cot, listening to every sound, frightened they'd come after her, and wondering who else knew. Because somebody did.

Why she'd even gotten stuck in that stupid job was anybody's guess. She'd applied for the prison sewing program. Would have helped if she knew how to sew, but others on the same work scheme didn't know how to sew when they started, either. They got lessons.

Amy still couldn't make a buttonhole worth a damn so she got stuck in dispatch, sending out boxes of garments in the truck that turned up twice a week. Her job was to pack the boxes, check the details on the packing slip, seal the boxes up. Most boring job on the planet—or it was until that particular box came back, returned from wherever and marked Attention Dispatch Department. The only person around with any authority to accept the box was Trish Tomes, the prison officer overseeing the project.

Amy had been going through the contents of the box, looking at every item. She was just holding a silk blouse up to the light, checking she wasn't imagining things, when Officer Tomes appeared behind her. Amy just about peed her pants. She yelped and pressed the blouse to her chest to try and slow her heart down. The woman had the stealth of a cat. Didn't matter how hard you listened, you'd turn around and there she was, standing right behind you.

Officer Tomes took the blouse from Amy, holding it up to the light while she looked it over. Then she dug through the box, frowning as she brought out other garments and checked them.

"I'll take care of this," she told Amy.

"But these are ours."

"I said I'll take care of it. Now go back, seal up the last of those boxes." Her tone implied she wasn't going to say it again. She gathered up the returned box and took it back to her office. When Amy looked up the next time, she could see her on the phone, talking to someone with that sour look on her face, every now and then glancing accusingly across at Amy.

But Amy wasn't stupid. She'd already tucked one of blouses down the front of her prison jumpsuit, then slept all night with it tucked under her mattress. Now here she was standing in line for breakfast with the blouse down the front of her jumpsuit while she waited for Stacy. What she'd discovered was something big—she just knew it was, and Stacy was the only one in this joint Amy could trust. She was also the one who'd know exactly what to do.

After several minutes, the doors opened and Stacy's crew entered, lining up for their breakfast trays, all chattering and checking out the tables to see whether anyone had been stupid enough to sit in their seat, then looking back down the line to see who they might be eating with. Amy fell into line with her heart jumping and her hands shaking. She waited until her oatmeal and juice box had been set on her tray, and when she turned, she caught Stacy's eye, indicating for her to sit with her.

Soon as Stacy came over, slid her tray onto the table and sat down, Amy looked left and right, and said, "Gotta talk."

Stacy dug her spoon into her oatmeal, screwed her face up in disgust as she stirred it around. "Sure. Go ahead."

Amy leaned forward and hissed, "I'm talking *real talk*. In private."

Stacy looked up from her tray, her expression grim. "Are you okay?"

Amy gave the adjacent tables another furtive once-over. Satisfied they weren't being overheard she leaned forward again. "I found something."

Stacy straightened in her seat, lifting her head and letting her gaze casually navigate the room before settling back on Amy. "Go on."

Amy took another quick glance back over her shoulder. "Can't. Have to show you. Bathroom."

Stacy got up and returned her tray to the counter along with her uneaten oatmeal, and pushed through the swing doors, heading in the direction of the bathroom. No point in leaving the meal until she got back. You leave your food unattended in this place, you never knew what might have been added to it while you were gone. Amy followed, placing her food tray back with her breakfast untouched, giving the area another wary scan before following Stacy.

When she got to the bathroom, two stalls were closed. A toilet flushed and Nyla Guthrie stepped out and looked from Stacy to Amy and back. "What?" she said in an accusing tone.

"Nothin'," said Amy.

"It's nothing. Don't worry about it," Stacy told her.

Nyla gave Amy a sour once up and down, then pushed through the bathroom door going back to the dining room, leaving Stacy and Amy both watching the second stall.

Impatient, Stacy went across and banged on the door with the side of her fist. "Hey, hurry it up, will ya?"

The toilet flushed and Cissy Pettameyer stepped out, a picture of ingratiating sweetness. "Good morning, ladies," she said with a sly smile as she moved to the basin and washed her hands, checking her face in the mirror.

Neither of them spoke, just watched her.

"Be like that then," Cissy told their reflections, and ran a smoothing finger along one eyebrow. "I'm just trying to be polite."

Neither Amy nor Stacy was taken in. Cissy was a poisonous, two-faced gossip who spread stories at a rate that would make the black plague look slow.

Stacy stuck one hand on her hip and shifted her weight. "You done?"

Cissy turned and ran her eyes right down to Stacy's prison issue shoes and back. "I guess."

She jerked her head towards the door. "Then get out."

After Cissy had gone, Stacy opened the door and peered out, then closed it, leaning against it so no one else could enter.

"So, what's so important? Are you okay, Amy? Is someone giving you a hard time?"

"No, it's not like that. I'm fine. But when I was working today, a box came, addressed to the prison, like they do sometimes. It had a Faulty Goods sticker on the side, so I figured it was just stuff coming back that had stitching problems with them or something." She paused and dropped her voice to a whisper. "But this was in it." She reached down into the front of her jumpsuit, pulled the blouse out, and handed it to Stacy.

"What is it?"

"You look," Amy said, hugging herself and jerking her chin toward the blouse in Stacy's hands. "I didn't know else who to tell."

Stacy checked the seams, the sleeves, the buttonholes and her eyes came back up to Amy, questioning.

"Keep lookin'," she said.

Stacy turned the garment, checking the collar, then the neckline. Her jaw dropped and she looked up, eyes wide.

"Well, holy shit," she said.

CHAPTER ONE

FOUR MONTHS LATER
DAY ONE: 1:56 AM—STACY

The car rounded the last bend into Becker Street and came to an abrupt halt. Right in front of them was a pack of reporters and TV crews surrounding the front gate and stretching halfway down the street. By the look of them, they must have had the place staked out since dawn. The instant the first person spotted the car, the crowd was in motion. In a matter of seconds the car was swamped, microphones and cameras pressed to the windows, reporters and news anchors pushing and elbowing each other and yelling questions while a couple of cops tried unsuccessfully to hold them back.

Stacy sat up in the back seat, peering out at the commotion. This was something she hadn't expected. This could be a problem.

She twisted around, looking out the side and rear windows, watching the chaos outside while Mrs. McClaine, who was sitting next to her, leaned forward, directing the driver to pull in as close to the front gate as possible. Meanwhile, Penny Rickman, Mrs. McClaine's secretary, got out of the car behind them and cut her way through the crowd, also pointing and yelling over the rabble, ordering security to push the media back, and to form a guard around the car while Stacy and Mrs. McClaine got out.

There was nothing like this when Stacy was sentenced three years ago. As she'd left the courthouse that day, a handful of supporters had lined up along the front steps, shouting and waving placards that said things like: "No mother should be in prison for wanting her child," and "Where's the justice in this country?"

Didn't make one iota of difference because she'd already been tried and sentenced. Seventeen years old she was, and on her way to Carringway Women's Correctional Facility for assaulting the social services lady who'd taken her baby away. And that was the last she'd seen of the outside world—would have been for the next two years, if it hadn't been for the Governor's new early release program.

Now, here she was free again—or at least, she would be if all these reporters weren't surrounding the place.

The car door opened to a semi-circle of space made by a wall of security guards. Stacy flashed Mrs. McClaine a glance, and when she got the "okay" Stacy got out, head down, hand shielding her face from the flash of cameras. The security guards closed in, forming one compact unit, and together they moved in through the front gate, up the front steps, and onto the porch.

While Mrs. McClaine turned to answer questions and pose for the cameras, Stacy took a second to ease the tension out of her shoulders, look the place over. Seemed kind of ironic that after all these years, here she was back at the very house she'd run away from.

Gayleen Charms, never would have made Mother of the Year. Child Services knew the house better than the mailman. Having a child at fifteen might have been the best thing that ever happened to Stacy, but being a teen mom hadn't been top of Gayleen's list of career choices. Gayleen had wanted to be a dancer. She wanted to live in the big city under the bright lights.

From the minute Stacy was born she knew she'd been the biggest mistake Gayleen ever made, that she'd ruined her mother's life. Fourteen years of being made to feel like trash finally made life on the streets a way more attractive prospect. Which was why Stacy had run away.

Standing here now, the place looked no different—same crappy house with the same dirty white paintwork, same clutter all over the front porch, same broken railing her mother still hadn't fixed in all the time she'd lived here. One of the conditions of Stacy's release was that she must live at this address for a minimum period of six months.

Like hell.

Stacy didn't intend staying six minutes.

To read more, visit
http://www.authorcatherinelea.com/

ACKNOWLEDGEMENTS

To all those who supported me in writing this book:

Laura Hunter: First reader, head cheerleader, supporter, writer. Without her, this book would have finished at chapter twelve. She kept me on an even keel through the stormiest seas and lit my way to the end.

Sara J. Henry, author of *Learning to Swim* and *A Cold and Lonely Place*: Rarely is a debut author fortunate enough to have someone of Sara's caliber give structural guidance, then top it off with an award-winning lesson in editing. I owe her more than I can say.

Richie Kray: Writing buddy, first reader, champion of the written word. He encouraged me when I was down and made me laugh when I should have been writing. But it was worth it.

Nikki Stuckwisch, author of *Code*: Writing buddy, second reader, ER doctor, go-to girl, extreme friend. She gives me strength when I need it most.

Loretta Giacoletto: Second-chair line editor. In ten pages, she taught me how to read like a reader instead of a writer.

79776126R00208

Made in the USA
Middletown, DE
12 July 2018